Other books by Fred Patten

Best in Show: Fifteen Years of Outstanding Furry Fiction (2003)
Reprinted as: Furry! The World's Best Anthropomorphic Fiction! (2006)
Watching Anime, Reading Manga:
25 Years of Essays and Reviews (2004)
Already Among Us: An Anthropomorphic Anthology (2012)
The Ursa Major Awards Anthology:
A Tenth Anniversary Celebration (2012)
What Happens Next: An Anthology of Sequels (2013)
Five Fortunes (2014)
Funny Animals and More: From Anime to Zoomorphics (2014)
Anthropomorphic Aliens: An Interstellar Anthology (2014)
The Furry Future: 19 Possible Prognostications (2015)
An Anthropomorphic Century: Stories from 1909 to 2008 (2015)
Cats and More Cats: Feline Fantasy Fiction (2016)
Gods with Fur: And Feathers, Scales (2016)
Furry Fandom Conventions, 1989-2015 (2017)
Dogs of War (2017)
Symbol of a Nation (2017)
Dogs of War II: Aftermath (2017)
What the Fox?! (2018)
Exploring New Places (2018)
Furry Tales: A Review of Essential Anthropomorphic Fiction (2019)

The Cóyotl Awards
Anthology

Edited by Fred Patten

The Cóyotl Awards Anthology

Production copyright FurPlanet Productions © 2019
Cover artwork copyright © 2018 by Kacey Miyagami
Cóyotl Awards logo by Jessie "Electric Keet" Tracer

Published by FurPlanet Productions
Dallas, Texas
www.FurPlanet.com

ISBN 978-1-61450-487-0

First Edition Trade Paperback July 2019

To

Sean "Duroc" Silva
who started the Furry Writers' Guild

and Kristina "Orrery" Tracer
who started the Cóyotl Awards

In Memoriam of

Fred Patten

A man of many fandoms,
who shared them with the world.

Fred Patten believed in the furry community passionately. Having been a member of the community from his early days, he spent his later years collecting and editing anthologies designed to highlight the best the furry fiction had to offer. We are proud to present his final collection, highlighting the modern masters of the genre with this volume, celebrating The Cóyotl Award winners and selected nominees.

Table of Contents

Foreword

by Mary E. Lowd

When I was a kid, I remember watching the Academy Awards with my mother every year—the red carpets, the fancy clothes, the musical performances, the inscrutable jokes, and all of those clips from movies, most of which I hadn't seen. My mother loves movies, and even if she hadn't seen them all, she'd have read and watched reviews of most of them. As I grew older and moved away, my mom and I couldn't always watch the Academy Awards together, but we'd still watch them separately and eagerly call each other during commercial breaks to talk about everything we'd seen.

Some years, I'd try to watch through all of the nominated movies before the awards; other years, I wouldn't have time, but I'd learn about which movies I wanted to make sure of watching later. Every year, I enjoyed the clips of great performances, the glimpses of characters and worlds contained in all of those movies.

Awards are a way to celebrate something you love. Behind the pageantry and the competition, there's simply a community doing good work and believing their work is worth telling others about, worth taking the time and energy to celebrate.

The Cóyotl Awards are a celebration. When I took over running the Cóyotls, I looked back on all the years I'd spent watching the Academy Awards, and I thought about how we could turn a simple list of names and titles into the kind of joyous pageantry that Hollywood movie stars enjoy… without, you know, asking a bunch of writers to fly across the country to a fifteen-minute ceremony and change out of their comfortable clothes. Fortunately, my awesome husband is an amateur singer/songwriter, and he looks great in a tux and antlers as our Mooster-of-Ceremonies. So, for the past five years, I've written him scripts that talk about every one of the nominated pieces, and he's composed a song to perform. We live-stream a ceremony where he tells jokes, sings his song, and presents plush coyotes to the winners of the awards. He may be the only who dresses up, but by the end of the presentation [currently at Furlandia, in Portland, each May], I hope all of the writers in the room (and watching the live-stream!) feel a little fancier, a little more acknowledged for the time they spend behind their keyboards. A little celebrated.

The furry writing community is doing good work, telling great stories, and that's worth celebrating. Please, enjoy some of that great work here.

All the best,
Mary

Introduction

by Fred Patten

The Cóyotl Awards are voted upon annually by the members of the Furry Writers' Guild, for stories of anthropomorphic fiction first published during the previous calendar year in the categories of Best Novel, Best Novella, Best Short Story, and Best Anthology. The stories do not have to be by members of the FWG. The winners receive an illustrated certificate and a trophy of a coyote pup plushie wearing a red bandana inscribed with "Cóyotl Award".

The Furry Writers' Guild got its start on the FurAffinity forums around May 2010, when Sean "Duroc" Silva and several others began discussing ideas for an organization for furry writers. The idea gained approval, and the FWG was officially started in April 2011 with Silva as its first president. He stepped down in 2013 and turned the leadership over to Sean "AnthroAquatic" Gerace. Later FWG presidents, voted upon annually by the membership, have been Renee "Poetigress" Carter Hall (2014-2016), Watts "Chipotle" Martin (2016-2017), Madison "Makyo" Scott-Clary (2017), and Watts Martin again (2017-2018).

"The purpose of the Furry Writers' Guild is to promote quality writing in anthropomorphic fiction and to inform, elevate, and support its creators." Membership is open to those who have had one short story, poem, or novel-length work featuring anthropomorphic characters or themes published in a paying qualifying market; or two short stories or poems featuring anthropomorphic characters or themes published in a non-paying qualifying market. Membership is currently up to 192 active writers and 9 associates (mostly editors). The FWG also promotes a "Furry Book Month" during October.

Almost as soon as the FWG started, the members (led by Kristina "Orrery" Tracer, Mary E. Lowd, and Renee Carter Hall) began discussing starting a literary award, to be voted upon by the FWG membership (all writers, as opposed to the Ursa Major Awards which are voted upon mostly by furry fandom's readers; or to a juried award, voted upon only by a committee). Silva supported this, and the Cóyotl Awards, administered by Tracer, began in February 2012. She ran them until the end of 2013, then handed the administrative duties to Mary E. Lowd, who added the trophies. The Cóyotl Award emblem was designed by Jessie "Electric Keet" Tracer, Kristina Tracer's wife.

The Cóyotl Awards had both a General and a Mature division in 2011, so there are two awards for that year. They have since been combined into a single award.

The first Cóyotl Awards ceremony, where the winners are announced, was held at RainFurrest in Seattle in September 2012. No ceremony was held in 2013, but a double ceremony was held at RainFurrest in September 2014. A ceremony was held again at RainFurrest in 2015, then at Rocky Mountain Fur Con in Denver in August 2016, and at Furlandia in Portland in May 2017 and 2018.

(My thanks to everyone who dredged up the dates on ancient e-mail discussions to put this history together.)

Don't we wish! Don't we wish!

The Canoe Race

by Daniel and Mary E. Lowd

The last camper had left. The cabins had been swept clean of the dirt from the tramping feet of a hundred teenagers. The dining hall had been swept and scrubbed free from the grease of a summer's worth of meals. The canoes had been pulled in from the lake and stowed in the boat house for winter. The fire pit had been emptied of ash. The gate on the road leading to Camp Riverwind had been locked.

It was finally time.

It started with a lone squirrel. Then another. Then a third, a fourth, and ten more leaped from the trees and skittered across the roofs of the cabins and dining hall. Finding no signs of humans, they moved to the ground, peered through the windows, and searched every nook and cranny before converging at the fire pit.

"All clear!" the squirrel band chittered in unison. The signal carried throughout the valley to the ears of raccoons, beavers, birds, bobcats, a moose, and a black bear.

The raccoons did not have to be told twice. They knew from years of experience that campers sometimes leave bits of food or, even better, shiny things to covet and fondle. The best treasures go to the quickest and cleverest raccoons. This year, the trash cans had been emptied, but not perfectly. The first raccoon found a few broken pieces of candy. The next found their shimmering wrappers. A third found craft beads in the dust beneath the picnic tables—one bead to slip on each claw, making her the most fashionable raccoon of the season. Having lost the race to the prime outdoor locations, the last two raccoons stationed themselves in front of the dining hall and waited for the beavers.

The two beavers waddled out of the lake and got to work. The trick to the dining hall was to gnaw a small hole in the corner of one door, just large enough for a squirrel to squeeze through in order to open the door from the inside. Once in, a careful search of the kitchen revealed a large collection of keys. After the two raccoons in the dining hall finished arguing over who saw the colander first, they used their nimble hands to help unlock the rest of the camp.

The scrub jays watched as the growing throng of critters raided the camp and declared victory over the previous inhabitants. But they were too busy making snide remarks to join in the celebration, cawing that they had been flying around camp all summer, and it was really no big deal. Besides, why celebrate the end of a camping season that had brought them so many seeds and other delectable scraps to enjoy? They did this every year.

When the others converged on the fireless fire pit and started singing songs, the birds decided it wouldn't hurt to watch the fools for a few minutes, other entertainment being scarce. And by the time the critters around the fire pit started singing, "Oh My Darling, Avian," even the grumpiest of jays couldn't resist joining in. Even the most superior bird must have some respect for the classics.

Everyone gave the two bobcats their space when they entered. No matter how playful and sweet a bobcat seems, no squirrel will ever trust a creature with claws that sharp and an appetite that carnivorous. The bobcats took their space towards one end of the rough semi-circle of animals, singing for some songs, and merely tapping their claws during the others.

The moose and bear were so late that they almost missed the entire opening jamboree. The larger creatures had learned, for their survival, to be somewhat more cautious around humans. Being big means being unable to scurry under a bush or up a tree at the sound of trouble. And humans could cause a lot of trouble. So they waited until dusk before making their way through the woods to the back of the gathering.

Animal noises are well-known to humans, but, apart from the ostentatious warblings of songbirds, few of their songs have ever reached human ears. The magnificent bellow of a bull moose is nothing compared to his sweet, rhythmic baritone when he rumbles, "Old Moose River." And, unlike chipmunk song, four-part squirrel harmony is always smooth and never squeaky. Raccoons are masterful crooners, but they have trouble agreeing with each other long enough to sing unison. The growly voices of bears and bobcats don't suit every song. But for a song like "On Top of Old Smokey," the punctuated roars are essential. Beavertail percussion completes the ensemble. The forest had never known sweeter songs.

Darkness came, the singers tired, and one by one they adjourned to the cabins for sleep. The raccoons, squirrels, and beavers shared one cabin, sleepy piles of fur too tired to fuss or fight. The bear had her own cabin, due to her bulk. The bobcats had a separate cabin as well, due to their claws and tempers. The moose and jays were most comfortable outside. All slept soundly, dreaming of the adventures this week had in store.

* * *

The campers rose bright and early to descend upon the dining hall. Two raccoons did most of the cooking, with some help from an assistant spice-squirrel. From the mix they found in the pantry, they cooked seedy pancakes for the birds and squirrels; bark-mulch pancakes for the moose and beavers; and fresh fish pancakes for the raccoons, bobcats, and bear. All had berries on top, but the bobcats insisted on smearing theirs around to make the pancakes look less like bread and more like meat.

After breakfast, each animal picked an activity of his or her fancy. The birds were suckers for macramé, weaving long strands of colorful fibers into sturdy ropes and bracelets. The squirrels joined them at the craft tables, but preferred to thread beads to make tiny necklaces.

Raccoons tried their hands at archery, as they did every year. In a rare feat of cooperation, two of them held the bow, two pulled the string, and one nocked the arrow and aimed. The first five times, the bow knocked them down and tangled them up, but the sixth time: *success!* The arrow sailed through the air and almost hit the hay bale target. This was an all-time camp record. The raccoons chattered with impish glee, eager to boast of their victory to the other animals. But they almost lost themselves to squabbling when none could agree which one of them was most responsible for the perfect shot.

Meanwhile, the beavers took a tour of the camp, analyzing the architecture from every angle. The cabins were built simply, using techniques the beavers had mastered long ago. The dining hall, on the other hand, was a never-ending source of inspiration: vaulted ceilings with exposed rafters, large windows with wooden shutters, a stone hearth in the center, and beautiful wood trim in every corner. The moose meandered along behind them, nodding his head from time to time. He understood very little of their shop talk, but enjoyed the company and pretended to follow along.

Suddenly, a feline scream rang out from the nearby hills. The bear and a bevy of birds hurried to help. When they arrived at the source of the sounds, they found two bobcats high in the treetops, fluffed up to twice their normal sizes. Apparently, they had taken the zip-line and found it more thrilling than anticipated. The scrub jays danced along the innocuous cable, cawing and cackling at the predators' misfortune. Eventually, the cats climbed down and spent the rest of the afternoon sulking over their hurt pride. The bear waited until they had left to take her turn.

* * *

The next day brought more of the same. The raccoons tried to convince the moose they could shoot an arrow between his antlers. The bobcats played with macramé string while trying to look dignified. And the squirrels and bear played hide-and-seek.

There aren't many places for a bear to hide. Trees provide little cover when the seeker is a squirrel. Buildings with large windows provide no cover at all. But the boat house was large, dark, and filled with canoes. It was worth a shot.

A minute passed and the bear had not been discovered. Then five minutes. Then ten. Twice, she heard the scratching of little paws racing by. Once, she was sure she heard the "it" squirrel open the door and peer inside, but he gave up before checking all the corners. It wasn't until half an hour had passed that the bear was finally discovered.

All the squirrels were impressed at her ingenuity. They hadn't believed a bear would fit between all of the canoes. They counted ten— no, twelve—canoes in total.

And then one squirrel got an idea. It's hard to say which one said it first. Ideas spread among squirrels faster than gossip among scrub jays. In an instant, the boat house was filled with the chittering of fifteen squirrels, all saying one thing: "Canoe race."

The animals had seen canoes on the lake every year, but never thought to float in them. The animals who liked to swim saw boats as unnecessary, and the animals who did not preferred to stay closer to the shore. But, the squirrels argued, practicality was hardly the point of camp. Archery and crafts were equally ridiculous, yet plenty of fun.

After the squirrels made their case at the evening fire pit circle, a brief but noisy discussion ensued. Who would be the judge? How would they propel the canoes, lacking human arms to paddle? In the end, they agreed that participants would be allowed to use whatever strategies they could devise, and the bear and moose would serve as judges. The rest of the animals formed teams by their species. Only the bobcats declined to participate.

The race would take place the following afternoon.

* * *

Breakfast the next morning was brief. Each team was eager to start preparing for the competition. The squirrels were sure they would win, since they came up with the idea in the first place. Squirrel logic. The raccoons were confident in their wealth of shiny objects, which could surely buy victory. The scrub jays claimed not to care about the contest at all. Birds shouldn't have to prove their obvious superiority to the flightless folks. But since the other animals needed a reminder, they would oblige. The beavers refrained from boasting almost entirely. They considered it unprofessional, and this contest was clearly a serious endeavor. Boats were, of course, merely a specialized kind of architecture.

By early afternoon, the entire camp had gathered at the waterfront. Four canoes were resting halfway in the water with their respective teams around them, having been dragged there earlier by the moose and the bear. The moose reviewed the rules. The first team to move their canoe to the center of the lake, as marked by an old buoy, and then return it to shore would be the winners. The bear let out a starting roar, and the race was on.

The first team to make progress was the squirrels. Half of the squirrels dragged a strange contraption of sticks and cloth into the canoe, while the rest pushed the canoe further into the water and climbed aboard. Once afloat, the contraption unfurled to reveal a bed sheet sail hanging from a tree branch mast. Bead necklaces secured the mast to a seat in the middle of the canoe. Crude though it was, the sail caught enough of the afternoon breeze to propel the squirrel team to an early lead. The squirrels cheered and congratulated themselves repeatedly on their cooperation and ingenuity.

The jays were prepared as well. They used long ropes of macramé to harness themselves to their canoe so they could pull it like a team of flying horses. At least, that was the plan. In practice, the canoe was heavy, and the birds were small. So, upon reaching the end of the rope, each bird met with a sudden jolt from the mass of the canoe and plummeted downward. Catching themselves mid-fall, they rose up again, gave the canoe a second tug, and the process repeated itself. Bit by bit, the canoe inched forward as the birds performed their strange, lurching dance.

The raccoons had brought no equipment, only currency: fourteen foil candy wrappers, thirty-six glass beads, and eight smooth, round stones that fit in a raccoon's paw just so. Since bribing the judges would be unsportsmanlike, the raccoons decided to hire the bobcats to push them. Half of the treasure would be paid in advance, and the rest would be awarded after the raccoons took first place. The bobcats, however, had no interest in raccoon trinkets and even less interest in approaching the water. Swimming was for fish, and fish were for eating. Not for emulating. The bobcats motioned to the dead fish they had brought for snacks. While the raccoons furiously defended the value of their goods and the worthiness of boat-pushing as a feline career option, their canoe sat motionless in the sand.

The beaver canoe was also motionless, and the two beavers were nowhere in sight. After some time, they reappeared dragging a second canoe from the boat house. The bear and moose looked at each other, but nothing in the rules prohibited multiple canoes. After placing the second canoe next to the first, the beavers disappeared into the woods. When they returned, they brought a carefully measured log, which they positioned between the two canoes. The next step was to fetch discarded planks of wood from the firewood pile, which slowly came together to form a platform on top of the log and canoes. The traditional cement for beaver construction was mud and rocks, but this project called for something stronger and lighter: fitted wooden joints. By gnawing grooves in the boards, the beavers created a rough approximation of the techniques they had seen in the dining hall ceiling.

Not far from the beaver construction zone, tensions between the five raccoons and two bobcats had gotten out of control. The raccoons had utterly failed to persuade the bobcats to help them. Since shiny objects and clever rhetoric had both failed, the raccoons resorted to theft and violence. Simultaneously. They grabbed the bobcats' fish and began to swing them wildly, slapping the confused bobcats repeatedly. The bobcats were stunned. This was their first time being fish-slapped by a frustrated gang of raccoons. Once they overcame their amazement, they slashed the fish to pieces and chased the raccoons all around the camp. The canoe remained motionless.

The harnessed team of birds continued to make slow but steady progress. To coordinate the rhythm of their tug-and-fall strategy, they began a squawking chant. To cope with the extremely strenuous task of hauling a large canoe through water, they worked out a rotation scheme for birds to sit on the boat and rest before returning to duty.

The squirrel racing team was the first to reach the buoy in the center of the lake, well ahead of the birds. For the return trip, however, the wind was against them, and the squirrels had no experience sailing into the wind. They tried facing the other direction and thinking really hard about the shore, but to no avail. Running around the canoe also had little effect. In an increasingly frantic attempt to turn around, they began to spin and swing the mast wildly. Surely some angle would make their boat go the other way!

Instead, the wild swinging made the canoe rock until it fell over, tossing the fifteen miniature sailors overboard. Squirrels are known neither for swimming nor for staying calm in an emergency. Each thrashed around desperately and ineffectually.

The birds didn't notice—they were lost in their chanting. The beavers, of course, were lost in their woodworking. And the bobcats and raccoons were busy chasing and being chased, respectively.

The moose saw the scene unfold and knew what had to be done. He waded into the water, deeper and deeper, until his hooves no longer felt the gravelly lakebed. Then his powerful legs began to kick in long, strong, cyclic strokes to propel him through the water. He was unintentionally majestic.

The drowning squirrels had just enough sense to climb on the shoulders and antlers of their savior when he arrived. It was a crowded ride back to the beach, but none of the squirrels complained. The black bear met them with sheets, curtains, and other stolen scraps of cloth that could serve as towels.

In the end, the birds were the first and only team to finish the race.

The awards ceremony was held on the floating platform that the beavers had built, where all of the animals fit comfortably, except for the moose who stood nearby. The bear awarded colorful ribbons to the scrub jays for placing first in the contest. Their victory caws were loud and long. When the caws died down, the squirrels stepped forward to present a special award of valor to the moose. The trophy was a wreath of tender branches taken from high in the trees and woven into a circlet. Finally, the raccoons presented themselves with a special award for Most Masterful Survival of an Encounter with Angry Bobcats. Their self-given prize was the very baubles they had originally offered to the bobcats as payment. The bobcats glared but said nothing. The beavers considered the sound construction and successful launch of their platform ship to be reward enough.

When the ceremonies were over, the squirrels began to dance. Bushy tails waved and twirled as the squirrels jumped and spun. Several of them joined paws in a circle and marched around one way, then the other, then into the middle and back out again. Each step was punctuated by high-pitched chitters of glee.

The raccoons were in a mood to celebrate, too. Two of them began to dance a foxtrot around the platform. Not to be outdone, another two started to tango. The fifth raccoon had no dance partner, but she had other skills. She picked up three smooth stones from the raccoon prize pile and juggled them. The bobcats soon found themselves covetously mesmerized by the movements of the very stones they'd spurned before.

The scrub jays were still tired from their extreme exertion during the race, but not too tired to show off a little. They took to the sky in vee- and star-shaped formations, ascending and then descending into loops and barrel rolls. Without a canoe weighing them down, they felt lighter and freer than ever before.

The beavers just sat back and enjoyed the show, proud of their handiwork that had made this floating party possible.

* * *

The morning of the final day of camp was spent cleaning up from the previous days of mischief and fun. The beavers disassembled their canoe platform. The bear and moose returned the boats to the boat house. The jays re-hung the curtains in the cabins. The squirrels picked up every piece of litter they could find. The raccoons grabbed brooms and swept the buildings clean of mud, fur, and feathers. Even the bobcats helped out, in their way, by sleeping on each of the beds a final time to make sure they'd all been returned to their original, comfortable conditions. Finally, the raccoons locked the doors, returned the keys, and camp was closed once again.

The animals met at the fire pit one last time, for the beginning of their annual parade. They had seen humans hold parades many times, marching along the forest trails almost every day of the summer. The animals didn't know what made these trails more special than the rest of the forest where the humans didn't walk, but clearly they were important. So, once a year, on the last day of camp, the animals held a parade of their own.

The moose led the way, stately and regal as he ambled among the trees. The squirrels scurried close behind, trying to keep ahead of the others while playing tag at the same time. The raccoons walked awkwardly with their arms full of treasures. The scrub jays flitted about above the throng, laughing at the idea of walking so far. The beavers discussed trail maintenance and erosion prevention methods. The bobcats argued about whether or not rocks became alive when juggled, and what one should do about it. The bear brought up the rear, soaking up the cheerful, lively sounds of her companions' conversation.

When they reached a clearing at the top of the highest hill, they sang a final song: "Kum-bear-ya." Then it was time to part ways, until next year.

Mina is a pampered Angoran Mau, a prize-winning show kitten. But she grows up, and discovers that life is more complex than a refined cat show.

Best of Breed

by Renee Carter Hall

My show name is Silver Willow, but he calls me Mina. The first two things I remember are my mother's scent and his.

* * *

GENERAL: The ideal Angoran Mau is graceful, of medium size, and well-balanced both physically and temperamentally. Males tend to be larger than females.

HEAD: A medium, smooth wedge. Muzzle gently rounded, should flow into wedge of the head. Firm chin. Ears medium to large, pointed and tufted, close-set and high on the head. Eyes large and almond-shaped. Neck slim and long.

BODY: Toned and slender, finely boned, with long arms and long legs. Paws small, dainty, and round, tufted between toes.

TAIL: Long and tapering with a full brush.

EYE COLOR: Acceptable colors include blue, green, or amber. Preference given for clearer, richer colors.

COAT: Single-coated, medium in length, silky and fine. Coat pattern of random, distinct spots with good contrast between spots and ground color. Arms and legs barred; tail banded. Distinct necklaces on neck and chest. Recognized colors: Cream (pale buff ground color with warm milk-chocolate markings), Smoke (pale silver ground color with jet black markings), Bronze (warm bronze ground color with dark brown-black markings).

DISPOSITION: Alert, affectionate, and intelligent. Basic literacy (see Testing Standards). Calm and cooperative. Pleasant voice, neither strident nor soft-spoken.

PENALIZE: Solid stripes or patches instead of distinct spots. Eyes with casts or rings of other color. Poor condition. Color blindness.

DISQUALIFY: Lack of spots. Short or kinked tail. Extra toes. Crossed eyes. Inability to speak and/or hear. Intelligence below Testing Standards.

* * *

I don't like the hotel where this show is. It smells like cigarettes and makes me want to wash my fur constantly. I follow Shawn through the crowd of cats and handlers. The cats flatten their ears and hiss when someone gets too close. We're all edgy, all bristling. I try to act as if I'm not, the way Shawn has taught me ever since I was a kitten.

"Easy," Shawn says, and he places a hand on my back as we get in line to register. I purr softly, trying to soothe myself. I don't mind the judging, but these hours before, the cats, the smells, the strange place, the *waiting*—these close in around me, and I'm glad for his touch.

The woman behind the table has me turn around so I stand with my back to her. Something beeps. "All right," she says, and when I turn around she is handing Shawn the papers he needs.

I follow him to the judging arena. "What number am I?"

"Six. Early, but not too bad." He shifts the big plastic bag he's carrying to his other hand.

I nod, thinking it through. Sometimes it's not good to be one of the first ones they look at. If they see someone nice near the end, the judges might remember her easier.

"How many are there?"

"Eleven in your group. About forty all together." He walks along the booths, looking at the numbers. "Here."

Each booth is the same: gray boards for walls, a slot to hold your name card, and a chair without a back.

Shawn puts his bag down and starts getting ready. First he takes out the purple cushion that goes on the chair. Then comes the sleek-shiny fabric that he tacks onto the boards behind me. He spends several minutes arranging it, putting it up, taking it down, muttering things, stepping back to look. The edge of one piece is torn, and he finds pins in the bag to fold it over and hide it.

"Now," he says, and starts on me with a stiff brush until all the loose fur is out. It feels good, and I smile as he gets to an itchy place. After that, he uses the soft brush, smoothing my coat. He works all the way to the tip of my tail, arranging it so it fans out over the purple satin.

"There." He takes my face in his hands. "Beautiful."

I like feeling beautiful. I like winning, because it makes him happy, and I hope I'll win today.

There is still an hour before judging starts. He checks his phone for messages while we wait. When I was a kitten, he read me silly stories to pass the time, so I wouldn't get nervous and sick. Now I don't need it. But sometimes I miss hearing his voice anyway.

Finally he looks up at me, and I know he's making sure everything looks right. "It'd be perfect with a necklace," he says with a sigh. "Silver and amethyst, with that silver fur. One of these days we're going to have to try you in something fancy, so we can really dress you up."

The fancy shows are bigger and cost more, but the prizes are bigger too. Here in the natural ones, I win ribbons and a little money. There, it would be more money, maybe even a contract for something. The thought of it flutters in my belly.

"Feeling all right?" he asks.

I nod.

He glances at his phone to check the time. "I'd better go." He takes my hands. His skin is warm against the pads of my fingertips and palms. "Knock 'em dead, kiddo."

It's the same thing he says to me at every show, ever since my first one. He squeezes my hands, then leaves. Handlers are allowed to be in the room during judging, but he says it looks better if he's gone. That way, if the judges ask me questions, they know he isn't trying to tell me what to say.

The first judge is a bald man with little glasses on his nose. "Good morning."

I smile without showing my teeth. "Good morning, sir."

"And how are you doing today?"

"Very well, sir, thank you."

He nods and writes something on his screen. "Will you stand, please?"

"Of course, sir."

He runs his thick hands over my fur. He smells strongly of cologne, and my whiskers twitch, but I stay still, even when I think of how long I will have to wash to take this heavy stink out of my fur.

He touches my face next, feeling my cheekbones, then has me walk to the end of the aisle and back. I do this slowly, placing each paw with care.

He nods. "Thank you. That's all." He scribbles something with his stylus and moves on.

The other judge is a woman. Her face is hard, with deep lines in it, but her eyes are soft and almost as blue as mine. "Good morning."

"Good morning, ma'am."

"Stand, please."

"Yes, ma'am."

She makes some notes, then holds her screen so I can see it. "Identify this, please."

"The number four, ma'am." I have seen the dot-pictures many times.

"Read this aloud, please."

I take the screen carefully from her. "'Without thinking highly either of men or of m… matrimony, marriage had always been her object; it was the only honorable pr… provision for well-educated young women of small fortune, and however uncertain of giving happiness, must be their… pleasantest pr-pres-*preservative* from want.'"

"That's enough. Thank you." She takes the screen back.

I sit down again and try to fan my tail out the way it was.

The last judge is a young woman I know from other shows. "Good morning, Mina."

I smile, but this time I feel it. "Good morning, ma'am."

She feels along my back, has me turn and walk, then thanks me and leaves.

My pads are slick with sweat, and my mouth is dry. Shawn comes back then, bringing me a cup of water. "How was it?"

"Easy."

He grins. "That's my girl."

From then, it's more waiting while the judges finish looking at everyone. I sit and fan my tail and watch people go by. Sometimes I think

I would like to see a show for people. There are so many breeds, all the sizes and shapes and colors, so different. I wouldn't know how to judge.

Finally the young woman comes back, smiles at me, and pins the ribbon up high on the drape where everyone can see it. A red ribbon, Best of Breed. I feel the purring bubbling up in my chest, but I pretend I don't even see the ribbon at all. After a few minutes, the bald man comes back with another ribbon. Best in Show.

We go afterwards to a place that sells frozen yogurt. I can't go in, but he brings me some in a cup, and I eat it on the way home. Strawberry.

I am so happy.

* * *

"Did you win?" Sanura asks as we come into the apartment. "I want to see."

I show her the two ribbons. She touches them carefully and speaks in a whisper. "Pretty."

My mother had two other kittens besides me. One was born very small and had a kinked tail and crossed eyes. He sent her away, I don't know where. I don't think she was ever named.

Sanura lives with us. Shawn says her name means 'kitten' in another language, one people used to speak far from here. When he first told me that, I had that feeling again of the sky being too high, everything too big, wanting to hide under the bed. How strange it was to think that there could be so many ways of saying the same thing. How sad that two people could be saying the same thing and not know it.

He bought me a toy shaped like a ball, that said hello in all the different ways when you pressed it in different places. I learned to say a lot of them. But Sanura liked to press all the places at once and make the voices speak fast one after the other. She laughed to hear them. The toy broke, and he didn't buy another one.

Sanura has faults, Shawn says. Her eyes are greenish-gold, not clear blue like mine, and her spots run together in stripes and blotches. I think she's very pretty, but he told me the judges only want certain things, and it would be a waste of time and money to take her even to the local shows. So I don't ask him anymore.

While Shawn pays the sitter, I take the little bottles of shampoo and conditioner out of the suitcase and give them to Sanura. She doesn't use them, but she likes to line them up and look at them. Sometimes she knocks them over and then lines them up again, purring, then puts them all away in a shoebox under her bed.

That night, after dinner, Shawn sits at the table planning for the next show. The table is covered with bits of fabric, blues and purples and silvers. He mixes them around, stares at them, then pours another drink.

I want him to read to me, but I know that what he's drinking will have him asleep soon.

"What the hell," he says, shrugging. He looks up and sees me. "Wanna move up, kiddo? Try something big?"

My tail lashes. "A fancy show?"

"Not yet. But bigger than today. Much bigger."

I relax a bit, twitching my tail back and forth while I think. "Do you think I'll win?"

He smiles. "Yeah. I think you can. Wanna try?"

I smile back. "Okay."

* * *

The next week, I go to the testing center to qualify. Shawn signs me in, but he has to wait while the woman takes me back to the testing room. She smells like too many flowers, and I try to keep from sneezing. I don't understand why humans wear so much scent. Most of them don't smell bad as long as they're clean.

First she feels all along my fur, fingers seeking out hidden things that listen or speak. It's not that different from what a show judge does, but her hands are quick and rough. Then she looks into both my ears with a little light. "All right," she says at last. "You're clean."

I sit down at the screen and touch where it says "Begin." A clock appears in the corner of the screen, counting down from thirty minutes. This test is longer than most, but it starts with the same easy questions. I touch the red shape, then the triangle, then the picture of the car, so they know I can read and see colors. The questions are different every time, and in a different order, so handlers can't tell their cats which answers to press when. Still, the flower-woman watches me the whole time through the window.

I finish in eighteen minutes and thirty-seven seconds. The screen chimes and shows my score. 100 percent. I know Shawn is already getting the computer message with the results—he's probably looking at it on his phone right now. I hope this means yogurt on the way home. I've gotten all the answers right before, but not on a test this long.

This time, I get peach, and when I ask him, he even brings out a little cup to take home for Sanura. While I eat, I remember how scared I was the first time I took a test. I thought I would get them all wrong and

Shawn would send me away like he did my other sister. But I only got four wrong, and for a kitten it was good enough to pass. I won my first ribbon that weekend, and after the show was over, I asked him why I had to answer the questions. I didn't understand then about the drinking, but that's what he was doing. The glass had only a few amber drops left in the bottom. The bottle was empty too.

"Makes them feel better," he said.

"Who?"

"The judges. That way they can tell off everybody who says we're breeding intelligence out. Makes it seem respectable." He had to say the last word three times before he got it right.

I still didn't understand. But I figured it out later. Making us pretty makes us not as smart sometimes. The judges want pretty *and* smart.

Sanura loves her yogurt. The cup is clean when she's done. I sit and stroke her fur as she falls asleep, and I wish she could win a ribbon sometime, too.

* * *

The bigger show is in two days, but Shawn is already thinking farther ahead. A thin package comes, with two long blue ribbons on sticks inside. At first I think he's bought a toy for Sanura, but then he tells me how the fancy shows have *talent*, which is where you do something special that not everyone can do. And in another place across the ocean, he tells me, they teach their cats to dance with fans or ribbons.

He shows me one on the screen, a slender seal-point with wide blue eyes, moving with ribbons flowing like water over glass. So beautiful. I long to move that way, but when I try, my steps are clumsy, and the ribbons tangle around my legs and tail.

"It's all right," he says. "It takes practice."

I know that birds are born knowing how to fly. I wish I had been born knowing how to dance this way.

* * *

We drive a long way to the show. I thought our city was big, but I was wrong. Shawn laughs at how big my eyes get as I stare out the window.

This hotel is nicer, and the room doesn't smell like smoke. The carpet is thick, the bathroom smells clean, and the shampoo bottles are a pretty shape. I put them into the suitcase right away so I won't forget.

He has a surprise for me. This city has a place where cats can stay with their handlers while they eat at little tables outside. He takes me there for lunch and orders me tuna salad. They don't have frozen yogurt, but I have something called sorbet, which is almost as good as it tingles cold on my tongue.

There are a couple of other handlers there, and I wonder if they're going to be in the same show. I also see a woman alone at another table, reading a screen while she eats her salad. I don't want to stare, but I can't stop looking back at her, wondering if she's lonely. Except for the testing, I've never been anywhere alone. It must feel so strange, so sad.

On the way back to the hotel, we pass by a public screen that shows a picture of a cat like me, only cream with brown spots. REWARD, it says.

"What's reward?" I ask him. It's not a pretty name, not like Silver Willow or Sanura.

"It means she's lost. Her handler doesn't know where she is. So he puts her picture on screens everywhere in case someone sees her. Reward means he'll give money to whoever finds her."

Lost. No handler. Alone. The thought makes me bristle and shiver.

"Don't worry." He puts his arm around me. "You'll never be lost."

Once we're back in the room, he shows me why. He takes my hand and shows me where to feel, at the back of my neck. There's a little hard thing there under the fur. He says it tells him where I am, so he can always find me.

I can't see anything for the tears. I hug him and purr as he strokes me. Never lost, ever. He is so good.

* * *

I win Best of Breed, and even though I'm still clumsy with the dancing, Shawn signs me up for the fancy show. He switches me from ribbons to fans and hires a man to teach me three times a week. I don't like the way the man looks at me, but my dancing gets much better, and that makes Shawn happy.

The night after my last lesson, after Sanura has gone to bed, I decide to dance for Shawn to show him how much better I am. His breath is already sharp and sour, but I put the music on anyway. I place my paws just so, slow and silky, careful to keep my eyes soft and heavy like the man told me.

I like this dance. The steps and turns blend into each other like water. The fans are easier than the tangly ribbons were, and I love peeking over them and making fluttering shapes in the air with them as I dance.

The room feels warmer. I step closer to him. His upper lip is shining with sweat, and his eyes widen as I approach. "Jesus," he mutters, "what'd he teach you?"

"Is it all right?" My heart races, and suddenly nothing matters more than his answer.

"Um… yeah." He shifts on the couch, looking uncomfortable. "It's… good."

I sit next to him. He smells different, and something about it makes me want him to touch me. I press against him, but he pushes me away. "*No,* Mina."

"But…" I can't use words for how I feel. Maybe another language has some. It's like wanting food, but bigger. It's like him stroking my back, but more.

"No," he says again. His voice is sharp and cold, and he goes to his room and shuts the door. I hear the lock click into place.

Is he afraid of me? I would not hurt him. I stand there, shaking, for a long time, and at last I go to my room and try to sleep. But all I can hear is his voice. Why is he angry?

* * *

The next morning, I hear him on the phone.

"I don't know, I don't know. I've got her signed up for the Diamond International in two months, for God's sake. I've already paid the fees. I've gotta do something." He pauses to listen, and then his voice turns colder than I've ever heard before, enough to raise the fur on the nape of my neck. "I'm not a fucking pervert." A long pause. "I just didn't want to do it this soon…" He sighs. "Yeah. I know. What's her number?"

He looks tired when I come out for breakfast. He heats a breakfast tray for me, then stares into his cup of black coffee while I eat.

"How are you feeling?" he asks finally.

I try to think of the right words. I feel different, but not sick. I don't like sitting still. I wish I could go dance, but the lessons are over. Most of all, I want to be close to Shawn. I want him to stroke me, a long time, everywhere. I want to go out with him to another place where we could eat together.

I tell him all of this. He looks angry at first, but then he scrubs his face with one hand and just looks tired again.

"I wanted to wait another year or so," he says at last, "but it sounds like you're ready now."

"Is it another show?"

43

"Not exactly."

* * *

"Don't worry," he tells me. "Just relax, and you'll be all right. He knows it's your first time."

Telling me to relax is not the same as feeling relaxed. The place smells strange and harsh, too clean, and the blonde handler woman smiles too much and too easily. I sip the catnip tea she brings me. I have to stay all night and sleep here. I want to go home. I want the itchy buzzing in my blood to stop.

I go into the room alone. The bed there is clean and soft, the lights are dim, and faint music plays from speakers in the ceiling. A large window takes up most of the wall by the door, and I see Shawn and the woman sitting there, watching.

I don't know what to do. There is a table in one corner with food trays and water, but I'm not hungry or thirsty. I sit on the edge of the bed and think about what Shawn told me. How we're making kittens, so they might look like me, might grow up to win ribbons and titles. This tom is a Triple Grand Champion, and from the way Shawn said that, I know it's important.

The door opens, and I catch the tom's scent before I see him. I hold on to the bed because I feel like I'm falling. He is spotted like me, only bronze. He is beautiful, and I want... I want...

He opens his mouth to taste my scent. As he sits beside me on the bed, I hear him purring.

Shawn didn't tell me I would feel like this.

I'm panting. He brushes his whiskers against mine.

"Don't be afraid," he whispers. "I won't hurt you."

And he doesn't. Not once.

Shawn and the woman watch from the glass. They talk to each other, but I can't hear the words. She blushes. When I look up again, after a long time, they are gone. It doesn't matter.

We couple all night, and too soon it's morning. "Did we make kittens?" I ask him.

The tom smiles. "Maybe. We won't know yet."

I groom his ear. "Even if we didn't, I liked it anyway."

Shawn comes for me then. He doesn't look like he's gotten much sleep, and his shirt is buttoned the wrong way. Then I smell the woman's scent mingled with his, and I'm happy for him. Coupling is so wonderful, I'm happy he got to do it, too.

* * *

The itchy, restless feeling is gone the next morning, but when I wake up I wish I had the tom's arms around me. It felt so nice.

Today is a day for lessons, and I spend most of it sitting at the screen in my room. Reading, spelling, math. Then, watching the video the dance teacher made of my routine, practicing more, moving just the right way in front of the mirror.

A package comes in the mail that afternoon: my costume, Shawn says, for talent. I've never worn a costume before, and I want to open the box right then.

"I have to go back and work a while longer," Shawn says. "We'll try it on later."

Work means sitting at a screen looking at rows and rows of numbers. I don't know what he does with them, but whatever it is, he gets money to pay for food and the apartment and to register me for shows.

"Did you finish all the lessons?" he asks.

I nod.

"Go ahead and take the practice test, then. And after I'm done, we'll see if the costume fits. Okay?"

I look at the box again. "Okay."

The test is easy. I only miss one, when I don't answer fast enough because I'm wondering what the costume looks like, and whether I'll be able to dance in it the way I do now.

My claws are sharp enough to cut the tape. I'll just open the box and look.

I slip into the hallway. Shawn's door is closed, so he's still working. Sanura's door is closed, too—sometimes she likes to have it shut when she plays.

The box is easy to open, and there are two more boxes inside it. One has something that looks like hair in it, black like my spots, with flowers and beads mixed in and slits for my ears to go through.

The other box is flat, and inside is something silky and pink. I take the costume out of the plastic, feeling the cool smoothness of the fabric against my finger-pads.

It's beautiful. It's the same thing the ribbon dancer was wearing when Shawn showed me, the thing he called a kimono. It has little flowers and branches all over it, delicate and swirling, and it shimmers from pink to pale purple in the light.

I slip it on. At first the weight on my fur, even such thin stuff, feels strange. I can't figure out how the hair thing is supposed to go, and it looks like it might hurt my ears anyway, so I leave it in the box. Then I go to the mirror in my room. And stare.

It's still me, but I look so different. The fabric ripples around me as I try part of the dance. It's perfect. I have to show him. I have to thank him.

I run to his door and open it. The desk chair is empty, and the screen is dark.

Then I hear something from Sanura's room. It sounds like his voice, so I open the door.

Sanura is lying on her bed. Shawn is lying on top of her, and he is doing with her what the tom did with me.

I remember how he told me no. I remember how he pushed me away.

I feel my fur bristling, my lips pulling back, my claws coming out. I lay my ears back and hiss.

Now I wish I had blotchy spots, or bad eyes, or even a kinked tail. I would not have had the tom then. I would have had him.

But Sanura has him. And all at once I hate them both.

"Go back to your room, Mina," he says. And I do.

I go back to my room and sit on the floor and shred the fans into little pieces, breaking the thin sticks that hold them together. I won't dance for him again. I won't dance for anyone.

Hours later, Sanura comes in. I'm still sitting on the floor, all the broken pieces of the fans scattered around me. I know I should get up. I'm hungry, but I don't feel like eating. I'm sad, but there aren't any tears.

Sanura sits beside me. She bats at the silky paper for a minute. "Mina, don't be mad. Please?"

I don't know what to say. Everything feels wrong. Then I look in her eyes. They look like a kitten's eyes, I realize. I've always known it, but I've never seen it until now.

One thing I have to know. "Do you love him?"

She thinks for a moment, stirring the bits of paper around, picking up one of the sticks and biting on it. It's like there's a right answer and she's trying to think of it, to pass a test. "Not like I love you," she says at last.

"Does he hurt you?"

She shakes her head, still chewing on the stick. Then she takes it out of her mouth and looks down at the floor, and her voice drops to a whisper. "Sometimes it feels good."

I want to ask more, but I hear Shawn coming. He stops in the doorway and sees the fans. "Mina, what *happened?*" His hands shake as he gathers up the pieces. "These were expensive!"

Sanura hunches low then. "I was playing. I'm sorry."

"These aren't toys. They're Mina's, and they're very important. I don't want you playing with anything in her room again, okay?"

She nods, eyes wide. "Promise."

Shawn dumps the pieces in the trash. "I'll order new ones tonight. They'll still come in time for the show. Now come on, both of you. Dinner's ready."

He leaves. I stare at Sanura. She puts her arms around me and rubs her head against my cheek. "Not like I love you."

I lean against her, closing my eyes and listening to her purr. She should be with a tom, like I was. She'd love to have kittens, and she never will. I feel like I'm reading a test where I don't even understand the questions, and there's no way I can know the answers.

* * *

The next day, we go to the testing place again, so I can qualify for the fancy show. Shawn doesn't say anything on the way, but I can feel him looking at me.

When I sit down at the screen and the test begins, I touch the first answers without thinking—the green square, the word "balloon," the picture of a fish. Then the next question appears, asking me to choose the picture with seven objects. It's the one with the paper clips, and I reach to touch the screen—and stop.

I don't want to be in this show anymore. And if I don't answer the questions right—if I don't pass the test...

The timer in the upper corner of the screen is still counting down. I watch the numbers, then look back at the pictures. I can't decide—but the test is just starting. Besides, if I miss the easy questions, he would know I'm doing it on purpose. I touch the paper clips, the word "tree," the birthday cake.

I realize I don't know what day I was born. I don't understand why that bothers me, but it does.

I touch the next answer without looking at the screen. Then the next. By then, my heart is pounding so much I'm afraid they'll think I'm cheating, so I give the right answers for a while until I calm down.

What will he say? Will we go back to the smaller shows? What if the judges ask me their questions and I don't answer?

The correct answer is fifty-three. I touch fifty-two instead. My finger-pad squeaks against the screen.

I glance at the status bar in the lower corner of the screen. Three questions left. Will that be enough? I skim through the little story, then press "She went to the store to buy milk" instead of "She went to the store to buy bread." I press "Wednesday" instead of "Saturday."

The last question appears. The timer says I have five minutes. I think about just sitting here and waiting until the time is up, but then he'd know.

He might know anyway. I've never missed this many, not since I was a kitten. Maybe I can tell him I'm sick. It wouldn't be a lie, really. I feel hot, and I keep swallowing back a burning taste in my throat. The screen shimmers in front of my eyes. I can't think anyway.

I stare at the question on the screen, but the questions circling around and around in my head are harder than how to spell "bottle." If I didn't go to the shows, would Shawn send me away? Where would I go? Who would give me food?

Then I feel a flutter inside that has nothing to do with my nervous stomach.

Kittens.

I press my hand against my belly, and there it is again. There they are.

I look back at the screen. I can't just think of myself. What if he waits until they're born, and then sends me away? What would I do?

I try to swallow, but my tongue sticks to the roof of my mouth. The timer says two minutes, seventeen seconds. I punch the right answer. The test is over. I hold back tears, watching the blurry hourglass until the results appear.

I've passed. By two questions.

I'm shaking when I go back to him. He asks why I missed so many, and I say they were harder. I don't know if he believes that, but on the way home I have to ask him to pull over so I can throw up, and he strokes my back and tells me it's okay, everything's all right, and even though it's not the truth, I let myself believe him.

* * *

Days go by, slowly at first, then faster. I go to coaching sessions with a too-cheerful woman named Ashlee who teaches me how to walk and turn and hold my arms the right way. At the last session before the show, she gives me a set of plastic alphabet blocks that rattle when you shake them. "For the kittens," she says. "Oh, it's so exciting! How are you feeling?"

The doctor tells me I'm feeling fine. At the appointments, I answer his questions and stay silent otherwise. I talk less than Sanura these days. And every night, Sanura comes into my room and lies next to me in bed, resting her cheek against my belly like she's listening to the kittens instead of just feeling them.

According to the doctor, they're due two weeks after the show. Shawn turned pale when he heard that and spent the next few minutes looking up the Diamond International qualifications on his phone. "Okay, we're good," he said then. "Don't worry," as if I had been.

If he notices any difference in me, he doesn't talk about it. He gives me anything I ask for, and I eat strawberry yogurt until I'm sick of it. Then, on the way home from the last doctor's appointment before the show, I decide to try for something else.

"Shawn?"

"Mm?"

"After the kittens come, do I still have to go to shows?"

"You can still go. Plenty of show cats have kittens."

He hasn't heard me at all. "I don't want to go." I mouth the words, but there's little breath behind them.

He glances at me, then back at the road. "What?"

I force the words out. "I don't want to be in any more shows."

Rain patters on the windshield. He turns on the wipers, and their squeaking rhythm fills the car. He grips the steering wheel tighter. He doesn't answer.

At last, in the driveway, he turns the car off, and we sit for a moment. The rain runs down the windows, blurring everything.

"I'm sorry, Mina." His voice is tight, like he's keeping more words inside him that might fly out if he isn't careful.

I think about the woman at the café, the one sitting by herself. I wonder where she went afterwards, and what it must be like to go wherever you want, stay there as long as you like, and then go somewhere else after.

Shawn says nothing else. He opens the car door for me, and we go inside.

* * *

The Diamond International show is held in the biggest hotel I've ever seen. The ceiling is mostly glass and so high up it makes my neck hurt to look at it. A fountain bubbles in the middle in the lobby, with green ferns all around and vases of white roses, and off to one side a man plays something quiet and rippling on a piano.

I've never seen so many cats in one place, every shape and color, tabbies and spots, longhair, shorthair, calico, toms and queens and kittens. Some wear sparkling collars connected to jeweled chains held by their handlers. One black cat even wears a kind of harness, a web of thin, glittering golden strands across her ebony fur. Men stare at her, then try to look like they weren't staring.

We get in line to register. I keep taking slow, deep, wondrous breaths, drinking in the different scents, cats and perfumes and roses. My kittens leap inside me, like they're caught up in it too.

Over in one corner of the lobby, I see a table laid with big plates of things to eat, little bits of cheese and fish on crackers. Cats wander around, talking to each other, and most are without their handlers.

"Can I go over there? Please? There's food."

He's ready to say no until I mention the food. I know he's worried that I haven't gained enough weight, even if it does make me look better at the show. "All right, but don't go anywhere else. I'll meet you there when I'm done."

I approach the table slowly, waiting for others to move away before I go near. I take a little cup of water that smells like catnip and mint, and then a cracker topped with a morsel of fresh salmon. I want to talk to someone, more than I've wanted anything in a long time, but I don't know how.

Next to me, a gray tabby with green-gold eyes takes a cracker, eats it in two bites, and gives me a smile with her ears up and her whiskers forward. "Fancy stuff, huh?"

I nod and smile back, not knowing what to say. She's not wearing any jewelry, so I can't talk about that.

"Did you try the shrimp? They're wrapped in bacon. Really good." She hands me one, and I nibble at it. "First time at a glitz?"

"Yes."

"Thought so. I haven't seen you around before, and I hit most of the big ones. Name's Cady. What's yours?"

"Hartley's Silver Willow."

She smiles, and at first I think she's laughing at me, but her eyes are too kind. "No, I mean your real name."

"Mina." As I say it, a rippling twinge goes through my belly, and I put my hand there.

She looks at me for a long time. She looks at my belly even longer. "Your handler's cutting it close, isn't he?"

"The rules say it's okay."

I don't like the way she's looking at me, the way she's listening so closely to everything I say and don't say. Like she hears what I'm thinking, how angry I am at Shawn, how I don't want to do any of this anymore. Like she would understand everything if I told her.

Two more questions wrong. That would have been enough.

"I'm all right," I say, but it sounds like a lie, even to me.

Her eyes fix on mine. "We've got an hour before lineup," she says. "Does your handler let you go places by yourself?"

I don't want to tell her I had to ask to cross the room. "I... don't think so."

Her whiskers drop a bit, but then she nods like that's what she thought I would say. She steps close enough to touch noses, close enough to share breath. She says nothing, but I watch her breathe in, tasting my scent.

A woman with long gray hair almost the same color as my fur comes up behind Cady. The cat glances at her and shakes her head very slightly, such a small motion that I almost don't see it. Then they move away into the crowd. My mouth is dry, and I lap at the flavored water to give myself something to do.

Shawn finds me a minute later. I'm glad he didn't see me talking with Cady. "Lineup's in two hours," he says. "Time to get you ready."

Getting ready means going to the room, sitting in a big oval tub while he scrubs my fur with gardenia shampoo. Suddenly all I can think about is that I've never seen a real gardenia. I've seen pictures of gardens with fountains and hedges and benches where you can sit and think. I wish I were at one now, someplace I could sit in the quiet and nobody would ask me anything, and maybe then I could catch some of these thoughts that are swirling around in my head like those ribbons I tried to dance with. As big as I know the world is, mine feels smaller now than it ever has before.

Shawn rinses my fur, combs more gardenia stuff through it, then starts drying it on low. He doesn't say anything except to tell me when to tip my head back or turn one way or another. Every time I look at him, I see him with Sanura, so I try not to look at him at all. I stare into the mirror, into my own eyes. I look scared, but I don't know why. I've never been nervous at a show before. The kittens move inside me, and I wonder if they feel the same things I feel.

Once my coat is dry and fluffed, he starts fixing up all the things we've never been able to do before. He puts a silver wig on my head, long hair that matches my fur. It looks silly, but I don't say anything. These are the kinds of things you have to do if you want to win. He brushes my teeth and paints stuff on them to make them look whiter. This close to him, I can smell the drink on his breath. He usually drinks after the show, not before. Maybe he's nervous, too. Next come pale purple covers for my claws, each one carefully glued on. My hands feel strange and clumsy when he's done.

At last he brings out a black velvet box. "I've got a present for you," he says, and opens the box to show me. A necklace lies on a bed of black satin, clear purple gems sparkling in silver.

I try to smile, because I feel like he expects me to. Finally he just nods and fastens the clasp at the nape of my neck.

"Mina," he says softly then, still standing behind me. His voice goes up a bit at the end of my name, and I realize he wants a response.

"Yes?"

"What you saw with me and Sanura that day, in her room. You know that's a secret, right?"

That's true. It was his secret.

"So you can't tell anyone."

Who does he think would I tell? Now I wish I'd gone with Cady. Maybe I can find her again somehow.

"Because if you tell anyone about it, if anyone finds out, I'd have to send Sanura away. Forever."

I wonder if Sanura even understands coupling. Or does she sit as I am sitting here now, and let him do what he thinks he needs to do?

He goes back into the room. I stay in front of the bathroom mirror and look at my reflection. I don't look like myself, but it's not just the silly hair and the necklace. I don't look scared anymore. And I'm starting to understand what I have to do, if I want to win.

I pick up the little shampoo bottle with the name of the hotel on it. I turn it around and around in my hands, like it's going to talk the way my old toy did, like it's going to say something in another language, something I should learn.

Sanura, I keep thinking. Sanura. My belly twinges again, as if the kittens know who she is.

Then Shawn is back in the doorway. "It's time to go down."

Again I try to smile, and I follow.

* * *

These fancy shows are different in other ways. Instead of the judges coming to us, they sit at a long table in front of a stage, and we walk along the stage when our names are called. I look for Cady in the lineup, but I don't see her or her handler anywhere.

"Number twenty-four, Hartley's Silver Willow."

I walk the way we've practiced, slow and smooth, gliding. My mind floats somewhere above the stage, past the judges. I know I'm supposed to look at them and smile, but I don't. I know if I look for Shawn in the crowd behind the judges, I will see him urging me to smile, so I don't look there either. And then my time is up, and they say my name again, and I leave the stage.

Shawn's angry with me. I can tell by the tension in his jaw, the darkness in his eyes. But he's trying not to show it because of everyone else around.

"You have to look at the judges," he says. "You have to smile at them, or we won't win. Just do it like we practiced, okay?"

But I can't, because when we practiced, I didn't feel this way. Back then, I felt like smiling.

We have an hour before talent starts. Shawn dresses me in my kimono, arranges the hairpiece with the trailing pearls and fake orchids, and gives me the pair of fans to hold. Then he takes me to the hotel bar, where he drinks a little glass of the amber stuff. He orders another one, drinks half of it, then looks around to see if anyone's watching, but we're the only ones there.

He pushes the glass over to me. "Here. Drink this."

I pick up the glass, sniff it, and pull back. Just the scent of it burns my nose.

"Drink it. It'll help you relax."

The man who filled the glass is at the other end of the long bar. He's looking at us, I realize, but Shawn stares at him with hard, dark eyes. The man looks away, and there's no one else, and then those hard eyes are on me.

I should put the glass down. It might hurt the kittens. I should walk out of the bar, out of the show, out of the hotel. But I don't know where I'd go.

"All at once," he says. "Like medicine. That's all it is."

I drink it in a single swallow that burns all the way down. Tears fill my eyes as I set the glass back on the bar, and I hold back a cough until the burning fades.

Shawn smiles, but it doesn't reach his eyes. "That's my good girl. Come on, kiddo. Let's go knock 'em dead."

I follow him out of the bar, hating him, hating myself.

* * *

My turn comes after a white Persian who sings some song I don't listen to. Everything feels fuzzy around the edges, like I'm wrapped in an invisible blanket. Maybe this is what Shawn likes about it.

I still don't see Cady in the lineup.

I glance out at the crowd, judges and handlers and cats. This, then, is my life. This will be my kittens' life. Good girls, ready to dance like they've been taught. And the ones with crossed eyes or kinked tails will wait at home for shampoo bottles and their handlers in their beds...

"Hartley's Silver Willow."

I jerk back to attention. From the emcee's expression, this is the second time he's called my name.

No. Not my name. Not my real name.

I step up onto the stage, find the spot where I'm supposed to stand, unfold my fans and hold them just so, and wait for the music to start.

The opening strains of a violin fill the ballroom. I know the next step, the turn, the flow of one movement into the next. I learned them all perfectly, when his happiness was mine.

I fold my fans up, carefully. They're expensive, after all. I stand, arms at my sides, while the music rises and swells and crests. I look at the judges, and fire burns in my belly, and I do not smile.

The music stops. The emcee looks confused. "Ah—that's contestant number twenty-four, Hartley's Silver Willow."

I stop in front of the emcee on my way off the stage. My tongue feels funny from the drink, but I shape the words carefully. "My name is Mina."

And as I step down off the stage, I see Cady in the back of the crowd, a gray shadow slipping out the ballroom door, out of sight again. I take a step to follow her—and Shawn's hand clamps onto my arm.

"What the hell was that?" He keeps his voice low as he pushes me out of the room and into the elevator. Once the doors close, he doesn't bother. "It cost me five hundred dollars to register for this. Five *hundred*. Plus the lessons and the coaching and all this shit." He yanks the hairpiece off me, the adhesive pulling out a patch of fur behind my ear. One of the trailing strands of pearls breaks, scattering the little beads across the floor.

The elevator doors open. He pulls me to our room and slams the door behind us. Then he takes a bottle from one of the suitcases and pours enough to fill one of the hotel glasses halfway. He takes one gulp, then another, then blows out a breath and closes his eyes. He sets the bottle and glass on the desk and sits down on the edge of the chair.

I sit on the edge of the bed. I don't know what's going to happen, but I already know that nothing's going to be the way it was, ever.

Shawn drinks in silence. I lose track of how many times he refills the glass, but the bottle is more than half empty already.

"I'm not doing any more shows," I say finally.

He barks a laugh. "Yeah, I kinda figured that." He takes another swallow. "So what *do* you wanna do, then, huh? 'Cause your qualifications are pretty slim."

He sets the glass back on the desk and studies me for a moment, then breaks into a lopsided grin. "Course, I know some people who might be very happy to pay you a few hundred here and there." He sits down next to me on the bed, his hand on my knee. "Not as high-class as the shows, but it brings the money in."

His hand slides under my kimono, cold between my thighs. He leans so close I can taste his breath.

"Ohh, now, don't look like that," he says, taking hold of my arm again with his other hand. I try to pull away, and he grips tighter. "Don't act like you didn't want it when you danced for me. You wanted me to fuck you then. Maybe I should've, huh? Maybe that would've kept you nice and happy and they'd be putting a crown on you downstairs right now. But no, I couldn't, you were too important, everything was riding on you."

"So you fucked Sanura instead?" The words taste gritty and sour in my mouth.

He laughs. "Tell you a secret, kitty. She likes it. She asks for it. And she's a damn good fuck for a retard."

I've only managed to pull off three of the purple claw covers while he's been talking, but it's enough to cut three deep lines in his neck. He jerks away, stumbling, pressing a hand to his neck. He stares at the blood on his fingers, like he doesn't know what it is or how it got there. It's enough time to get the bottle and bring it down hard. He trips over the chair, pulling it down with him. I hear his head hit the wall.

At first I think he's dead, and my stomach knots from a mixture of terror and satisfaction. Then I realize he's still breathing. I know this sort of sleep; it lasts a long time.

I take off the claw covers and the kimono. After a moment to think, I find the silver necklace from earlier, safe in its box, and put it on. It was a gift, after all, and silver means money.

I want to take the little shampoo bottle, the conditioner, the lotion, all lined up on the mirrored tray. But none of the luggage is small enough for me to carry without looking suspicious. A handler might send their cat on an errand, but not carrying a suitcase, and I've never needed a little bag of my own.

There's nothing else to take. I step over Shawn, open the door, and walk into the world alone.

* * *

It starts in the elevator, with a sudden warm rush down the fur of my legs, soaking a dark splotch into the carpet. The first pain hits me soon after. Distantly I hear the bell ding, but by the time the doors open, the pain has passed. I'd planned to look for Cady or her handler, to ask everyone I could find where they might be. But the kittens have planned something else.

There are no safe places here. I have to get as far away as I can before he wakes up. With that button under my skin I can never be lost. He might even have it hooked to his phone.

I make my way out of the hotel from a side entrance. It's getting dark, and the streetlights are flickering on. I rest against the side of the building as the pain grips me again, and once it passes, I move on. The street feels too exposed. I find an alley, dark, safe, and double over against the next wave. They're closer now. Soon.

I huddle behind a huge metal box of garbage. The smell is awful, mostly rotten meat and urine, but I feel protected. The pain comes again, familiar now. This time I push against it, and one by one, they are born.

I wash them and bite them free. They smell like nothing I've ever smelled before, and I breathe in their scents again and again. I want to rest now, forget everything else for these precious first minutes, but there's one more thing I have to do.

I find a piece of glass nearby, sharp and straight and easy to hold.

It hurts. It hurts so much, but I cut until the button comes free. My back feels warm and wet, and I'm shaking. I throw it as far as I can, but it's not very far.

The kittens are crying. They're so tiny, but so strong. One is blotchy like Sanura. One is smoky gray, no spots at all. One has a bronze coat just like the tom. All of them are beautiful and perfect and mine. They press their paws against my belly, and I hear myself purring as they start to nurse.

Then eyes come out of the darkness. Green eyes. Yellow eyes. Water-blue. Two queens and a tom-who-isn't.

"Showgirl," one whispers.

I flatten my ears and spit. No one will touch my kittens. No handlers. No cats.

Green-eyes comes close. She doesn't smell angry. She touches noses with me.

"I'm not going back," I say. "I'm lost. Forever."

She nods. "So are we."

And then, someone I know. Tabby stripes and gold-green eyes and Cady's scent. "It's all right. They're with me."

The world has gone gray, and I don't know if I'm really saying the words or not, but I try. "My sister…"

"We'll find her. Don't worry. It'll be okay." Her voice floats in the gray.

They lift me up, away from the blood and the button he'll find. A van is parked nearby, and Cady helps me into it. I don't know where we're going, but the others tell me about warm beds and food. *Safe,* they keep saying, *away,* and that is all I need.

I hold my kittens close. Someone asks me my name, and tired as I am, when the old title swims up out of the gloom, I push it away again. "Mina," I reply softly, whispering it to each kitten, singing it to myself, sharp as a shard of glass, bright as a purple stone. "My name is Mina."

Dan drives a big truck, a Kenworth with a dragon on the door. He's been driving it since the war. His soul was killed in the war, and his dragon is all he has left.

Buffalo, Coyote, Horse, Snake, and Lonesome Woman help him find his soul again.

Dragonman and Lonesome Woman

by Vixyy Fox

"Hey, Dan!"

Hearing no response, the dispatcher stepped into the small trucker's lounge and stood where his presence was obvious. The big driver folded the newspaper down around his fingers so it was bent in half, and then looked over his 'half' reading glasses.

"Yeah... what?"

"I'm glad you're so quick to jump at a job; I got a load if you want it. It's not much, but it'll pay some bills and maybe buy you an extra tank of diesel."

The large man gave a deep sigh. "I hate charity work," he grumbled, but he was at a point where he had to take it. His breath smelled heavily of stale cigarettes. On the stand next to him was an old cup of coffee half full of cold black liquid and floating butts. He carefully picked it up and tossed it into a large open garbage can a few feet away. Some of the liquid sloshed on the wall.

He sighed. "Sure... all right... give it to me. It's better than sitting around here collecting dust."

Leaving his newspaper on the chair, he followed the dispatcher as he limped back to his small office. Paper littered the desk but on the wall were mounted neatly arrayed clipboards representing the trucks he had out on the road, their loads, and their destinations.

"I told ya to come on full time with the company," the dispatcher said as he walked. "The bosses have given me explicit instructions that the good loads go to company truckers first and all the rest to the ones who just hang around… that would be you."

Dan pulled a pack of Lucky Strikes out of his shirt pocket and shook up two from the crumpled paper container. He offered one to the dispatcher when he turned to look at him. "You know me, Pat. I don't let nobody mess with my truck. The minute I sign a contract with the company, they become part owners in my life. I'll take the peanuts, thank you very much. If the old girl was a living creature, you know I'd marry her."

"Sex with a truck," snorted the dispatcher as he accepted the cigarette. "Thought I'd heard it all but that one takes the cake; icing and all."

"That's not what I meant, and you know it." He chuckled, as he clicked the top back and spun the knurled knob on his lighter. "Your mind is always in the gutter."

They paused as the cigarettes were puffed into clouds of smoke. He flipped the lighter closed with a click and looked at the plain Red Ball on it. It was a reminder of better times.

"I'd settle down if'n I found the right woman; you know that, Pat. She'd just have to be really large, and able to haul a good load."

The dispatcher laughed and pulled a clip board off the wall. "It's not exactly like when we were driving with the Red Ball Express, is it?"

"Red Ball… now there's one for the history books. You and me logged a lot of miles over in Germany. Sorta hated for it to end… but…" He turned and looked out the door of the office so he wouldn't have to look at his friend. He hadn't forgotten the mine and the fact that Pat had lost his shifting leg to it. That's why he was a dispatcher now and not a trucker still. Pat was not supposed to be the one driving that night, but Dan had found some German hooch and hadn't been in any shape to be behind the wheel. Pat had done double duty for his friend to keep him from getting court-martialed. They were closer than best friends… war will do that to people. After Pat was shipped to the rear, Dan volunteered for every dangerous job there was, and hadn't touched a drop of booze since. He ended up getting himself a Bronze Star which he mailed to Pat with a forged letter from the commanding General awarding it to him. Pat had worn it on his uniform when they met the driver at the train station on his return from Germany, never once even hinting to his friend that he was aware of the deceit.

"Forget it," Pat said, reading his old comrade like a book. "That was a long time ago. I got on with my life, Dan. Look at me… I got a wife and kids, three dogs, a house, and even some goldfish. Whadda you got? A truck?"

Dan turned back to him and smiled. "Not just any truck, ya old fish-faced pencil pusher. She's a Kenworth; and the best one on the road."

"I saw the dragon on the door," the dispatcher said to him quietly. "It brought back a lot of good memories."

The dragon was the same one Pat had personally painted on their Army duce and a half against strict orders about such things. On that one he had used dark colors so it wouldn't stand out at a distance... but it was there. The brass, in a rare mood of understanding, had seen it while not actually seeing it. The dragon was Dan and Pat's personal talisman.

"Yup," the trucker replied from around the fist holding his cigarette, "Wanted to surprise you. Thought maybe it would get me an extra load or two. Whatayagotforme?"

"Potatoes."

"Spuds? Well, hell... at least it ain't pigs. I hate the smell of pigs... 'bout makes me want to puke when I get down wind of 'em. Not like hauling 105 ammo."

Pat drew in a lungful of smoke and then let it back out again. "Pigs won't blow you up, Dan," he said softly. Then he gave him a look that the driver knew only too well.

"What's the catch?" he asked suspiciously.

"The load's in Idaho and you have to drive there empty. Told you it would get you on the road and not much more. The company will tanker your fuel to the destination which is L.A., but you have to pay your own fuel to the farm, and again home from L.A."

"Empty from L.A. too? Jesusssssssss, Pat, why don't you just shoot me and get it over with. I'm dying a slow death here."

"Call me when you get into L.A. I got a few favors outstanding and I can probably get you a load to carry back."

He held the clipboard out with a pen on top of it so Dan could sign for the trip. "It's the very best I could do for you, pal. You're the last independent here... you know that. I told you a long time ago to move to Chicago. Texas just isn't cutting it for the truckers wanting to stay free."

"Yeah," he said, signing the document. "Big whoop. Chicago, the mob, and a nickel will get me a cup of coffee." He looked up at the dispatcher and saw the other man's look of hurt feelings. "I didn't mean it like it sounded, Pat. I was referring to moving... Chicago... and ... well... up there I get owned too. Thanks all the same, pal; I do appreciate the thought."

Pat held out his hand, and the two shook, the hand shake moving into a bear hug.

When the hug ended, Pat told him, "We've come a million miles or so since way back when, Dan. I ain't gonna let a comment about coffee and the mob get me all riled up. I sure wish you would settle down, though. If'n you had a good woman of your own, we could do some really good barbeQ's. You know, like a family… maybe have a beer together?"

"Yeah… sure… some day, Pat; right now I gotta get to Ida-hoe."

Pat took the clipboard back, scribbled his signature under Dan's, and then again on a fuel chit. Taking out his wallet, he removed a five and handed it with the chit to the big trucker. "Dinner's on me tonight. Take the chit to the pumps and they'll fill your tanks; then you're ready to roll."

"The company buying me a tank of fuel is ok, but I can't let you buy me dinner," he said holding the money out to the dispatcher.

"And why the hell not? You haven't been to the house in forever, and I get tired of seeing you living in that damn truck."

"Martha don't like me; that much is as plain as the nose on your face. I don't go where I'm not welcome."

Pat looked at him for a moment, and then smiled his most disarming smile. He had once gotten the drop on a German Sergeant with his smile, handily knocking the man's rifle aside when he had smiled back and then taking him prisoner.

"She loves you, Dan, same as me… she just has her ways, is all." He took the bill and stuffed it into the trucker's shirt pocket. "Don't cross the desert. Go around it. You don't have a definitive time to be there, and the extra fuel is for the extra miles. Just show up and they'll load you when you get there."

"You being superstitious on me?" the driver asked. "What's wrong with the desert?"

"Martha…" he began, but Dan interrupted him.

"Martha's an Injun, and full of superstitions. These are modern times, Pat. You of all people should know better. Dammmmmm… you seen the world."

"And I didn't like what I saw much, either. White medicine didn't keep me alive when I got home, Dan; it was Martha and her Comanche people. Her brother Sammy was a Marine Code Talker, for God's sake; that's why she was a volunteer at the Army Hospital where we met. She was doing her part like everyone else, and she was right to bring Sammy in to see me; he's one fine Medicine Man."

"Him and his dances, and his totems… yeah… and all that mumbo jumbo; we've had this conversation before. I don't believe in that or any other religion… damn… the conversation is old and ya ain't gonna make a believer out of me. Reality is the road, and that's it."

"That's right… we have had the talk before," replied Pat, becoming suddenly angry. "It's not just God you gave up on, you gave up on the world too, Dan. The war got you just the same as if you'd been blown up like me. You hide in that damn truck of yours. You stay on the road for weeks at a time, and what do you have to show for it? Not a damn thing! Come to the house. We're a family there… you could be included."

Now it was Dan's turn to look hurt. "I better get moving," he said softly.

"Yeah… maybe you'd better."

The trucker turned without a word and walked out of the office.

"Don't drive through the desert at night!" Pat yelled after him.

Dan's right arm came up waving the trip ticket. His left dropped down, and from his hand the green of the five-dollar bill fluttered to the floor like a leaf.

* * *

The tractor trailer roared along at a steady sixty miles per hour. The full moon lit the road almost as well as the truck's headlights. Dan had stopped at the 'last diner for the next 200 miles', but opted to put his money into the fuel tank instead of his stomach. Ten cents for a coffee, was hardly cheap, but he convinced the waitress to fill his thermos rather than dump the fried-out remains of the huge coffee urn in the sink. It was nasty, but he was used to nasty, and it would help keep him awake.

Then it was twenty-five cents a gallon to the pump for diesel… 'Pay the attendant please, thank you very much'. He topped the tank out, counted his change carefully to the penny, and then allotted himself exactly two cents for a liquorish rope before heading out on the dusty road. The road in question was a two lane stretch that most of the truckers avoided if they were able. Driving the desert during the day was unbearable except for the real diehards. The temperature had topped out at 108 degrees the day before, and the arid sands had actually seen hotter. Those were days that the truckers would put a bale of hay in each window and then soak it with water. As they traveled, the evaporating water cooled the cab just enough to get them through. Some of them even installed a water tank on the roof of the cab so the cooling effect would last a longer amount of time without the need to stop. To Dan it was a challenge, but he preferred the night when it was cooler naturally… screw the bales of hay, those would just mess up his paint job.

Ten miles out from the diner he saw an old man standing beside the road. At first look, he appeared to be a lump of shadow exactly like the cactus that populated the area. As the truck approached he grew in detail. The shadow moved slightly and his head turned back to look at the oncoming truck. The man's eyes reflected the light just like those of an animal. He didn't have his thumb out, nor did he hold up a painted cardboard sign announcing his destination and that he had just had a bath; but he did watch Dan come, and the driver knew his eyes were on the truck as it passed and as it progressed into the distance. The driver shivered, goose bumps forming on his arms. He might have passed it off, but the shiver and superstition caused him to glance down at his gages. The engine temp was well into the red zone.

"Cripesamighty!" he yelled, his body automatically beginning the down shifting and braking. With each downward movement of the gear shift, he saw the temp needle dip slightly, and then move back up, which was a sure sign the problem was not with the indicator. Dan was an old timer, which meant he was meticulous about checking the gages. There had been no problem ten miles back when he left the truck stop, nor even a mile back just a few minutes before; everything had been fine. That meant there was a more than good chance there was no damage done, but he had to act quickly.

With a final pishhhhhh of the brakes, the truck came to a shuddering halt. Both of the cab windows were open and Dan heard nothing outwardly that suggested anything wrong. Nor did he smell the tell-tale smell of hot fluids. Glancing at the temp gage, he was gratified to see that it had slid back down into the high area of the green arc, but he would still have to check the radiator's water level.

"It'd be just my luck you'd have a busted hose out here in the middle of nowhere, and you can betcha no one would be by for a good day," he grumbled to the truck as he set the brake.

Grabbing his old army issue flashlight, he stepped out of the cab, walked to the left front, and opened the side panel so the tractor could breathe a little easier. The extra airflow would cool the water in the radiator a little more before he opened the cap. Walking to the other side, he did the same thing, and then mounted the fender and was shining his light down into her guts when a voice from nowhere startled the living crap out of him.

"Ya got problems?"

He banged his head on the top panel, and almost fell off the fender. His initial gut reaction was to scream and throw his flashlight, but he caught himself. Army training kicked in… he had spent too much time close to or actually behind enemy lines to give himself away like some green behind the ears driver... but he did yell for all he was worth when he identified the source of the voice.

"CRIPESAMIGHTY AND GAWDDDDD DAMMMMMMMM... DON'T EVER DO THAT!"

"Do what?"

Dan found himself looking into the eyes of the old man he had passed on the road. He suddenly felt silly. The fellow had had no reaction to his tirade. Instead, he stood calmly watching him. The driver had the unexpected mental image of a large Buffalo standing in a field... and then the vision passed. He sat heavily on the fender of his truck, and held a hand over the area of his chest that suddenly hurt. "You'll give a fella a heart attack by sneaking up on him like that."

"Didn't sneak... you had your head in by the growler."

Dan flashed the light at him, and the man didn't squint against its beam. "I don't grind my gears," he countered, feeling slightly insulted. "What are you doing way the hell out here anyways?"

"Waiting for you."

"Now that's just creepy as hell," he fairly shouted.

"Why?"

Dan could hear the truck's engine ticking over behind him. He felt the heat coming off of the radiator and blowing back past him. For a moment it was all he heard... and felt... and then he slid off the fender to stand in front of the man in a confrontational way.

"If you're looking to highjack me you may as well forget it. The trailer's not loaded, and even if I did have a load it wouldn't be anything 'cept spuds."

He sized the other man up and figured him to be in his late sixties. He, on the other hand, was late thirties, and in some sort of shape... well... as in good a shape as his constant life on the road and smoking three packs of cigarettes a day allowed for. He spit on the ground.

"Shouldn't spit out here," said the other man.

"Why the hell not?"

"Cuz it's the desert and water is precious."

"I'll be out of the desert by sunup tomorrow morning."

"Don't think so."

The big driver backed a step, and spread his feet slightly, readying himself. "And why not?"

The old man shrugged, and said something in a language Dan didn't understand.

"N' what's that supposed to mean?"

"Gut feeling. Check your engine temp. I think it's back down."

Pat's last words to the big driver began to echo through his brain... 'Don't drive through the desert at night'.

"How'd you know about my engine temp?"

The man smiled. "You stopped sudden like, and when I come up, you had the side panels up... you opened both of them. You wouldn't a done that 'cept for heat. I might be old but I'm not stupid."

Dan felt how tightly he was holding the flashlight, and forced himself to relax his grip. He suddenly felt stupid giving in to the feelings of being creeped out the way he had.

"You need a ride?" he asked the old man trying to cover his confusion.

"Yup... could use one, I s'pose. My sister is ill, and I travel to be with her."

"Well, why the hell didn't you stick your thumb out when I passed? I woulda picked you up."

The old man looked at his right hand. Slowly he put his thumb up and then held it in the space in front of himself, looking back at the driver. "Like this?"

Dan frowned, not sure if the old man was now making fun of him. "Yeah, that'd work."

The fellow smiled in the glare of the flashlight, and Dan realized he had never stopped shining it at him. He also figured that the desert wanderer had not been making fun of him; he was probably just not all there.

"OK," he said. "I'll check the radiator, and then we'll continue from here provided the temp went back down and the radiator is full. Otherwise we turn around and head back to the truck stop, but you're still welcome to share the cab."

The old man nodded, but said nothing.

"What's your name?" Dan asked him.

"Buffalo."

"You got a first name?"

The old man nodded, never cracking a smile. "Buffalo."

"OK then, what's your last name?"

He still did not smile. "Buffalo."

"Dang... How about I call you Buff?"

He nodded. "Sure."

Twenty more miles down the road and the old man had not said so much as one word. Dan was sipping on some of the sour-tasting burned coffee. He offered 'Buff' some but the man had simply shaken his head no.

"Dang, but the time flies," the driver said conversationally.

"Yes," agreed Buff, "But it does not fly; it stampedes like the herd in a thunderstorm. It runs blindly, never seeing the cliff until it is too late."

Dan looked at him. "What in hell does that have to do with time? You're a strange old bird, ya know that?"

The old man smiled this time, and it was an honest smile. "If'n I was a bird I could fly like your time."

Dan snorted, took a sip of his coffee and then spit it out the window, tossing the rest of the cup off with it. "That was just a bit too bad even for my taste."

A small man dressed only in a loin cloth and wearing some sort of animal skull headpiece jumped into the middle of the road holding up his hands, palms towards the oncoming truck, as if he were going to physically try and stop it.

"HOLY MARY, JOSEPH, AND THE CHILD!" yelled Dan, swerving the truck to the left and mashing down on the brakes. For a long moment the trailer wanted to continue straight, teetering on the verge of jackknifing. As the wheels screeched, Dan went through the gears like a mad automated machine, not even thinking of the motions he was having his body complete. Five hundred yards later, his rig, once again straight and stopped, sat beside the road with its engine ticking over quietly. It was as if the modern monster had not even disturbed the still of the night. A quick check of the undercarriage with the flashlight showed no evidence that he had hit the little man. The driver now stood behind the truck shining the light off into the distance. His nose twinged at the smell of burned rubber. He was fuming because this meant he would have to be changing the tires sooner than he had anticipated, and that cost big money. Unlike many of the large trucking companies, he did not run recaps which were cheaper, but more dangerous to use.

"This night is beginning to really, really grate on my nerves," he said into the darkness.

Buffalo came up and stood next to him. "He's back there," the old man said softly, pointing to an area of darkness. "I think you scared him with all the noise."

Dan looked at him, his disbelief clearly seen even in the low light of the moon. "I scared him?" He deliberately placed his hand on his own chest for emphasis. "I scared him? Dang, Buff, that's the second heart failure I've almost had tonight, and both within an hour of each other."

"The other one didn't count." The statement was said without humor, without anger, without irony... it was just a statement. "Come with me and we will find this Trickster."

"Trickster?"

"It was Coyote. His heart attack was meant to happen. Turn off your light and we will walk up the path to find him."

A hundred yards up the road, the pair stopped, and Buffalo called into the night. "How, Coyote."

"How," came the reply. The voice was higher than normal, though it had a clear masculine quality to it.

"You did not trick us, Coyote. You have failed in your joke. Come; show yourself."

The smallish man seemed to separate from the shadows of the nearby brush. He was no more than four and a half feet tall. Dan made to raise his flashlight but Buffalo's hand was on his arm.

"Moon is enough," he said simply. "She gives us light with which to see."

To Dan's eyes, the light was only sufficient to show the newcomer as a small shadow, somewhat larger than his surroundings.

"Buffalo? What are you doing with the Dragonman?"

The old man turned back to the newcomer. "Yes," he replied. "I have found Dragonman before you, little brother, so that is another coup for me. How is our sister?"

"She lives, but we need to hurry."

Dan, watching the exchange, felt another chill. The name 'Dragonman' did not quite jell in his mind, but it was obvious that they were talking about him... and who was this ailing sister?

"What in hell do you mean by jumping into the middle of the road like that?" he demanded. "You got a death wish or something? Damn near run you over like some sort of wild dog." He turned and spit on the ground.

"I am not a wild dog," the little man told him flatly. "I am Coyote."

"You were damn close to being a speed bump! I'm packing it up and hitting the road, Buff. You want to come along, do so... otherwise... well... otherwise... just..." he made a frustrated sound, "Otherwise; that's all."

He turned and stormed back to the truck. Buffalo and Coyote watched him as he walked.

"You're sure this is the one?" asked the little man of the other.

"Yes. He is like my people. He has sacrificed much, though not joyfully. He has left a good part of himself behind in this recent war, and he does not know how to fill the hole. There is no joy in his heart. This machine is his only happiness."

Coyote sighed. "This is not going to be easy."

Buffalo smiled at him. "Where is your spirit, little one? You are the 'Trickster'. I have seen you do great things. I am sure you will be equal to the task."

The smallish man chuckled. "Remember that Pawnee brave?"

Buffalo chuckled too. "Oh my, yessssss… that was a good one."

The truck's horn blasted out one long lonely note, piercing the quiet like the ancient roar of a real dragon.

"That fits," said the little man.

"Yes… it does, doesn't it?" replied Buffalo. "We need to go before he leaves us. He certainly is a peculiar sort of human, but he has been through much. We will have to be patient."

"You're sure he's *the one*?"

"Yes, Trickster. I am very sure."

Dan was about to slip the truck into gear and ease down on the accelerator when the rider's side door opened and the dome light flashed on and then off again as the door was closed. Both men had gotten into the cab. It was a bench seat, so Coyote slid to the center and Buffalo sat on the right.

"I am sorry I scared you," the little man told Dan, holding out his right hand for a shake. It was the way he held his hand that told the driver he was not used to the custom.

Dan took his hand and then squeezed it firmly, shaking it up and down. "Not a problem," he replied. "Just next time you try that little trick, you're liable to end up road kill."

He made to let go, but Coyote held on to his hand and continued shaking it.

"Ok…… ok…… enough…" Dan finally said, ending the strange hand shake.

"I was desperate," Coyote told him. The bleached bone of his headpiece, and the black painted lines on his face gave him an almost comical appearance in the half light of the truck's dashboard indicators.

"I'd be desperate if I looked like you too. You dress like this on a normal basis, or did I miss Halloween?" The trucker chuckled, and then what Coyote told him seemed to sink in. "Oh… I don't suppose you're gonna tell me why you were desperate?" he asked, starting the truck back down the road again. He moved through the gears slowly; automatically double clutching to keep from grinding them.

Buffalo gazed out his window and into the distance as if he were looking for something.

"I am afraid for my sister," said the little man.

"Hell, if I had a sister, I'd be afraid for her too, but that hardly constitutes a dire emergency now, does it?"

"She is dying."

Dan spit out the window, and then reached up and grabbed the lanyard of his horn. Pulling it, he held it until the air in the system had run low enough that the horn faded to nothing. This left him with no air for braking, but he knew the system would pump up again in a matter of seconds... besides, the road was straight, and there was no other traffic.

"Why did you do that?" the little man asked him.

"It chases the demons away."

Coyote and Buffalo exchanged a look.

"Besides that," the trucker continued, "If you ever say the word 'death'," he paused to spit out his window again, "You have to spit, or it'll come looking for you."

Coyote leaned over Buffalo, and both of them spat out the window.

Dan chuckled, and actually smiled. "You guys are too much. So continue; tell me about your sister."

"She is dying," Coyote said, and then leaned across Dan's chest and spat out of his window, blocking the driver's view of the road. Dan pushed him back roughly.

"What in hell are you doing!?"

"Spitting, like you said."

"For crying out loud, do it out Buff's window. I have to see the road, or we'll drive right out into the desert, and end up breaking an axle."

"Drive?"

"Oh, for Pete's sake!" Dan was about to call him a bonehead, noticed what was sitting on the little man's head, and thought better of it. "OK... let's assume you've lived your entire life out here in the middle of nowhere. Look... you turn the wheel in the direction you want the truck to go, and it goes there... simple." He turned the wheel to the left, and the truck went into the left lane. Then he moved it to the right, and the truck moved back to the right lane.

"OHHHhhhhhhhhhh..." Coyote said, his mouth dropping open slightly. "It is not a living thing then?"

Dan laughed out loud. "It is to me, but no, it's a machine. You act like you really have lived your whole life in the desert."

"Yes... this is true."

The trucker glanced at him, and then back to the road, smiling. If it hadn't been that he was so far out in the desert, he might have suspected Pat of setting up a huge practical joke.

"RRRrrrriggghhhttttttttt... OK... tell me about your sister."

"She is dying."

Dan spit out his window, and Coyote leaned across Buffalo to spit out that side. Part of his dribble came back in the wind and landed on Buffalo's face. The old man wiped it off, and then without comment, made the smaller man trade places with him so he would have the spot all to himself. Coyote promptly stuck his head and upper torso out of the window. He let out a happy yowllllll, and his animal skull head piece went flying off into the night. Buffalo grabbed him by the straps of his scanty loin cloth and dragged him back into the cab.

"Tell him," he instructed the little man.

"She is dying...," they all spat again, "And we need your help to save her."

"We?"

Dan looked over at him, and stifled the laughter which bubbled to the surface. Where the head piece had been, Coyote was completely bald. This made his long hair, which streamed out from the sides and back look even funnier. He turned his eyes back to the road and almost had his third heart attack of the evening. In the distance, and on the edge of the light his headlights produced, stood a very young and naked woman. As the truck approached, she began to run in the same direction the truck was traveling. As she ran, her body flowed into the form of a horse which easily kept pace with him. Glancing at the speedometer, he saw that he was clipping along at sixty-five miles per hour.

Coyote yelled out the window to her. "HOW HORSE!" He was then taken again with the exhilaration of the wind in his face and leaned out far enough that he would have fallen except for the firm hands of Buffalo holding on to the strap of his loin cloth and to one leg.

"You should stop slowly this time," the old man said to Dan, his face not even cracking a smile.

"Right... sure," the driver replied, beginning to move down through the gears again. "And you hold on to slick britches there so he doesn't fall out under the wheels."

"He has no britches."

"Exactly my point."

* * *

The girl, at first glance, appeared to be no more than fifteen and a Native American. She stood looking at Dan appraisingly. He for his part held out a blanket he had snatched from the sleeping berth.

"You need to put this around yourself."

"Why?"

"Because you're naked as a Blue Jay."

"That is a bird. Don't be silly; birds are not naked, they have feathers."

"Just put the blanket around yourself; you're making me nervous as hell. It ain't proper to run around naked. Didn't your mother ever teach you the rules and all?"

"I will wear it if you help my sister," she told him, standing erect and defiant.

"What is this?" he asked, holding the blanket in front of himself so he only saw her from the neck up; "Sister night? Fine, I'll help; just put the blanket around yourself."

The girl smiled a disarming smile and allowed Dan to slip the blanket around her shoulders.

"Now then... what's wrong with your sister?"

"She is dying."

All three men turned and spat on the ground.

* * *

Dan found himself driving over rough ground. Having promised to help, he cursed himself for being stupid and gullible, and then detached the trailer, leaving it by the side of the road. His reasoning was simple... as light as the trailer was empty, it would still be too cumbersome to pull through the sands he might encounter. The tractor, on the other hand, was still compact enough that he could easily get it in and out of where he had to go; which he had been assured by all three people was not that far off the road. The mission was a simple one: get to the ailing sister, pack her up, and move her out.

"OK," he told them as they stood in the light of the headlights. He was pacing back and forth in front of them like his old Lieutenant explaining their destination and cargo. "I don't know what exactly is going on here, but I gave my word, and my word is my bond... always has been... always will be." Under his breath he mumbled something about being snookered by a woman. "Now the way I see it, the objective of the mission is that we go in, get your sister into the truck, and then get her into town where the doctors can look at her. What's her name anyways?"

"Lonesome Woman," all three of them said at once.

Dan stopped pacing and looked at them. The age spread was from what appeared to be about sixty-eight to fifteen years, and they were all claiming this woman to be their sister.

"Now this is some sort of family," he told them, not bothering to explain his thought. "OK," he continued, "Lonesome Woman... I'm guessing that she's too ill to walk or she would've come into town by now. That would explain the need for me. Woulda been nice if'n I had a jeep instead of the Kenworth. Where exactly is she?"

"I can show you," Coyote said, "But we will have to climb to the top of your machine."

Dan had immediately said 'no climbing on the truck', wanting to protest that they would scratch the paint, but then he relented. He had to know the direction. Removing his shoes he climbed with Coyote to the top of the cab, where they scanned the night.

"She is there," the small man said pointing.

Dan didn't see anything. He was about to say something sarcastic, when he saw a flicker of light which might have been a very far-off campfire. Measuring distance in the dark out on the desert was a tricky business at best.

"There?" he asked. "I seen ghost fires all over the desert... you sure it's not one of those?"

"Yes."

"What in hell is she doing living way the f... ahhh... Why does she live way out there?"

"It is her home. You live in this machine... she lives out there." He held up first one hand and then the other as he said this, and then brought the two together and smiled at the trucker.

"Now how do you know where I live? Oh hell... never mind. I'll get down first and then help you so you don't fall," he said, but the little man had already bounded down ahead of him. His bare feet had no trouble with the truck's painted surface. Dan cringed with the metal thumps of his feet hitting the hood.

When the big trucker managed to get back on the ground, he patted his shirt pocket and pulled out his pack of Lucky Strikes. Shaking the pack, he placed the cigarette that popped up between his lips. He was quite surprised when the girl plucked it away.

"It is a good idea... we shall smoke the pipe and then we shall go to Lonesome Woman."

She held out the cigarette to Dan, so he could light it for her. He obliged, pulling out his Red Ball lighter, and as he watched, she deeply breathed in the smoke and then blew it up into the air, reciting something with her eyes closed.

"The first smoke is always for the Great Spirit," she said looking at Dan when she opened her eyes again. She then passed the cigarette to

Coyote. He repeated the process and the prayer, as did Buffalo after him. The old man then passed the cigarette to Dan and they all looked at him expectantly.

"What?" He asked them.

"Aren't you going to give thanks to the Great Spirit?" asked the girl.

"For what?"

There was a shocked stillness, and Dan distinctly heard the engine of his truck ticking over as if it too were disappointed in him. He placed the cigarette in his mouth, and let it dangle there, obstinately refusing to give in.

"Get in the cab if you want to go, otherwise I'm hooking the trailer back up and getting the hell out of Dodge."

Buffalo turned to go back to the truck, but the girl and the little man stood whispering to each other, both of them making pointed gestures in the air with their hands.

"Well?" he asked them.

"You are not the one," Coyote said, crossing his arms over his chest.

"Yes he is," hissed the girl at him. "Lonesome Woman is dying and all you care about is a prayer?"

All three men spit on the ground.

"Why do you do that?" the girl asked, her voice rising in slight distress. She was very agitated, and Dan thought she might cry.

"Any time you mention death, you're supposed to spit," he told her, taking the time to spit on the ground after he said the word. "It's something I got to doing when I was driving for the Red Ball over in Europe."

"So you acknowledge death, but you will not acknowledge the Great Spirit?"

All three of the men spit on the ground again.

"I told you he was not the one," intoned Coyote.

"Perhaps when we get to Lonesome Woman, she will be able to help him," offered Buffalo. "He has suffered much of which you know nothing. You have not walked in his moccasins, Horse."

"You think he is the only one who has suffered? What about our people... the Trail of Tears... Wounded Knee..."

"Fine!" Dan told her, standing square in the yellowish light cast by the truck's headlights. "Just... fine... I'll say a prayer if it will get you moving."

Dropping his lit cigarette to the ground, he crushed it out under his foot, and took a fresh one from the pack. Holding it up to the sky, he yelled out, "This one is for you, Great Spirit!"

He put it to his lips and thumbed his lighter. The lighter flamed and then the flame went out as the driver tried to light up. He thumbed the lighter again and the same thing happened. Taking the cigarette from his lips, he blew down into the lighter to clear it out, and then shook it down in case it was getting low on fluid. Thumbing the knurled knob again, he smiled as the flame sprang up all bright and cheery. He watched it for a full three seconds before putting the cigarette back between his lips and moving to light up.

The flame went out.

Turning, he threw the lighter as far out into the night as he was able, and then cursed when he realized what he had done. "Son of a bitchhhhh... that was my Red Ball lighter."

Looking back to the threesome, he dropped the cigarette to the ground and growled, "Whoever is going, get into the truck, and not a word."

They had been driving across the desert for better than an hour, and other than a soft smattering of an unknown language between the three, it had been very quiet. Dan was becoming increasingly aware of the young woman sitting next to him, and he was more than just a little bit uncomfortable with it. She had an animal-like smell to her that he found very appealing. He tried to think of what it reminded him of... and then he realized that it was the smell of horses. It reminded him of his uncle's barn when he was just a child.

She noticed him looking at her and smiled. Dan quickly turned his eyes back to front... where the road should have been. In reality, he saw nothing there that even resembled a trail. What he was driving over was no more than a vast expanse of sand and scrub brush. He did feel fortunate in that it was flat and the cactus was sparse. Like a ship in the middle of the ocean, he was now steering by the small compass mounted on his dash board, which Horse was holding his flashlight on.

"More to the right," Coyote told him. His mouth was almost on the driver's ear as the little man was laying up in the sleeping cabin with his face down so he could look out the windshield.

Dan suppressed his annoyance, steered a point more to the right by the compass, and was rewarded with the front tire hitting a hole, causing the truck to shudder.

"Damn!" he cursed.

Buffalo looked at him from the shotgun position. "Why do you say bad words?" he asked softly.

"Because I can," Dan replied acidly, swerving his wheel to avoid a large cactus, and down shifting.

He was traveling at only twenty miles per hour and felt a great risk in even going that fast. All he had to do now was break an axle, and then they would all be stuck.

"I suppose your Great Spirit would not approve of that, either?"

"I think he would not."

Dan reached up and grabbed the cord for the air horn and then leaned way out the window. Yanking the cord down and holding it, he screamed obscenities at the night, letting the horn cover his words, until the air in the system was again depleted.

Coming back into the cab, he looked at the old man and smiled. "Now I feel better."

"You did not spit."

"I didn't say death."

As soon as he said it, he made a sour face, realizing what he had done, and leaned out the window to spit. Buffalo and Horse did the same on the rider's side, and Coyote leaned across Dan's back to spit out of his window, narrowly missing the driver's ear. Dan, coming back in, caught him between himself and the seat, and sat back harder than he needed to on purpose.

"AHHHhhhhhhhhhh…… AHHHhhhhhhhh…" the little man yelled.

Horse grabbed him by the arm, pulling him back upright, and he banged his head on the ceiling of the cab. When Coyote had his balance back, he licked a finger and stuck it in Dan's ear, which caused the driver to curse again… the word 'death' found its way into the tirade, and all four were once again spitting.

Dan abruptly stopped the truck and set the brake. Getting out, he walked several yards into the night. When he was a distance from the tractor, he yelled as loud as he could, trying to get himself back under control. When he stopped yelling, he stood with his hands on his hips listening to the silence of the desert. The way the area swallowed up his shout made him feel very small, as did the bright moon and the stars over his head. That was when he heard the unmistakable sound of a rattlesnake.

As his eyes adjusted, a form took shape on the ground in front of him. At first, it looked like a large rock, and then it grew, slowly expanding, and unfolding, if those were the right words. It continued in this fashion until it became the full silhouette of a woman. The whole time this was happening Dan heard the unmistakable sound of the rattle. Had he been bitten? Was this the effect the venom was having on him? He felt no pain… he had no shortness of breath… he…

The figure moved towards him, until he could see just her eyes from within the shadows of everything else. They transfixed him and he could not move. He heard the rattle again.

"Who areeeeee youuuuuu?" she whispered, and her voice had a hissing quality to it.

"How, Snake," said Coyote's voice loudly from the driver's right. "This unworthy unbeliever is Dragonman. His loyalty is like that of the Coyote. Over the years he has remained faithful to his friend, seeing to his needs above his own from the silent shadows of his machine. He only leaves his side when he is required to travel."

This was an admission that even Dan would not have breathed out loud, but it was the truth. Dan had no money of his own, because he had set up a college trust for both of Pat's children with whatever was left over at the end of the month.

The shadow's eyes shifted to the area on Dan's right. The big driver knew the little man was there, but he didn't dare move to look.

"Sooooo... This is your hope..." It was more of a statement than a question.

"How, Snake. He is not hope... he is reality," said Buffalo's voice from Dan's other side. His voice was still quiet, but it had a strength to it that Dan had not noticed before. "He is also like the Buffalo. He has sacrificed much in his lifetime for the good of the many and has never asked anything for himself."

"How, Snake," said the girl's voice from the right. "He is like the Horse. I have traveled far and wide with this man, and I have found no fault in him that cannot be rectified with proper guidance."

The rattles sounded again, and the woman began a small circular dance, shuffling her feet and singing softly. Dan could taste the powdery dust she was kicking up, and the more he looked at her, the clearer became the details of her person. She was naked from the waist up, and was full breasted. She wore a skirt that hung to her knees. At first he thought the skirt was made of individual ropes, the ends knotted, but then he saw the ropes moving on their own, and he realized they were snakes. Her face and upper torso were painted a chalky white, which gave her a pale ghostly sheen. Her hair, which moved with the dance, was long, and fell over her shoulders in its bounty, and there was a cactus flower in it.

Buff, Horse, and Coyote joined in the sing, dancing in little circles where they stood. Though there were no actual words, Dan was sure what the song was about. It was a simple thanksgiving to God... The Great Spirit. His heart told him he should join them, but he clamped his lips together and refused to say anything at all.

When the four finally stopped it became very quiet.

In the silence, Dan asked quietly, "Am I dead?"

Buff, Horse, and Coyote all spat on the ground at the same time. The snake woman looked at them, and Horse volunteered, "When 'death' is mentioned you must spit… it is Dragonman's custom, and we honor him by doing as he does."

The snake woman smiled, then bending slightly spat upon the ground.

Turning back to them she said softly, "Mother Earth approves. Lonesome Woman is a short distance straight ahead. She heard the roar of the beast and is waiting."

As the words were spoken, her form began to change again, seeming to dissolve before their eyes. Always there was the sound of the rattle, until she was once again on the ground in the form of a huge Diamondback. As she moved off the rattle noise faded away to nothing.

"Well," said Dan quietly, "Thank you all for sticking up for me, I guess. If your sister is just ahead then we better get moving. Who was that, or do I really need to ask?"

"That was Snake," replied Buffalo softly. "She is closest to the earth. Her message of Mother Earth's acceptance is a good sign."

When he was back in the truck, the driver breathed a sigh of relief. They had really stood up for him. It had been a long while since he had spent time with anyone other than Pat; and he knew their relationship hadn't been doing too well since he had gotten back from the war. For a long time now it was just him and the truck. It was rare when he even allowed anyone to sit in the rider's seat… and here they were. He was actually rather happy for the company.

The feeling quickly left him when Coyote stuck a wet finger in his ear again.

"Do that again and you just might die!" he yelled, jerking back in his seat and turning so he could see the smaller man. He was greeted with a large smile made larger than normal by the long set of canine teeth that were just a little too close for comfort. Immediately, with the word 'die', they were all hanging out of the windows and spitting.

"OK," said Dan pulling himself back inside the cab, and trying to pin Coyote behind him on the seat again. This time the little man was too quick for him. "Let's get her rolling."

Reaching up, he pulled the horn lanyard giving one long blast, and two shorts as if he were the engineer on a train. Coyote reached up and pulled the horn cord next. Dan let him, without saying anything. Horse pulled it after that, and when Buffalo looked as though he was undecided, Dan smiled and told him, "Go ahead... it's all right."

"Chasing demons," said the old man, smiling, and then he leaned across Horse and pulled the cord.

* * *

As they drew close to their destination, Dan's first impressions were sketchy. There was the camp fire, the light of which he had been steering towards, and there was a woman sitting next to it. The only other thing in sight was a lone tree. It did strike him as odd that there would be a tree all by itself out in the middle of the desert. He thought he remembered it from a photo essay in an old National Geographic. There had been a group of Native Indians standing around this one tree in the middle of nowhere. It had to do with a ritual something or other, but the thought quickly passed from his mind as he down shifted and braked.

Checking the fuel gage, he saw that he had a good three quarters left in both tanks. This would be more than enough to get them back out of the desert, and halfway to Idaho if he wanted.

With a pishhhhhing sound of the brakes, the truck rolled to a stop, and in a move that was unlike Dan, he turned the engine off. Normally, the trucker, acknowledging custom more than anything else, would leave the truck sit idling for hours. The argument was for keeping the engine warm and the oil flowing allowing for proper lubrication. The common concept was; that starting an engine was the hardest thing on it, wear wise. 'It's all about friction', he could hear the old motor pool sergeant telling him, 'An engine was made to run, not start and stop, start and stop... 'sides, an engine takes more fuel to start up than it would use in an hour of idling.'

Buff, Coyote, and Horse piled out of the cab as soon as he stopped. They went to the woman sitting next to the small camp fire, and greeted her, each squatting down and holding her hands, then kissing her on the cheek. Dan, climbing down out of the cab, walked around the front of the truck, and lagged behind, his big hands firmly shoved into his pockets.

The three turned to him expectantly and smiled.

"Ma'am," he said nodding to the woman sitting next to the fire. She seemed old and haggard, and then at the same moment, he saw her as young and beautiful. The two images flickered back and forth as if fighting for dominance, and then they combined and seem to settle on an image of middle age, not too much older than Dan was himself.

"Achowea," she told him. "May the blessings of The Great Spirit be upon you. Please forgive me that I do not stand, but I am older than I look, and the years have taken their toll."

The trucker nodded, coming closer. "So I've heard from your family. I'm here to take you into town to the doctor. I figure if we leave now, we could make it easy by sunup. I'll even spring for breakfast, how's that sound?"

"It sounds delightful, Mr. Petersen," she told him, "But I am not going to be leaving this place. It is my home."

Dan looked at Buffalo, and the old man looked back at him. There was just the slightest trace of a smile on his lips. His expression held no clear meaning.

"How is it you know my name? I never told anyone, not even your family here."

She smiled a Mona Lisa smile. "I know many things."

"I was under the impression that you ... well... you needed medical assistance," he told her.

"I am dying," she told him matter of factly.

All four of them spat on the ground, and the old woman was actually taken by surprise.

"It is his custom to spit when 'death' is mentioned," explained Coyote, spitting again as did the others. "Dragonman says it keeps death... (spit)... from coming for you."

"I see," she said, and then said something else in the soft tones of the language they had been speaking in the cab of the truck. Coyote, Horse, and Buffalo spread out in a semi-circle around the small campfire and sat on the ground. "Please, come and sit, Mr. Petersen. Keep me company till the dawn."

"What happens at dawn?" he asked.

"The Great Spirit will come for me, and I will complete my life."

"You're going to roll over and die then... just like that?"

Coyote, Horse, and Buffalo were about to spit again, when he stopped them. "Guys... it's OK... you can't always spit death away, so let's hold off on that one for awhile."

The three swallowed, and the old woman chuckled.

"They all think very highly of you to follow you in your custom like that," she told him.

"I don't know how that could be possible. We all just met tonight. They could hardly know me from Adam."

"Knew him," mumbled Buffalo. "He wasn't anything like you."

Dan let it pass as bad humor.

Finding a vacant spot that seemed to be reserved for his bottom, he slowly sat on the ground close to the old woman. He noticed that her eyes sparkled in the fire light as if she was yet full of life; the type of person who would enjoy every second she was given to live.

"These three have been with you your entire life, silly man creature," she told him. "That you choose not to recognize this fact simply reflects on your humanity."

Horse rose, Dan's blanket now tied around her shoulders like a loose dress. She moved away from the light, and when she came back, she had an old coffee pot that she sat on the glowing coals near the edge of the fire. "You first met me in your Uncle's barn," she said without looking up. "I was simply among the many horses that he already possessed… but it was a way I could be close to you without suspicion. You were always meant to be a traveler. I knew this, and I watched over you when I could."

"That's impossible," he told her. "You're no more than fourteen… fifteen tops."

She looked at him, and he remembered her face… only it was the face of the horse… the one in his Uncle's barn that had been so gentle; the one who the other horses seemed to show great respect. He remembered their voices; all whispering in the shadows of the barn… of how honored they were that she had come.

She rose, and walked to the area behind Lonesome Woman, and knelt there.

"You were lost in the woods," said Coyote from close to his right. The little man had moved without the trucker ever realizing it.

Dan saw him as if for the first time, and also saw the wild Coyote's face. "You!" he whispered.

Coyote nodded. "I am not a dog as you supposed."

"You led me home and then disappeared. No one would believe me. My mother was so… she was crying. I couldn't have been more than five. They thought a wolf had gotten me."

"A Coyote is loyal to his family," the little man told him. "You are family. I could hardly leave you to the wolf."

"I'm also off my nut, you can be sure of that," he added. "Pat told me not to drive the desert at night. I'm going to wake up any time now in the back of the truck's sleeper soaked in sweat, and probably dehydrated."

The coffee pot began to percolate. Dan's eyes were drawn to the noise.

The woman said something to Horse, and she moved her position, kneeling directly behind her and untying her hair. The woman's hair fell down over her shoulders, and Horse looked very sad.

"I asked her to comb out my hair a final time," Lonesome Woman explained to the trucker.

"Final time," he mumbled, watching the flames dance in the fire. They seemed to keep rhythm with the coffee pot's bubbling noises. "You want real good coffee," he said softly, ignoring her inference that she was to die, "You need to put an aspirin in the pot."

"I was with you in Germany," Buffalo told him from where he sat. The old man was sitting further away from the fire than the others. "I know the pain you suffer because of what you saw there."

"You don't know the half of it," Dan told him.

"The herds of my people used to cover the plains. So many were their numbers that when the herd moved, great clouds of dust would completely obscure the sun until it appeared to be night. We did as The Great Spirit asked, and gave of ourselves gladly for the sustenance of The People. Then came a different people, and they did not hold life as sacred. They wantonly killed us until the plains were scattered with our bones and we were almost no more. What you saw was no more or less the same. Not all people are good. The Great Spirit asked that you help stop these people, and you did, even though you knew you might be killed. In this, you too are Buffalo."

A breeze rustled the few leaves left in the tree, and Dan looked up at it, seeing its silhouette against the stars in the sky.

"Tell me why you are so angry," Lonesome Woman said quietly, and her voice seemed to be in the center of his thoughts.

The trucker looked to her after a moment of his mind wandering through his past and found that he and Lonesome Woman were now alone by the small fire. She had risen, and was carefully pouring him a cup of coffee from the old pot. Except for the small noises of the camp fire, the silence of the desert engulfed them. Her appearance had changed slightly. She now seemed younger than she had been. She wore a long blue skirt, a white blouse, and her hair fell long over her shoulders.

He was about to give her one of his curt trucker responses as an answer, when she looked at him, and he saw that there was no... badness... about this woman.

She smiled. "I am neither large, nor can I haul a heavy load. I believe those were your requirements of a wife?"

"I did say that, didn't I?" he replied sheepishly. "What's your story?"

She handed him the battered tin coffee cup she had just filled.

"I am this tree, and this tree is me. My people lived in this place eons ago when it was not a desert, but a lush forest. The Great Spirit told us that we would have to move, which is a hard thing for a tree. He said things were to change, and in order to survive, my people would have to leave. To everyone else, there seemed to be no choice in the matter, but I was stubborn. I told Him that I would not leave. In this place, which was my home, I would wait for my mate. He was gracious and granted me my way, though it was a foolish way. He told me, however, that when I did not find a mate he would be back for me. As the world changed the tree stayed the same. I lived on… always waiting, but when the sun rises tomorrow morning my wait will be over."

She placed the coffee pot back by the fire and sat back on the ground. "I am sorry, but I have no aspirin for your coffee."

He sipped it, burning his lips on the metal of the cup. Through the pain, the taste of the coffee filled him. "It's delicious," he told her.

"This is what it was like when I lived with my people," she told him. Moving a hand up and over her head, the night sky changed, as did the area around them. Dan smelled the mottled smell of a jungle, and felt the moist heat. There were loud and shrill animal cries in the air. There were sounds of movement among the trees, which were all just like the one singular tree she had told him was her. The magnitude of the sounds made it plain that there were very large animals close by.

"Creatures very similar to your dragon lived in my home," she told him "A home where I have lived since the creation of the world… and then it changed very quickly, just as The Great Spirit said that it would."

Fire and Ice… Fire and Ice… and the scene around them changed again and again and again, until it was once more the desert sky under which they sat.

"All that time… through all the changes…I persevered. I waited for my mate whom I knew would come one day. Because of my endurance and faithfulness to this dream, I came to be known among the totems, all of whom became my friends. Now they are distressed that I might not be among them any longer. I have told them that death is a natural occurrence for all living things."

"Sometimes it is," he replied softly.

The weight of the coffee cup on his finger made him automatically sip the brew. This time the heat of the cup was a comfortable warmth on his lip, and the taste of the coffee was good. It gave him a feeling of rest… of peace… of home.

"Why are you so angry with God?"

Her question was simple, and direct. It took him by surprise. He started to tell her he was not angry at God, but at the world. Life was just unfair and hurtful. He stopped the reply before it started. He decided to be truthful with her and with himself. The war changed him. He had seen things that were just too horrible to imagine, and then, right after that, the person that he loved closer than a brother had been mutilated, and taken away from him... the one person he might have been able to confide in... who would have helped talk him through what he felt, and it was his fault that this had happened.

"It's His world. He created it, and us, and He's doing a poor job of running it... that's all."

"By this you mean what?"

"I was in Germany. Sure... it was war and in war people die," he paused to spit on the ground. "You can handle that, but what you can't handle is the glut of death... the killing of the innocent. Bad people come to power, and suddenly it's ok to wantonly kill. Exactly the same way Buff said concerning his own people. We can't give life, but we sure as hell can take it away."

The air around them became frigid and the ground changed, becoming covered with snow. There was the sound of mechanization in the air. A convoy of trucks moved slowly along in the distance, all upshifting and downshifting; making their way along a road that had been sabotaged to the point that it could hardly even be called a road. Dan stood and watched them. The trucks all had red balls painted on the doors.

"That's where we were heading... over there," he said, standing and pointing at a fenced-in factory-looking place with the coffee cup. "It's called a concentration camp."

He felt a hand on his arm. Turning, he found Lonesome Woman standing next to him.

"It's all right," she told him. "I can do this one last time before I have to leave. We have the time."

"Do what?"

"Help you."

"Thought I was the cavalry riding to the rescue here, not the other way around."

She frowned.

"Bad choice of words?" he asked.

"Perhaps. More than these people have suffered at the hands of others. The image of 'cavalry', to the ones I hold closest, is not a good one, but the thought was a sound one. We all wish to be the ones helping... and we all wish for the help of a stranger when we need it most."

"Well... that was us," he said, pointing toward the trucks. HQ sent a flash message, ordering us to this place empty. That really confused us.

I mean, normally we got the most dangerous assignments… ammo… explosives… stuff like that."

"What happened?"

"They wouldn't tell us anything. Half way there they loaded us with food, some cooks, their camp kitchens, and then they led us in. Lonesome… the people in that camp could hardly be described as being alive. We were more than shocked. Actually that's putting it mildly. Most of them were scared of us. What's one more man in a uniform? Didn't take 'em long to understand that we meant freedom."

The area around them changed. They were now standing in the midst of people who were skeleton thin and dressed in rags. Dan was able to pick out a few of the faces; this surprised him. Without even knowing it, he dropped his coffee cup to the ground and began carefully picking his way through the crowd looking for one particular face.

"Erick!" he called out. "Erick!"

There was a tug on his pants leg and a small boy was there holding his arms up to the big driver. Dan scooped him up immediately and clutched him to his chest. Tears streamed down his face. "You're alive… you're alive… Oh please God; I prayed… I prayed so hard, Lonesome… Oh please God, I prayed; let him live!"

As he spoke the words the child went limp in his arms as his life ran out like the final grains of sand in an hourglass.

The scene faded and Dan found himself standing in the desert again, his arms empty. His face was wet with his tears, and he stood trying very hard to control the memories that now flooded his brain. The showers… the ovens… mounds and mounds of mass graves…

Lonesome Woman bent and picked up the tin coffee mug. She held it upside down and shook it gently as if freeing the last drops to water the arid ground.

"And for this you would hate God?"

"Who else better to blame? There was no reason for that child to die. We were there. He had survived the worst part of it. Why didn't God listen to that one prayer?"

"Among the many prayers?"

"Yes… among the many."

"I don't know. There has never been an answer for this question."

"I got drunk after that. I found a dead guard, and there was a bottle next to him. He had drunk half of it and then shot himself. God knows I might have helped him pull the trigger if he'd been alive when I found him. So I stole a dead man's bottle and drank the other half. Pat drove for me the next morning and lost his leg because of it. It was my fault… and in the end, I lost the best friend I ever had."

"What position would your truck have been in if you were driving that day?"

"Lead position."

"What happened to the lead truck that day?"

"He got caught by a King Tiger tank; blown up and then machine gunned. One of our Thunderbolts hammered the bastard before he could get any of the rest of us."

"Losing a leg is not the same as losing your life," she told him.

"You did not lose a friend," said another voice. "You chose not to let him back inside your Hogan."

Dan turned and found Buffalo standing on the fringes of the campfire. His back was straight, and he wore a Buffalo headdress complete with the horns. On his chest was a warrior's breast plate of bone. His age was transposed by the dignity he now wore as the Chief of his people.

"People die in war. It is the way of things… but your friend did not die."

Horse stepped into the light. She was dressed in buckskins.

"In life, you live," she said simply.

Coyote came forward. He had his headpiece back, and looked the same as when he had jumped in front of Dan's truck. "In death," he said, and then spat. "Your memory lives on, even if there is no one to remember you."

"We are all one with The Great Spirit," they said at the same time.

Dan turned and looked away from them. The first indications of the dawn were in the sky. Taking the pack of cigarettes from his pocket, he thumbed one up and put it between his lips. Putting the pack back into his shirt pocket, he patted his pants leg looking for his lighter, and then cursed when he remembered he had thrown it away.

A hand came into his line of vision. It held the Red Ball lighter. Turning, he saw Buffalo's unsmiling face. He accepted the lighter, and then looked back at the other two people. They both nodded to him.

The driver thumbed the lighter open, and spun the knurled knob. The flame sprouted like a merry little flower, and he watched it dance for a moment before holding the lighter and the cigarette up toward the sky. Bringing them back, he placed the cigarette between his lips again and lit it. He breathed the smoke deeply into his lunges. He felt a great sense of calm come over him. As he blew the smoke out, his eyes saw the sun peek up over the horizon.

He turned to say something to Lonesome Woman, but found her lying on the ground shivering.

"It begins," said Buffalo, moving to kneel beside her. Raising his face towards the rising sun, he began a chant.

Horse came and knelt next to him, and held Lonesome Woman's hand. Coyote knelt by her feet, and in the low light of the dawn his eyes met Dan's. They were pleading with him to do something... anything.

Looking back at the sunrise, the trucker dropped his cigarette and crushed it out under his foot.

"Buff... stop the chant. You brought me here to help, so what say let's do something other than wait for death."

He deliberately did not spit. The other three did spit and then looked at him expectantly.

"You must spit, or death will come for you," said Coyote. "You said so."

"So I did," replied the driver, bending down to pick up Lonesome Woman. "Maybe if he does, he and I can have a good face to face, and I'll be able to talk some sense into him... that or he's gonna kick my butt, but either way it's at least something. Buff, you get the door. We'll put her in the cab. She can sit between us."

"The Great Spirit is coming with the sun," said Coyote.

"Good,' Dan told him, settling back on his feet and adjusting for the weight he now carried. "Your job is to slow him down."

"Slow him down?"

"Yeah... tell him some jokes... show him a card trick or jump in front of him like you did my truck... just buy me some time."

"What are you going to do?" asked Horse.

"Me? I'm not going to do a damn thing, but the truck is gonna run like hell. I'm taking Lonesome Woman out of this place. Maybe if I can get her back to Pat's, his brother in law can do something. Pat tells me he's quite the Medicine Man. It's at least a chance. That beats waiting around for her to die."

Turning to the lightening sky, he yelled, "Did you hear that, Great Spirit? I said 'DIE' and I didn't spit! Bring the old boy on, because I got a few things I want to tell the both of ya!"

As Horse and Coyote watched, Dan and Buffalo placed Lonesome Woman in the cab of the truck. Horse whispered to the little man, "What do you say now?"

"I think he is the one," he replied quietly.

The big tractor's starter shrieked and the engine turned over, complaining just a little about being woken up. As the engine warmed, Dan got back down out of the cab and walked back to the pair.

Holding out his hand to Coyote, he told him, "Try not to be a speed bump in life."

The little man shook with him, and then gave him a funny look. "What does that mean?"

"It means; don't jump out in front of any more trucks."

"Just in front of The Great Spirit?"

"Yeah… forgot that one. Good luck, old son."

Turing to Horse, he extended a hand to her too, but she embraced him instead. "Please hurry. I will lead the way so you will be able to find your way out."

"Where I'm going, hun… you won't be able to follow. You just get me started, and I'll do the rest."

She nodded in understanding.

Moving back to the truck, he stood by the front bumper looking at the sunrise. The truck's engine was purring in his left ear. It was a sound that had always pleased him.

"OK, Big Chief," he said softly to the morning sky. "This one time, you're going to lose. You can't have her… she means too much to too many people. It's just something you're going to have to live with. You can take me in her place if you want, but I doubt it's much of a deal for you. Because of that, I'm going to make you this one time offer and throw in the truck. I think you know she means the world to me, but she's all I got other than the clothes on my back. It'd be best all the way around if you just agreed. I just wanted to tell you in a friendly way before we get started, cuz I think this might get just a bit ugly before we're through. Oh… and the three that came and got me? Those are good people you got working for you. Ya otta give 'em a raise, and maybe tanker the fuel on their next trip out."

Taking his pack of Lucky Strikes out of his shirt pocket, he thumbed one up, and put it between his lips. In sudden inspiration, he turned and walked back over to Lonesome Woman's tree, and placed the pack at its base. Lighting the cigarette, he snapped the lighter closed and placed it carefully on top of the pack.

"See ya round, old buddy," he said softly. "We had a good turn together."

Moving back to the cab of the truck, he climbed in, slammed the door closed, and then tossed his cigarette out the window. Lonesome Woman sat in the middle, and Buff was sitting shotgun. Lonesome was leaning against the old man, clutching the blanket he had given her from the sleeping compartment. Her complexion had paled.

"You ready?" Dan asked Buffalo.

"Yes."

He then placed a hand on Lonesome Woman's, and she smiled weakly at him.

"You stay with me, hun, and everything will turn out OK."

She nodded.

The trucker eased in the clutch, grabbed the gear shift, and deliberately ground the gears getting it into first. He looked over and smiled at Buffalo. The old man smiled back. His lips formed the word 'grinder', but he did not speak the insulting word.

Dan eased the truck out, and turned until he was heading in the opposite direction. Looking over, he saw Horse standing waiting for him. She had stripped off her clothes, and as he approached, she began to run. Within a few yards, her body had changed into that of a horse, and she was easily leading him as he went through the many gears, building up his speed.

"Lonesome," he called out above the sounds of the engine, not taking his eyes off the area ahead of the truck.

"Yes?" she asked him, her voice sounding weak.

He reached over with his shifting hand, and placed it on hers for a moment, until it was time again to shift the gears.

"You remember my criteria for choosing a wife?"

"She must be a large woman," she said so softly that Dan had a hard time hearing her. "And she must be able to haul a heavy load."

"That's right," he said loudly. "And I figure you been carrying that load for a long, long time. That makes you the perfect candidate. What say you and I get married? I mean… I don't know if that's exactly what you would call it in your language, but it works for me if it will for you. I figure it this way; if the Great Spirit wants you then he's going to have to accept a package deal… that'd be the both of us and the truck, too."

She smiled. Reaching over, she placed her hand on top of his shifting hand, "You don't have to do this," she managed.

"I know I don't; but I want to. Buff… you're our witness. A Chief is better'n any preacher I ever knew. Speak the words."

The old man nodded, and pronounced loudly, "I witness this to The Great Spirit; Dragonman and Lonesome Woman are now mated."

Dan looked down at the speedometer, and then out the window. In the early light of the morning, he saw Horse running ahead of them. He was up past sixty now and still building up speed. He glanced in his driver's side mirror. In its reflection he saw the cloud of a sand storm moving in front of the morning sun and sweeping towards the lone tree. Close to the tree he saw what appeared to be a dog, sitting calmly, waiting on the approach of the storm. The thought of the bravery of the little man jumping out in front of the sandstorm like he had the truck made him almost choke. He almost cursed, but he stopped himself. Now was not the time... not now and not ever again.

Looking back to the front, he found he was beginning to outdistance Horse. Buffalo called his name, and he looked over at him. The old man pointed at the horn lanyard.

"Chase the demons," he told him.

Dan nodded, and reaching up, pulled the lanyard down and held it there for a long moment. When he looked back, Buffalo was gone, and it was now only him and Lonesome Woman in the cab. She shifted her position to lie against Dan, and her touch was pleasing to him.

He was all the way through the gears now, and holding his foot hard to the floor. In side mirrors, he could see the dust storm approaching, sweeping up and eclipsing his own trail of dust. The speedometer was now approaching one hundred miles per hour. He pulled the lanyard again, and the horn sounded out in defiance. He held it there for a long time... and the speedometer finally pegged at 120.

Simultaneous... a word that encompasses many and many things happening all at the same moment.

The horn eased to nothingness as the air system depleted. Perhaps the pump had broken... perhaps and perhaps and perhaps...

Dan saw the shadow of the approaching ravine... it was long, and wide, bottoming out some one hundred feet below. Out of instinct, his right foot came off the accelerator and mashed down on the brakes but the pedal went to the floor without effect.

The sand storm caught up to them, and sand poured into the cab through the open windows.

"Hang on to me, love!" he yelled. "This is going to be just a bit bumpy!"

Lonesome Woman did hold on...

And as the big Kenworth sailed off the edge of the cliff, Dan suddenly felt weightless. Letting go of the steering wheel, he clung to the woman who clung to him.

* * *

Pat stood focusing his binoculars, looking over the edge of the ravine. A hundred feet below them, and almost five hundred yards down the length of the chasm was Dan's truck. It seemed in perfect shape; just sitting there waiting for them to find it. As he watched, his brother-in-law climbed into the cab. Within a minute he saw black smoke shoot out of the dual exhaust pipes, and a second later the sound of the engine starting up reached his ears.

"Damn," he muttered. "How in the hell did it get down there?"

Standing next to him, her eyes squinted against the harsh light of the desert, was his wife. Her face wore no expression for the sake of her husband. In her mind she offered up a prayer for the man she had met only a few times.

Dan Petersen was missing for better than two weeks before Pat had gotten a call from the Texas Rangers. They had found a trailer abandoned by the side of the road out in the desert. Checking the plates they traced it back as one of the many trailers owned by the company he worked for. When he called headquarters and reported it, he told them he was going to go out and look for the trucker. He was told not to bother, the man was just an independent… they could pick up the trailer later. With a few choice words from his Army days, he resigned, slamming the phone down so hard he broke the receiver. Regretting that he had broken the phone, he carefully held the two parts together long enough to call Martha. She had then called Sammy. Sammy, in turn, called the family, and they had all piled into their pickup trucks; which all pulled horse trailers.

Dan wasn't blood related, but he was a close enough friend of Martha's husband to have been automatically included in the group whether he wanted the privilege or not. In the way of a wife, Martha knew how close the two men were, and it hurt her to see how crushed Pat was that the trucker had rejected their offer of family. Again, for her husband's sake she had said nothing.

The truck's engine turned off and Sammy stepped back into the open where they could see him. Using his hands, he told them there was no one with the truck. Pat felt relieved, and yet still distressed. He had warned Dan about crossing the desert at night, but the stubborn moron wouldn't listen to him.

Martha talked to the men who had come with them, instructing them to fan out. They would work a large teardrop search pattern. When Sammy got back up from the ravine, the three of them would then follow the tractor's tracks back to the point of origin. By sunset, they would all meet at Lonesome Woman, camp there for the night, and then come back in. If they didn't find the trucker's body by then, they would hold a funeral ceremony for him at the tree, and then come back in the following day.

When Sammy made it back up from the ravine bottom, he and Pat stood together examining what was left of the truck's tracks at the edge of the ravine's face.

"He wasn't braking, that's for darn sure," said Sammy. "Looks to me like he was going mighty fast, too… had to be for the truck to be so far down the gully like that. Darned if I can explain why it's in as gooda shape as it is. Off hand I would say she was ready to roll, Pat, but it will take some doing to get it out of there. The edge of the cliff isn't strong enough to hold up to a wrecker. Best bet would be a crane, but I doubt you'll find anyone wanting to come all the way out here even for salvage rights."

Pat looked at the ground, and then out at the truck. "He had to be doing over a hundred to make that distance. Even if he had landed on all four wheels, though, he would have broken every axle, and then flipped and burned. It don't make any sense."

They heard what sounded like a dog barking. Looking up, they saw a Coyote in the distance. It was sitting and watching them.

"Where did he come from?" Pat asked of no one in general.

"He's been watching us since we got here," said Martha.

"Not like a Coyote to let himself be seen like that," Sammy muttered. "I think there's more here than face value, but I'll be darned if I can figure it out."

They traveled slowly for two hours without talk. Sammy then dismounted to look at something on the ground.

"Was an unshod horse run through here," he said looking up at Pat. "'Bout the same time frame as the tire tracks. Might mean something… might mean nothing."

"Sammy…" Martha then spoke in her native language. She had a hand over her eyes and was staring off into the distance. "There is something different about Lonesome Woman."

She pointed, and Sammy looked up. From the ground he couldn't see it, but when he re-mounted his horse, it was easy to see. There were two trees in the distance now… not just one.

"That's not possible," he said.

When they were within a five hundred yards they dismounted. Sammy began a Medicine Chant as they walked the horses closer.

Pat had only heard about this place. It was considered sacred among the tribe. When a person had problems, they would make the trip into the desert alone and talk to Lonesome Woman. The tradition said that she would help you see clearly so you could make things right.

"Sammy?" he asked.

Sammy stopped singing and looked at him. "I don't know, Pat... really... there's only ever been one tree."

A hundred yards out Pat could see clearly where the tire tracks had stopped next to the trees, then made a loop and headed back out in the direction from where they had come... towards the ravine.

"The road's off in that direction," Sammy said nodding in the direction the tracks initially came from. "Your friend was definitely here." He then knelt and examined the ground closer. "I'll be durned... these sure look like Buffalo tracks."

He looked over at his sister. She in turn, reached out and took Pat's hand. This was not meant as an aid so he could walk better. She knew that Dan Petersen would not be returning, nor would they ever find his body. Pat sensed it in her touch, and nodded to her.

"It's ok, hun... I'll be all right."

They walked up to the trees, both of them looking strangely healthy for being in such an arid place. That was when Pat saw the lighter sitting on top of the pack of Lucky Strikes. Tears came to his eyes. Bending down, and almost losing his balance, he picked them up.

He looked up at his wife, showing her what he'd found. "He only smoked the damn things because they had a red ball on the pack like his lighter," he explained. "It meant something to him; suppose it should have to me, too."

Stepping back a pace, he stood at attention and saluted.

"I'll see you in the next life, old buddy," he said, and then paused, his words sticking in his throat. In a softer tone he said, "You stupid dumb ass son of a bitch... I told you not to drive the desert at night."

Sammy had taken a small drum down from his horse's pack and had begun a chant. Martha joined in. Pat, lowering himself to the ground with a little difficulty, added his voice... the chant was meant to be a comfort for the living... for those left behind.

If the new tree could have spoken to him... it would have told him not to be so damned sad.

It would have told him that his old friend was finally happy. Dan Petersen... the last independent trucker in those parts of Texas... had reconciled with the Creator of All Things and had found himself a fine wife in the process.

It would then have given him a long bear hug, and told him simply: "I love you too, Pat."

"*I knew that there were people who'd done tattoos, implanted whiskers and claws, but so far there'd only been rumors that there were people trying to go full-on 'furry.'*"

A news feed podcaster has to follow up any lead to keep ahead of the competition, so Alex interviews a furry fan who has had surgery to turn himself into a "real" anthro wolf (or cat).

Chasing the Spotlight

by Tim Susman

There are no shortcuts. You learn that pretty fast no matter what business you're in. I'm in my late thirties (okay, very late thirties), and I know all about the get-rich-quick crazes, from the tech stocks of the late 90s and early teens back to crazy land speculation and tulip markets. Didn't stop me from going in with two friends on WhisperWare. Yeah, I know, you've never heard of it. Best way I can describe it is it was Talk2Talk without the good marketing plan or the financial backing. Or the advanced engineering.

Anyway, I wised up, and now I run a news feed called WhispOWorld (little shoutout back to WhisperWare), which at the end of last year was listed in the top 50 North American news sites. Not too bad, and got a little bump in my ad revenue, enough to afford an upgrade to my feed throughput. Making people wait two seconds to see my articles was killing me. At least now it's down to one and a half, so there are a couple million more who'll wait before moving on.

It's a lot of work right now. I've had to give up on having any romantic life in the last couple years just to keep the rankings up, because when I'm not posting stories, I'm researching. My readers send me tips every day and I can't just toss them out, even the ones who send me stories about their cats every day, because you never know what's going to be the one that shoots you into the top ten.

So I get this tip one morning from a guy in L.A., right in my neighborhood, who says his neighbor came back after doing some plastic surgery, real "weirdo cutting-edge stuff." I get that one a lot too. But he attached a blurry picture, and it sure looked like the person had cat ears.

I knew that there were people who'd done tattoos, implanted whiskers and claws, but so far there'd only been rumors that there were people trying to go full-on "furry." It's hard to keep secrets in this day and age, when everyone has cameras in their wristphones, but there are still places—the military, company boardrooms—where they have the cameras blocked.

This guy said that since his neighbor'd come home, she hadn't been out of the house. Groceries had been delivered later that day, but the car hadn't moved. He didn't know much about the neighbor: a first name, Charlene, and he'd thought she was an agent based on phone conversations he'd overheard. Weird for an agent to be undergoing that kind of procedure, but then again, they were hungry for anything that gave them an edge.

I looked again at the photo. It was hard to tell whether the ears were real, but the photo was blurry, so she was either moving fast, or in low light, or both, which implied some level of secrecy. The posture also screamed secrecy: hunched over, wearing a long trenchcoat in the middle of July. The photo was clearly from a home security camera, pointed outward to capture interesting things the neighbors might be doing; even though the guy had tried to edit out the timestamp, he wasn't that good with photo editing, and also it explained why a photo that looked like it was taken in the evening wasn't mailed to me until the following morning. A lot of people in L.A. used HomeSec cameras and then reviewed the footage the next morning.

The address was only an hour drive away if I left before two. The feeds in the top 10 every year say that they run their news with 90% work and 10% gut. I looked back from the G-Map to the photo, and my gut said: go for it. So I went for it.

* * *

The address led me to a largish house off one of the canyons halfway to Malibu. I had to dig out the right fake permit to get my car past a checkpoint, but there was only one. The houses in this neighborhood were closing in on a hundred years old, big and elegant, in various states of upkeep. "Charlene's" house was one of the smaller ones, a little ranch-style job with a front yard obviously kept up by gardeners, overhung by palm trees. No ocean view, but at least the illusion of privacy.

I parked a little ways back from the house and walked up, looking across the road and around. I counted three houses visible from here, any one of which might house my informant. I resisted the urge to wave to him.

This house had security cameras on it as well, which there was no point in me avoiding. I adjusted the pen in my pocket, making sure the 360-camera in the tip was clear of the fabric, and walked up to the door, through a yard of short grass and rosemary bushes. The flowers and herbs smelled sweet, but as I got closer to the house, it smelled of old wood and brick, nice paint job notwithstanding.

I pulled aside the screen door and knocked on the wood door behind it. Two peepholes: one for the human behind the door, one for the camera. I smiled for both and waited.

Shuffling movement behind the door. I waited politely. The lower peephole darkened, and then a voice—a male voice—said, "Who are you?"

"WhispOWorld News Feed," I said. "Entertainment Industry division." For actors and agents you say "Entertainment Industry," and "division" makes it sound like you're part of a big operation. The automatic response gave me time to adjust to the fact that it wasn't Charlene who'd had the surgery, but a client of hers, probably.

"Jesus," he said. "Go away."

I expected that. "What I'm offering is the chance to control your story. The first one to break is the one that gets quoted and reported, and I work with you to make sure that the story is the one you want to see out there. If you wait, you're going to be the subject of a lot of stories that won't care or even try to get your perspective."

There was a long pause. "Call my agent. She's setting up the press release."

"What's her number?"

He gave it to me through the door. I pulled it up on the phone and connected to my earpiece as it rang.

"Extraordinary Talent Representation, Charlene Norris speaking."

She had a manufactured plastic voice that sounded creepily like my secretary. If my informant hadn't told me that she was a real person, I would've guessed that she was computerized voice response receptionist. "Hi, Charlene," I said. "Alex Roberts, WhispOWorld News Feed, Entertainment Industry Division. I'm trying to interview your house guest, and—"

"Absolutely not." She cut in crisply. "I'm preparing a release to go out to the top ten news feeds tomorrow. You can wait along with everyone else."

"Or," I said, "I can publish the photo I have with an article that I write myself without any facts other than what I've seen. I'll publish your name and a description of the surgery and we'll just let the story come out on its own, right?"

"You don't have anything to publish."

"I have a photo that shows cat ears. I've got a voice on record. I can dig through local plastic surgeons."

She didn't respond right away. I turned away from the house so I could breathe the fresh scent of the flowers more than the house. "I can dig through furry boards. I have people who know them."

"I can have the press release out in an hour."

This was probably not true, and if it was, then it would be a cookie-cutter press release, or else it would ruin her attempt to push the story out at the right time. Entertainment people don't read news in the middle of the day. They read it from 7-10 in the morning, over coffee, and then again from about 8-10 at night. Sure, they follow big stories as they hit, but if you really want someone to notice a story, usually you drop it around 7 or 7:30.

"Well," I said, "go ahead. I'll have my story out around the same time, and we'll see if your manufactured press release or my authentic footage gets more play."

It was a bit of a gamble, but if she really was trying to keep the lid on this, then having someone else publish a "behind the scenes" at the same time as she was trying to keep control of the story—a full-time job for the first day or three it was out—would be a hassle she didn't need. "I'm not worried," she said, which meant that she was. If she really wasn't, she'd have hung up.

"What I'm offering," I said, "is an interview allowing him to tell his side of the story, written up by an actual journalist for a top-fifty news feed." She would probably assume that meant worldwide. "I've been picked up by CNN, USN, USA Today, Boingboing, and TechToday. Your story will get play, and it won't be from a press release."

"If we'd wanted that, we could've contacted a feed ourselves," she snaps.

"But you didn't. And now you don't have a choice." I step back. "Did I mention that I'm outside your house right now? Lovely hydrangeas. The feeds will be coming to you before you know it."

"Don't publish my address!" She collected herself. "All right. You will call him Lon, the wolf-man. You won't ask him any questions about the procedure."

"Seriously?"

"The doctors have a very specific way they want to present the procedure. As a lay-person, he isn't qualified to talk about it."

I look again at the house, carefully groomed, new paint covering old bricks. Even the walkway is manicured, with those stupid little solar lights that look like black mushrooms and don't work. "As the guy who underwent the procedure, I think he's the most qualified to talk about the experience."

"You can ask him about his experience, but focus on his future plans. He was unconscious for a lot of it."

"Still, they prepped him for it, right?"

"Mister Roberts. I am not ordering you, nor am I asking you for a favor. I am warning you that if you publish something that incorrectly describes this procedure, you may be liable, and this group of doctors will come after you. They actively monitor their online image and they will shut you down."

That made me stop and think. Worse than not getting this story would be getting shut down. After the infamous "CISPouts" of last decade, the regulators were getting better about preventing capricious blackouts, but warranted ones, from a powerful group that was on alert for misinformation... Yeah, that could happen. That would drop my feed from top fifty to top five hundred. In California, maybe. Depending on how long it lasted. Sometimes you could reverse a blackout just by pulling the offending article. Sometimes, if they wanted to make a point, or they didn't like you, or if they were dicks, it would take a week.

That would mean I'd have to either start from scratch or find some other kind of work. In other words... "Yeah, okay. Fine."

"All right. Hold your phone up to the door. I'll transmit the lock codes over it." She started dialing another number before I even got the phone all the way up.

And that is how I got my first look at Lon, the wolf-man. He was just putting away his phone when I walked in—probably getting instructions from Charlene. He asked me if I wanted a glass of water, and showed me to a stylish wood chair with deep purple cushions. The house had the same kind of manufactured comfort feel inside as it did out, with an artistically arranged set of wall tablets showing mountain scenes, probably downloaded—no, wait. The same woman appeared in three of them. Vacation photos, then.

On the coffee table between the chairs lay three books, all glossy picture books: Movie Stars of the 20th Century, One Day In Los Angeles, and The Art of Battle Sun. The carpet looked a little dusty, but otherwise clean, and the chairs had a little bit of animal fur on them. Maybe she had a pet, or maybe it was Lon. I checked the pen-camera's transmission on my phone and made sure it was recording back at the apartment, then settled back into one chair.

He came back with two glasses of water and sat in a matching chair across from me. The sun coming through the roof panels lit him from above with a slightly disconcerting light.

Fine gray fur covered his face. Two triangular ears stuck out from the side of his head. If they'd been on the top, it would have looked much better. His eyes, though shaded by the sun, were clearly blue, and his nose had also been resculpted, jutting out a few inches from between the eyes in a protruding muzzle. From the pink nose down to the upper lip was a straight drop, gray-furred like the rest of him. He had not much chin to speak of, but I didn't know if that was a result of the surgery or not.

The same fur covered his hands, sporting dull doglike claws rather than fingernails. The backs of his hands were the same grey as his face, but when he lifted his hands from the water glasses, I saw white fur on his palms and up along the underside of the wrist. His loose sweatshirt and pants hid the rest of him, so I couldn't see any more of his altered skin, nor whether he had a tail (he hadn't appeared to when he went to the kitchen), but he appeared to be in pretty good shape.

Honestly, he didn't look as bad as some of the photomorphs I'd seen, or the computer-generated characters from any of a dozen films of the past decade. Didn't look as good as some of them, either, but he wasn't jarring enough to make me squirm.

In fact, I set down the water and got his name (Lon) and his age (twenty-eight), just as if he were any normal-looking person I were interviewing about the clothes he was wearing, or something. Then the first odd thing happened.

He reached out for his glass of water, and then looked down into it, the way you might if you tended to forget what you'd poured and wanted to make sure it was the right thing before you drank it. He paused in the middle of telling me that he'd been born in Arizona, and an expression of distaste crossed his face.

At least, that's what I think it was. With his rebuilt face, it might have been something different. But I'm pretty sure it was distaste. He sighed and reached into his water glass and fished out a hair with the crook of one of his claws. He held it, looked at it a moment, then wiped it off on his pants.

So far, I hadn't seen nor heard a cat or dog. I'm pretty sure it was one of his hairs. I waited politely while he picked up his water and drank, checking my glass for stray hairs, but when I started questioning him again, I had something else in the back of my mind.

I've seen a hundred stories about people doing bizarre things to themselves, and all of them are either some kind of rebellion (like the guy who stuck a pair of knives through his nose) or some kind of call for attention (the girl who implanted a flexible screen in her back and showed nude photos of herself on it). There was a body mod gaining in popularity that allowed you to implant your phone into your wrist, with the receiver and mouthpiece implanted into your ear and face, but that one was just for, I don't know, people who lose their phone a lot.

So I'd expected Lon to be of the attention-seeking variety, especially with an agent writing a press release about him. Hell, I'd pretty much formed that opinion the moment I saw the address of the house. But the way he wiped the hair off on his pants, well, in that moment he reminded me of the eighty-year-old man catching sight of the name of his college girlfriend tattooed on his shoulder.

I've been doing this long enough that I can shift gears without it being too obvious. So I went on with some of the standard questions. "Where do you live?"

"Eagle Rock," he said.

"I'm sorry," I said, and he laughed at that. Relaxed a little. "In the Struggling Actor Suites?"

"Something like that." He took a drink of his water. His smile looked weird. I couldn't tell if it had been built to look that way or if it was just his human smile on an alien face.

"So, this procedure... What made you decide to undergo it?" I wanted badly to ask him more about the particulars of the procedure, because it looked incredibly detailed: skull reconstruction, skin grafts for the fur, and reshaping for the ears, not to mention the claws on the hands. But that fell firmly into the realm of things I wasn't allowed to talk about. I wasn't even sure if I could ask him if it was painful or not. I figured if he told me, I'd use it. No doubt he was under the same orders from his agent.

"The technology. I always felt like I wanted to be an animal..."

"So you're a furry, then."

He nodded, slowly. "But I didn't want to do it like one of those people with the tattoos and the wire whiskers. I had a plan. I got an agent, she says she can get me parts in movies."

"Playing..." I was trying to imagine.

"Horror at first, probably." He looked down at his hands, turned them over in the sunlight. "But hopefully more serious things later."

"What about living your life? You know, going down to the Starbucks, out to the grocery store, out to eat?" I gauged his mood. Probably we weren't close enough for a "No Pets" joke yet.

"This is L.A." He scratched at his face, around his whiskers. "You haven't seen weirder things than me walking into a Starbucks?"

"Does that itch?"

Lon dropped his hand fast. "A little," he admitted. "They said it would." And then he said, fast, "But I feel great. Everything looks great, and it's the best move I ever made. Even if I don't get a movie job for a while."

That felt rehearsed, especially the smile. Under all the fur and surgery, he was still an actor. I'd seen enough actor's smiles to know. "Does it still hurt? I imagine it wasn't an easy procedure."

I could say that; it was speculation. He didn't rise to the bait to tell me more about it, though. "Here, it aches a little," he pointed to his face, "and here," and to his backside.

"There? Oh, you have a tail."

That same expression of distaste crossed his face again, more than a flicker. But he brightened and nodded. "Yeah."

"I'll get pictures of it later, if that's okay." He nodded, so I went on. "Have you been in touch with other furries? Are there other people interested in this?"

"Oh, uh, sort of. I mean, they know I was going to do it, but they haven't seen the results yet. I've been telling them to tune in tomorrow." He smiled, more genuinely. "They're all pretty excited."

"I'm sure." There was something else there, too. I asked another rote question while I figured out how to get at it. "What about your family? Girlfriend, boyfriend, parents?"

He shook his head. "I haven't told my parents. And I don't have anyone—well, not local. I have sort of an online long distance thing. She's in Madagascar, though."

"Has she seen the pictures?"

He frowned. "I wanted to send her some, but Charlene—my agent— she said I'm not allowed to send out any."

"There'll be some with my article."

He looked me up and down, peering close. "You have one of those shirt-button cameras?"

I shook my head. "Any other people know?"

"Couple of the guys at my work at the restaurant. I just told them I was going in for cosmetic surgery. I didn't give them details."

"Told them it was to further your acting career?"

He nodded. "It's an excuse, here in L.A."

"You feel like you have to make excuses for it?"

"I'm chasing my dream, but it's not a dream everyone would understand." Rehearsed, again. "I think people should respect the choices other people make. I'm not hurting anyone, am I?"

I shook my head. It was almost convincing enough to believe, but I knew the real reason. It was to be different, to be noticed. To be famous. That's what everyone in L.A. was striving for, the carrot we were all chasing as fast as our artificially tanned, liposuctioned, Home-Toned thighs could move us.

If he was going to stick to his sham, I wasn't going to press. It'd only upset him and then my interview would get cut short. So I let him get away with it. "What are your plans for the future?"

He relaxed, back on his script. "Like I said, my agent's working on some acting roles for me. I'll have to start small, I know that, but I think I'm good enough to work my way up to some major roles."

If his agent told him he'd be a big star, she was leading him on. Big stars are faces that the audience wants to sleep with. Reality wasn't too big on his priority list anyway. He was sitting here thinking he could manipulate the system and score his day in the sun out of it. Not a chance.

Course, it wasn't completely out of the question that he was actually just a furry who wanted to be his totem animal or whatever, and had enough sense to think through a way he could make that pay off. But guys like that didn't move to L.A. to pursue an acting career. They saved up their money and did their plastic surgery with wire whiskers and tattoos and maybe claw-hands, and they hated media attention because people made them out to be on a par with the guy who had his legs broken in three places and set with two-inch gaps in between the breaks so he could stand six inches taller (if you haven't seen the YouTube, it's hysterical—he falls down a lot). I'd done a couple articles on those body-mod freaks back when I was playing around with what kind of content brought the most clicks. Freaks are about the number three type of click-magnet, behind celebrities and funny cat pictures, just ahead of conspiracy theories.

"Best of luck," I said. "Mind if I get that picture now?"

He frowned. "Of the tail," I said.

"Oh. Yeah, hang on."

He went into a back room and came back out a moment later wearing a white t-shirt and shiny red gym shorts. The tail hung down limply over the shorts. It didn't look bad: uniformly grey on top, white underside. It wasn't as bushy as a wolf's tail should be, but maybe they couldn't get the long fur to stick, or something. I snapped a couple shots from different angles with the camera on my phone and added a couple subtle filters, the kind that make it look better but not fake.

He turned around, and I got a few more shots of his face, hidden behind that actor's smile, and his body, posed in actor's poses. I asked a few more general questions while we were doing that, and by the time I'd finished, I had enough to make up a post. I was already composing it in my head.

But something nagged at me still. I knew I could get something up in an hour, counting the time it took me to get home, but I hated the feeling that I was leaving something on the table. The oil-slick agent didn't want me to talk about the procedure—or the doctors didn't want me to talk about it—but Lon's attitude about his surgery, the bright-and-sunny "I feel fantastic" routine coupled with the shadowy glimpses of his real feelings, made me feel like he'd been misled. In which case I could write about that without violating any of the doctors' protocols. Just writing about how a patient felt about a procedure didn't open me up to libel.

But I'd have to get him to tell me honestly how he felt about it. So I turned on my charm, and stepped up the thing actors are most susceptible to: flattery. The problem was, I couldn't flatter him about his looks, because if I was right, he wasn't happy with them. "Hey," I said, extending a hand, "I really appreciate this. I know your agent forced this on you after I showed up at your doorstep, but you've been really up-front with me and I think it's a great story. It'll really help get your career going."

"You're welcome," he said. "You seem pretty straightforward. I'll look forward to seeing the article."

"Yeah," I said, "I'm going to do a good job. It helps that you're a smart guy, level-headed. I mean, so many of the subcultures get lambasted in the media because the guys just go over the edge, right? They expect everyone to understand them and love them for who they are. You can really see objectively and you made a pretty smart decision, to get what you want and make it work for you in your life. It's been a real pleasure talking to you."

A hint of a genuine smile crossed his face. "Thanks," he said. "You seem like a good guy too."

Now for the hook. "Oh, I'm just telling it like it is. You're the kind of guy I'd love to sit down and have a beer with."

With that, I walked to the door, opened it, then hesitated as though I were just getting an idea. "Hey… You want to? Have a beer, I mean?"

"Why?" His eyes, ice blue in that extraordinary face, fixed me. With his fierce, suspicious expression, if he'd been in black and white, I could totally see him in "The Wolfman" at that moment.

I shook it off. "Come on. I usually put together my articles In a bar anyway," I lied. "There's a great place just half a mile away, they brew their own beer and everything. You can still have beer, right? Your metabolism isn't all messed up inside?"

"No," he said, and then, "no, I shouldn't."

But he wanted to. I could tell. "Come on," I said. "Toss on a hoodie and those sweatpants, and nobody'll see you. Get out in public, have a drink. My treat."

He narrowed his eyes. "You're trying to get more out of me."

"Off the record." I shrugged when he didn't move. "Look, I like you, and you seem all cooped up here. I just thought it'd be nice for you to get out. I'll drive, so you don't have to worry about the traffic cams snapping your picture. Pull the hoodie down over your face. Your agent never has to know."

He bit his lip, which looked a lot more painful with his long canine teeth. "Off the record?"

"Sure."

"Can I see you post the article?"

I shrugged again. "Absolutely."

He shuffled his feet. "All right," he said. "Be right out."

He came out with an oversized L.A. Vikings hoodie, the hood pulled down mostly over his eyes, and didn't say much else on the way there, just watched the scenery go by. I was tempted to roll the window down so he could stick his head out, but I didn't think he'd appreciate the gesture. I kept my thoughts to myself until we pulled into the brew pub.

There are a rare few places (and people, for that matter) that can survive changes in style and society, and they tend to be the ones who can either reinvent themselves for each new era, or are so universal that they transcend the vagaries of society's A-list mentality.

The brew pub was not one of those places. I guessed that it had been trendy back at the turn of the century, but you could just see in the décor and the uniforms that it hadn't changed much since then. The list of microbrews was still on the wall, but I'd wager half of them hadn't been ordered since the latter Bush administration. Yellow paint had flaked off much of the trim, revealing brown underneath, and there were some obvious cracks in the plaster.

But the waitstaff, both the balding bartender with the paunch and the attractive young waitress, greeted us cheerily and took a couple minutes to ask us about our taste in beers. Lon kept his hoodie down until the waitress, Julie, asked if he had some makeup on. Then I said, "Go ahead, show her," and to her I explained, "he's auditioning for a film. Just getting him a little bit of a pick-me-up first."

"That makeup is amazing. You do that yourself?" She peered closer.

"Sort of," he said, and cleared his throat.

"Well, you look totes legit. Let me get your beers up."

We sat in silence for a bit. "See?" I said finally. "Just tell people you're in a movie and they hardly blink twice."

"Yeah." He sounded surprised, maybe grudgingly appreciative. His head turned from side to side, taking in the bar without the hood over his face. "This looks like a cool place."

There were a few people at the bar, regulars by the look and the time of day. "Seems cool enough to draw a crowd back. Neighborhood hangout."

"Yeah. I don't really have a place like that. My friends and I work weird shifts, so we don't get together anywhere. And now…" He looked down at his furred hands.

"Right." I tapped the table. "You know, I bet your friends, of all people, will be cool with it. All people need is just time to get used to it." Hell, I was getting used to it after just an hour. "And you've always got your family." He slumped. "Do you talk to them much at all?"

"Look," he said. "I thought you had an article to write."

"Okay, okay." I pulled out the tablet and started dictating, composing on the fly so he could hear the paragraphs. But he didn't seem to be listening after the first couple. He stared off around the bar, at the regulars and the waitress, until she came over from the bar with our drinks.

"So what film are you tryin' out for?" She set the glasses down and looked over at Lon.

He gaped. I cut in. "They're remaking 'The Wolfman.' You know, it's been another twenty years, so…"

"Oh my God," she said, "if you don't get the part, there is no justice in the world."

"Thanks," he said, though he didn't seem grateful for the assist.

"You guys enjoy the beer," she said, and walked back behind the bar. "Give me a holler if you need anything."

When she'd left, Lon gulped down a couple swallows of beer and then slammed the glass down on the table. I rattled off another paragraph and then said, "Everything okay?" When he didn't answer, I said, "Lon?"

"You done your article?"

"Uh, yeah. Just need to drop some pictures in." I called up the text and started adding photos from the pen-camera.

"My name's David," he said.

"David?"

He took another gulp. "My agent picked the name 'Lon' for me."

"I can see that, I guess," I said. "I mean, it creates an association, right? That's what you want."

"'Association,' right." He didn't look at me. "This association sucks."

I frowned. "Lon Chaney, right?"

"Yeah. The wolf man." He did look at me, then, and my expression must have given away my confusion. "I'm supposed to be a cat."

"A... Oh." I could see it now: the shorter muzzle, the thin triangular ears. The less bushy, ropy tail. I had assumed that they just didn't have the expertise to build out a full wolf's muzzle. Lon Chaney in the original "Wolfman," or Del Toro in the remake, both of them have just short human-faced muzzles.

"Doctors couldn't tell either," he grumbled. "My agent said there's no movie parts for cat people. But I look enough like a wolf, you know. Enough. Doesn't matter to her, I guess."

"Sorry, man," I said.

"Man." He laughed, and lifted his beer, then put it down again.

"Well, maybe you can be..." I thought as fast as I could. "Look, you can start out with the wolf thing, right, and then work your way into some cat roles later."

"I thought it'd be cool," he said, slumped down farther over the table, almost resting his head on crossed arms. "I thought they could do it right. They said they could."

"It looks good to me," I said, lying only a little bit. "The fur is really impressive and the face." I gestured around my nose and chin. "Face is awesome."

"It's okay." He did lift his head a little bit at that.

"And the tail—wow."

That got him animated. He lifted his head and his eyes sparked. "That thing is pathetic," he said. "It just fucking sits there like a limp rag. I knew they couldn't put any muscle control into it, but still, I thought..." He sagged back into his chair. "I don't know what I thought."

I didn't say anything. Here, I thought, we were getting to it finally. "And the fur smells funny," he said. "It gets into everything. And the ears don't move either. " He tapped claws on the table and then held them up. "These don't retract."

He seemed to be running out of steam, so I nudged him along with another question. "So why are you going along with all this stuff your agent's putting out? This 'best move I ever made' stuff?"

"Oh, it is," he said. "I don't... I don't regret it. Even if the movie stuff doesn't pan out..."

I waited, but he shut up. So I nudged again, gently. "The procedure must have been pretty expensive, though. Is being in communion with your animal spirit worth that?"

Still, he didn't say anything. I ran some numbers in my head. "Four hundred grand? Five hundred?"

He stared down into his beer. "Upload your article," he said finally. "What?"

"I wanna see you upload it. Then... Then I'll tell you what it cost."

I shrugged, not letting on how excited I was at the prospect of hearing behind the scenes. "Sure," I said, and set the tablet down on the table. I did a little formatting work, tapped a small, unobtrusive checkbox he didn't notice, and then hit the big Publish button. He watched the screen clear and the message come up: Your article has been published.

"All right," he said. "I got a deal from the clinic. Because I had an agent and a movie deal—well, movie possibilities—they cut me a deal and my agent paid part of it. Cost me fifty thousand out of pocket."

"Uh-huh." So about the price of a car. Not too bad. "What's the deal?"

He licked his lips and then picked up his beer and took another drink. "I just have to be a positive model for the procedure," he said when he put it down. "They have some other people interested, they have to get some more people into the pipeline." He shut his mouth quickly, and then said, "Program, I mean. Into the program."

"Right." I nodded. I could follow this up without asking him any more about the procedure itself, couldn't I? "So have you talked to any of these others?"

"A few. I got some contact info, and one of them's responded to me."

"Must be hard keeping up that positive attitude all the time."

"Nah. I'm really a pretty positive guy." He lifted his glass to drain it. "You know, I could've ended up like—uh. Worse. Could've ended up worse."

"Mmm." He was really bad at hiding when he knew something, at least on one beer, which figured; probably if he'd been in a medical procedure, he'd been dry for a while. "Like those others, you mean." I watched for his reaction to confirm my guess, and then went on. "I read about them."

My gambit paid off. His eyes got saucer-wide. "Oh, shit. Where? They told me nobody knew, that they'd been shipped off to Mexico or something."

"That's what I heard."

He leaned across the table. "What else do you know? Are they alive?"

The waitress, seeing the empty glass, came over. I held up two fingers before she could even ask if we wanted more. She nodded and picked up the empty glass, returning with it to the bar.

"I don't know," I said. "I just asked a couple of my sources before coming to see you." Keep the lie vague and simple.

"That was what I was most afraid of," he said. "I mean, they promised they knew better now, but they didn't tell those other guys that they were going to end up living in a foreign country, right? I was scared they'd finish me up and say they still had to get better, that they were going to send me away, or..." His voice dropped to a whisper. "Kill me."

"I'm pretty sure they're not allowed to kill you," I said, but he watched too many movies, apparently.

"Well, of course they're not allowed." He kept whispering. "But those other guys, they just disappeared. One of them was a furry a friend of mine knew. Everyone thinks he went in for gender reassignment surgery and has a new identity, but I saw his name come up on one of the computers in the facility I was in. I checked, and nobody's heard from him since his surgery."

"Maybe he's just in hiding. Maybe they paid him off."

"Yeah." He nodded, and sat back in his chair as the waitress brought two more drinks. "Yeah, probably." But his eyes stayed wide, and he gulped down the beer as though it would keep him real, keep him here and visible.

"Look, I think if anyone were going to—to disappear you, they would've done it by now. Your agent wouldn't have let me in to talk to you, or publish that article." I sipped some of my own beer, barely tasting it.

"Unless I don't fall in line," he said. "Unless I start talking about the problems."

Privately, I doubted that there was a powerful cabal banking on furry body-mod being a wave of riches, so much that they would wipe out anyone who stood in their way. That sounded more like one of the millions of bad one-man films you can catch on the Tube.

"So I have to call up these prospective people, and get on the net and tell everyone how cool it is. I have to pose for pictures and smile and do the movie parts. And I'm a positive guy, I am. But, but—" He gulped down a little more beer, quickly. Half the glass was gone. "You know what the worst part is? The worst part?"

I had difficulty imagining. "What?"

"The worst..." He burped. "The worst is that all these new kids are going to be going in but they're going to come out better. In a few years when they say they'll have working ears, they really will. They'll have a tail that, you know, that curls, and does something." He made a strange noise, between a cough and a hiccup, and I didn't realize what it was until he wiped his eyes and left a dark, damp trail in his fur. "And I'll be stuck like this. I can't afford another procedure. I'll be watching the operations get better and better and I'll be, like, this old relic." He sniffed and wiped a hand across his nose.

"Hey, your friends, and the furry community, they'll still love you." Half of me raced to keep him from breaking down to the point that he couldn't give me any more useful information, and half of me recited these facts to myself so I wouldn't forget them, committed his lines to memory. "They're not that shallow. Are they?"

"No." He sniffed again, and wiped his eyes. "But they'll still look down on me. They'll pity me. And I'll pity me, too." He lifted the glass and drank, then put it down. "I probably shouldn't be d-drinking this."

"It's good for you." I finished my first glass, and slid my other full one over to him. "You can have mine. I need to drive."

"No, I'm okay." He sighed.

"Come on. It'll help."

He finished his second beer and reached out for my glass. "You're being really nice to me," he said, and burped again.

"Well, you know, you helped me out with the story. And now that it's published, it'll be harder for them to come after you. If they change their minds, I mean."

"Yeah." He smiled, and pushed the empty glass away from him, and then he sat and thought in silence while I composed the rest of my article in my head.

I felt a little sorry for him. He really wasn't in it for the attention. He just wanted better ears and a working tail. I've never really understood furries, but hey, there were half a million people around the world who understood him perfectly, which is probably more than I could say for myself. So more power to him. And the more I thought about that, the more I thought that maybe there was an industry out there dedicated to giving these people what they wanted for exorbitant amounts of money, and that they would not be the first industry in the world to promise beyond their capacity to deliver. Maybe there was a lot of money in that market.

Great, if so. If they were lying, manipulating and blackmailing this poor guy, and if they'd "disappeared" the others somehow, that'd be a terrific story. I could insinuate all of that without stating it outright, could say things like "nobody has heard from the mysterious first participants in this program since they entered it, but their existence is on record" without lying.

This was gonna be a big story, all right, and once I finished my article, once I published it to the Outbound folder and not the Draft folder (that was a little trick I played on David, but to be fair, an actor should know that nothing is really off the record), the world was going to see it with my name attached. There'd be follow-ups and I was one of the few people who had the ground floor access on it. This was the best break I'd ever gotten. The story had a conspiracy, it had body-mod freaks, it had a celebrity (albeit a minor one), and, of course, it had a cat.

That was worth a top ten ranking for sure.

Henrietta, a chicken, is eager for babies, but her eggs don't hatch; so she adopts an orphaned fox kit.

Henry the fox grows up thinking that he's a chicken. But he still has a fox's instincts.

Which will win out—nurture or nature?

Fox in the Hen House

by Mary E. Lowd

The eggs never hatched. Henrietta and all her coop-mates laid eggs every day, and every day the Coopmaster came and took the eggs away. No baby chicks. Henrietta had so much love in her feathered breast and no one to spend it on.

Only nine inches below the slatted floor of the coop, a cold and hungry litter of fox kits waited for their mother to return. One by one, the kits closed their eyes and fell into a patient sleep. Their breathing slowed. Their hearts slowed too. Still, the mother did not return.

But one kit was not patient. His heart beat fast, and his nose twitched at the smells that drifted down to him from between the wooden slats. The musty, dusty, warm-blooded smell of chickens tantalized him, filling his nostrils.

While his littermates waited for a mother that would never return, losing themselves into the sleep that becomes death, the impatient kit followed his nose out from their den and into the chicken coop above. There, he found a new mother.

Neither Henrietta nor any of the other chickens in her coop had seen a fox before. Chickens don't often live long after seeing a fox, and the last massacre of that particular hen house had left no survivors to tell the tale. The Coopmaster had ordered replacements from the local feed store and raised them from eggs. None of them knew the haunted history of their home. Thus, when Henrietta saw a small, pointy, red-furred face peek into the coop, she wasn't frightened. In fact, her first thought was, "Why, what lovely plumage! I do believe it's exactly the same shade of red as my own!"

Henrietta was smitten. She was the only red hen in her coop; all the others sported black, white, or checkered feathers. Clearly, she and this little creature were meant for each other. She would call him Henry.

And so Henry became a chicken. He was invited into Henrietta's nest where she sat on him, keeping him warm with her thick, soft feathers. All the hens doted on him and offered him all the grain a growing chick could want. But Henry wasn't a chick, and he didn't want grain. He wanted eggs.

The eggs weren't serving any better purpose—in fact, none of the chickens knew why they laid them. Day after day, they laid the mysterious, pearlescent objects, and day after day the Coopmaster came to take them away. So, when Henrietta's little red-furred chick began to crack eggs and lick out their viscous, slimy insides, none of the hens begrudged him. Better, they thought, that Henry eat the eggs than that the Coopmaster steal them. That dirty thief!

The chickens treasured Henry and hid him carefully from the Coopmaster. If the Coopmaster stole their eggs, there was no telling what else he might steal, and they couldn't stand to lose their baby.

For his part, Henry reveled in the attention from his coop full of clucking new mothers. He loved the warm pressure of Henrietta's weight perched on top of him, pressing him safely into the nest as he slept. He enjoyed the gentle tugs and tickles as various chickens took turns preening his fur with their beaks. His life was a blur of warmth and touch and safe, comfortable smells. And, of course, the eggs were delicious.

As Henry grew, the chickens began to speculate about him. He looked so different from the rest of them. He hadn't changed shape as he grew, sprouting wings and talons like they'd expected. He'd merely grown larger and sleeker. His smell was sharp and dangerous. Terribly exciting! Why, it made their hearts flutter!

Eventually, one of the youngest hens—Calliope with the loveliest, downiest, white feathers—suggested that Henry might not be a hen. He might be a rooster.

All the hens were atwitter at the idea. A rooster! In their hen house! Oh my! Some of the more romantically minded hens had dreamed of meeting a big, strong rooster some day.

A black-checkered hen named Dorrit, the fattest in the coop, swooned at the very idea. The other hens had to fan her with their wings until she recovered, rousing from her faint only to exclaim, "Oh Henry! You are the handsomest young rooster I could imagine!" Then she turned all shy and hid in her own nest with her head tucked under her wing for the rest of the day.

After that, the chickens began to court their young squire. Some sang songs to him in warbling voices; others followed him around, plying him with eager compliments. As always, Henry loved the attention.

Dorrit plucked flowers from the garden to bring Henry. He was quite flattered, but he had no use for flowers.

Calliope dug up worms for Henry. Those tasted funny and squirmy in his mouth. They weren't rich and yolky like the eggs, but their flesh burst satisfyingly under his teeth. Henry approved and asked Calliope to teach him worm-hunting. As the two of them spent more and more of their afternoons together, hunting worms and gossiping, it became clear to all the hens that Calliope had gained Henry's favor.

At a word from Henrietta, the other hens stopped courting her son. If he'd chosen Calliope, there was no need to confuse the young couple. No, indeed, it was time to give them space to get better acquainted. And time to prepare the wedding!

The big day was set for a week hence. Under Dorrit's direction, the chickens plucked flowers and vines from the garden to decorate the coop appropriately. At Calliope's suggestion, they gathered worms for a special feast. And Henrietta arranged for them to build a new, larger nest for Henry and Calliope to share, discreetly hidden at the back of the coop, behind a screen she wove out of straw.

While the rest of the hens worked industriously on the wedding, Calliope strolled with her handsome husband-to-be around the edges of the farmyard. His presence close beside her made Calliope nervous, and her presence close beside him made Henry's heart pound with anticipation.

Calliope's white-feathered body was plump and tempting; her neck slender and appealing. Henry felt an urge, deep in the pit of his stomach, to nuzzle her neck, caress that plump body with his muzzle. He didn't understand the feelings, but they were strong and exciting.

On the night before the wedding, Henry confessed his confusion to Henrietta. As any good mother should do, Henrietta assured her son that his feelings were completely normal. On the morrow, it would all make sense. "Don't worry," she said. "I know you love Calliope, and you'll make her a good husband. As you are a good son. And a good rooster. Just follow your instincts, and let your feelings for Calliope be your guide."

Henry was reassured. He did love Calliope. She was far and away the cleverest of the chickens in the coop. On their walks, she'd told him many stories, sharing her insights on the world and on the political intrigue between different chickens in the coop that Henry had never noticed before. He could listen to her musical voice cluck away, filling his ears with ideas and stories, forever.

The wedding was a solemn affair. All the chickens arranged themselves in a circle around Calliope and Henry. Each and every one of them had prepared a few words to say. Chickens have a lot to say. And they all got their turns—wishing Henry and Calliope happiness, reminiscing about old times, and making promises to support the two of them in their future together. And, of course, hoping for them to have many children.

Then the newlyweds went inside to enjoy their newfound marital bliss while all the other chickens stayed outside, to give them their privacy.

The new nest was made from the freshest straw and had been lined with fragrant flower petals. It was plenty large. Calliope roosted in the middle, nervously preening her neck feathers, and Henry curled his body around hers.

"My bride," he said, pressing his muzzle against her breast.

"My love," she clucked, tracing the tip of her beak down the curve of his ears. A tingle of excitement shot through him at the touch.

Henry opened his mouth a little and breathed softly against her. Calliope's feathers ruffled under his breath. He touched his teeth to her neck in a touch as soft as hers. He nipped lightly, playfully at her like the kit he used to be, and he felt her heart race under the breast pressed against him.

Calliope, suddenly, held herself very still. She didn't understand the feelings racing inside of her. She expected to feel love for her husband. Instead, she felt only fear.

Henry, however, was unaware of the change in his bride's feelings. His own feelings were running high, and everything in him said to press himself harder against his wife. He tightened the grip of his jaw, feeling his teeth press into her plumage. A hunger inside Henry roared for him to bite harder against her tender, delicate neck in his mouth. Overwhelmed with love for his bride, Henry followed his instincts.

Calliope began to struggle, but then her body shuddered and fell still. A satisfying crack between his teeth and the hot flow of blood into his mouth told Henry that he was doing what was right. Nothing could feel more right than the glorious taste that exploded in his mouth. He felt himself overcome with a blind urge to rampage and ravage, working his jaws until white feathers flew around him.

Henry had never eaten a meal so amazing, so succulent, so filling. Immediately, afterward, Henry fell into a deep, contented sleep.

In that sleep of satiation, Henry dreamed a disturbing dream. He was a tiny kit again, nestled under his mother hen's feet, and he was watching all the hens in the coop fly about in a crazed, frightened flurry. "Where is Calliope? Where is Calliope! Where has she gone?" they all clucked. Every chicken was in a tizzy, and Henry felt guilty. Though, he didn't know why.

The clucking changed, as chickens began to bock, "She's dead! She's gone! Someone has killed her!"

Then Dorrit squawked and flapped her wings, commanding the attention of all the chickens in the coop. They roosted around her, settling down and quieting themselves to hear what Dorrit had to say. She turned to the assembled crowd and announced, "The killer is none other than…"

Henry awoke in a fever. Although he'd lost himself in his passion, Henry knew what he had done. He'd eaten his beloved. His wife. His Calliope. His tender, tasty, delicious Calliope… Henry's mouth watered at the memory of her flesh on his tongue. He felt power surging inside him, as if he'd finally realized who he was. He had woken up into himself for the first time and all his life was like a mad play.

Henry wanted to share his insight with Calliope, but the feelings that welled up in him at the thought of her were complex and shifting. Love. Regret. Hunger. And an insatiable desire to feel her hot blood pumping onto his tongue.

Faster than he could think, Henry's feet carried him out of the chicken coop and into the yard. His eyes shone with a mad light as he looked, blinded with bloodlust, at the chickens who'd raised him. Loving clucks turned to screeches of horror as Henry flew at the hens.

Feathers flew in the air.

Henry tasted blood again and again, until there were no more chickens. Only a mad fox, shaking limp carcasses in his mouth, mere feathered bags of flesh and broken bones. His belly was too full to eat anymore but his tongue still screamed for the taste of hot blood.

When finally the Coopmaster came with a gun, Henry darted into the forest behind the farm. He ran through the underbrush, haphazardly dashing without knowing his way. The speckled light filtered down through the trees, dappling his red coat. And, only now, did his sight begin to clear. Only now did he realize: Calliope, Henrietta, all the chickens… were gone.

Henry found a hollow, rotting log, smelling of earth and wood like the place he was born, the place his littermates had died. He knew what he was now. And what he had never been.

The next few weeks were hard. Henry was used to living in a warm hen house, eating eggs, and listening to the friendly clucking of the hens. He was used to the feel of soft feathers and the gentle preening of careful beaks. He wasn't used to working his paws numb, scratching out hollows in the cold dirt ground; or hunting for his food; or falling asleep to melancholy silence alone.

Henry was like the kit he had been before he found the warmth of the hen house and Henrietta had named him. Except, now he was grown, and he could take care of himself. He could find his way through the forest. He was lean and strong, a deadly predator. He was a fox again.

But he missed his chickens.

You won't recognize this version of "The Three Little Pigs".

Rearview

by Sean Silva

Those eyes.
Those fiery, malevolent eyes.

They were still there, staring at me through the rearview mirror. And they'll probably follow me forever, like the headlights of a car trailing behind me on a dark lonely back road. I just wish I knew whose they were. Because even though that was my plump face and stubby snout looking back at me in the reflection, those eyes certainly weren't mine. They hadn't been mine for quite sometime now.

That's when a loud noise startled me, causing my focus to shift away from the mirror and over to the darkness that stretched out beyond the glass. The jarring cacophony of a car horn brought my senses back to reality, and my ears began twitching as I heard what sounded like hundreds of little feet running across the roof of the vehicle. I must've dozed off again, probably because of the continued rhythmic drumming noise coming from the heavy downpour.

Yet... it was mesmerizing in a way, listening to the rain hammer on the car while I watched the lights from passing vehicles illuminate all those tiny droplets of water. It made them glisten as if someone had dumped a bag full of diamonds all over the windshield.

Then my eyes moved over to the road, and I watched vehicle after vehicle rocket by me from where I had parked my car on the shoulder. They were streaking down the highway in a line of endless taillights, looking like a trail of glowing ants as they marched along a black canvas. They were still traveling, though, which was what I should've been doing. That's when I realized I couldn't continue to sit here and stare out the window when I knew damn well it wasn't safe for me. I had to find a way to get moving again, even though I didn't have the foggiest idea where I was headed or what I was going to do when I actually got there. Not like it really mattered. I just had to go.

I needed to get away.

After a couple more vehicles passed by I reached down with my thick cloven hand and grabbed the key, which was held in the ignition's tight grasp. I turned it one slow, agonizing click, hearing the soft jingle of the other keys imprisoned on that cold metal ring. Then I mouthed a quick prayer, begging for it to please start as I turned the key the remaining distance. The car moaned and growled, protesting like a sick, angry dog that didn't want to get out of bed. I finally released the keys.

That settled it. The car was dead, and I was stranded. All on the one night I happened to leave my cell phone on the dresser. It's what I get for leaving in such a hurry.

"Damn," I muttered before taking in a shuddering breath. Then I rubbed my snout with my wiry haired arm, aggravating the already irritated skin. It itched even worse now, burning me with an agonizing, relentless ache that wouldn't go away. It just wouldn't stop, kind of like all the other things happening to me back at home.

And that seemed to be the trigger, because it brought everything rushing back to me in a sudden flood of thoughts and images. It overwhelmed me, to the point where I couldn't even think straight, and I started panicking and twitching nervously in the seat, frantically looking around for any possible way to make it all stop. But no, my mind just continued running out of control and I didn't know what to do, but yet, I could see all those things flashing in my mind over and over again until it was impossible to see anything else.

Why? Why was this happening to me? I just didn't understand it; none of it made sense anymore. There were… those things. Odd, strange things going on… like my stuff, it was out of place all over the house. I mean my wallet, my keys, my medications, even the damn toothbrush wasn't where it was supposed to be. Nothing was where I remembered it—nothing.

And then there was the money that vanished from the lockbox, and the open windows and the unlocked doors and the missing clothes, and the—oh god… those bleach stains in the carpet.

What were they?

I don't remember them being there before, ever. And I don't know why, or where they came from, it was… it was all driving me insane. I mean, if someone had been in the house, I would've smelt them, right? There would've been scents all over the place, but there weren't. There was just… that odor. Like disinfectant or something, and it was everywhere, all the time, but I don't remember using it. So I… I figured I was going crazy. I couldn't eat, I couldn't sleep, and it was all coming at me so fast I didn't know what else to do, so… so that's when I knew I had to leave. I had to get away.

But where? Where could I possibly go, completely out of the blue and in the absolute dead of night, no less? It was a crazy notion, but… really, what choice did I have?

At first I thought about going to see Garvis, since the last time I talked to him he'd just bought that wood cabin up by Badger Flat, but then I remembered he was out of the country with his business partners on something important, which was so like him. He was always off gallivanting somewhere, trying to pretend like he didn't have problems just like the rest of us. Some brother he was. Not that he'd want to talk with me anyway, but I had a better chance with him then I did Woodley.

Woodley… had it really been that long since either of us bothered to speak one word to each other? The last time was… it had to be the day daddy went to trial; and that was…what—like twelve years ago. Maybe more.

It felt like such a distant memory now. Some sort of fantasy, like those stories they used to tell us all before bedtime. Back when the three of us were just little pigs without a care in the world… when we still acted like brothers. Like friends. Back when momma was still alive.

So… so that was about the time I decided to get in the car and start driving. I couldn't depend on my brothers to help me. That I was sure about, and I'd figure out someplace to go eventually, on my own.

Which is how I ended up here; with the rain pounding on the car harder than ever before, as if those tiny little raindrops were somehow laughing at me incessantly. I just wanted it all to stop. And it did once a pair of headlights brightened up my rearview mirror like the eyes of a predator stalking its prey under the cover of night. So I froze, rigid like a statue for a couple of seconds before I sunk into the driver's seat ever so slightly, hoping to get a glimpse of the vehicle in the mirrors. Unfortunately, the blinding light drowned out everything else, and I felt my heart flutter a little in my chest. The term sweating like a pig seemed strangely ironic at that moment, because if I were actually able to sweat, I would've been pouring buckets right about then.

Who was it? A cop? Or maybe this was the person who broke into my house and did all those things to me? No, no, no, I mean that was just crazy, right? Someone wouldn't go around following me like that, now would they? Would they?

My back twitched against the seat as I watched a shadow burst from the driver's side door of the vehicle behind me. It streaked toward my car, flowing like death on the prowl as it looked for another soul to steal. I didn't hesitate to reach for the door, making sure it was securely locked. The shadow eventually migrated to my side front window and rapped on the glass with a single dull claw. It looked like the pointed beak of a hawk frantically trying to get through to a rodent on the other side, and it made me swallow a heavy lump in my throat. I couldn't help but stare at the wet glass for a few seconds before I finally reacted and cracked the window.

"Car troubles?" the dark figure questioned, his tone slightly elevated so I could hear him over the passing cars.

My snout flexed, sucking in a quick burst of air as I tried not to grunt. He was a wolf. I could tell that much by his hot earthy breath, and it made me wonder if he was trying to catch a whiff of my scent too. Could he smell my fear? Were his instincts sharp enough to pick up on that?

"Y—yes," I finally replied as I cracked the window a little further, trying to get a better look at him.

Even though less of the talking figure was distorted by the sopping wet glass, it still didn't help. I couldn't see his entire face, partially because the dark red hood he was wearing kept his head shrouded in a shadowy veil, leaving only the faintest glimpse of gray fur visible around the wolf's protruding muzzle. But when cars roared by, they temporarily illuminated his visage and I saw those teeth—and those eyes, standing out against the darkness. It definitely startled me.

"Where's ya headed?" the wolf asked.

His voice—it was deep. Very masculine, and it enticed me in a strangely pleasant sort of way that I couldn't quite pin down. It wasn't so much that he had a country vibe to his voice. It was more like he sounded uneducated, but there appeared to be a genuine, homey charm to him which made you take notice. And the fellow seemed awfully benign given that he was standing next to a busy highway out in the pouring rain. Maybe he really was trying to help me out? Regardless though, I still had to think of something. I mean, even if this wolf wasn't the one doing those things to me, I couldn't let him know I was running away.

Come on dammit, think.

"Fl—Florin... I'm going to Florin," I replied with an adolescent-like stammer as I locked onto the wolf's fiery golden eyes, which seemed to lure me in like a cobra enchanting its prey.

"Florin? Ain't that just south a' Manning?"

I pondered that for a moment, a little unsure myself before I finally answered him with a nod.

"You're a long way from home, ain't ya? Well, you're 'n luck, cause I'ma headed right by there. I'll give ya a lift."

"Well, umm… I—I don't think I—"

"Hey, don't worry 'bout it," the lupine insisted as he backed away from the car door. "Let's jus get ya outta the rain."

I hesitated stepping out of the car, as if I'd somehow been glued to the seat. But I finally pried my hoofed fingers away from the steering wheel and opened the door. The noise of the rain increased dramatically as I got out of the vehicle, so much so, I would have to shout if I wanted to be heard, especially when another car drove by and drowned out all the other sounds. The wolf headed back to his larger vehicle, his bushy gray tail swaying to and fro like a hypnotist swinging his watch.

I moved around to the rear of my car and opened the trunk of my small hatchback. I grabbed my duffel bag from inside before slamming the door and locking the car with a push of a button on the keys. The lights flashed on my vehicle as I turned and rushed over to the wolf's sedan, watching as he opened the passenger side door and began fumbling around in the car. Another vehicle sped by, blinding me for a moment as it flew past us and sprayed fine droplets of water on my face.

When I got to the other car, I could hear his radio blaring, and I saw the wolf had a child seat strapped into the passenger side and was struggling to get it loose. This struck me as odd. Why did he have a pup carrier but no pup? Then another car sped by, showering us with more water from a dip in the road, and it reminded me that I needed to get moving.

"It's okay. I'll sit in the back," I said before opening up the rear door.

The wolf nodded in agreement and headed around to the driver's side. I threw my bag into the car and got in, quieting the noises outside with a slam of the door. I could hear the radio more clearly now, the song "Brick House" thumping through the aged, tinny sounding speakers on the dashboard. My lupine driver stepped inside and immediately shut the radio off before situating himself behind the wheel, adjusting his tail and lowering the hood on his red coat. It made me feel like I was in the back of a damn taxicab.

"Sorry 'bout that," the wolf said as he looked over at the child seat. "I jus dropped my little one off at her grand mama's place. It's pretty rare I have passengers anymore, if ya know what I mean."

Deep down, I knew I should've let things be and not inquired more. But the pup carrier was nagging at my brain for some odd reason, and

Lord knows why, I just couldn't let it go. Maybe it was because of the nerves.

"I thought it was against the law to have a carrier in the front seat?"

The sentence just shot out of my mouth, and I wanted to slap myself as soon as I said it. Then I saw an irritated look wash over the lupine's face as he glared at me through the rearview mirror.

"Only if ya face it forward and ya have airbags. But in this piece a junk—" he paused, just long enough to shake his head, "airbags weren't even heard of yet."

Way to make friends, jackass. Now shut the hell up so he can drive. "Sorry—I… I was just curious, is all."

That seemed to satisfy the wolf because he glanced at his side mirror and pulled out into the line of vehicles littering the highway. We were going. Thank the Lord, we were finally going. As long as it was away from here. Anywhere but here.

"So let me introduce myself," the wolf said in a chipper tone. "The name's Mike Hooten, but my friends call me Hooter."

I hesitated when those eyes of his found mine through the rearview mirror. I knew what he wanted. I knew what I was supposed to do, but the words had trouble coming out.

I had to say something though, so I eventually dribbled out the reply, "I'm Ben." *No—no, don't give him your real name, idiot.*

"What? No last name?" Mike asked, switching his eyes from the road to the mirror again. "Do I gotta get all huffy and puffy to get it outta ya?"

He chuckled at that, but I certainly didn't see the humor in it. My mind was far too occupied to think rationally, let alone clearly.

Quick—a name. Give him a fake one, hurry. "It—it's Huffington."

Crap. That sounded ridiculous. And I watched as Mike gave me the most perplexing look, which made the hairs all over my body stand up straight. I must've been shaking like a dang fish out of water.

"Ya alright there, partner? You sure look like sumthin' has ya all knotted up. You ain't in some kinda trouble, are ya?"

There was heat in his voice now. He knew something wasn't right. I needed to quell his curiosity—and fast.

"No—no, good heavens, no. It's just… I—I had a bad week at work and I… I'm just getting away for awhile."

"Oh… well, okay. Jus don't get your little tail in a twist or nuthin'." He laughed again, and he seemed surprised that I didn't find his clever pun equally amusing. "Lighten up there, ol' boy. I ain't one a' those big bad wolves like your momma used to tell ya about back when you was younger. I'm just a guy tryin' to help another guy out, is all."

I didn't respond. I didn't know how to, and Hooten seemed to catch on because he turned his attention back to driving. We rode in silence for the next ten miles or so, listening to the rain beat on the car while streaking headlights flew past us in both directions. It caused everything to go by in flashes; from light to dark, light to dark. It made my eyelids heavy. Made me want to sleep. But I couldn't, and not because I didn't want to.

It was because I hadn't had a good night's sleep in well over a month.

And I really didn't know what to do about the situation. I mean, the sleeping pills didn't help, that was for dang sure. They only caused me to feel even more paranoid about the whole thing, and the drinking simply made everything worse. But if I kept this up, I'd most certainly lose my job. I'd lose it all, and then what? I'd just… I didn't want to think about it. The thought of what might happen… it was down right scary. That's when I felt the panic building up again, getting ready to boil over inside and I started shifting around in the seat, trying to keep myself calm.

Don't do it, Ben. Not in here. Please… not right now.

"So, Mr. Huffington, why ya goin' to Florin?"

That jarred me. It sounded so weird hearing a fake last name come out of Hooten's mouth, but at least it snapped me back to attention. I felt the sudden swell of panic begin to subside. But now my thoughts were racing to catch up with me, and I couldn't help wondering if maybe I had fallen asleep. Did I black out? Did I miss something important? I met the wolf's eyes in the mirror before I dropped my head and stared into my lap. I tried to think of a reply, but it was hard because I knew his eyes were still there, staring at me.

Why? Why did he have to toy with me like this? Why couldn't he simply shut up and drive? Or just kill me now and get it over with? What was he waiting for?

An answer? Maybe an answer would get him to stop glaring at me with those eyes.

"I'm going to visit my brothers," I muttered back. "One lives in Florin, and the other lives just up the hill near Badger Flat."

"Sounds like a good deal to me. So what's the occasion?"

"Oh—uhhh, it—it's family business. Nothing I really want to talk about though… if you don't mind?"

"Not a problem. I can relate when it comes to family matters. Got enough problems of my own."

"Thanks, I apprecia—"

And that's when a phone started ringing.

Hooter began fumbling around in the center console, causing the car to swerve a bit as the phone continued to blast that annoying chime. It sounded like the shriek of a crying piglet set to an obnoxiously upbeat electronic tone, and it made me feel like my ears were going to start bleeding at any moment if it didn't stop. Finally, Hooter picked up the device and looked at the screen. But when I saw a wretched snarl form on the edge of his muzzle, it made the muscles in my back tighten so much I nearly grimaced from the sudden twinge that crawled up my spine.

"Sorry I… I gotta take this," Hooten muttered. I could almost hear his teeth grinding as he spoke. Something about this phone call was going to be bad. Really bad.

I choked on the aching lump in my throat as I watched the wolf flip open the phone and raise it to his ear. Then I heard a strident, almost piercing howl of a voice resonate through the speaker, and it was so loud, even I could hear a few choice words clearly. That's when I knew I had made a *really* big mistake. I should've never gotten into this dang car.

"Hey!" Mike shouted, slightly pulling the phone away from his ear as the yelling intensified. "Wai—wait a damn minute. What the hell ya screamin' at me for?"

The voice answered, and it became muffled when he moved the phone back against his head.

"Now look here, I came by when I was supposed to, aw'ight? I can't help it if ya got your—"

Another pause, and my hoofed fingers began digging their way into the worn leather seat. The muffled voice was getting louder now. More aggressive.

"Well, if ya didn't invite every Tom, Dick, and Harry over to your momma's house, then maybe I wouldn't be interruptin' nuthin', now would I?"

I heard a laugh come through the phone before that voice started howling again. It made my stomach turn a bit, especially when I caught the sound of Hooten's tail brushing against the seat. He was getting pissed.

"No! You're the one who screwed things up. Now don't you go blamin' all of this on me."

Hooter didn't even realize that he was drifting onto the shoulder until after the right side tires started banging against the rumble strips. Then he swerved the car back onto the road, and my head nearly smacked into the side window.

"No. Screw you, ya stupid bitch. And don't you bring Kayla into this mess either, ya hearin' me? You leave my daughter out of it!"

There was more talking on the other end now, but it quieted down, and not in a good way. Hooten's tail hammering against the seat told me that much.

"Don't you threaten me like that. If you take my daughter away from me, I swear to God I'll—Mary Ann? Mary? You—"

That's when he pounded the phone against the wheel before throwing it onto the dashboard with a loud crack. And even though I couldn't see much inside the dark vehicle, I was sure something had to have broken. Hooter slammed his paw against the steering wheel, then he repeated it a few more times, producing a solid thumping sound that made my tail twitch inside my pants. I had been quietly begging for that conversation to end as quickly as possible, but now I was beginning to regret that wish. I attempted to take a breath, but the tension hovering inside the small confines of the car seemed to suck the air right out of my lungs. It felt thick and oppressive and so much worse than before. Much, much worse.

The wolf hung his head down and breathed in a heavy sigh before muttering, "I'm... I'm sorry ya had to hear that. It's jus..."

I don't know how, but I managed to inhale enough air to start speaking. "It's okay, I—I understand that... you know, these things happen," I replied, but it sounded fake as soon as the words escaped my mouth. Probably because they were. I wanted to say something, anything, I didn't care what, just as long as it changed the conversation.

"Yeah, but I..."

The wolf trailed off, and I watched him bend over slightly in the seat. Hooten belched, then he let out a groan as he dropped one hand from the wheel. The car swerved again, and when Hooten finally straightened back up, he was panting.

"Hooten... maybe we should stop. You don't look so good."

He nodded with a rumbling growl, and a few seconds later he flipped on the right blinker.

A blue sign with bright white lettering reflected in his headlights that read, "REST STOP 1 MILE AHEAD". The wolf sped up, and when he got to the exit he tore down the off ramp before quickly parking the car in one of the many empty slots. He stormed out into the rain, slamming the door behind him as he put his paw over his muzzle and raced for the men's bathroom. And just like that, he disappeared into the darkness.

Only two lights appeared to be working here, and none of them were near the facilities. It made the place look completely dead, other than a couple of cars which littered the small parking lot. There was no movement inside any of them, though. I had a sneaking suspicion the people had probably stopped just to get some sleep. Yet here I was, sitting in a stranger's car while he ran off to throw up in the restroom.

I contemplated leaving. My brain kept shouted at me, *"Just get your bag and run, you idiot. Go!"*

But when I looked over at the bathroom, I couldn't help feeling bad for the poor schmuck who was in there. That must've been his wife on the phone, or a soon to be ex-wife from the sound of it. She was probably screwing around, making life miserable for him and his daughter. What a horrible way to live. And for a moment, just a moment, everything that had been happening to me over the last month or so seemed to fade away. Yeah, sure, I may have been a freaking mess, but at least this wolf had tried his damnedest to help me out. Even though it sounded like his life was going to hell in a hand basket. And what did I want to do? Run away. Good Lord, Ben, at least try and do something decent for the guy in return.

And that's when I decided to step out of the car.

I ran toward the bathroom, feeling the rain assault my head as I attempted to block it with one cloven hand. Not like I could see much of anything, and I nearly tripped when my right hoof clipped some of the busted up concrete on the walkway. When I finally did get to the door, the smell just about knocked me backward. I covered my snout, which didn't help much with the stench as I heard Hooten gagging in one of the stalls. Then there was a heavy, clumpy sound of fluid being expelled from his body as it hit the toilet water below, which made me belch in my mouth. He coughed and choked, muttering something like 'fucking bitch,' and I wondered if maybe I was better off just going back to the car. But I stepped inside anyway, hearing Hooten spit and hack into the toilet before he flushed away the evidence. When he came out of the stall, the wolf was wiping his muzzle with the back of his arm, and his eyes drifted up to meet mine. It was those eyes again. The ones that were clouded with anger and hatred, and they were just looking for a place to channel it as the wolf stomped toward me.

"Hooten? You alrig—" I started to say, but I didn't get the chance to finish my question.

The wolf grabbed me by the collar, and I felt my feet become light as he swung me toward the wall. I heard something break behind me, and a sharp pain bit into the back of my skull. It made my entire body feel woozy and energized simultaneously, sending out sharp twinges through my nerves that made all my limbs want to jump and contract in a spasm. And that was it. That sensation, it ended up being the last thing I remembered as a bright flash lit up behind my eyelids.

* * *

"Do I fuckin' look alright to you?" a voice said just as my eyes suddenly popped open.

My head hurt like hell, and I heard the tinkering of glass hitting the floor when my senses started to come around. What a way to wake up. This place was dark, and it smelled like piss and vomit. My snout twitched from the stench, and I zeroed in on those eyes when everything else started coming back into focus. They were lupine eyes too, belonging to a wolf who for some reason had grabbed me by my shirt collar.

Who the heck was this guy?

"What are you—get off me!" I shouted, moving my arms in-between his so I could push outward and force them apart. "Who the hell do you think you are?"

Glass crunched underneath my hooves as I pushed the wolf away and turned around, glancing at the broken mirror behind me. I brushed the back of my head and checked for blood. There wasn't any. Just a few small pieces of glass stuck in my hair.

How in the world did I end up in a dirty public restroom with this guy? Dammit, my fucking head.

I rubbed the back of my skull and turned my attention to the wolf, who was now backing away while shaking his head. He looked down at his paws, as if he were going to start crying like a flaky little pansy. Guy must've lost his mind; some drunk, homeless bastard by the looks of it.

"Look, Ben—I'm… I'm sorry, 'kay? I… I jus lost it," the wolf said when he finally shifted to make eye contact with me. "I'm under a lot of stress and… I'm really sorry."

Ben? Who the hell is Ben? "I'll say. What the fuck is wrong with you, anyway?" I said, half pissed, and half trying to figure out what the heck was going on.

"Look, I… why don't I jus go back to the car and call ya a cab, alright? It's the least I can do after… well, this." He motioned with his hands toward the mirror and added, "Again, I—I'm really sorry."

I could hear the wolf heading toward the door just as I turned around and looked at the mirror. That's when I saw it. A nice piece was still hanging there, about ready to fall off and shatter all over the floor. What a waste. So I made sure to reach out and save it from obliteration. It was big and sharp and pointed—you know, like a broken piece of glass should be. I grabbed it with my cloven hand and pulled it free, and thankfully my porcine skin was so rough that it didn't even slice through me when I gripped the chunk of mirror a little bit tighter.

"Yeah. Yeah, I bet you're sorry. Real sorry," I thought to myself as I turned back to the wolf and started walking toward him. *"I'm gonna make sure of it."*

* * *

When the world came back to me, it did so in a panicked flash of awareness, like you do when you wake up from a horrid nightmare. I noticed it was still dark out as I blinked away the haze, and that's when I came to realize that I must have blacked out or something. But yet, I was still inside the car, parked on the side of the road just like I had been before Hooten...

Wait. No. No, this wasn't my car. This was Hooten's car. So then... why was I in the driver's seat, and where the hell was Hoo—

Then I smelt it. A pungent, burning odor assaulted my nostrils like someone had waved smelling sauce in front of my face. And when I moved my hands up toward my snout, the scent just got stronger and stronger. It saturated everything, and I wanted to turn on the interior light so I could see it with my own eyes, but I didn't need to because... that smell, it was too distinct.

It was blood. Dried blood... and it wasn't mine.

"No. No, no, no—please, no," I muttered to myself, trying not to panic as I looked around the cab with my hands held in the air so I wouldn't touch anything. "This—this can't be happening. Not to me, please. It just can't—it—"

And that's when I finally saw them.

They were right there, staring back at me from my dark, sad reflection in the rearview mirror. It was them. It was those eyes. Those fiery, malevolent eyes.

But this time... there was no question as to whom they belonged to.

This time... I knew they were mine.

They always had been mine.

Who is River? He doesn't really know, himself.
He finds out on the Night of the Blood Moon.

Son of the Blood Moon

by Bill "Hafoc" Rogers

"River! River, where are you?"

River jerked his hand back from the purse, momentary guilt stopping him. He went to the living room. Mom was sprawled in the big recliner, her eyes unfocused and wild with fear.

"I'm here, Mom."

Tears welled in her eyes. "Don't go out at night. Don't go out under the full moon," she muttered.

River topped off her glass of peach brandy. The ice had all melted, but from experience, he knew that she wouldn't notice that at this point. He edged the filled glass across the pattern of water rings on the end table until it touched her hand. Automatically, she picked it up and raised it to her lips. Drunk as she was, she didn't spill a drop. Practice makes perfect.

"I'm here, Mom," he said, watching her drink. "Don't worry."

She set the glass down and dropped off to sleep again. He made sure she was really out this time. Then he went back to the kitchen. Her purse was on the table. He opened it and got the car keys out. Thirty seconds later he was out the door, walking to the driveway in the light of the rising full moon.

* * *

River Greene loved his mother, of course. He must love her. Everyone loved their mothers, right? But he wished she hadn't eaten so many mushrooms or dots of acid or whatever the hell it was she'd taken at that New Age, neo-pagan, tree-hugging, hippie commune where she'd lived when he was born.

"Fetal alcohol syndrome," Dr. Blandings—that idiot—called it. River didn't think much alcohol was involved. Mom was a binge drunk, not a constant one, and her binges had started only a few years ago. But she'd been high on something back in that commune, and it hadn't done him any good in the womb.

He didn't mind the trapped, jittery feeling he got when he was stuck indoors, or the way he couldn't pay attention in school. It kept him from getting good grades. Why should he care about that? It kept him from learning what he should. Who needed to know English or math anyway? But the hair-trigger temper that got him into fights with the other boys when school started each Fall until he'd showed them their proper place in the order of things, somewhere beneath him. That... *That* he wished he could control.

It was Halloween. It was time to go to Rick's. Everyone went to Rick's, wherever it happened to be at the time, and tonight's location was a great one. He'd found it himself on one of his long rambles in the woods.

It was an abandoned farmstead on what was now public land, off the side of a road that had once been more important. What used to be the house was a square hole in the ground, the barn a tangle of silvered, rotting timbers, but there was a tractor shed with a good roof.

Best of all, nobody ever went out there. One reason was that the abandoned farm was said to be haunted. Supposedly there had been axe murders there, and the ghosts of the slain and of the murderer's dog pack still haunted the place in the nights. It was a good, scary story. River knew every detail of it. Why shouldn't he? He'd been the one to make it up and start spreading it around about a year and a half ago.

He'd left the rusty minivan that was all his mother could afford parked in the driveway, away from the house as far as he could leave it without seeming too unusual. The muffler was good, replaced just last spring. He started the van, reasonably sure his mother wouldn't hear it, backed out, and headed for Main Street.

Somewhere east of town, at the edge of cell phone range, he turned off the state highway onto 38 ½ Road. The minivan handled the gravel road just fine, even after he drove past the sign that said, "SEASONAL ROAD - NOT SNOWPLOWED BY THE COUNTY ROAD COMMISSION" and the road became nothing more than two rutted wheel tracks through the woods. He maneuvered along the ruts with precision, turning outside their straight line from time to time to go around a mud hole or a place where a particularly large tree had fallen across the road five, ten, or fifty years ago.

He kept watching the woods to his right; he knew where he was going, but things looked different at night, so he wanted to be careful. Soon he saw a gleam of light off the road, downhill. Carefully, he eased the minivan off what road there was and down a barely-visible trail, brambles scratching its undersides and its theoretical paint as he went.

He picked a good hiding spot for the vehicle with an expert eye. Finding just the right place in the trees to avoid being seen had always come naturally to him. It wasn't that likely they'd be found out here in the depths of the State Forest anyway, but Officer Dagner had to know there'd be a party somewhere around town on Halloween Night, of all nights, and he'd be looking. There was no reason to make it easy for that pig.

There were half a dozen other cars and trucks parked nearby already. He didn't recognize two of them. Sniffing for danger, River walked around to the open side of the three-sided, metal-clad, abandoned farm shed that was the center of tonight's party.

Rick had provided a fine set-up, as always. He had a folding table as a bar, with a couple bottles of rum someone had bought or stolen, and mixers. He had a cooler of canned beer on ice. He'd strung low-powered lights in paper lanterns; their colored light made the place almost cheerful. A fire burned just outside to keep off the chill, and a boom box played heavy metal. Not loud enough, of course, but at least there was music for the ten or twenty partiers.

"Hey, Greene Man!" Rick shouted, lifting a beer. "Fix yourself a cocktail."

River smiled, waved, and went to the booze table. "Cocktail," huh? That was a pretty fancy word for the drinks he might make here, but it didn't matter. He didn't plan to drink much, or anything. His mother did that. He hated it when she got drunk, however convenient it might make sneaking out at night and doing whatever he wanted.

He poured himself a big plastic cup of cider, picked up the bottle of dark rum, and tipped it toward his glass, keeping his back turned so nobody could see that he wasn't actually pouring any into his drink. Someone had brought caramel corn too, his favorite. He grabbed his cider and a handful of the caramel corn and went to Rick.

"Cheers," he said, lifting his cup.

Rick lifted his beer in reply. "Your harem's here."

"Oh? I don't see Cass."

Rick laughed. "Autumn and Tiffany aren't enough for you?"

River shrugged. "The more the merrier. Who's the dark one in the corner?" She was tall, whoever she was, and a bit heavy, but with muscle, not fat. Her hair was as black as River's and he sensed, almost scented, something dangerous about her.

"I don't know, she came with Jake's crowd, I think. So did that other guy, the jock who's trying to pick up Autumn."

"Someone's trying to pick up Autumn?"

Rick grinned. "Sic 'em."

River sighed. People just wouldn't learn to leave his women alone. There he was, some no-neck, steroid-addicted jock who thought he was hot stuff, chatting to Autumn and Tiffany near the open side of the shed. And here he'd thought he might have a party without any trouble.

"Evening, girls," he said, walking over. "Enjoying the party? Care to go out for a walk in the moonlight?"

"Hey, kid, find your own chick," No-Neck said, unobtrusively—he thought—making his ham-hand into a fist.

River smiled. "I did find my own." He finished his cider and dropped the cup. "Shall we go, girls?"

"Hey, kid, I warned you…"

No-Neck tapped River's shoulder with three stiff, outstretched fingers. That was all it took to set River off.

He was unstoppable in a fight. He wasn't that big and he didn't seem that strong, but he was *perfect*. When The Rage took him he didn't fight, he *was* the fight. Every move was like a dance step, beautiful, instant, and instinctive.

River was aware of moving quickly, of turning and bobbing for some reason he didn't understand just before a fist swung through the place his face had been a moment before. He felt blows on his fists and on his feet. It was more intense than anything else in his life, yet it seemed far away at the same time. He stopped his dance. No-Neck was on all fours on the ground at his feet, trying to breathe.

"I'll kill…" No-Neck said, and tried to rise. He hadn't had enough yet? Fine. River began dancing again. The knuckles of his left hand bled and his right foot hurt from a powerful shock. No-Neck was flat on his belly this time. No-Neck tried to get up, but he was finished, clearly. There was no need to start the dance again. River just kicked him in the ribs, twice, hard as he could, to explain the situation to him.

"Stay down," River said. No-Neck stayed down. From behind, River heard a smattering of ironic applause. "Ring up another win for the Champion," Rick said.

Tiffany looked annoyed. "Jesus, River, why do you have to take guys down so hard like that?"

"It's his own fault, Tiff. If he'd just back off I'd let him go, and if he'd stay down once he's down, I'd let him. I'd leave him alone. You've seen this before. You know how I work. I don't need to hurt them; I just need them to *back off.*"

"Hmff," Tiffany said. "As if you owned us. C'mon, Autumn, let's get another beer." The girls stalked off without a backward look.

River sighed. That was it for those two, for tonight at least. Well, he could charm them back later. Or if he couldn't, there were other women. There were always other women.

He needed to calm down. He should go outside and smoke one of his mother's cigarettes. He stepped over No-Neck and headed out under the moonlight. Something about the woods always calmed River and cleared his head, especially at night under the stars.

* * *

He inhaled the tobacco smoke, held it, and blew it out while looking up. It made a little cloud in the clear air above his head that barely moved in the still air. The stars were brilliant in the clear sky, and the full moon was still rising higher.

He spun on his heel, tossing the stub of the cigarette aside, before his mind registered the reason. He'd heard something, a faint rustle in the brush behind him. The dark-haired stranger from the party stood there, still twenty feet away. She smiled.

"No normal human could have heard me coming," she said.

"Who are you?"

"My name is Rhiannon. And you are River Greene. When I came here today, I came for you."

"The line forms in the rear."

She laughed, silently. "It does, doesn't it? Charm the ladies and move on to the next; that's your style. I know a lot about you. How you want many… girlfriends… and how you fight to keep them. How you must dominate the other men around you."

"I'm glad my little fistfight impressed you so, but No-Neck back there is like all football jocks everywhere. He's a fine bully when nobody fights back, but when you do fight back, he's stupid and easy to take down."

"Nonsense." She stepped close to him now, and something about her made him shiver. "You fight like an artist. And I know more about you than that."

River rolled his eyes and turned away dismissively. "Please. Do tell me all about it."

"You were conceived on Easter." He thought she said Easter, but she seemed to pronounce it a bit differently than most people did. "You were born at midnight on the night of the first full moon after Yule, the Ice Moon, and the most powerful full moon of the year."

"Oh, God, it's that pagan crap my mom's into."

"God and Goddess," Rhiannon corrected. "Your mother never told you about your father, did she? She is reluctant to have you go out after dark, especially on the night of the full moon. Am I wrong?

"You are more alive than other people. You want to live life by the light of the sun, moon, and stars, running free in the woods, savoring it to the full. Your friends want to hide from life inside boxes by the light of compact fluorescent lamps. Your senses are sharper than theirs, your reactions are quicker. And you know things. You knew about the axe murderer who lived on this farm, didn't you?"

"I made all that up."

"Did you? Did you make up that story? It's an interesting question. Did you magically know about those horrors, hushed up and forgotten so many decades ago, or did your making up the story cause those horrors to have-happened, way back there in the past? For dreams, and some other things, can pass backward and forward through time.

"Regardless, you know the story of this farm. You know how Blain chopped his family to death and hanged himself, or so his neighbors thought. His family was found in pieces, and their blood was on the axe, but that doesn't mean the axe did the cutting. He was hanged, but that doesn't mean he hanged himself. You know of his pack of spectral dogs, which haunt these woods even yet. You really shouldn't call them dogs, though. It's rather insulting, don't you think?"

She reached a fingertip toward him. He wanted to run, but he couldn't. She touched him. The moonlight dimmed, and her face changed. She had sharp, erect ears, shaggy silver fur, a long muzzle full of fangs, and her eyes glowed.

And then she was normal again. River shook his head and blinked. "What are you?" he croaked.

"We go by many names. You don't know our proper name, but you do have a name for us. As with so many other things, you know the truth, don't you? So, River Greene, what am I?"

"Werewolf. You're a werewolf, but that's insane. There's no such thing."

Rhiannon laughed silently again. "That's right. I'm not a werewolf. You don't know what you know, and you didn't see what you saw. It's an illusion caused by indigestion and the rum you drank, no doubt."

He hadn't had any rum. The cigarette had been one of his mother's, though. God—and Goddess, if you please—only knew what might have been in it. That had to be the problem. He was going to get his own cigarettes from now on, that was for sure!

She grabbed his collar and spoke with terrible intensity. "Listen to me, River Greene. You are not like the mere humans around you. You are special. You are better. You were born on the night of the Ice Moon.

"Tonight is the night of the Blood Moon, and tonight it falls on Samhain; on Halloween, as modern humans call it. Tonight you can join us at the Hanging Tree at midnight; true midnight, when the Moon is highest, not midnight according to some mindless human clock. Then, and only then, you can become your true self.

"Or you can miss your one chance, go home to your little box filled with fluorescent light, and hide from life as do the humans around you. You can collect welfare and steal your mother's peach brandy and her cigarettes and tell yourself you didn't give up your one chance to *live* and be special. Which will it be?"

He stared at her and nodded, not sure what he was agreeing to. "But that's not all of it. There's something more."

"Yes. The change must be paid in human blood. You must bring a blood sacrifice when you come."

She released his collar and turned to leave, toward the deeper woods, not back toward the abandoned farm. "I think you will disappoint us," she said, over her shoulder. "But there is still time, if you want to be your true self."

"But I don't know where the Hanging Tree is."

"Yes you do, River Greene. You have the power. Either you know where the Hanging Tree is, or you can go where you think it is and it will come into being when you arrive there. I would like to know which of these is true, but there's no way I could tell the difference."

She walked into the shadow of a red pine and was gone, as if she had never been there. Perhaps she hadn't.

* * *

He shook his head as he walked back into the party shed. It felt like he was waking from a dream.

"Ah, the mighty fighter returns," said a familiar voice, louder than the Heavy Metal music from the modest sound system. It was Cassandra, the third of the girlfriends who ran with him at the moment. She, Tiffany, and Autumn were at the bar-table. He went to them, not sure whether he wanted their company or whether it was a hit of rum he craved.

"Glad you could make it," he muttered, pouring himself another glass of cider with a good dash of rum in it this time. The girls looked to be angry at him. Why?

Tiffany raised her nose and curled her lip. "Where's your new girl?"

"Who?"

Autumn chimed in. "The black-haired one. Rhiannon, someone said her name was. She followed you out. Are you done with Rhiannon already?"

River stifled a chuckle. He'd been sure Tiff and Autumn were done with him for the night, if not for keeps, after the way he'd decked No-Neck in front of them, but trust jealousy to bring them back!

And some "new girl" Rhiannon had turned out to be. She wanted to meet him at the Hanging Tree, wherever that was, and bring a blood sacrifice. He had a pretty good idea that "blood sacrifice" in this case meant a lot more than a ceremonial scratch and a drop or two of blood on the ground, into a fire, or onto a contract with Dark Powers. It was true that Cass, Tiff, and Autumn didn't mean any more to him than any of the others he'd had, but turning one of them over to be killed by werewolves—as if there were such a thing as werewolves—was way too much even for him.

"She's not my new girl, I don't want anything to do with her, and I don't want to talk about it." He took a slug of his drink and almost choked. He'd put too much rum into it.

"Ooh. She turned you down, did she?"

"No, Cass, she did not."

"Yeah, right. She turned you down, or what else could it be?"

"She did *not*!"

But Cass wouldn't shut up about it. What story could he come up with to make her stop bugging him?

Cass was still going and going and going. "Nice to see the stud get humiliated for once. I bet she…"

Why not try the truth? Rhiannon was crazy, that was reason enough to avoid her. "She thinks she's a werewolf," he said.

Cass blinked. "What?"

"She thinks she's a werewolf, and she seems to think I'm a werewolf, and she wants to meet me at the Hanging Tree when the moon is highest so we can turn into giant dogs, and I don't want to talk about it. Could I have some more rum?"

Cass hooted. "We gotta go! We gotta go to this Hanging Tree and watch this. I bet she crawls around on the ground and yaps and snarls and everything."

"I'm not going. I've had enough running around in the woods with crazy people tonight. In fact I think I'm going to head home now before Mom wakes up."

Tiff said "He's leaving a party early? That's unnatural. Somebody's shocked our Great Fighter. I think he's telling the truth. I think Rhiannon really *did* say she was a werewolf."

"We gotta go see this! It'll be a hoot to see…"

"Cassandra," River said with all the patience he could muster, "with your name, shouldn't you be the one who tells people *not* to do stupid things?"

"What are you talking about? Where's this Hanging Tree? The Moon is almost overhead. Let's go!"

"Cassandra! We'll just get lost in the woods!"

But she, Tiff, and Autumn were leaving. Growling with exasperation, River followed.

* * *

They were lost in the woods, as he'd said. Now he was just trying to find his way back to 38 ½ Road, so he could find Rick's and the minivan and go home. Ahead, in the moonlight, the trees thinned. With the women following him, he walked into the light and stopped, dumbfounded.

The center of the clearing held a twisted tree, scarred and lightning-blasted, that reeked of death. Standing around its trunk were twelve people with dark hair and eyes that gleamed strangely in the moonlight. Rhiannon was the thirteenth.

"Welcome, River Greene," she said, and her teeth gleamed in the moonlight. "So in your heart of hearts you wanted to join us after all! And you have brought us not one human, but three. You've outdone yourself!"

"River, this is not funny," Tiff said. "We're leaving."

"Yes, you do that," Rhiannon said. "Get a good head start. Go, now. Not you, River. Come to us. It is time! Join hands!"

Heart pounding with excitement, River walked to join the circle at the Hanging Tree. He held Rhiannon's hand in his right and a tall man's hand in his left as they faced the scarred, horrible trunk. A rotted wisp of rope dangled from one of the branches. Somewhere behind him he could hear the women trying to leave through the brush. It sounded as if they might have started to run.

But he couldn't care about that now. Words in a strange language welled up from somewhere… from everywhere. He felt ice flowing through his hands and his heart, and suddenly it was beyond "believing", it was simply "knowing" it was all true. The circle was complete, and the midnight of the Blood Moon had come!

Everything twisted. He fell to his hands and knees as a painful shock seemed to burn every atom of his body.

River blinked. The moonlight seemed bright as day now. The thirteen other people of the circle changed as he watched, one by one, starting with Rhiannon on his right ending with the stranger on his left. They melted, sank down, and where humans had stood, wolves now stood in their places. But terrifying as that might have been in itself, these wolves were huge, and their eyes burned with an intelligence that was human, or even greater than human.

The wolves raised their muzzles to the moon and howled. River raised his muzzle with them.

He bleated.

Eyes wide, he looked at the wolves around him, and at his own body. His legs were spindly and ended in cleft hooves. The shadow of his head, as clear as a shadow under noonday sun to his changed eyes, showed that he had huge ears *and antlers.*

"Help me! Something went wrong!" he tried to say. But all that came out of his throat was gasping and a strained moan.

The wolves could still laugh and it was the most horrible thing he had ever heard. Rhiannon nipped his flank, drawing blood. He jumped. "Run, leaf-eater," she said, in a terrible growling voice. A voice filled with excitement and hunger. "If you run well, there is a chance—a *small* chance—that you might survive this night."

White tail flagging high in terror, River turned away from the Hanging Tree and leaped, bounding through the woods, quickly catching and passing the frantic human females. They had meant something to him once, something more than a threat, something more than slow meat to slow down the wolves so that he might have a chance to escape. He felt a ghost of the mind he had lost and the horror and sorrow of losing it, but only running mattered now.

Give the Pack credit. Rhiannon gave a fair, slow count of ten before moving. Then, howling with joy, the Pack leaped as one onto the trail of their fleeing prey. Their silver fur and white fangs gleamed in the merciless light of the Blood Moon.

A jackalope wife takes off her rabbit skin dress to dance.
What happens when her rabbit skin dress is burnt?

Jackalope Wives

by Ursula Vernon

The moon came up and the sun went down. The moonbeams went shattering down to the ground and the jackalope wives took off their skins and danced.

They danced like young deer pawing the ground, they danced like devils let out of hell for the evening. They swung their hips and pranced and drank their fill of cactus-fruit wine.

They were shy creatures, the jackalope wives, though there was nothing shy about the way they danced. You could go your whole life and see no more of them than the flash of a tail vanishing around the backside of a boulder. If you were lucky, you might catch a whole line of them outlined against the sky, on the top of a bluff, the shadow of horns rising off their brows.

And on the half-moon, when new and full were balanced across the saguaro's thorns, they'd come down to the desert and dance.

The young men used to get together and whisper, saying they were gonna catch them a jackalope wife. They'd lay belly down at the edge of the bluff and look down on the fire and the dancing shapes—and they'd go away aching, for all the good it did them.

For the jackalope wives were shy of humans. Their lovers were jackrabbits and antelope bucks, not human men. You couldn't even get too close or they'd take fright and run away. One minute you'd see them kicking their heels up and hear them laugh, then the music would freeze and they'd all look at you with their eyes wide and their ears upswept.

The next second, they'd snatch up their skins and there'd be nothing left but a dozen skinny she-rabbits running off in all directions, and a campfire left that wouldn't burn out 'til morning.

It was uncanny, sure, but they never did anybody any harm. Grandma Harken, who lived down past the well, said that the jackalopes were the daughters of the rain and driving them off would bring on the drought. People said they didn't believe a word of it, but when you live in a desert, you don't take chances.

When the wild music came through town, a couple of notes skittering on the sand, then people knew the jackalope wives were out. They kept the dogs tied up and their brash sons occupied. The town got into the habit of having a dance that night, to keep the boys firmly fixed on human girls and to drown out the notes of the wild music.

Now, it happened there was a young man in town who had a touch of magic on him. It had come down to him on his mother's side, as happens now and again, and it was worse than useless.

A little magic is worse than none, for it draws the wrong sort of attention. It gave this young man feverish eyes and made him sullen. His grandmother used to tell him that it was a miracle he hadn't been drowned as a child, and for her he'd laugh, but not for anyone else.

He was tall and slim and had dark hair and young women found him fascinating.

This sort of thing happens often enough, even with boys as mortal as dirt. There's always one who learned how to brood early and often, and always girls who think they can heal him.

Eventually the girls learn better. Either the hurts are petty little things and they get tired of whining or the hurt's so deep and wide that they drown in it. The smart ones heave themselves back to shore and the slower ones wake up married with a husband who lies around and suffers in their direction. It's part of a dance as old as the jackalopes themselves.

But in this town at this time, the girls hadn't learned and the boy hadn't yet worn out his interest. At the dances, he leaned on the wall with his hands in his pockets and his eyes glittering. Other young men eyed him with dislike. He would slip away early, before the dance was ended, and never marked the eyes that followed him and wished that he would stay.

He himself had one thought and one thought only—to catch a jackalope wife.

They were beautiful creatures, with their long brown legs and their bodies splashed orange by the firelight. They had faces like no mortal woman and they moved like quicksilver and they played music that got down into your bones and thrummed like a sickness.

And there was one—he'd seen her. She danced farther out from the others and her horns were short and sharp as sickles. She was the last one to put on her rabbit skin when the sun came up. Long after the music had stopped, she danced to the rhythm of her own long feet on the sand.

(And now you will ask me about the musicians that played for the jackalope wives. Well, if you can find a place where they've been dancing, you might see something like sidewinder tracks in the dust, and more than that I cannot tell you. The desert chews its secrets right down to the bone.)

So the young man with the touch of magic watched the jackalope wife dancing and you know as well as I do what young men dream about. We will be charitable. She danced a little apart from her fellows, as he walked a little apart from his.

Perhaps he thought she might understand him. Perhaps he found her as interesting as the girls found him.

Perhaps we shouldn't always get what we think we want.

And the jackalope wife danced, out past the circle of the music and the firelight, in the light of the fierce desert stars.

Grandma Harken had settled in for the evening with a shawl on her shoulders and a cat on her lap when somebody started hammering on the door.

"Grandma! Grandma! Come quick—open the door—oh god, Grandma, you have to help me—"

She knew that voice just fine. It was her own grandson, her daughter Eva's boy. Pretty and useless and charming when he set out to be.

She dumped the cat off her lap and stomped to the door. What trouble had the young fool gotten himself into?

"Sweet Saint Anthony," she muttered, "let him not have gotten some fool girl in a family way. That's just what we need."

She flung the door open and there was Eva's son and there was a girl and for a moment her worst fears were realized.

Then she saw what was huddled in the circle of her grandson's arms, and her worst fears were stomped flat and replaced by far greater ones.

"Oh Mary," she said. "Oh, Jesus, Mary and Joseph. Oh blessed Saint Anthony, you've caught a jackalope wife."

Her first impulse was to slam the door and lock the sight away.

Her grandson caught the edge of the door and hauled it open. His knuckles were raw and blistered. "Let me in," he said. He'd been crying and there was dust on his face, stuck to the tracks of tears. "Let me in, let me in, oh god, Grandma, you have to help me, it's all gone wrong—"

Grandma took two steps back, while he half-dragged the jackalope into the house. He dropped her down in front of the hearth and grabbed for his grandmother's hands. "Grandma—"

She ignored him and dropped to her knees. The thing across her hearth was hardly human. "What have you done?" she said. "What did you do to her?"

"Nothing!" he said, recoiling.

"Don't look at that and tell me 'Nothing!' What in the name of our lord did you do to that girl?"

He stared down at his blistered hands. "Her skin," he mumbled. "The rabbit skin. You know."

"I do indeed," she said grimly. "Oh yes, I do. What did you do, you damned young fool? Caught up her skin and hid it from her to keep her changing?"

The jackalope wife stirred on the hearth and made a sound between a whimper and a sob.

"She was waiting for me!" he said. "She knew I was there! I'd been—we'd—I watched her, and she knew I was out there, and she let me get up close—I thought we could talk—"

Grandma Harken clenched one hand into a fist and rested her forehead on it.

"I grabbed the skin—I mean—it was right there—she was watching—I thought she wanted me to have it—"

She turned and looked at him. He sank down in her chair, all his grace gone.

"You have to burn it," mumbled her grandson. He slid down a little further in her chair. "You're supposed to burn it. Everybody knows. To keep them changing."

"Yes," said Grandma Harken, curling her lip. "Yes, that's the way of it, right enough." She took the jackalope wife's shoulders and turned her toward the lamp light.

She was a horror. Her hands were human enough, but she had a jackrabbit's feet and a jackrabbit's eyes. They were set too wide apart in a human face, with a cleft lip and long rabbit ears. Her horns were short, sharp spikes on her brow.

The jackalope wife let out another sob and tried to curl back into a ball. There were burnt patches on her arms and legs, a long red weal down her face. The fur across her breasts and belly was singed. She stank of urine and burning hair.

"What did you do?"

"I threw it in the fire," he said. "You're supposed to. But she screamed—she wasn't supposed to scream—nobody said they screamed—and I thought she was dying, and I didn't want to hurt her—I pulled it back out—"

He looked up at her with his feverish eyes, that useless, beautiful boy, and said "I didn't want to hurt her. I thought I was supposed to—I gave her the skin back, she put it on, but then she fell down—it wasn't supposed to work like that!"

Grandma Harken sat back. She exhaled very slowly. She was calm. She was going to be calm, because otherwise she was going to pick up the fire poker and club her own flesh and blood over the head with it.

And even that might not knock some sense into him. Oh, Eva, Eva, my dear, what a useless son you've raised. Who would have thought he had so much ambition in him, to catch a jackalope wife?

"You goddamn stupid fool," she said. Every word slammed like a shutter in the wind. "Oh, you goddamn stupid fool. If you're going to catch a jackalope wife, you burn the hide down to ashes and never mind how she screams."

"But it sounded like it was hurting her!" he shot back. "You weren't there! She screamed like a dying rabbit!"

"Of course it hurts her!" yelled Grandma. "You think you can have your skin and your freedom burned away in front of you and not scream? Sweet mother Mary, boy, think about what you're doing! Be cruel or be kind, but don't be both, because now you've made a mess you can't clean up in a hurry."

She stood up, breathing hard, and looked down at the wreck on her hearth. She could see it now, as clear as if she'd been standing there. The fool boy had been so shocked he'd yanked the burning skin back out. And the jackalope wife had one thought only and pulled on the burning hide—

Oh yes, she could see it clear.

Half gone, at least, if she was any judge. There couldn't have been more than few scraps of fur left unburnt. He'd waited through at least one scream—or no, that was unkind.

More likely he'd dithered and looked for a stick and didn't want to grab for it with his bare hands. Though by the look of his hands, he'd done just that in the end.

And the others were long gone by then and couldn't stop her. There ought to have been one, at least, smart enough to know that you didn't put on a half-burnt rabbit skin.

"Why does she look like that?" whispered her grandson, huddled into his chair.

"Because she's trapped betwixt and between. You did that, with your goddamn pity. You should have let it burn. Or better yet, left her alone and never gone out in the desert at all."

151

"She was beautiful," he said. As if it were a reason.

As if it mattered.

As if it had ever mattered.

"Get out," said Grandma wearily. "Tell your mother to make up a poultice for your hands. You did right at the end, bringing her here, even if you made a mess of the rest, from first to last."

He scrambled to his feet and ran for the door.

On the threshold, he paused, and looked back. "You—you can fix her, right?"

Grandma let out a high bark, like a bitch-fox, barely a laugh at all. "No. No one can fix this, you stupid boy. This is broken past mending. All I can do is pick up the pieces."

He ran. The door slammed shut, and left her alone with the wreckage of the jackalope wife.

She treated the burns and they healed. But there was nothing to be done for the shape of the jackalope's face, or the too-wide eyes, or the horns shaped like a sickle moon.

At first, Grandma worried that the townspeople would see her, and lord knew what would happen then. But the jackalope wife was the color of dust and she still had a wild animal's stillness. When somebody called, she lay flat in the garden, down among the beans, and nobody saw her at all.

The only person she didn't hide from was Eva, Grandma's daughter. There was no chance that she mistook them for each other—Eva was round and plump and comfortable, the way Grandma's second husband, Eva's father, had been round and plump and comfortable.

Maybe we smell alike, thought Grandma. It would make sense, I suppose.

Eva's son didn't come around at all.

"He thinks you're mad at him," said Eva mildly.

"He thinks correctly," said Grandma.

She and Eva sat on the porch together, shelling beans, while the jackalope wife limped around the garden. The hairless places weren't so obvious now, and the faint stripes across her legs might have been dust. If you didn't look directly at her, she might almost have been human.

"She's gotten good with the crutch," said Eva. "I suppose she can't walk?"

"Not well," said Grandma. "Her feet weren't made to stand up like that. She can do it, but it's a terrible strain."

"And talk?"

"No," said Grandma shortly. The jackalope wife had tried, once, and the noises she'd made were so terrible that it had reduced them both to weeping. She hadn't tried again. "She understands well enough, I suppose."

The jackalope wife sat down, slowly, in the shadow of the scarlet runner beans. A hummingbird zipped inches from her head, dabbing its bill into the flowers, and the jackalope's face turned, unsmiling, to follow it.

"He's not a bad boy, you know," said Eva, not looking at her mother. "He didn't mean to do her harm."

Grandma let out an explosive snort. "Jesus, Mary and Joseph! It doesn't matter what he meant to do. He should have left well enough alone, and if he couldn't do that, he should have finished what he started." She scowled down at the beans. They were striped red and white and the pods came apart easily in her gnarled hands. "Better all the way human than this. Better he'd bashed her head in with a rock than this."

"Better for her, or better for you?" asked Eva, who was only a fool about her son and knew her mother well.

Grandma snorted again. The hummingbird buzzed away. The jackalope wife lay still in the shadows, with only her thin ribs going up and down.

"You could have finished it, too," said Eva softly. "I've seen you kill chickens. She'd probably lay her head on the chopping block if you asked."

"She probably would," said Grandma. She looked away from Eva's weak, wise eyes. "But I'm a damn fool as well."

Her daughter smiled. "Maybe it runs in families."

Grandma Harken got up before dawn the next morning and went rummaging around the house.

"Well," she said. She pulled a dead mouse out of a mousetrap and took a half-dozen cigarettes down from behind the clock. She filled three water bottles and strapped them around her waist. "Well. I suppose we've done as much as humans can do, and now it's up to somebody else."

She went out into the garden and found the jackalope wife asleep under the stairs. "Come on," she said. "Wake up."

The air was cool and gray. The jackalope wife looked at her with doe-dark eyes and didn't move, and if she were a human, Grandma Harken would have itched to slap her.

Pay attention! Get mad! Do something!

But she wasn't human and rabbits freeze when they're scared past running. So Grandma gritted her teeth and reached down a hand and pulled the jackalope wife up into the pre-dawn dark.

They moved slow, the two of them. Grandma was old and carrying water for two, and the girl was on a crutch. The sun came up and the cicadas burnt the air with their wings.

A coyote watched them from up on the hillside. The jackalope wife looked up at him, recoiled, and Grandma laid a hand on her arm.

"Don't worry," she said. "I ain't got the patience for coyotes. They'd maybe fix you up but we'd both be stuck in a tale past telling, and I'm too old for that. Come on."

They went a little further on, past a wash and a watering hole. There were palo verde trees spreading thin green shade over the water. A javelina looked up at them from the edge and stamped her hooved feet. Her children scraped their tusks together and grunted.

Grandma slid and slithered down the slope to the far side of the water and refilled the water bottles. "Not them either," she said to the jackalope wife. "They'll talk the legs off a wooden sheep. We'd both be dead of old age before they'd figured out what time to start."

The javelina dropped their heads and ignored them as they left the wash behind.

The sun was overhead and the sky turned turquoise, a color so hard you could bash your knuckles on it. A raven croaked overhead and another one snickered somewhere off to the east.

The jackalope wife paused, leaning on her crutch, and looked up at the wings with longing.

"Oh no," said Grandma. "I've got no patience for riddle games, and in the end they always eat someone's eyes. Relax, child. We're nearly there."

The last stretch was cruelly hard, up the side of a bluff. The sand was soft underfoot and miserably hard for a girl walking with a crutch. Grandma had to half-carry the jackalope wife at the end. She weighed no more than a child, but children are heavy and it took them both a long time.

At the top was a high fractured stone that cast a finger of shadow like the wedge of a sundial. Sand and sky and shadow and stone. Grandma Harken nodded, content.

"It'll do," she said. "It'll do." She laid the jackalope wife down in the shadow and laid her tools out on the stone. Cigarettes and dead mouse and a scrap of burnt fur from the jackalope's breast. "It'll do."

Then she sat down in the shadow herself and arranged her skirts.

She waited.

The sun went overhead and the level in the water bottle went down. The sun started to sink and the wind hissed and the jackalope wife was asleep or dead.

The ravens croaked a conversation to each other, from the branches of a palo verde tree, and whatever one said made the other one laugh.

"Well," said a voice behind Grandma's right ear, "lookee what we have here."

"Jesus, Mary and Joseph!"

"Don't see them out here often," he said. "Not the right sort of place." He considered. "Your Saint Anthony, now…him I think I've seen. He understood about deserts."

Grandma's lips twisted. "Father of Rabbits," she said sourly. "Wasn't trying to call you up."

"Oh, I know." The Father of Rabbits grinned. "But you know I've always had a soft spot for you, Maggie Harken."

He sat down beside her on his heels. He looked like an old Mexican man, wearing a button-down shirt without any buttons. His hair was silver gray as a rabbit's fur. Grandma wasn't fooled for a minute.

"Get lonely down there in your town, Maggie?" he asked. "Did you come out here for a little wild company?"

Grandma Harken leaned over to the jackalope wife and smoothed one long ear back from her face. She looked up at them both with wide, uncomprehending eyes.

"Shit," said the Father of Rabbits. "Never seen that before." He lit a cigarette and blew the smoke into the air. "What did you do to her, Maggie?"

"I didn't do a damn thing, except not let her die when I should have."

"There's those would say that was more than enough." He exhaled another lungful of smoke.

"She put on a half-burnt skin. Don't suppose you can fix her up?" It cost Grandma a lot of pride to say that, and the Father of Rabbits tipped his chin in acknowledgment.

"Ha! No. If it was loose I could fix it up, maybe, but I couldn't get it off her now with a knife." He took another drag on the cigarette. "Now I see why you wanted one of the Patterned People."

Grandma nodded stiffly.

The Father of Rabbits shook his head. "He might want a life, you know. Piddly little dead mouse might not be enough."

"Then he can have mine."

"Ah, Maggie, Maggie...You'd have made a fine rabbit, once. Too many stones in your belly now." He shook his head regretfully. "Besides, it's not your life he's owed."

"It's my life he'd be getting. My kin did it, it's up to me to put it right." It occurred to her that she should have left Eva a note, telling her to send the fool boy back East, away from the desert.

Well. Too late now. Either she'd raised a fool for a daughter or not, and likely she wouldn't be around to tell.

"Suppose we'll find out," said the Father of Rabbits, and nodded.

A man came around the edge of the standing stone. He moved quick then slow and his eyes didn't blink. He was naked and his skin was covered in painted diamonds.

Grandma Harken bowed to him, because the Patterned People can't hear speech.

He looked at her and the Father of Rabbits and the jackalope wife. He looked down at the stone in front of him.

The cigarettes he ignored. The mouse he scooped up in two fingers and dropped into his mouth.

Then he crouched there, for a long time. He was so still that it made Grandma's eyes water, and she had to look away.

"Suppose he does it," said the Father of Rabbits. "Suppose he sheds that skin right off her. Then what? You've got a human left over, not a jackalope wife."

Grandma stared down at her bony hands. "It's not so bad, being a human," she said. "You make do. And it's got to be better than that."

She jerked her chin in the direction of the jackalope wife.

"Still meddling, Maggie?" said the Father of Rabbits.

"And what do you call what you're doing?"

He grinned.

The Patterned Man stood up and nodded to the jackalope wife.

She looked at Grandma, who met her too-wide eyes. "He'll kill you," the old woman said. "Or cure you. Or maybe both. You don't have to do it. This is the bit where you get a choice. But when it's over, you'll be all the way something, even if it's just all the way dead."

The jackalope wife nodded.

She left the crutch lying on the stones and stood up. Rabbit legs weren't meant for it, but she walked three steps and the Patterned Man opened his arms and caught her.

He bit her on the forearm, where the thick veins run, and sank his teeth in up to the gums. Grandma cursed.

"Easy now," said the Father of Rabbits, putting a hand on her shoulder. "He's one of the Patterned People, and they only know the one way."

The jackalope wife's eyes rolled back in her head, and she sagged down onto the stone.

He set her down gently and picked up one of the cigarettes.

Grandma Harken stepped forward. She rolled both her sleeves up to the elbow and offered him her wrists.

The Patterned Man stared at her, unblinking. The ravens laughed to themselves at the bottom of the wash. Then he dipped his head and bowed to Grandma Harken and a rattlesnake as long as a man slithered away into the evening.

She let out a breath she didn't know she'd been holding. "He didn't ask for a life."

The Father of Rabbits grinned. "Ah, you know. Maybe he wasn't hungry. Maybe it was enough you made the offer."

"Maybe I'm too old and stringy," she said.

"Could be that, too."

The jackalope wife was breathing. Her pulse went fast then slow. Grandma sat down beside her and held her wrist between her own callused palms.

"How long you going to wait?" asked the Father of Rabbits.

"As long as it takes," she snapped back.

The sun went down while they were waiting. The coyotes sang up the moon. It was half-full, half-new, halfway between one thing and the other.

"She doesn't have to stay human, you know," said the Father of Rabbits. He picked up the cigarettes that the Patterned Man had left behind and offered one to Grandma.

"She doesn't have a jackalope skin any more."

He grinned. She could just see his teeth flash white in the dark. "Give her yours."

"I burned it," said Grandma Harken, sitting up ramrod straight. "I found where he hid it after he died and I burned it myself. Because I had a new husband and a little bitty baby girl and all I could think about was leaving them both behind and go dance."

The Father of Rabbits exhaled slowly in the dark.

"It was easier that way," she said. "You get over what you can't have faster that you get over what you could. And we shouldn't always get what we think we want."

They sat in silence at the top of the bluff. Between Grandma's hands, the pulse beat steady and strong.

"I never did like your first husband much," said the Father of Rabbits.

"Well," she said. She lit her cigarette off his. "He taught me how to swear. And the second one was better."

The jackalope wife stirred and stretched. Something flaked off her in long strands, like burnt scraps of paper, like a snake's skin shedding away. The wind tugged at them and sent them spinning off the side of the bluff.

From down in the desert, they heard the first notes of a sudden wild music.

"It happens I might have a spare skin," said the Father of Rabbits. He reached into his pack and pulled out a long gray roll of rabbit skin. The jackalope wife's eyes went wide and her body shook with longing, but it was human longing and a human body shaking.

"Where'd you get that?" asked Grandma Harken, suspicious.

"Oh, well, you know." He waved a hand. "Pulled it out of a fire once—must have been forty years ago now. Took some doing to fix it up again, but some people owed me favors. Suppose she might as well have it...Unless you want it?"

He held it out to Grandma Harken.

She took it in her hands and stroked it. It was as soft as it had been fifty years ago. The small sickle horns were hard weights in her hands.

"You were a hell of a dancer," said the Father of Rabbits.

"Still am," said Grandma Harken, and she flung the jackalope skin over the shoulders of the human jackalope wife.

It went on like it had been made for her, like it was her own. There was a jagged scar down one foreleg where the rattlesnake had bit her. She leapt up and darted away, circled back once and bumped Grandma's hand with her nose—and then she was bounding down the path from the top of the bluff.

The Father of Rabbits let out a long sigh. "Still are," he agreed.

"It's different when you got a choice," said Grandma Harken.

They shared another cigarette under the standing stone.

Down in the desert, the music played and the jackalope wives danced. And one scarred jackalope went leaping into the circle of firelight and danced like a demon, while the moon laid down across the saguaro's thorns.

Sokolai and his six gengineered dog-brother soldiers are in the ruins of a house. They are starving to death. They are dying of thirst.

They are supposed to protect the humans. But how can they protect the humans if they are all dead?

Pavlov's House

by Malcolm Cross

Once I was strong and believed, now I am small and unbelieving.
– Anonymous German Soldier in Stalingrad, 1943

* * *

The dream always starts the same way.

A drop of rain seeps through the shattered rock-block beams that now serve as a ceiling, and falls into the child's eye. The rain is deadlier than the tank shells that blew the upper storeys of the housing block to rubble, better able to penetrate the building and kill the inhabitants.

This is how: A biowarfare spore, gengineered in a corporate lab and released during the Eurasian war, has survived for forty years in the water cycle. It has been dried to dust and picked up on the wind, laced the clouds, and fallen to earth over and over until, at last, the spore contacts human tissue. The spore's cortex ruptures, spilling its gengineered payload.

From the child's eye the payload travels to the mother's hand, and from her hand to all her children. Within twenty minutes they are all dead. Spasming, wheezing, kicking, dying. It takes the family longer to asphyxiate than it took the spores to produce fast and extreme anaphylactic shock, making every tissue bed in their bodies uncontrollably swell.

Setzen, Eversen, Sokolai, Stolnik, Eberstetten, Ereli and Steinfelde stop drinking the rain water.

They have been told they are immune, that the fast biowarfare agents are tuned to specifically kill human beings, and they are only dogs built to superficially resemble human beings. They are not sure whether or not to believe it, because the corporate labs that gengineered the spores, and later told the world that the spores were a safe way to end the war, were the same labs that later gengineered the dogs, and told the world that they and many similar products under development would be ethical, willing slaves. Not many people believe the claims Estian Incorporated used to make, these days.

There is no water in the house except for the rain. When the revolution began, the water was cut off. By the time the brothers had barricaded themselves in the house—they call it that, though it's actually a small apartment block—there were only rusty dregs in toilet cisterns. The water boilers had been siphoned dry, and the plumbing was so empty it did not gurgle.

There is an empty bucket, lying beside the dead eldest child. On the second day the family in the basement had been drinking from it, and offered to share with the brothers, even if they were dogs, because there was a story in their holy book in which a woman gave water to a dog and was blessed for it. Other than that, the people of Tajikistan do not like dogs, and they do not like the brothers. The brothers had politely refused. After all, the family were civilians, and the brothers had been hired from their home, far away in the Middle American Corporate Preserve, to protect civilians.

The buckets lasted the family until the third day, when the revolution ended. The family did not want to leave the building, after the revolution's end, because the revolutionaries had lynched their father from a street light when he came out to see if it was safe to leave.

Drip by drip the bucket fills with rainwater. Setzen watches the surface of the water dance, his mouth dry.

He has spent ninety-six hours killing people. He has not slept. His judgement is fuzzy. He and his brothers used their guns to kill the revolutionaries who came to remove them from the house. He and his brothers used their fists to kill the revolutionaries who came to remove them from the house. He and his brothers used their teeth, their feet, their knives, bricks and pipes torn from the walls, scavenged grenades, and a bottle of cleaning alcohol to kill the revolutionaries who came to remove them from the house.

The reason the revolutionaries killed the family's father is, he thinks, that bottle of cleaning alcohol. The brothers should not have set that revolutionary alight and thrown him from what was left of the third floor, but the revolutionaries did not fucking understand that they would never take the brothers out of the house, alive or dead, because the brothers were dogs who had been genetically engineered to kill human beings more quickly and efficiently than even the biowarfare agents could.

But no matter how deadly Setzen is, he is also thirsty. He has not had any water for four days. He has not eaten in four days. Four sleepless days, in which he has killed fifty-seven people.

Sixty-two, including the family, if he alone were responsible.

The dream, up to this point, is factual memory. From here on it diverges with what really happened.

Setzen is afraid of the water. He feels like he will piss himself, he feels like the fur all over his body has been set alight, he feels like a real dog—a four legged dog—that is about to be kicked. He is afraid.

Setzen drinks the water. At first everything seems to be alright. He laps it up with his tongue, and his tongue does not swell. His heart does not race. His throat does not close up. He can breathe easily. The water tastes cool and fresh. For the first time in days he is not thirsty.

The rest of the brothers join in, lapping at the rain, holding tin cans up to the drips, shuddering in fear of the spores until they have sipped enough water to feel the cool, clean sensation of water in their mouths. Their thirst is quenched, and they forget to be afraid. They decide, after guilty discussion, to move the family to the latrine corner of the basement, which has already been fouled, because the corpses are soiled with leaking shit and there is nowhere to bury them. They cannot throw the corpses from the third floor position until nightfall, because they will have to expose themselves to snipers.

Brothers upstairs cry out that there is an incoming assault. It is time to fight. Setzen feels glad. He cannot fight the biowarfare spores, but he can fight the enemy.

A bullet bores into the top of his head, splashing blood and pink-grey slime out of his caved in skull, and crashes into the poured concrete floor beneath Setzen.

This really happened. The revolutionaries had taken control of the government and deployed the sympathetic remnants of the Tajik army's special forces to kill the brothers with hypervelocity armour-piercing rifles—which could also penetrate crumbling rock-block beams, if properly aimed with wall penetrating radar. Setzen was really dead.

But Setzen didn't drink the water first, it was Sokolai. That is what is different, that is what makes it a dream, that is why Sokolai can dream of the fresh taste of the cold water, and why he dreams of Setzen's head being broken through with agony so terrible that Sokolai cannot even dream it, only scream as he wakes up, scream and howl like an animal, as

163

though he is experiencing unimaginable pain. Sokolai is not experiencing that.

He is experiencing what it feels like to be powerless to help his brother Setzen. To be powerless to help himself.

It hurts.

* * *

There were four windows. Sokolai moved from one, to the next, to the next, to the next, all without exposing himself. A smooth roll of shoulder against paint, ducking beneath the sill, edging back into the room, back again. There was a good line of sight on the street from three of the windows, but the fourth one was on the other wall, showed him the neighbours.

The neighbours weren't going to attack. The neighbours were having a barbecue.

The neighbours were out in their yard, under equatorial sunshine, throwing a garden party on gengineered green lawns that were soft underfoot, walking happily around talking to each other, and Sokolai was inside, alone, seeing broken glass everywhere it wasn't.

There was a car in the street, and there were three people inside, and none of them were revolutionaries. Sokolai was sure of that. There weren't any revolutionaries in the car, or even in the country. The three people in the car weren't revolutionaries, but Sokolai had to check. Had to squint, had to stand there with his heart thumping and his tail slack and his fur on fire and a tight feeling in his guts until he had *seen* that one of them was black, and the other two were white and pale-pink coloured, too pale-pink to be Tajik. Tajiks were pale-pink-olive coloured, different enough that Sokolai could tell in full sunlight, similar enough that he couldn't in shadow.

Sokolai moved from window to window, and watched the car drive itself away, its three passengers unaware that they'd been watched by a gengineered monster with a hunting rifle locked in his gun safe. He'd tried to give the ammunition to one of his brothers to keep, but his hands had shaken and his mouth had grown too wet and hot, like he needed to pant the heat out of himself, and he hadn't been able to bring himself to do it. So he had the rifle and the ammunition, and he knew, roughly, how to aim so the bullets would still hit the three passengers in their heads even after being knocked off course by breaking up on impact with the car roof.

"Socks?" Ajay always called out softly, before knocking. The thumps at the door didn't startle Sokolai. "Can I come in?"

"Yeah."

Ajay came in. He had a tray with cookies and milk on it. "Heather and Limmy are picking out a movie. They wanted me to ask if you'd join us, but I knew you'd say no, so, I brought you a snack instead." He smiled, beautifully.

Sokolai knew, every time Ajay smiled, why Ajay and Sokolai's foster-brother Michael had been in love for so long. Michael, whose family had adopted Sokolai after Estian Incorporated had been legally outmanoeuvred and forced into emancipating Sokolai rather than selling him into slavery, had always loved a pretty smile. Michael had, in fact, taught Sokolai how to smile when they were both eight years old.

Sokolai tried to remember how to smile, but just then, he couldn't. "Thank you," he murmured. "You're right, I don't want to watch a movie."

"It's okay." Ajay kept smiling, bright enough for the both of them, and set the tray down on the side of Sokolai's bed, pulling a dent in the perfectly folded sheets. "Anyway. Here's a snack, so you don't have to sneak around."

"Thanks," Sokolai repeated.

He watched Ajay smile and leave the room, and Sokolai couldn't quite remember how to smile.

He could remember learning. Michael had stuck his fingers into the corners of Sokolai's mouth and lifted them, and that was the first step to smiling, and somehow in the years between childhood and adulthood Sokolai had forgotten all the steps after that and smiled when he felt happy.

Now he couldn't remember how. Maybe because he didn't feel happy.

It was nice, being called 'Socks'. It reminded him of Michael. Michael and Ajay and Heather and Limmy had all been a couple, one of those couples where there are four people instead of two, but while Sokolai was working in Tajikistan Michael and Ajay and Heather and Limmy had broken up, and when he came home Michael was living somewhere else, and Sokolai didn't have anywhere to live, so Ajay and Heather and Limmy had let him move back in even though Michael had moved away.

Sokolai missed his brother Michael. Sokolai had more than five hundred brothers all exactly like him, and only one—Michael—who wasn't the same at all.

Sometimes, in the dream, it was Michael in the house in Tajikistan. Michael who got hit in the eye with the drop of rainwater, and swelled up and died. Michael, who sipped the water first, and convulsed so hard he bit his tongue off. Michael, who got shot in the head in that one happy moment where it felt like there was a fight on its way, a fight to win.

Sokolai ate the cookies.

Sokolai drank the milk.

Sokolai checked the windows, couldn't stop himself, couldn't do anything to shake the invasive paranoia that made him go and look, made him check, as if there'd be a guy climbing up who Sokolai would need to stab, to kill, to rip and tear—

Sokolai took the tray back to the kitchen.

"Socks? Are you sneaking around?" Heather squinted over her shoulder, next to Limmy on the couch.

It was uncanny. She was almost as good as Sokolai when it came to noticing people, but Sokolai could smell people close by, and he didn't think Heather could. He'd been quiet, though. Hadn't made a sound. And the screen was on, volume up. You wouldn't think anyone could hear past it.

"Yes," he said at last, leaning around the door frame. "I was just putting the dishes back."

"Come and sit with us," Limmy said, shuffling to the side, making space by climbing up into Ajay's lap.

"Okay." Sokolai sheepishly clambered over the back of the couch, slumping down among all of them, amongst their love and care and kindness, their warmth.

Heather ruffled his fur between his ears, like a dog, even though she had to stretch up high to reach.

"How'd you know I was sneaking around?" he asked quietly, while someone struggled with a sailing boat's ropes on the screen.

"Hm? Oh." Heather smiled. "You're so big you block the internet signal, a little, standing in the hall. The movie loses a frame or two, the resolution drops a little bit."

"Really?" Ajay tilted his head, squinting.

Limmy slid bonelessly down Ajay's lap, until his head was at stomach level, and his heels were on the floor. "Too small for us to notice. It's all her genetweaking, her scrambled brains."

Heather stuck out her tongue. "My parents cared enough to give me the best, even before I was born. I'm not even slightly scrambled, and neither is Socks." She stretched up and kissed his fuzzy cheek. She stopped, though, looking up at him.

Ajay leaned in from the other side, kissed Sokolai's cheek too. "It's okay, Socks," he said gently.

It wasn't okay. He couldn't sneak past Heather watching a movie. He couldn't do what she did to see if someone was in the hall or not. He couldn't protect them if the revolutionaries came, he couldn't protect Michael, he couldn't protect anyone, nobody else understood how much danger they were in because they weren't paranoid shell-shocked messes.

Sokolai wasn't crying, or anything. But they all knew what it was, when he went stiff like that, when he stared, when he had his ears perked up high to listen. They all knew.

"It's okay, Socks, it's okay," Limmy said, head now in Sokolai's lap.

Maybe Sokolai was part of the couple that had four people in it, even if he always slept alone, and never kissed back. He wasn't sure. He was sure about one thing. It wasn't okay. He very, very gently pushed Limmy's head out of his lap and stood up.

"Socks?"

"It's not okay," he said.

"It's really okay, Socks, it's—"

"It's *not*! So stop saying it is."

"Why isn't it?" Limmy asked, voice hardly a whisper from where he lay sprawled on the floor.

"I'm not supposed to be like this!"

Ajay sat up straighter, mouth a hard, thin line. "Be like what?" he demanded.

"Broken. *Defective.*"

"Socks…" Heather reached out to him. "You're not defective."

He stood still, afraid that if he moved he'd hurt them. That if they touched him, he'd hurt them. "I was made to be brave," he whispered. "I'm supposed to be brave, but I'm not, and you treat me like that's okay. It isn't."

They held him like he was one of them and said they loved him.

He didn't hurt them. He was still afraid.

* * *

The purpose of checking the windows was survival. The purpose of making sure his gun was clean was survival. The purpose of eating food was survival. The purpose of drinking water was survival. There wasn't any purpose except survival.

Clean the gun clean the gun clean the gun. Guns could jam. Sokolai's gun had jammed. He had taken that gun from the dead revolutionary's hands, on day two. He'd had to break the revolutionary's fingers, because the revolutionary had been dead just long enough that his hands were stiff but not so long they were soft, and the gun wasn't very clean, and it had jammed, and *he could have died.* So now he had to clean the gun.

The gun was a hunting rifle. The one he'd taken from the revolutionary's hands. Except revolutionaries carried Kalashnikov assault rifle ripoffs, so why was Sokolai cleaning a hunting rifle?

He felt confused.

Disoriented.

That was dangerous. Being confused meant not knowing what to do. Not knowing what to do made him vulnerable. If he didn't know what to do, he could die. He didn't mind dying if it was a choice he made, when he took a risk, when he decided to be brave. He didn't mind dying if he decided to die.

He could decide to die.

He sucked on the hunting rifle's barrel. He spat it back out.

He'd heard a loud noise, like a mortar round, and he didn't want to die. He hadn't decided to die. He didn't want to die. He could be brave if he knew why he was dying but if the bullet came through the wall and burst open his head he wouldn't know why he was dying and he didn't want to die. He would happily die if he did so trying to protect Ajay and Heather and Limmy and Michael, but if he died he couldn't protect them and he didn't want to die. He couldn't taste cool clean water if he died, he didn't want to die.

The loud noise came back. A bang on the door.

"Socks?"

He had to protect Limmy he had to protect Limmy he had to protect Limmy he had to protec—*"Fuck off! I'm cleaning my gun,"* he yelled, raw-throated.

The door stayed shut.

Nobody was coming in the door, nobody was coming in the door, he'd fucking *kill* anyone who came through the door, nobody was supposed to come through the door or the windows fuck no the windows the glass was broken they could get in quietly, nobody was watching the windows where was someone to watch the windows where was Setzen? Setzen was supposed to be watching the windows no wait no fuck Setzen was dead Sokolai had to watch the windows.

The street was clear. No bodies hanging from street lights. When had that been cut down? Nobody had cut it down, Setzen hadn't gone out to cut it down.

Setzen cleaned the gun. Guns could jam, if they weren't cleaned.

Somewhere, a small voice told him he wasn't Setzen. The voice was the part of him called Sokolai, the part that said words and thought things and had feelings and killed people and used reflexes and was a person and *fuck* that part of him, Setzen hated that part of him because that part of him wasn't even strong enough to stop him from checking the windows when there was nobody out there, nobody trying to kill him.

Eversen hated that part of him too. Eversen was sitting on the roof under a pile of rubble making sure nobody snuck up on them. Eversen wasn't dead, Eversen wasn't even there, but that didn't matter. None of them had been given names until they'd been emancipated, they'd been given squad designations like Black-Four and Grey-Seven and Yellow-Ten, and if one of them died in training they were replaced and the replacement was Black-Four or Grey-Seven or Yellow-Ten instead. They'd been mass produced, a factory run of clones, that was how it worked. It worked so well that even after fourteen years of pretending to be individual people with names they could go to Tajikistan without preparing and fight better than the special forces, because special forces were only intensively trained for two years before being deployed, and they'd been trained since before they could remember thinking in words. They were all the same. Exactly the same. So it didn't matter if Setzen was dead, Sokolai could be Setzen instead.

Stolnik didn't agree.

Stolnik said he was behind the door with Limmy, and that Limmy and Ajay and Heather had called him over because they were worried about Sokolai, but Stolnik didn't believe that for an instant.

Stolnik knew he was using the dead family's shirts to bind their legs together so they'd be easier to carry without flopping all over. Sokolai knew that was what Stolnik was doing, and Sokolai trusted Stolnik. They were part of a team, part of a group working for the same goal, and Sokolai's part in that group was to clean the guns, and his brothers were doing all the other things that had to be done, and Stolnik should stop staring at him and go and do what he was supposed to do which was get the dead family ready to toss out of the house.

"We're out of the house, Sokolai."

"You're off schedule," Sokolai told Stolnik.

Stolnik wasn't doing what he was supposed to. Stolnik was just standing there, looking at Sokolai. Sokolai had trouble thinking about that, so he put down the gun and started looking around for a shirt in his dresser drawers. Stolnik had to tear up the shirts. That was what he was supposed to do, so Stolnik found one and started ripping it up.

"Stop it, Sokolai," Stolnik said.

Stolnik kept tearing the shirts because that was what he was supposed to do to survive. If they kept the family's bodies down there they'd rot, spread diseases—maybe the brothers couldn't catch those diseases because the family were human, but they'd been gengineered to be fairly close to human, and dogs could probably get sick from decaying dead bodies, couldn't they? Or because they were scavengers, maybe they couldn't?

"Stop tearing up your shirts." Stolnik took Stolnik's hands and held them, and then Stolnik didn't know who he was anymore or what he needed to do to survive.

If he wasn't supposed to do that, what was he supposed to do?

"I'm having trouble focusing right now," Sokolai managed to say. It took an effort because making noise meant you could be overheard, and that meant someone could triangulate your position off the sound of your voice and shoot you, and Sokolai didn't want to be shot, he didn't want to die.

"Sit down." Stolnik took dog and made him sit down on the bed.

When dog had been very little, had been too little to think properly, he had thought that all barking was just barking and you had to bark just right. Hadn't been aware that barking was mostly words, words that could go together. Dog hadn't understood that standing in Grey-Four's place meant that he was Grey-Four all of the time, not just when he was standing in Grey-Four's place in training. Hadn't understood he was a person.

He'd only been 'Sokolai' at the Emancipation, and nobody had explained anything then, either. He'd thought it was some kind of new training exercise, and then they'd told him he was a seven-year-old child and that he had to go and live with a family, but there were new words he'd never heard before like 'she' and 'her' and 'mother', and.

And Sokolai got confused sometimes.

He held his hands over his eyes while Stolnik picked up the hunting rifle.

The hunting rifle *k-tanged*, the noise it made when the bolt was thrown back with a round loaded, and the unfired round landed on the sheets, bounced twice.

Stolnik stared at it. "You loaded the fucking gun?"

"What's the point of owning a gun and not loading it?" Sokolai asked, unsteadily.

Stolnik didn't reply. Just took the ammunition, and the hunting rifle, and the knife on the table, and went downstairs for a bit, then came back upstairs with Ajay's smell faintly on him, like they'd been talking. The smell went away fairly quickly, Sokolai's sense of smell wasn't very good. Almost human.

"Were you going to kill yourself?" Stolnik asked.

Sokolai didn't answer.

"I could smell your spit on the barrel. You put it in your mouth."

Sokolai still didn't answer.

"None of us have killed ourselves, you know. I don't know why, and I've thought about it myself sometimes, but not one of us have actually done it."

"We ate them."

Stolnik didn't answer.

"We changed our minds because we were hungry and gutted them like deer and threw their guts out with the shit buckets, and we ate them."

Stolnik still didn't answer.

"Why don't I feel bad about it? I'm supposed to, I know that, and I don't. Why am I caught in paranoid fear for my life, when I'm safe, and why don't I give a shit about cutting open an eleven-year-old girl and eating her fat, just because her corpse was fresh and we'd already thrown the revolutionaries' bodies off the third floor?"

Stolnik got up and shut the door.

"Why do I feel bad about the wrong thing? Shouldn't I feel guilt? I feel guilty, I guess, on an intellectual level, but I don't face up to it. Shouldn't I be having nightmares about that, instead of about Setzen dying?"

Stolnik came back, and leaned against the wall between two of the windows. Sokolai fought down the urge to get up and check them.

"Well?" Sokolai asked.

Stolnik let his jaw go slack, slung it left and right until it clicked, and finally shut his mouth. "Did you get implants or did they put you on the hormone patch?"

"I got implanted testicles in high school," Sokolai said. "Did you get those?"

"I think we all got new balls, eventually, but I was on the hormone patch for awhile." Stolnik stared at him. It was a little like looking in the mirror. "I met this guy who said he worked as one of our trainers, once, out in Colombia. He said they cut our balls off so they could regulate our brain development."

Sokolai stared back.

"He said with the right mixture of puberty and drugs, they were going to fuck with our brains so we wouldn't respond to emotional trauma, wouldn't develop post traumatic stress disorder, just wouldn't give a shit. Not about death, dismemberment, not about eating meat crawling with maggots, nothing." Stolnik tilted his head slightly. "When did they give you implants?"

"I didn't get balls until I was seventeen," Sokolai said. "I was on the patch until then."

Stolnik shook his head, and shrugged. "They got it half right with you, I guess."

"I guess."

"Personally, I threw up. I mean, I kept her down for an hour or two, but as soon as I was alone, taking my shift on the third floor, I threw up."

"I didn't."

"Cried like a baby about it, too."

"That help?" Sokolai clasped his hands together. Stared at the floor.

"A bit." Stolnik's jaw clicked, unseen. "Cathartic. Think about it, feel it, deal with it."

Sokolai stretched out his fingers. Squeezed them back together. "I didn't cry."

Stolnik came closer. Patted Sokolai's shoulder.

"I always figured I was a coward. Didn't confront what I did. Ran from it. Made myself a monster." Flex his fingers, squeeze his fingers. Over and over. Something to focus on. "But I guess I was already a monster, and the cowardly part was thinking I wasn't, huh?"

"We're all monsters, Sokolai. That's how they made us."

* * *

After talking to Stolnik, Sokolai still wanted to kill himself. Make Sokolai go away, *really* go away, not just get confused and think he was dog, or one of his brothers. But it turned out that Estian Incorporated hadn't made him to kill himself. After all, a product that destroyed itself wasn't any good, was it? Maybe that was why he was more afraid of dying like that, hurting himself, than he was of machine gun nests.

So Sokolai went to Azerbaijan, when the crowdfunded civil war kicked off, and the population all chipped in to hire mercenaries to kill their president.

It was a kind of democracy, and it was a kind of suicide. The first teams into the country went in with the government fully aware of why they were there—after all, you didn't run a crowdfunding campaign for millions and millions of New Dollars without it being fucking obvious what it was for. Except the army was too incompetent to kill him.

Oh, Sokolai *tried*. He volunteered for all the risky shit, all the shit he could die for happy. Pulling his wounded brothers in out of sniper fire, distracting UAVs and automated turrets so someone else could get a lock, but he couldn't bring himself to switch off his chameleon gear, couldn't bring himself to step out in front of a gun.

He wondered, sometimes, whether or not it was the devil who made him. If the Catholics were right, and there was a hell, surely it had to resemble being set on committing suicide, and being too much of a fucking pussy to actually do it.

The house ahead was a good firing position. Clear all around, great sightlines, thick walls. He wanted to die, but a churning need to survive in his gut pushed him onwards with the rest of his brothers on the patrol. So far Sokolai had seen two of his brothers die—they'd tried for a medevac, but had been unable to get them out in the six hours stabilizing them had bought—and fifteen get taken to one of the field hospitals they'd snuck into Baku's underground parking lots, but so far he hadn't had that kind of luck. Maybe he'd have that kind of luck in the house. It was worth trying.

Edane opened the door with a 23 millimetre shell from his Light Anti-Materiel Weapon that shattered the lock, and Sokolai kicked what was left of the door down, pushing in first, ahead of the others.

A man in a tactical facemask, a goggle-eyed collection of six lenses winking as he looked up, gun rising, died before Sokolai could stop himself from pulling the trigger. It had been a reflex, pure, simple, perfect. If he'd been any slower than that, the man would have killed him. But the man was incompetent, and so was his friend on the far side of the entry hall, who fell back into a row of mail delivery lockers like a split water balloon, body and black uniform visibly warped around the 23 millimetre shell that must have detonated just right to splash the friend across the tiles like a bucket of paint.

It was quiet, while they checked the bodies. Sokolai smiled, thinly.

"I'm going to find a position up near the roof," Edane said. "If they bring the tanks, I should be able to knock 'em out if I can get an angle on the top armour. You coming?"

Sokolai shook his head slowly. "I need five. Give me a minute to eat something and I'll be up with you."

"Sure thing." Edane slapped his shoulder, and went through the shattered glass security door to the house's stairwell. The house, the house was more of a small apartment block, to be honest.

Sokolai shut his eyes, and took a deep, deep breath. He could smell raw meat and charring and sewage. He smiled again.

He felt happy. He could smile, just like Michael taught him. He didn't know why he felt happy. Was he supposed to feel happy?

He lifted the dead man's phone, and thumbed on the translation program his EWAR kit had installed. The last outgoing message blinked into English.

Khadija, you must not be afraid, daddy will come home when everything is safe.

No, daddy would not be coming home. Daddy was lying on the floor with his head puddled out, like Setzen's.

Sokolai shut his eyes, hard, and thought about Setzen. Thought about it until his heart shuddered in his chest and he was so afraid he felt like his body was too tight, and he looked at the phone again. Searched around for a family photograph, and compared the man in the picture to the ruination of blood on the tiles at Sokolai's feet.

Sokolai dry-retched.

Sokolai hated himself.

Sokolai wished he hadn't had to kill the man. Sokolai wished the man had given up like the other Azerbaijani soldiers. Sokolai wished the man had stayed home with his family.

Sokolai's eyes were wet. He wasn't crying, but they were wet.

He lifted his own phone, went to the nearest window, checked for the enemy, went to the next window, letting part of himself just move, live, breathe, do everything needed for survival, while he called home. The phone rang twice, and Michael picked up.

"Socks?"

"Hey, Mike?"

"Yeah? It's good to hear from you. The gang called, asking about you. Aren't you, like. Over *there*?"

"I am." Sokolai wiped at his eye, and rested his head against the window frame, staring across at the mouth of a street between two buildings, waiting for the enemy. "This. This is a weird question, but you taught me how to smile, and, and I think I'm figuring out some of this myself, but. Can you teach me how to *cry*? I'm not a monster if I can cry, right?"

"I. Jesus, Socks. I don't know. We could give it a shot." Michael was quiet, for a little bit. "Are you okay, Socks?"

"I—I might be. Listen, when I get home, you, you have to teach me. Okay?"

"Okay."

"I have to go now. Bye."

"Bye. Take care of yourself."

"I will." Sokolai killed the connection.

Then he went upstairs, and helped Edane to kill seven more combatants. By the time he'd killed the fifth, he didn't care much about it anymore, he didn't give a shit, they were just *targets*, but Sokolai took photographs with his rifle's camera.

Later, when he'd learned how to cry, looking at the pictures would be cathartic.

For now, Sokolai let himself survive.

"The Analogue Cat" shows bioengineered furries equally as subservient pets, as a rebel underclass among themselves, and as interstellar explorers for mankind.

Tozer stands out among them all. And among the humans, as well.

The Analogue Cat

by Alice "Huskyteer" Dryden

When you wake, you wait a few moments for your eyes to come online. You can manage without them, but it's pleasant to lie in the dark warmth and purr while the blurred pixels slowly crystallise into your world. You stretch a striped arm and extend your claws until the pink quick shows, then pick up your other arm and lock it into position. Stretch. Extend. The joints move with ease and the claws, opaque white on this paw, click smoothly in and out. It's time to begin.

You're a second-generation Bengal. Your parents were grown in the wombs of human women who needed the money or wanted to do something shocking, but you were conceived the natural way—if there can be anything natural about the tangle of DNA that makes up a Pet— your sire and dam carefully selected by your breeder.

It's at training school, which you and your classmates call Kittygarten without knowing why it's funny, that you notice the difference between you and the others. You think more deeply, ask more questions, get in trouble more often. At the end of the course, you're ready to go off with your new owners. The fad for Bots is over, and it's all about Pets now. You were sold before you even opened your eyes, to a family with three boisterous kids. You put up with having your tail and ears pulled in return for their uncomplicated love. With the parents, it's different; you're expected to keep your golden fur groomed nicely and mince ahead of them on a lead so they can show off to those who have a less expensive breed, a mere Bot, or no companion at all. You miss your friends from Kittygarten, don't see other Pets except for brief meetings on walks. The neighbours bring their black cocker round sometimes, and he's alright, but, again, he doesn't think like you do. You were the pick of your litter and everything about you is perfect, from the delicate tufts of fur on your ears to the apricot fluff of your belly. Each spot and stripe is regular and correctly sized.

You go blind when you're not quite full-grown, a breed fault, and your owners take you back for a refund. The kids protest, but are quelled by promises of a dog Pet next time. The breeder is kind, just has you neutered and throws you out on the street rather than put you to sleep. You survive on wits and whiskers for five long years, until your golden, patterned coat is masked by dirt and your perfect ears are nicked.

By now the third generation of Pets has come along. They're smarter than their parents, many of them crossbreeds sprung into life without a careful breeding programme, and they want to be recognised as people. The Bots take up the call, as if they've been waiting all this time for someone else to kick off. There's activism, and you're a part of it until it gets too violent for your tastes. Victory comes at last, and with it new rights, like the right to work, and the surgery that will give you new eyes. The sponsored ads that go with free healthcare are a small price to pay for vision. Not just vision, either; there's night sight, close-up, and Cloud access, all snug behind your eyelids and hooked with hairsbreadth wires to the living circuitry of your brain. You're not quite a Pet any more, but not quite a Bot either; something in between, non-binary. You see the world from twin cameras hidden behind green lenses of one-way glass. You don't mind so much, these days, that the breeder stole your sex years ago. You pick a new set of pronouns to go with the changes in your body, and a new name: Tozer. You're the Analogue Cat.

Now you find that the firsties and the second-gens are an embarrassment the third generation hopes will die off quickly, and sometimes helps to get there. Most of the first-gen are already gone, their lives short, simple, and largely happy. The seconds start to follow but you hang on, whether by chance or by some freak of genes. At thirty-eight you feel used up, your striped and spotted fur losing its plushy thickness and the skin loose around your shrinking neck, but you hang on. You're not sure what for. You don't fit. These days, people want everything to be discrete and sharply defined: on/off, male/female, good/evil.

You're an analogue cat in a digital world.

One night, as you take the moving walkway home from your sorting job at the recycling plant, popup ads flickering at the edges of your vision, a group of fourth-gen dogs walks by. They're young, have never known a world where Pets are promised to an owner before they're even born. One of them pretends to stumble and grabs your left arm, feeling under the bicep with a thumb. Then everything goes dark; they've used a jammer so you can't call for help over the Cloud, and it's knocked your eyes offline.

"Liberation!" you hear, and smell the booze on dog breath. You hiss and struggle, feel your claws connect with a nose, then one of the others has your paws pinned behind your back. There's a stab in your arm, a flood of warmth, and pain so sharp you fall and can't move. It takes you far too long to pass out, and when you do, the uncaring walkway carries your body onwards.

You wake with a stump where your arm used to be. The dog vigilantes hacked out the chip that, in the old days, allowed your owners to trace you if you got lost or stolen, and the wound became infected. You look from your stump to the Bot standing beside your bed, waiting for you to come round. It was this Bot who found you dying on the walkway, stopped the bleeding and carried you to hospital. This Bot has checked back every day while you lay sucking in air and fluids, as your system hovered between reboot and shutdown.

Her name's Min.

Your new arm is emblazoned with advertising logos, but you don't mind. It's stronger than the old one and can feel no pain. It's resistant to heat and cold. You soon get used to working it, and a lot of the time you forget it hasn't always been part of you. But it's the other paw, the warm, soft one with its bundles of fragile nerve endings, that you slip into Min's three-fingered hand one afternoon soon after your release from hospital. She takes it gently in a grip that can exert meganewtons of pressure, touched in more ways than one.

Analogue Pet and digital Bot have a lot in common; like you, Min has made decisions about who and what she is, and she's had her body modified to suit the female identity she's chosen. Her torso is cylindrical, the glossy red of lipstick. When you sit together in the park, her chest is warm against your body, and something deep inside it ticks like a slow purr. Because of the Cloud link behind your eyes, you and she can talk silently, for hours, even when you're apart. You hadn't realised how lonely you'd been until you weren't.

You get a better job, working for a space programme newly reactivated as the planet's resources run low. Just cleaning up at first; then, when they realise your eyes can overlay blueprints and instructions, building components. Nobody makes Bots any more, and few people will voluntarily have their eyes taken out, so your attributes are rare and valuable - almost as much as a pedigree Bengal once was. The fourthers working at the programme treat you with an awkward respect, even though they've had the university education you could never have imagined for yourself. Pretty soon, nobody will count Pet generations any more.

You become even more valuable the day a fire starts in the laboratory next door to your office. The sprinklers are having no effect, but you reach out into the white heat with your prosthetic arm, flicking switches off and grabbing burning material away so the flames die for lack of fuel. You lose half your whiskers, and can't wear the arm for a week because the heat it conducted has blistered your stump, but at the hospital you discover the programme has paid for an ad-free upgrade to your eyes, and when you come back to work the Director herself summons you to her office to thank you personally. She's run disaster analysis, and you've saved the project from losing precious time, money, and perhaps people. She's looking at you thoughtfully, and you wonder if she's having trouble with your pronouns, but when she speaks, it's of the programme.

She tells you about the mission: about the star the scientists have identified as having the ability to support life. They think there are planets. They can't tell for sure. But once they get someone out there, get them on the surface of a new world, they can send a signal back with the coordinates, and start the processes that will ensure food and shelter for the first wave of colonists. You ask why not an unmanned probe, and she explains that nobody knows what's out there, so no computer can be programmed to deal with all the possible eventualities. It takes the living to improvise.

A fresh start for anyone who wants it, she says. A society in which all are equal, truly equal. You ask what the problem is.

She describes the spacecraft, how the process is automated except for one crucial stage when controls must be operated. How the terrible forces involved fill human eyes with red mist, and render human hands too heavy to move. She conjures up clumsy, big-boned bodies pressed flat against the floor, and inflexible spines snapping. But perhaps you, Tozer…she says. And you feel your tail twitch with excitement in a way it hasn't for years.

Then she tells you how long it will take. For you, a couple of weeks; for Earth, a couple of centuries. In that time, they'll build bigger and better craft, overcome the technical obstacles, and get ready for mass transportation. But someone has to go first. Because you can't send thousands of men, women and children into space without knowing what awaits them. Send one Pet, though, and they're a hero whatever happens.

You mention your age—you know no other second-gens still living— and she says, bluntly, that you need only survive long enough to send the signal; then she relents, and tells you your medical records indicate you've got plenty of time.

You say you'll need to discuss it with someone first. But when you talk to Min over the Cloud, she can tell your heart is already up among the stars, doing something nobody else has done or can do. Discovering a world that's yours from the start.

And now here you are, waking up on the cusp of a new life. You're bound to be disorientated; that's why this recording is playing for you. And if it's playing, then you're alive. You've reached your destination. There's a planet below you that will be your new home.

You remember it all now, don't you? I know you'll succeed in your mission. You're the Analogue Cat, neither Pet nor Bot, and you can do anything. And once you've landed, set up your camp, and sent the signal on its long journey home, there's another task for you.

Weight and space were too critical to take along so much as a gram of surplus, but the flash memory in your eyes holds a set of blueprints, and a compressed backup of my memories and personality. Whether you salvage scrap from the capsule or use the equipment you've been given to mine and work the metals, eventually you can make a new body and install me in it. However it works, I'll still be your Min, your only Min. I shut myself down back on Earth the day you left; I didn't want to live without you.

I'm waiting, Tozer. I love you.

Who killed Alex Richards?

His old pal, Mike Harrison, investigates.

Muskrat Blues

by Ianus Wolf

The phone was ringing when I stepped into my office in the early afternoon. I barely had time to rush to my desk before my answering service would take the call. Then I would have had to go through the rigmarole of calling them up and getting the message right after someone had left it. I took a second to catch my breath once I had the receiver in my trotter. Rushing across the office isn't good for my leg, and I'd just been on a decent hike through the city after closing things out with my last client. I'd had to inform a deer that his doe was stepping out on him just like he suspected. I felt for him, with what I've known of heartache.

Finally, I put the phone to my ear. "Harrison," I said through a few heavy breaths by way of hello. A new client would at least know they'd properly reached *Harrison Investigations*.

"Hello, Mike," said the growling voice of Grimaldi, a cougar police detective who I recognized from the first syllable. "I'm giving you a courtesy call."

His voice was just somber enough in its neutral, official tones that I had a bad feeling. "What kind of courtesy call?"

"Alex Richards is dead," he answered flatly. Grimaldi wasn't the kind to beat around the bush or take his time with bad news.

My snout sank a little bit, and my eyes closed. Alex and I went back a long time. Back as far as the days when I was on the force, even so far as taking the fall with me when the department needed a couple patsies for PR and decided a wounded pig and a loud-mouthed muskrat wouldn't be much of a loss. We'd gone through entering the private sector together and helped each other back and forth through the process of getting licensed and occasionally pooling our resources on cases. He also kept his ear to the ground for me about anything that might lead to finding Michelle. I gave him a pittance each month out of pride, even though he'd have done it for free. I hadn't seen him the last few weeks owing to both of us being busy on cases. Now he was dead.

"Where?" I asked.

Grimaldi sighed on the other end of the line. "Now Mike, this is police business. Unless someone's paying you—"

"Where?" I said again.

"Damn it, Mike, this was a courtesy; don't make this hard on me."

"I'm not asking to be cut in; I just want to know where it happened."

There was silence for a moment except for light, agitated breathing. "We found him along a trail in Migorsky Park. You don't want to see him, Mike. He's torn up and—"

I hung up and didn't let him finish. I told my somewhat bum leg to stop whining because we had places to be. Like Migorsky Park and wherever all the pretty police tape was marking the area.

* * *

I'd caught a cab to the entrance of the park to give my leg a rest and avoid the hassle of parking so close to downtown. It helped some, but I still had to make my way through the trail. I was used to the slight limp slowing me down just a little and working around it when I had to. It was a memento from my last official case with the police. I'd say you should see the other guy, but he's in Oak Lawn Cemetery and the funeral was closed casket.

The day was making my leg worse though. Between my client and hearing about Alex, it was too full of reminders of Michelle, which always made the leg flare up. Michelle, the beautiful brown-furred bunny that shared a bungalow with me for a couple years and always put off the idea of actually getting married. Who would have drinks and game nights with me and Alex and whatever skirt he was into that week. Who worried about the life we'd have trying to make it together. And who, once she knew I was going to walk with a limp for the rest of my life, forced me to come home to a half-empty little bungalow and a letter scented with stale perfume.

I pushed the memories out of my thoughts, because all they could do for me right now was make it harder to walk. And I was coming up on the part of the path where yellow tape had cordoned off an area. I could see Hank Grimaldi, already back from whatever payphone he'd used to call me. When the tawny cougar looked up and saw me, he rolled his eyes and stalked up to meet me in his ill-fitting suit. Even before he blocked me, I could tell he hadn't been lying about Richards.

The plump little muskrat body was lying in its own half-dried pool of blood just off the trail, surrounded by a few smaller pools here and there in the grass. From where I was I could vaguely tell some of him was missing and see occasional glimpses of white bone. Any clothing was ripped to shreds. I could make out one glassy eye staring at nothing while uniformed officers tagged spots on the ground and collected bits of extra evidence. The whole thing almost made my gorge rise, but I had plenty of experience at pushing that back down. Then Grimaldi stood in my way.

"Mike, this is a police investigation. What are you doing here?"

"Checking up on an old friend. Want to tell me what happened or should I just start disrupting things around here in nice, perfectly legal ways?"

Grimaldi gave an exasperated sigh. "He was found late this morning by a Labrador taking a morning jog. Probably would have been found earlier, but it's a Saturday and not as many early risers. The Lab called it in; we came out and found him pretty much as you see him. We questioned the dog, but there's no reason to think he's a suspect. No blood on his breath, no connection to Al—to the deceased. Clearly, this is a predatory killing, so we're going to investigate the area, see if we have anyone with a history of stalking or other priors, but…" The cougar trailed off, spread his arms wide, and gave me a look.

I snorted and nodded. It was something you got used to in this city when you were one of those species certain folks look at as a lesser creature. Hunting anything on two legs had been illegal for a long time on paper, and for the most part it worked. Most inhabitants of the world at large and our fair city at least managed to see people like me as…people on some level. But everyone also knew there were still certain neighborhoods you didn't get caught in after sundown if you lacked claws and fangs, or at the very least antlers or horns.

When a predatory killing did happen, the department made a token effort to investigate and sometimes found their culprit. But unless they already had teeth impressions or a specific scent sample on file that we could match pretty quickly to a known suspect, the case would get cold practically before the body had a chance to. No one really wanted to sweat too many resources over some defenseless leaf-muncher that was in the wrong place at the wrong time. Grimaldi and I both knew this.

Yet when I looked around him at the scene, something bugged me about it. Something in the back of my mind.

"Hank, we both worked predatory killings back in the day, right?"

The cougar nodded. "Yeah, of course. You had the nose for it."

It wasn't said as a compliment, just a statement of fact. Grimaldi was always an odd one. He had to balance a certain personal respect that had grown for me with his belief that certain species never belonged on the force. He wasn't the sort to use words like "porker" or "ham hock"—at least not to my face—but he'd always clearly had a definite opinion about the order of the world and everyone's place in it. Still, that couldn't keep him from admitting that no bloodhound or pure-bred wolf could beat my snout when it came to literally sniffing out clues.

"Yeah, and I still do, but right now I'm using my eyes. What's wrong with this picture?"

Grimaldi looked over his shoulder. "You mean besides the dead PI?"

I let that little reminder that I wasn't a cop anymore go unchallenged. "Right, we can tell immediately that's Alex. What about every other predatory killing you've investigated? Unless they're caught in the act, we usually don't find a body; we find bones. Bones that have been cleaned and discarded somewhere and take forever to identify. Not to be crass, but why's there so much left of him?"

He looked back again for a moment, a frown appearing on his muzzle when his head turned my way. "Maybe the killer was interrupted."

Even he didn't sound convinced, and I wasn't going to let that go. "Right. Our killer was interrupted, then the body sat for several hours to be discovered by your jogger this morning. Think about it, Hank. Think like a cougar. If you were going to go through the trouble of killing...me for argument's sake—"

"Jeez, Mike!"

"Just hear it out and think. If you'd gone predatory, and you were going to all the effort to kill me in the dead of night based on that, would you just leave most of the meat lying around for hours?"

He rolled his eyes and bit his lip, tail twitching nervously. He wouldn't look at me. Good. It was handy sometimes to make people uncomfortable. Makes it a little more difficult for them to come up with a convincing lie.

"No," he said finally, looking back over where the body lay. "No, I wouldn't."

"So why does he look like that? Something is rotten here."

Whiskers twitching, Grimaldi looked up for a few moments, then shook his head. "It doesn't matter."

My black eyes widened. I couldn't control the angry squeal that came out of me and caused several of the patrolmen to look over. "My curly tail it doesn't! You're honestly going to tell me—!"

"Mike," the cougar interrupted, putting a paw on my arm to get my attention. He looked back at me and there was something in his face that vaguely resembled sorrow. "Look at it my way. Even if I point that out to the higher-ups, they won't spend the resources on it. It'll still just be a predatory killing and we'll run down the appropriate leads. In the end, that's all that'll happen no matter what. I've made it to where I am because I know how the system works."

I reined myself in. Of course, he was right. Nothing would be done. At least not by the police.

"Fine," I said. "At least let me go over there and pay my respects to the dead."

Grimaldi saw the look on my face. "Mike, you can pay your respects when he's—"

It was my turn to grab his arm. "Hank, it's Alex. Richards deserves better than just being a short obituary and a single case file gathering dust on a shelf." I looked away and took my trotter off his suit. "He deserved better than a lot of things."

That worked at the cougar. Grimaldi hadn't been fully on board with hanging Alex and me out to dry, but he certainly hadn't done a thing to stop it. That was how the system worked, and how Grimaldi always worked the system. After just a moment, he stepped aside and extended his arm back. "Since you two were so close," he murmured. Always aware of potential politics, he was neither condemning nor officially condoning my own personal investigation. He was just giving me a few seconds to say good-bye.

I walked up and pushed up the tape to duck under it. Some of the uniformed officers—most notably an angry-looking Doberman—scowled at me as I stepped into the scene but didn't say anything. I had the blessing of the detective, and they'd seen it. So taking a deep breath, I went over to what was left of Alex's body.

That inhalation filled my snout with the stench of old booze and offal. I let out an involuntary little grunt. Breathing regular-like, I didn't quite notice it. Most of it must have dissipated and settled in the night. But if you got a good whiff, you could get a clear sense of that rotten, fermented smell around the body.

I turned to one of the friendlier looking patrolmen, and asked the husky, "Lot of alcohol?"

He just nodded, giving his nose a little rub. I saw that Alex's belly had been opened up from some wound or other, explaining the odor that had assailed me. When someone's guts come out, the smell is naturally bad enough, but if they've also been drinking a lot beforehand, it'll all but destroy any other smell in the area. That meant there was no use trying to sniff out anything if the body's condition would blot out all other scents.

It really was even less pretty close up. Bits of him were mangled to different degrees. His throat was torn away, just like anyone might expect. As I stepped closer, I saw one arm draped over his body and stripped in many places of its meat. I could see bloody bone almost up to the elbow before the rest seemed more or less intact. When I looked up and down the body, I saw a few more wounds that looked like teeth had ripped a chunk out of him, but nothing with any fervor. It was almost like the killer started with the arm, but then lost their gumption. Then they tried to hit some other points and just couldn't finish the work. So they left him like that, hoping police would make the assumptions Grimaldi already had.

But when I really looked at it, this didn't look like the ravening of someone gone predatory psycho. This looked more like someone trying to cover up a killing who had the teeth for this sort of work, but not the stomach for actually taking apart what they saw as a person. Between that and everything else, it seemed more like maybe a hired thug trying to throw someone off the trail.

I knelt next to Alex and started a light patting of his pockets while I made the motions of paying my respects. I wasn't interested in anything big, just trying to find any little clue that police might miss when they were casually stripping and labelling him as another victim. My eyes stung a little when I thought of it, but I bit it back and focused on the task. In one of those pockets, I found a matchbook that I palmed casually without looking at it. The patrolmen didn't notice, but I bet Hank did and didn't care one way or another. The modern calling card of business establishments didn't count as anything important in this case. I didn't find much else, and I was tired of standing there in my friend's blood.

"I'll find him, Alex," I promised my friend in a soft whisper. "I'll find him…and I'll make him wish he'd never been born."

* * *

My first stop had been to visit Alex's office. The matchbook in his pocket was for a club called Menagerie that operated primarily in the evening, so I had a little time before following up on it. We kept keys to each other's offices, which meant that it was easy to at least try and piece together what he was working on.

To anyone who didn't know Alex, his desk would have been a chaos of disorganized notes and papers with no rhyme or reason. But

I'd worked with him enough. I knew how he kept things and how he worked cases. Just to the right from where he'd sit was an open file with papers and pictures from a construction site. That would be his current earner, the case that was paying the bills. I thumbed through it and found notes relating to Hanlon Construction and his clients—from the name I couldn't really pronounce, I guessed a coyote tribe—all pointing towards Alex being paid to gather info on a project just outside of town called Regal Acres.

Just the name Hanlon Construction was suspect. The Hanlon family had been known to skirt the law and had enough power and wealth to rarely see the inside of a courtroom. If Alex had been caught snooping around in their business, that might be motive enough for murder. Though the Hanlons were lions. If one of them was going to kill a plump little muskrat, they probably wouldn't leave leftovers. Unless they wanted to make sure it couldn't be traced back to them and had hired someone to make it look a little more random. It was something to look into, but the whole thing seemed a little too sloppy for a family so used to covering their tracks.

Looking through the other papers on the desk, I found a mishmash of minor cases that he'd either already closed out or was trying to collect for. Nothing that really called out to me as a motive for killing, a lot of the people and places listed weren't even predatory sorts from all the indications. I looked through each one, hoping for any lead, anything that might point towards what got Alex killed. Nothing there tugged at me; I kept coming back around to Hanlon Construction and possibly Menagerie.

On the left, I found a pad that Alex always kept for personal musings. It was where he jotted down things that didn't belong in an official casefile. On the top page, he just had a long-distance phone number and a name: *Dr. James Rennick, L.A.* with a single word: *Possible?*

That was how Alex worked on some things. Just enough to jog a memory or thought in his mind that would be meaningless to the rest of us. I took the note and put it in my pocket, just in case. After a couple more hours going through the office, making a few notes of my own, I decided it was finally time to go change and see about the night life at a little club called Menagerie.

* * *

I felt fairly dapper in the one good suit I owned. Even my hat was a nicer one than my day-to-day wear when I stepped into Menagerie. It was a nice, quiet nightclub with a welcoming atmosphere. A band played some upbeat swing on a stage while guests dined at tables surrounding a mid-sized dancefloor. From the first glance around, the place lived up to its name. I saw wolves mingling with rabbits, mice working their way between herds of cats that didn't seem to mind their presence one way or another.

I'd read about places like this that were on the rise. The whole idea that the atmosphere would welcome everyone no matter their species to come and have a good time, no intimidation, no worry about whatever history between them. It was an understood rule that bad attitudes need not apply and would be tossed out.

I'd always been skeptical about these places, but as I stepped up to the bar to order a rum-and-Coke, I noticed that the joint seemed to be working out well. As if music and social lubrication really had become some kind of universal language for inhabitants of a city to set aside their differences and just have a good time. Watching people at the bar, I could see that this was probably Alex's sort of place. They were laughing at each other's jokes and generally having a good time no matter who was around. It almost made me regret my preference for quiet drinks at home with just a few friends. Almost.

While I got my drink, I showed the chipmunk bartender and one or two other folks near me Alex's picture. They all pretty much confirmed that they'd seen him around the last couple weeks but that he'd never seemed in any kind of trouble. They remembered him as the boisterous overweight guy who liked to watch the fox sing.

A little while into it, I heard the applause and looked from the bar to the stage. I understood what they were talking about when a fennec vixen stepped up to the mic in a shimmering, light purple dress that hung down to the floor. As it sparkled under the lights against her russet fur, she began to fill the place with a torchy number sung in a dusky voice. She was quite the knock-out as she sang about rustling bushes and looking up trees to find that special man.

For a few songs I sat and enjoyed the view. I scanned the crowd for anyone that looked like a potential killer, but came up goose egg. Maybe the sound and the look of her was distracting me. I could see why Alex had become such a regular here, but I was starting to realize this probably had nothing to do with his death.

That was when someone tapped me roughly on the shoulder and made me turn on the barstool. I swiveled to see an angry feline face pressing close to mine. Eyes glared out of yellow-tan fur graced with a top shock of mane cut back around the rest of the face. It was a style some young lions went for these days.

"Hey! Yer in my favorite seat."

The lion was all heavy breathing and looming intimidation, stopping just short of baring his teeth. Maybe a few years younger than me, in his twenties, and showing off as much of his well-worked muscle as he could through the short sleeves of a button-collar shirt. So much for the brotherhood and the common language.

I glanced around to see the audience at the bar watching our little show. So I looked down at the seat, checked it all over, and turned back to the feline. "Funny. Looks like every other seat in the place to me. Why not try another one? I think they're all pretty similar."

His eyes widened and he growled in my face. "I'm warnin' you, porker..."

"Brutus," the bartender said with a warning tone that seemed pretty daring for a chipmunk, "play nice."

Brutus turned a look of pure rage and frustration on the bartender, and I noticed a very large gorilla in a dark suit had inched closer from a corner of the place. Then the feline turned his glare back to me, his claws flipping out and retracting in time with the heaving of his chest.

His breath was on my face, and I was just about ready for a dust-up. Sure, I'd get hurt, but I knew they wouldn't let things get to a point of murder with that burly bouncer waiting in the wings. The place did have its reputation to worry about, given what they were trying to be. That was when I saw the singer out of a corner of my eye coming to the side of the bar. That fennec vixen with the dusky voice.

Suddenly, I just didn't care about the stool anymore, or my pride. I saw something worth going after much more as she put a cigarette in her muzzle and started rooting around in her sequined bag for something to light it with. I didn't even look back at the lion as I slipped off and headed for her, saying, "All yours, pal."

I didn't pay attention to the insult he hurled at my back. He could play the big bad king of the jungle all he wanted while I took in the scent of her and reached into my pocket. She wore a perfume that was equal parts floral and pheromone. The type designed to make a man think of her as a proper lady, while burning with a desire to take her somewhere and treat her like a woman. I flicked my lighter and held it out to her.

She looked at me for just a moment in surprise, then smiled and held out her cigarette to the flame. "Wow, a real gentleman. Almost an endangered species these days."

"I like to think we're still hanging on." As she pulled her cig back and took a few puffs, I flicked the lighter closed and slipped it back into my pocket. "I'm Mike. Mike Harrison."

She offered her paw. "Lucy. Delighted."

I took it gently. "Heck of a last name."

"Ooh, charming and clever," she said with just a playful hint of mockery. The fennec looked over my shoulder. "Your friend over there is boring holes in your back. I think he's still not satisfied."

"He and I are not affiliated," I said with a shrug. "And I'm not in the habit of satisfying men. I find the present company much more enjoyable."

Lucy gave me a coy little chuckle. "Not bad, not bad. I'd be careful though. I've seen Brutus get riled up and land people in the hospital. And they weren't…well, like you."

"Oh, I can handle myself if I have to." I leaned against the bar. "Some of us aren't so defenseless as you'd like to believe."

She raised her eyebrows and shrugged, taking another drag.

"Though it does beg the question, why's he still allowed in here? Thought this place was going for a certain kind of reputation."

"Oh, they've kicked him out a few times, told him never to come back. But Daddy has money. So he goes whining to Daddy, and Daddy comes here and offers them a nice little sum to lift his son's banishment with the promise he'll be good. Then he's good for a little while until something sets him off, and it's 'round the mulberry bush again."

"Huh. And who is Daddy, if you happen to know?"

"Dicky Hanlon. I'm sure you've heard of him."

I hadn't wanted to make assumptions just because he was a lion, but here was a connection to the Hanlons, right in a club Alex had been to recently. Most people in my circles had heard of Richard "Diamond Dicky" Hanlon. Legitimate businessman—as far as any hard evidence was concerned—with at least a few family interests in the city. He wasn't the biggest guy in the city, but he was at least well-in enough to have his own clout. And his primary business interest just happened to be Hanlon Construction, the company Alex had been looking into. Interesting.

While I wanted to see about getting to know her better, the mention of Hanlon reminded me why I was there. I fished in my coat pocket for the picture of Alex and showed her my credentials.

"You seem like you're here often enough. You seen this muskrat around? Maybe saw him get into some kind of trouble with our man Brutus, or someone like him?"

Lucy took the picture and stared at it for just a few seconds. It looked like she was trying to recall him, then she shook her head.

"I know I've seen him here a lot, but I never saw him get into any trouble. I do think I've seen Brutus talking at him once or twice. 'Fraid

I don't see many people down here when I'm up there." She handed the picture back to me. "Speaking of which, I'm due to get back up and do another set. Thanks for the light, Mister. Come see me again sometime."

With a little wink at me, she gracefully slipped off the stool and made her way to the stage, leaving me in the wake of that perfume. For just a moment, I forgot about Alex and thought all those thoughts any man will think about a vixen like that. Was nice to know I still could.

But with a glance over my shoulder at Brutus, my mind returned quickly to my dead friend. I stared into my one drink and thought a few moments. Maybe Lucy Delighted, singer extraordinaire, hadn't seen anything, but maybe the lion hadn't been coming to this establishment by accident. Maybe as a favor for Diamond Daddy getting him out of trouble, he'd taken out a snooping private eye. Though one or two things didn't wash with that; it would be pretty gutsy to show up here so soon after killing someone. Or maybe that famous temper of his finally just went too far and he was trying to act natural while getting Diamond Daddy's help to get out of it. I'd have to see when I went around to Regal Acres the next day.

A big paw grabbed my shoulder and spun me to face two-hundred-fifty pounds of angry lion and bad breath.

"We still got business, porker!" Brutus roared, apparently thinking that glance at him meant it was time to settle the score.

For the first second when I looked at him, I thought about how this might be the guy that had torn up Alex. And very, very briefly, I thought it might be good to take him up on his offer to dance and show him just what an angry swine could be capable of.

I looked at him, narrowed my eyes, and muttered in a low voice, "Think you wanna take me, kitty? Think you have what it takes to knock me down?"

He growled, for the benefit of everyone around us. "I'll break you in half!"

Brutus probably could. Then I'd either wind up in traction or we'd wind up in a cell for disturbing the peace. Neither of which would do well to prove or disprove what happened to Alex. I managed to keep the corners of my mouth from turning up for another half a second, curling my fists. Then I leaned forward and kissed the lion on the nose.

"Then call me sometime, big boy," I whispered very loudly with just a little lily-of-the-valley lilt in my voice. I scooted around Brutus while he stood there sputtering and others started laughing around him. I walked quickly but casually out of the bar, making sure I didn't show too much of a limp.

I didn't think I'd get much more useful info out of the place for the night, and I knew a tussle with Brutus right there and then wouldn't get me anything but a few new injuries. I'd just have to keep it in mind and see what I could find out the next day. Still, sometimes I just love messing with carnivores.

* * *

After a decent night's sleep and a morning of checking the papers—the story about a dead muskrat was brief and buried on page six, ending with the usual "police have no leads at this time"—I drove my way out to Regal Acres after noontime. I had a good breakfast of a spinach and apple omelet at a diner I know then made a couple calls and found out that Hanlon was currently overseeing some aspects of the project himself. I figured I'd actually get there just after lunchtime and see if I could talk to the big man. Maybe see how he reacted when I mentioned Alex.

When I arrived, I pulled into a development on the very edge of our fine metropolis. I could tell by the model house at the end of the drive and some of the frames that were going up and being worked on by various men that this was going to be an upscale place. Somewhere for the wealthier element of the city to get far enough away, for a while, from the sprawl of the dirty commoners like myself. I also noticed a trailer set up that had all the indicators of a temporary office.

I found space for my little jalopy close to that trailer, driving past the hard-hat-wearing beavers working on timber frames while a few elephants and rhinoceroses worked at pouring concrete for upcoming foundations. The whole place seemed surprisingly up-and-up as I went into the cramped trailer, working as hard as I could to hide any trace of my limp. I only knew Hanlon by family reputation, and stopped short when I saw the powerful, middle-aged lion sitting behind a well-organized desk going over paperwork.

Richard Hanlon possessed a thick body that fully filled out his dark blue tailored suit with its subtle pinstripe pattern. Rings glittered from a couple of his fingers, displaying where he got his nickname for those in the know. A deep brown, perfectly styled mane with a shock of black at the top surrounded his yellowish tan face when he looked up and made me stop just in the doorway. Everything about him read of a man completely in charge of all around him, and his quiet poise was more intimidating than any of his son's bluster could ever have a hope of being.

He looked me up and down once with discerning yellow eyes, and without a hint of frustration, judgment, or any real emotion asked in a deep bass voice, "Is there something I can help you with?"

I took another couple steps in and removed my hat. I had to fight myself not to wring it nervously. Normally I pride myself on letting nothing rattle me, on being that guy who's cool in the face of the odds and so on. But Diamond Dicky's gaze was a force to be reckoned with all its own. It said he was the strongest guy in the room and that he was so sure of that, he had no need to prove it whatsoever. Still, this was for Alex, and I couldn't show fear to someone like him. So I let my breath out and spoke as clearly as I could.

"Mr. Hanlon, my name is Mike Harrison." On ceremony, without even thinking of it, I walked to his desk and extended my trotter. It was just what I did during introductions, and I was so busy trying to act natural, it happened almost automatically.

To my surprise, he simply leaned forward and took it cordially. "All right, what brings you here, Mr. Harrison?"

I had planned to bring up Alex and see his reaction. That stare of his though, told me that he wouldn't rattle easily. I thought maybe I should come at it slow, from another angle.

Releasing his larger paw, I leaned back from the desk. "Well, it's a little complicated. For starters, I had a run-in with your son last night at a club called Menagerie."

Hanlon leaned back in his chair with a frown. He gave an exasperated sigh that ended in a rumbling growl and pinched the skin between his eyes. Without another word, he reached for his right desk drawer.

I froze, and I think my heart stopped for a moment. In that second, I expected a gun to come up in his paw. That he wasn't even going to waste time using his claws, that he was just going to get rid of a nosy swine without a second thought. Because he could do it, and I'd foolishly stepped into his domain and meddled in his business.

The planet started spinning again when he brought out a thin leather-bound book and pulled an expensive fountain pen from a well on his desk. He looked up at me with that piercing stare as he opened a checkbook.

"Let me be frank. I don't want to know what Brutus did to you or how he acted. I just want to know how much it will cost to make it go away. Completely."

Shock kept me from speaking for a few moments. He was being perfectly genuine, and for just a second I thought about naming a number that would take care of a few months for me. But there were more important matters, and since I was already here, I had to press on. "Well, Mr. Hanlon, it's not about me. It's about a detective friend of mine by the name of Alex Richards."

With a confused expression, Hanlon twirled his pen between his fingers. "Alex? What's he got to do with this?"

Everything was getting a little murky. "You know Alex?"

"Yes, in a manner of speaking. Did he and Brutus get into some kind of trouble together? Is that why you're here?"

Curiouser and curiouser. "You haven't read the papers this morning."

"I haven't had the chance." He groaned and rubbed his eyes again. "You're telling me they made the papers somehow?"

I decided to hit him with it and see what happened. "Then you don't know Alex is dead?"

He looked up at me, that powerful controlled stare still hard to read. Then again, I make it a habit of reading difficult looks. There was definitely surprise there, possibly even a little dismay?

"You're serious?" he asked.

"Found yesterday in Migorsky Park. It was supposedly predatory. Or at least made to look like that." I was about to mention Brutus's bluster and potential for violence, but felt it might not be the time to accuse Diamond Dicky's son directly of murder.

Hanlon sighed. "That's a shame. I actually liked Alex, what I knew of him." He thought a moment. "And after meeting my son and experiencing his…personality, you think he might have had something to do with it."

The talk was still cordial, so I answered honestly. "The thought had crossed my mind."

Hanlon shook his head and leaned back in his chair. "Mr. Harrison, for all my son's faults, and I am aware they are many, he's simply not a killer. His violent temper is largely bluster that I've become accustomed to paying for, for his mother's sake. I also feel it safe to say he wouldn't have harmed Alex."

"So you weren't worried that he was snooping around your site here?"

The lion gave the barest of shrugs. "There was nothing for him to find. Despite my reputation and any other business endeavors in which I may or may not be involved, this is merely the future of luxury living. For those that can afford it."

"You sure Brutus was aware of that? No chance he might have been trying to do you a favor? Or that his temper got the better of him?"

Hanlon shut me up with a direct stare. "Careful, Mr. Harrison. Your theories could come close to slander. I take it that you and Alex are—were—in the same business. As I've already said, despite the way he handles himself, Brutus would not have harmed Alex. They had recently become friends."

That was where my jaw dropped. "Say again?"

"Allow me to explain and absolve my son in your eyes. We first noticed that a muskrat was watching the site from across the street several weeks ago. Since we had nothing to worry about, we let him be. He didn't disturb work, and my employees merely began to think of him as a regular fixture around here. Then Brutus came to visit me one day and was up in arms that someone was watching the site, asking if he should go 'tune the muskrat up a little' I believe was his phrasing."

"I can believe that."

"So in an effort to show him how we actually do business, I instead had him stay while I invited your friend in for a drink of some very good brandy I keep in my desk drawer. He was perfectly forthcoming about who had hired him and why. The coyote tribe had made no end of trouble for me during the permitting process, claiming this was some 'sacred land' in some way or other. They hired him to try and find another way to shut us down."

"Which according to you, he was never going to."

Hanlon gave a hint of a smile. "Precisely. Everything happening here is perfectly legal down to the last bit of paperwork. No one cares about a bunch of native mumbo-jumbo, but Mr. Richards explained that he was being paid regularly and had to continue gathering information. Nothing personal on anyone's part."

"So Alex would keep watching the place on their dime, and you would just leave him be? And he and your son started, what? Palling around?"

"You should have seen the two of them after a couple drinks. Peas in a pod, strange bedfellows, call it what you will. They started cutting up while we were talking, laughing about the whole thing, and soon Brutus wanted to buy Alex a few more drinks."

I couldn't help a little smile. "Yeah. That was one thing Alex always had going for him. Guy could talk and laugh and make just about anyone feel at ease."

"Indeed, I noticed. I felt it was actually good for Brutus. Seemed to calm him down a little when Alex would make him just laugh something off with a few comments, if the way he talked was any indication. I've had to make fewer trips to Menagerie since then."

That caught my attention. "Menagerie, huh? So that's where they'd go carousing?"

"That was one club among many, yes. Brutus showed Alex to the place one evening I believe. My son says that Alex became quite smitten with a singer there and started spending more time there than in any other club. A fox, if memory serves."

"Can't say I'd blame him; I've met her." Suddenly, something fit into place. "And if Alex is that sweet on her, your son probably wouldn't take kindly if he thought someone was horning in on his friend's action would he?"

Realization came into Hanlon's powerful eyes and he gave a bittersweet sort of smirk. "No. No he definitely wouldn't. I know he's going to take this news very hard. I take it that satisfies what you need to know?"

"Well, it rules a few things out. Thanks for your time, Mr. Hanlon. Sorry if I caused any offense."

"Think nothing of it," he said and studied me for a moment longer. "I take it the reason for these questions is that the police are ineffectual in this matter as they often are in…certain deaths. If your investigation should bear fruit, I would like to hear about it. If need be, I would like to offer any and all resources at my disposal to see justice is done."

I took his meaning loud and clear. "Thank you, Mr. Hanlon. I'll be sure to do that."

"Call me Richard." He rolled his eyes and showed humor for possibly the first time with a little smile. "Or even Dicky if you prefer."

I just chuckled a little and started to head out. "So Alex really had a thing for that fennec, huh?"

"According to Brutus, he was going in to watch her every night after a while, trying to find out everything he could about her."

"Well, she is definitely something."

I walked out of the trailer with a mingled feeling of relief and frustration. I'd ruled something out, but it essentially put me back to square one. Just to be sure, I figured I'd talk to some of the workers, see if the stories matched.

Just about everyone I talked to said the same thing. Alex was a known fixture around the place, and he and the boss's kid were just about bosom buddies after the initial meeting. During a moment when I talked to a burly hippo in a tank top that was spreading concrete smooth, I realized completely that Diamond Dicky was telling the truth and that the Hanlons probably had nothing to do with Alex's death.

I began to wonder about the coyotes that hired Alex. Maybe they wouldn't have taken too kindly to finding out he was having drinks with the people that he was supposed to be watching for them. I knew very little about the culture of the local tribes, but I had to wonder what they might do to someone they saw as a traitor. Maybe they'd each just take a bite of him after he was dead, some kind of symbol of repayment or something. Or maybe I was just grasping at straws.

I needed to clear my head and think things through before I went rushing into someone else's domain again, so I spent the next few hours in my office before heading home. I did the best I could to put Alex out of my head and finish some work on cases that actually paid me. Still, he was always there, at the back of my mind, making me wonder just what could have happened to my friend.

* * *

I grabbed the bag of cheap mixing soil and poured some into the blessedly oversized tub. It was one of the things I insisted on getting, back when Michelle and I were setting up the bungalow. When we were paying for it out of two incomes rather than me barely managing to keep the place with my clients and the little pension I was granted. I turned on the water and started mixing it all up.

Sure, it's part of what creates the ugly rumor that we're dirty, but there's no denying I do my best thinking and relaxing when I'm having a good wallow. The mud just feels nice against my skin, and I even know of some wealthy swine that pay top dollar for imported soil in their own mixing rooms. Personally, I never noticed any difference between that fancy stuff and the basic dirt I got in bulk to make mine.

Once the tub was ready, I sank myself down into it and felt the cool of it all envelope my skin while it warmed slowly. I set my head against the edge of the tub, closed my eyes, and started running through facts.

Fact One: Alex's last case in the notes on his desk had him watching Hanlon Construction's upscale housing development called Regal Acres for a group of coyotes.

Fact Two: The last place Alex was apparently seen alive was Menagerie, and people remembered him.

Fact Three: The good folks down at the Regal Acres site had seen Alex around but none of them ever ventured to Menagerie with Brutus and Alex.

Fact Four: Brutus just wasn't quite cut out as a predatory killer psycho and wasn't a suspect anymore, if Diamond Dicky could be believed.

Fact Five: Diamond Dicky was very believable, and it wasn't in his best interests to leave a body lying around a park when he had a whole host of new foundations in which to store one.

Fact Six: Not one person I talked to at the Regal Acres development seemed to react the wrong way to Alex's death. No one seemed to want him gone or care what he saw.

The more I rolled those through my head, the more I began to think that Menagerie and Regal Acres were just dead ends. The next day, I'd have to look into the people who'd hired Alex. Would they really murder him for being seen with his mark? And what about that doctor he was looking into all the way out in L.A.? I'd have to take some time to look into him too, though it seemed like a long shot. Something still wasn't adding up when I heard the clicking at the front door.

It was smooth, someone working the lock in a way that most people wouldn't notice. But I knew all the noises of my house, and despite my relaxed state to sort things, my nerves were still on edge for any such disturbance after what happened to Alex. I hopped out of the mud bath just as I heard the lock turn and the door open. No time to get dressed for a visitor.

I slipped quietly out of the bathroom and to the closet across from it quickly, using a towel to brush up any hoofprints or drips on the hardwood floor. He was pretty good, moving more quietly than one would expect and coming around a corner just as I'd stopped closing the closet door, leaving a little crack. I'd planned on waiting for him to sniff me out, then rushing him right out of the closet and hoping on the element of surprise. I didn't recognize him as I peered through that crack or as I got a better whiff and took in the smell of badger and cigarettes. He wore a long coat that could easily hide the sawed-off shotgun he was carrying, which grabbed most of my attention.

He wasn't sniffing for me, so I didn't have to leap out of the closet into his face as I expected. No, he headed straight for the bathroom. Which meant he knew exactly where to go and someone—because this was obviously a hitter for hire—had told him that and the time I would likely be most vulnerable. Had he been watching the house? Peering through a window to see when I went into the bathroom so he could do the deed?

The badger opened the door and took a step in, his shotgun raised. I'd guess he planned on firing as soon as he saw his target. Now was the time to move.

I burst out of the closet just about the time he started to relax his shotgun. Despite being slippery, I knew enough of how to handle myself in that condition. I was used to it, which was more than I could say for my would-be killer. I made sure to grab the gun in both trotters and cram it back against him, not giving him the opportunity to gain control and bring it to bear. The badger wrestled with me, displaying some good reflexes and trying to shake me away as he snarled.

I'd love to say that I fought the good fight, bum leg and all, and that I bested the killer: turned his shotgun to him, questioned him, and solved it all when he cracked. But the reality is that he started to push me away and I shoved forward again, already feeling like I was about to lose the struggle. Mud dripped on the tile, and luck intervened when his feet slipped out from under him and I came tumbling with him. He was taller and wider than I am, and the only cracking he did was when head slammed hard into the marble corner of the bathroom sink. As soon as I noticed he was limp under me and I looked up to see the smear of red on that corner, I was pretty sure the fight was over.

It was a little effort to roll him over, and once I saw the wound and the glassy look in his rolled up eyes, I knew the sink had done for him as well as any gun. I'd hoped to get some answers out of this guy, but I wasn't too annoyed. Better to be alive in this case. And I did have other ways of getting information off of him.

Like I mentioned before, I always had one of the best noses in the business. Most pigs do, even though people write us off in a lot of ways in favor of more imposing individuals. That's kind of our major advantage in a world full of creatures that think less of us. They underestimate us in all the ways that can really matter at certain times. So I leaned down to the body to get some answers.

I pushed my snout in close. I worked to separate the mixture of scents into individual components. I pushed past the smell of fresh blood and cordite and tossed them aside. I inhaled the pungent aroma of badger and then mentally set that in another place from some of the other smells. His still warm body told a tale of all the places he'd been. He'd indeed been to Menagerie as well as a few other places in the city I could sort out. I needed more though. I needed to find every individual scent as I snuffled over him, thinking only of how to identify each one.

Then I finally found it. A unique bouquet of something I recognized from the last couple days, and just underneath that, something that should have been impossible. Once I sorted those out, the rest of my brain began running the numbers on everything that had been right in front of me the whole time. I thought I had a pretty good idea what happened to Alex. I thought there was a chance I'd just destroyed the weapon, but not the actual hand that had wanted him dead.

If I was right, there was nothing I could really prove to the authorities, no evidence I could bring to Grimaldi that would give him the power to follow the lead further. But I could do enough to confirm it for myself before I did anything rash.

As for the body, I just closed the door to the bathroom for the time being. Odds were good he wasn't the sort of guy someone would report to Missing Persons anytime soon, so he could keep. If push really came to shove, I knew of several ways to get rid of a body. Yet another thing people don't think of when it comes to pigs.

I found a clock and headed for my phone. Getting cleaned up would also have to wait just a little bit. It was already settling into evening, but it wasn't quite so late on the West Coast, and I had a long distance call to make.

* * *

I took a back door into the club. It was late enough that most of the crowd had gone, but I was hoping one person would still be there. Hoped that the customers had cleared away but that some of the staff were still closing up.

Moving through a dingy back hall, I found what I was pretty sure was the door I was looking for. I could hear the sounds of tables being broken down in the front, making enough noise that I wouldn't be noticed. More importantly, light was still streaming out from under that door.

My leg hurt like hell, and I just wanted to go home, but I pushed open that door. It didn't even creak, but the little cardboard star someone had hung on it did flap a little. When I closed it behind me, the fennec jumped and turned in her dressing chair. Her eyes went wide. She hadn't even had time to get out of her dress yet.

"D-Detective!" Lucy said, forgetting to put that sultry, smoky sound into her voice. She recovered quickly. "You startled me. I didn't expect you to pay me a personal visit."

She was doing pretty good. Not a trace of nervousness in her voice after the initial shock, just that same coy attitude from before.

"No, I imagine you didn't," I said casually, my fingers hooked into my belt and pulling my coat back. "Especially not after you sent that cheap bruiser to try and tie up loose ends."

She turned back away from me, making a show of nonchalantly taking off some jewelry. "I don't know what you're referring to. Were you attacked in some manner? You should go to the police."

"You played it so cool that first night I came in, I had a hard time believing the truth myself. You made just enough mistakes though. I'm sure it's easy for you to get guys to do anything if you get close to them, maybe make them think they can get a little piece of the action. But something rubs off when you do that. Especially when you're not drenched in that expensive perfume yet." I took another step closer. "And you still love your gimlets, Michelle."

That froze her. If I had needed any more proof, that would have been it. It was only for a second, but it was enough.

"I...I don't know who—"

"Save it!" I scoffed, with an angry snort. I tried to calm myself down. I didn't want to startle her too much. "You're the same height. Just a little work would have fixed your ears, not too difficult. And it's pretty easy to go from brown to russet and change your pattern just a little. Though I bet that new muzzle and those teeth cost you a pretty penny. That is something Doctor Rennick out in Los Angeles specializes in, isn't it?" I'm sure after a while, I sounded more hurt than furious. "Turning people into something they're not, for Hollywood."

Her head drooped. She didn't speak for almost a minute. I half expected her to keep up the act, to shout for someone out front, but instead she just sighed. "Not officially. No one wants records of surgery like this. He...does it off the books if you have enough. But you can work something out if you're willing to..." She shuddered a little. I didn't need her to continue.

"Why, Michelle?"

"That's not my name anymore, dammit," she growled through clenched teeth, almost trying to remind herself. "I'm Lucy." I was only now seeing the way the agitated twitching of her tail through the hole in the seat didn't look natural.

"Why all of this, then? We were happy together. We could have been...could have been even more. Why create this new person?"

"Happy?" she said with more than a little scorn. "You think constantly living under a cloud of worry is happy? You think knowing that neither of us could ever protect the other is happy? Imagining what someone might do to us as soon as they saw you limping alongside me on a bad night? You think it wouldn't have happened someday, eventually, to a couple like us?"

"You mean like what happened to Alex?"

She quieted then, her shoulders dropping again and her scorn spent. My chest was already heavy from hearing her say those things, but I had to press on.

"Did you do it yourself, or did you send some bruiser after him too?" I asked, almost not wanting the answer.

She hesitated a moment. "He... He came into the club the other night. Not to enjoy the place, but because he'd finally figured it out. It was when he'd heard me sing 'This Nose Knows' that he got suspicious. I hadn't even thought when I put it in my set how much I used to sing bits of it when...before. He had a few drinks while he was waiting to make sure it was me, then he came into this room. Told me how he'd done his research, found out who I was. Once I spilled it and begged him not to say anything, he said he was going to tell you, and he left. I followed him. He'd had enough to drink that he was willing to walk through that park at night. I wasn't going to hurt him, was just going to beg him not to say anything. It's... It's even worse for someone who tries to pass for what they're not than being...what we are."

She was actually crying, though I couldn't tell if they were genuine tears of remorse or just another lie.

"After I was following him for a bit," she continued, "Alex turned. He started screaming at me. Telling me how I broke your heart. He was angrier than I'd ever seen him. I had a knife I kept in my bag. These claws are for show; they're useless for protection. I got it out. I just wanted to scare him off or threaten him or I don't really know what. Things just got more heated and he tried to leave again, and I was so scared of what would happen, and... and..."

"And then he was bleeding on the ground—somehow," I finished for her.

She still wouldn't look at me from her chair and nodded.

"Then you had to cover it up," I said and paused for a moment. I had assumed some bruiser, possibly even the badger that showed up at my place, had maybe done the deed and definitely done the clean-up. But she'd just said they were alone...and there hadn't been time to find someone...

I felt the bottom drop out of my stomach while I took a step closer to actually see her teeth. "So you actually used your new pearly whites to take care of that. Realized how lucky you were that the alcohol would cover your scent."

To her credit, Michelle gagged at the memory. "I knew what it had to look like. I knew the sort of thing the police wouldn't dig too deep into. You'd ranted and raved about it enough times before." She had to take several breaths. "It was...awful. I did as much as I could. Spit most of it into my bag, then threw it into a dumpster. And the taste...oh, God, I can still almost taste it! Nothing washes it out! *Nothing!*"

She was about to go into hysterics; I could tell. She'd been pushing it all down, trying to go on, but now it was out. Her body was hitching, her ears twitching, and that vulpine muzzle she'd traded so much for was working up and down like she was about to really scream.

I had all I needed and reached into my coat pocket. I tossed the envelope from it onto the dressing table in front of her. It caught her off guard enough to stop her hysterics. She was curious now, a shaky paw reaching for it.

I'm pretty sure Michelle was about to ask what was in it when the shot went off. I put the gun right to her temple so that she wouldn't feel a thing. It was an unregistered throwaway, something I'd actually learned while working with the police. Brains and blood were already splattered to the side of the room and her body sat there limp while I wiped any trace of myself off of the snub-nosed revolver and dropped it to the floor next to her chair. The whole thing took just a couple seconds, and I beat hooves out the back door before the sound of running feet could even come close to her room.

The envelope contained a typed confession, a suicide note. It included how she'd wanted to sing just one more night before ending it all. It explained who she actually was, and the things she'd done. Well, more or less. At the time I wrote it out, I didn't know just how far she'd gone to try and cover her tracks. Even if I had, I still probably wouldn't have included that. I wrote that she'd hired some thug to gnaw at Alex, and that's where it would stay. Most of the truth would come out, but Michelle wouldn't have to live under it.

I'd briefly thought about calling Diamond Dicky for some of those resources he'd promised. I didn't want her to suffer whatever they'd put her through though. This had turned out to be something so personal that I had to take care of it myself.

I didn't do it out of love lost or love unrequited. I did it for Alex Richards. A loud-mouthed, overweight muskrat who drank a little too much. A guy that also picked me up in the darkest days, when all I wanted to do was just lie down and do nothing. A friend who apparently cared more about my broken heart than I ever knew. Who'd gone above and beyond to try and fix it and ended up bagged and tagged because of it.

The way I looked at it, my cute, nervous rabbit died just a couple years after she left me, and I'd mourned her for a few years more. What I'd done was put down a deranged vixen that murdered one of my best friends to keep her secret. Her death would be an open-and-shut case of suicide, just like a muskrat's death might have been an open-and-shut case of a random predatory murder.

No one saw me leave that alley. I trundled on home in the dark, with a few secrets to take with me to the grave someday. Yet thankfully, my leg wasn't bothering me nearly as much as it usually did.

The Mesoamericans—the Mayas, Aztecs, Toltecs, Zapotecs, Tlaxcalteca, and other pre-Columbian North and Central American peoples—had many gods. The important ones were mostly human, but many of their minor gods were animals. The nineteen months of the Mayan calendar included several named after animal gods such as K'ayab the turtle, Muwan' the owl, Xul the dog, and Zotz the bat.

According to Wikipedia, "In Aztec mythology, the Centzon Totochtin are a group of divine rabbits who meet for frequent drunken parties." They are the children of Patecatl the fertility god and Mayahuel, the goddess in charge of the maguey plant, a principal ingredient of tequila. So non-stop drunken parties with booze and sex comes naturally to them.

But what happens when one of the Centzon Totochtin—the four hundred rabbits—decides that there should be more to life than drunken revelry?

400 Rabbits

by Alice "Huskyteer" Dryden

Eighty-Six-Rabbit woke up with a hangover. As far as he could remember, he had woken up with a hangover every morning since he and his three hundred and ninety-nine siblings, the Centzon Totochtin, were born of the union between Patecatl, god of fermentation, and Mayahuel, goddess of alcohol. It didn't seem to be getting any more enjoyable.

He wobbled his nose, sending ripples of pain across his skull like wind through a field of maize, and lolloped unsteadily over to the big obsidian mirror. His eyes might have been two beads of dried blood, the skin inside his ears was pale, and when he poked out his tongue it was frosted with white.

"This has got to stop," he said to himself.

"Hey! Keep the noise down!" Three-Twenty-Three-Rabbit staggered into the burrow, still clutching an empty bottle which had, at some stage, contained pulque. "What a night, huh? That was one amazing party. Wasn't it?"

"Was it?" Eighty-Six-Rabbit eyeballed his brother. Late-born and late-numbered, Three-Twenty-Three was ranked among the lowest in seniority of the four hundred sibling gods. The real big quesos, Twelve-Rabbit and upwards, wouldn't even have given him the time of day. He had a nerve, telling Eighty-Six to keep it down.

"What was so great about it?" Eighty-Six asked. "Tell me one thing."

One of Three-Twenty-Three's ears drooped. He pushed it upright with a paw, only for the other to flop down over his eye.

"Well...there was...how about..." He scratched his whiskers. "Actually, Eightsy, I can't remember the first thing about it. And that's what made it so amazing!" he finished triumphantly.

"Don't you ever want to do something different with your evenings? And don't call me Eightsy."

"Different?" Three-Twenty-Three's eyes bugged out as he thought. "Like...drinking mezcal instead of pulque?"

"No, I mean, like dancing. Playing rubberball. Going to watch a human sacrifice. We could even just stay in and talk. When was the last time two of us had a conversation that wasn't about who took the last aspirin?"

"But what about our duties?"

Each of the rabbit siblings was in charge of a particular aspect of drunkenness. Eighty-Six was the god of attempting to chat up your best friend's betrothed. His favorite sister Fifty-Five was the goddess of attempting to chat up your best friend. Three-Twenty-Three, being a more junior rabbit, was responsible for the inability to tie your shoelaces. Since shoelaces would not come to Mesoamerica for another three hundred years, he was frequently at a loose end.

"We don't all need to be at every single party, all the time. I'm pretty sure a few of us could take the night off every now and then."

Eighty-Six became uncomfortably aware that Three-Twenty-Three was wearing the expression of someone who has opened a bottle of pulque, only for the god Quetzalcoatl to fly out of it in the form of a winged serpent.

"I just think there might be more to life than getting drunk," he concluded.

"More to life than...!" Three-Twenty-Three's eyes bulged, and he clapped a paw over his mouth. Eighty-Six thought he was probably going to be sick, but instead he went haring out of the burrow and down the warren, tripping over his paws and crashing into walls as he tried to hop and thump his hind foot for danger at the same time.

"Two-Rabbit, Two-Rabbit!" he yelled. "Come quick! Eighty-Six-Rabbit has lost his mind!"

Two-Rabbit was the leader of the siblings, and, on the frequent occasions when their parents were busy with other affairs of fermentation and alcohol, represented their ultimate authority. None of the three hundred and ninety-nine had ever seen One-Rabbit; legend had it that the moment he was birthed he had embarked upon a binge of such divine proportions that his corporeal elements had fractured across space and time, allowing him simultaneously to attend every party since the age of the Jaguar Sun, as well as those yet to come. This bending of the laws of the universe was thought to be the origin of the term 'bender'.

"This had better be good," Two-Rabbit pronounced, glaring at Eighty-Six, Three-Twenty-Three, and sundry brothers and sisters who had popped out of their burrows to see what was going on. "I'm trying to draw up the duty roster for the party Tlazolteotl, Goddess of Sexual Misdeeds And Their Forgiveness, is holding tonight."

That was a top gig. The rabbits drew themselves up, trying to look alert, bright-eyed, and ready to party; not easy when the effects of the last party are still draining from your system.

"I'm just saying." Eighty-Six swallowed. "I know we do important work, helping people relax, enjoy themselves and make stupid, regrettable decisions, but we've been doing it since we were born and, frankly, it's getting a bit dull. Tiring, too. I'm sure we'd all be better for a night off every once in a while. Maybe stay in and read a good codex. The humans have invented this stuff called cocoa, it's quite nice apparently…"

Two-Rabbit's bloodshot eyes looked him disapprovingly up and down, and Eighty-Six trembled.

"Eighty-Six-Rabbit, you are a deity. An anthropomorphic personification of drunkenness, no less. Anthropomorphic personifications of drunkenness don't get bored. We don't get tired. And we don't put our feet up with a mug of hot mashed beans when we could be out partying!" Her glare swept the assembled rabbits, daring them to disagree. "Am I right?"

There were hasty cheers. Paws punched the air.

"Party! Party! Party!"

With a twitch of her ears, Two-Rabbit silenced the chant.

"Eighty-Six-Rabbit, I am disappointed in you," she said. "This is not the behavior I expect from a rabbit of double figures."

Eighty-Six waited to see what punishment would be meted out. He had heard that Two-Rabbit could demote her siblings to more menial jobs, though it hadn't happened for centuries. He didn't fancy being the divine personification of slamming your finger in the taxi door, or of why not make it a vindaloo instead of a madras.

"Since you think so little of our sacred customs," Two-Rabbit continued, "you are welcome to try this crazy notion of 'sobriety'. But you will try it away from here, so none of your brothers and sisters are tempted to follow your example. Depart, now, and return when you have learned some sense."

Eighty-Six hopped slowly up the warren and into the world above, his white tail bouncing as he went. His sibling gods watched him go with twitching noses and quivering whiskers, but nobody said a word. Only Three-Twenty-Three mouthed something that might have been 'sorry'.

* * *

"Sobriety," Eighty-Six-Rabbit said out loud. Until Two-Rabbit used the word, he had not even known how to describe the opposite of drunkenness. Now, for only the fourth time in his life, he was sober to watch the sun go down.

That first drink-less night had been hard. It wasn't just the longing for pulque, a hunger and thirst rolled into one that no amount of cocoa, maize or beans could sate. Only his fierce determination had kept Eighty-Six dry. In the end, he had broken leaves off a maguey plant and drunk the honey-water, the base from which pulque was made, just to get the faintest shadow of the taste which had been mother's milk to him.

What was a divine sober rabbit supposed to do in the evenings? It was all very well to talk about rubberball and priestly ceremonies, and on the second evening, when he felt a little less like a dried-up husk of last year's corn than he had on the first, Eighty-Six tried both these entertainments. But they were no fun without his brothers and sisters there to talk to. Besides, whenever someone in the audience opened a bottle of pulque, he felt the pull of his divine duty to keep them company, and he had to move away before one of his siblings showed up.

The next night he tried going to a dance, but it seemed nobody could do anything fun without involving alcohol, and he crept away early. He made himself a nest in the grass and tried to sleep through the partying hours, but he was too used to keeping nocturnal time to get much rest. As soon as the sun rose he started walking, in the hope of tiring himself out before the next empty night.

Foregoing pulque was still hard, but he had become used to his body's grumbles about it. Worse than the pain of sobering up, right now, was the pain of homesickness. He missed his brothers and sisters powerfully. Of course they had argued; how could they not, with three hundred and ninety-nine of them, plus the mysterious One-Rabbit who may or may not have been present, all crammed into a burrow, and all in a permanent state of either inebriation or its aftermath? But Eighty-Six, like all rabbits, was a sociable creature. The world felt very cold and silent without the warmth and noise of his family. He wanted to sing off-key with Two-Hundred-Four while Thirty-Three played the log drum. He wanted to be grabbed round the middle by One-Hundred-Fifty-Three, who got all huggy after the first few bottles. He wanted to discuss the question of life, the universe and everything with Forty-Two. He wanted to form a line with his paws on the hips of the rabbit in front and conga until his feet left the earth and they were dancing across the sky, the way they did at particularly good parties when the entire tribe was gathered together. That always really annoyed the Four Hundred Gods of the Southern Stars, snooty, fun-hating bunch that they were.

He missed his job, too. He hadn't asked to quit, just to take a little time off every now and then. Sure, it had been hard, but at least he went to bed feeling as if he'd achieved something. On the occasions when he could remember going to bed, that is. He had been good at his job; everyone had said so, even Two-Rabbit, before she cast him out. Who was encouraging partygoers to chat up their best friends' betrotheds now? Three-Twenty-Three, probably. He was bound to be making a mess of it.

Weary of his wandering and his thoughts, Eighty-Six lay down on the side of a hill and stared at the sky. He had never before noticed the colors, how the daytime blue faded through yellows and pinks to the deep red of blood, then a rich indigo across which trod the moon and the stars. The breeze brought him scents of flowers and the nighttime noises of scurrying animals.

With a bottle in his paw and few dozen of his favorite siblings around him, it would have been just perfect.

Maybe if he went back and told Two-Rabbit he was really, really sorry...

"No," Eighty-Six said to the moon and stars. He'd only been trying for four nights; he wasn't about to admit defeat. He just needed to stop hanging around the places that reminded him of home—and anywhere alcohol might be found. Let Two-Rabbit wonder and worry about what had happened to him, if she cared. He had already discovered sunsets. Now Eighty-Six was going to find out what else there was in the world.

After that night, he avoided human and divine company alike. He wandered the arid regions and the lush, tropical forests, climbed cloud-capped mountains, and swam in the turquoise sea. Lonely though he was, he could not help noticing the new clearness in his mind, and his sharpened senses. The foods he ate tasted better than they had done when his tongue was dulled with pulque. He was awake for sunrise and sunset, and he could enjoy both without screwing his eyes up in agony. When he hopped and skipped in the sand, he neither lost his balance and fell over nor felt as if his head might be going to come off.

Above all, he could think properly. His brain was like a cocoa bean freshly popped from the woolly enclosure of its pod, all glossy and gleaming. He could remember things he had long forgotten, like obscure minor deities with seven-syllable names. He composed little songs and poems in his head as he travelled. To pass the time, he listed his siblings in numerical order, analyzed their characters, and remembered a nice thing about each of them. The sights he had seen and the thoughts he had had during the course of one day, he actually remembered when the sun came up again. What's more, they were worth remembering.

It was in this state that he happened upon Tlacuache, the opossum, whose place in the world was to create rivers. No one was entirely sure how this task had fallen to him, but he was pretty good at it, for an opossum. One moment Eighty-Six saw something gleaming in the distance, the next he heard a rumble, and before he knew it a river was flowing past him, with Tlacuache panting after it.

"Oh, no, you don't, friend Rabbit," said Tlacuache when he saw him. He held up a pink paw. "I know who you are—you're one of the Centzon Totochtin. Well, I can't get drunk today. I have to finish this river. Isn't she a beauty?"

They admired it together as it coursed across the plain, straight and wide, and glittering like a lost temple full of treasure.

"Don't worry, Tlacuache. I'm not here in an official capacity. I'm... taking a break."

The opossum's beady little eyes grew beadier and littler, but he didn't press Eighty-Six for the details.

"Want to help me for a while?" he offered.

"Sure."

So they drove the water across the plain, herding it along the correct path as it carved a channel and flowed into it. Sometimes Tlacuache grabbed himself a fish, while Eighty-Six-Rabbit nibbled the plants that sprang up along the banks. When evening came they rested and watched the sunset together. Eighty-Six, exhausted from his hard work, fell asleep at Tlacuache's side. In the morning, when Tlacuache asked if he would help him again, he readily agreed.

Together, they brought water down from the mountains and across the deserts. Plants sprang up in their wake, and little fish jumped for joy in the currents. Eighty-Six and Tlacuache caught the fattest and least cautious of them for dinner. With each river, Eighty-Six had lasting, physical proof that he had helped to do something good. His old job never delivered that, although he supposed there were a few happily married couples out there who, without realizing it, had Eighty-Six to thank for their union.

The opossum was peaceful company, and he called Eighty-Six-Rabbit simply Rabbit, as there was no need to distinguish him from his brothers and sisters. He taught his new friend to make cocoa, and they drank it while they watched the sun sink into their river, turning it blood-red, and the moon rise to coat the ripples in silver. Life was…cozy.

One evening, as they dangled their feet in the day's newborn river, Eighty-Six-Rabbit told Tlacuache all that had happened. The opossum listened quietly, with the occasional nod or hiss.

"I'm sorry for your troubles, Rabbit. I really am," he said at last.

"It's not your fault."

"Well, it kind of is. You see, I invented pulque. Didn't you know?"

Eighty-Six-Rabbit supposed that he had known, once, before the fog of alcohol took the knowledge from him.

"I gave it to the humans and they really ran with it. Hit it right out of the rubberball park." Tlacuache whiffled his nose. "I sometimes wonder if I did the right thing."

"Keeps them busy, I suppose."

Tlacuache nodded. "Beats all that war stuff. They haven't got the recipe quite right yet, though. Mine's still better."

"Yeah?"

The opossum produced a bottle. "Try for yourself…oh. I suppose not."

He sighed deeply, pulled off the bamboo stopper with his teeth, and upended the bottle. Eighty-Six watched his white throat bob as he swallowed. It had been a long day of river creation; he was hot, tired, and most of all thirsty.

"I suppose one can't hurt," he said. "Just…open it quietly. I don't want any of my siblings showing up."

When he woke, the sunlight stabbed at his eyes, and he slammed them shut again. Why was his burrow so bright? Then he remembered, and cautiously raised his eyelids to see Tlacuache peering anxiously down at him.

"I guess your tolerance isn't what it was," said the opossum, helping Eighty-Six to sit up. "Are you all right, Rabbit?"

"What did we do last night?"

Tlacuache didn't answer. Eighty-Six stared out across the landscape. It was moving and shimmering, and it continued to move and shimmer even after he blinked hard and rubbed his eyes. He held a paw in front of his face. It was in perfect focus.

He looked again. From horizon to horizon, a wide band of shining water ran. It looped. It meandered. It went back on itself. It even flowed briefly uphill, though as Eighty-Six watched it ran out of energy and fell back, leaving a lake behind.

"Yeah." Tlacuache scratched the back of his head and yawned. "We made a river."

* * *

Eighty-Six-Rabbit said goodbye to Tlacuache, and apologized for the river.

"Don't worry about it! Happens to me all the time!" Tlacuache said. "Are you sure you want to go? You've been a big help."

Eighty-Six took a last, wistful look at the bright morning and its brand-new river, then shook his head.

"No—I need to go back and do my duty. Two-Rabbit was right; you can take the drunken rabbit god out of the party, but you can't take the party out of the drunken rabbit god."

And he hopped away, while Tlacuache watched him go from the river bank.

It was a long journey back to the warren, and all Eighty-Six wanted when he arrived was a nice eight-hour nap in his burrow, but when he arrived he found that Ninety-Two had promoted herself into it. By the time he had kicked her out, with a great deal of noise and foot-thumping, it was evening, and the rabbits' duties were beginning. Eighty-Six checked the roster and found he had been already been assigned to a party in the Underworld, which suited him fine; he was feeling pretty low anyway.

The Lord and Lady of the Underworld welcomed them with open arm bones. As the pulque began to flow, Eighty-Six felt himself growing loud and brash and happy, just like he used to be. Warmth spread through his body. Why had he cut himself off from who he was? This worked. This was right. He couldn't escape his destiny? Well, then, he would embrace it. He would be the loudest, brashest, happiest drunk of the family. He would drink more and party harder than any other rabbit.

He shook himself from ears to tail, and resumed his role as if he had never left it. Now he had tasted Tlacuache's original recipe, the regular mortal pulque was as water to him, and he downed it at a rate that astonished his siblings and had the Lady of the Underworld checking the cellar anxiously in case her supplies ran out.

As he urged a recently deceased spirit to try it on with the long-dead fiancé of her best friend, on the grounds that the best friend was scheduled for several decades more of a long and happy life, he felt the thrill that comes with doing your job, and doing it well.

It was a long, loud and successful party, which broke up only when the God of the Morning Star had to leave in order to create the new dawn. Then Tonatiuh, Lord of the Sun, said he'd better be going too, and the rabbits went home. Except for Twenty-Rabbit, the deity of Risky Showing Off, who accompanied Tonatiuh for a while in the hope of persuading him to bounce the sun along the sky instead of carrying it as usual.

The resulting hangover wasn't easy to shake. It took several bottles of pulque, so that when Eighty-Six arrived at the next night's party he was already feeling lively. It was only a mortal wedding, but it ended up lasting nine days, during which time no fewer than fifty of the guests made advances on their best friends' betrothed. Of these, thirty-two were coldly rebuffed, six were slapped, eight were removed from the happy couple's Atemoztli card list, and four discovered that they and their best friend's betrothed had, in fact, been made for each other all along.

From then on, Eighty-Six's status as the guarantor of a great evening was legendary. Gods and goddesses booked his presence at their parties months in advance. He did feast days, wakes, birthdays and religious ceremonies, although for some reason he was never in great demand at engagement parties. He drank and danced with his brothers and sisters, and carried on long after they had collapsed. He slept through sunset and partied until the morning star had faded into the day. He had no time to sober up between parties, so he suffered no aches, pains or troubling thoughts, and he forgot that he had ever wandered the world as a solitary rabbit. Once or twice, when the room was whirling hard around him, he even thought that he glimpsed the shadowy form of One-Rabbit, always dancing a few steps ahead and out of reach.

He might have gone on this way for all of eternity, if one evening he hadn't staggered, pleasantly buzzed, into the wrong burrow, and found Three-Twenty-Three frantically splashing water over his ears.

"What's wrong, bro?"

Three-Twenty-Three turned his bedraggled head.

"Oh, hey, it's the poster boy for alcohol poisoning. Don't worry. You wouldn't understand."

Eighty-Six took a seat with the exaggerated care of the drunk pretending to be sober. "Try me."

"I'm tired, Eightsy. My throat's like sandpaper and if you picked me up by my tail, my eyeballs would fall out. I don't think I can get through another night of this."

Eighty-Six crinkled his forehead. A memory from the dim and sober past was thundering towards him, flooding his mind with the force and brightness of a river flowing true.

"Have you ever seen a sunset?" he asked his brother. "Really seen it?" He reached out a paw to smooth Three-Twenty-Three's rumpled fur.

"Hey, knock it off. I'm not your best friend's betrothed, you know."

"Oh, please. I mean: let's take the night off."

Three-Twenty-Three stared at him with bulging eyes, just as he had so long ago, but this time the eyes were filled with hope.

Eighty-Six made cocoa, and the two rabbits sat cozily together as their siblings set off for their assigned parties. They enjoyed a pleasant conversation, went to bed early, and awoke to watch the sun come up. Nobody appeared to have noticed their absence, since three hundred and ninety-nine rabbits are hard to keep track of, although Eighty-Six's favorite sister Fifty-Five did tell him that if he didn't wipe that self-satisfied smirk from his muzzle and stop looking so indecently cheerful, she would clock him one.

That night he threw himself back into the proper lifestyle as if the break had only sharpened his thirst, and the next night, and the next. The night after that, he noticed that One-Four-Four was looking a little ragged around the edges, and he took her dancing. When he woke refreshed, Two-Hundred-Eighteen, who had feasted on flatbread and milk before going out and thus remained more sober than his siblings, asked him if he fancied playing a board game.

Word spread, and soon more of his brothers and sisters came in secret to question him about the mysteries of time off. Eighty-Six found himself writing down cocoa recipes, and then organizing a rubberball league. In order to fit all this into his daylight hours, he drank less at night, so he spent less of his free time feeling like a hollowed-out gourd. He even began, when he found one of his siblings drinking hard on the eve of an important match, to tap them on the shoulder and suggest they call it a night.

It wasn't long before he extended his services to the human and divine partygoers, whispering a hint into receptive ears that stopping now would result in an evening of slurred speech and pleasantly lowered inhibitions, rather than an embarrassing scene, apologies, cleaning bills, and nicknames like Mixcoatl Who Should Not Mix Pulque And Mezcal.

Curiously, he was more in demand than ever before.

As he hopped down the warren on the eve of the rubberball finals, feeling better than he had for centuries, he caught sight of a paw sticking out from one of the burrows. It clasped a bottle of pulque, and it trembled. Automatically, Eighty-Six reached for the bottle.

"You!" The head and shoulders of Two-Rabbit emerged from the burrow, followed by the rest of her. Her eyes glowed dull and red, and her upper lip was pulled back to show her buck teeth. Eighty-Six noticed for the first time how sharp her claws were—for drawing up the rotas, he supposed.

Eighty-Six had known he was living on borrowed time. His actions could not forever escape the notice of Two-Rabbit, who made it her business to know the departures, arrivals and blood alcohol levels of all her siblings, and now he had delivered himself to her on a golden platter. If he apologized right now, and downed a few pulques for good measure, he might escape demotion to God of Projectile Vomiting, which was the nastiest thing he could dream up at the moment.

Instead, he tightened his grip on Two-Rabbit's bottle, and drew it from her grasp with a firm, practiced motion.

"How dare you, Eighty-Six-Rabbit? I'm going to make you the God of Being Projectile Vomited Upon! What have you got to say for yourself?"

Two-Rabbit was larger than the other siblings, so that Eighty-Six had to stand on his hind legs to look her in the eye, and speak the six words that would undoubtedly seal his doom.

"When did it stop being fun?"

Two-Rabbit's top and bottom teeth clicked together. Eighty-Six covered his eyes with his paws and braced for the attack. When it didn't come, he peeped cautiously through his claws at Two-Rabbit. She was shaking.

"When...when One-Rabbit left," she whispered. "When he left me in charge of you all. I draw up the rotas and then I have a drink to forget what a dull job it is, and to wash away all the complaints I get from rabbits who think they deserve to go to different, better parties, and then I have to get up and do it all over again, day after day until Huitzilopochtli is born of Coatlicue to destroy us all."

Eighty-Six blinked. He hadn't known about Huitzilopochtli, and he didn't much care for the knowledge.

"I've worked so hard," Two-Rabbit continued, staring glassily at a point above Eighty-Six's head, "and I still can't keep up with One-Rabbit. I can't even keep up with you!" She swung her gaze back to her brother. It was filled with loathing, but also, Eighty-Six thought, with fear.

"Me? I haven't had a drink for..." Eighty-Six tried to work it out. He hadn't deliberately stopped drinking; it had just happened, as he found other things to do. "It doesn't matter!" he burst out, as it dawned on him that it really didn't. "We don't need to be drunk all the time. What's fun and free about that?"

"I think you'll find," Two-Rabbit said, shuffling her paws, "that 'drunken rabbit god' is both your classification and your job description."

"We're the gods of partying! You said so yourself! Shouldn't things be a little more relaxed? Why can't we party because we want to, not because we have to?"

"This is anarchy, little brother. We were put into this world to preside over social situations where alcohol is present." Two-Rabbit was sounding dangerously like her usual self again.

"And we're doing it. Have you heard anyone, god or mortal, complain that their parties didn't have enough drunken rabbits? Someone's always in the mood, even if they're not on the rota. It just works. This is what you were afraid of, isn't it? This is why you sent me away when I suggested we might all drink a bit less. You didn't want anyone to sober up and discover the secret—that we don't need the rotas, and we don't need you."

It was a long time since Eighty-Six had made such a long speech. With three hundred and ninety-eight siblings, he hadn't had much opportunity. That was probably why his mouth was so dry.

Two-Rabbit lay on the floor of the warren, deflated. Her ears lay flat and limp along her back, and her eyes were like obsidian mirrors.

"Then what am I supposed to do?" she asked.

"There's a whole world out there, Two-Rabbit. Take a break. Wander. Learn to play the turtle drum. You can even make rivers!"

"That's disgusting, Eighty-Six."

"Not like that!" He cocked an ear. Somewhere in the distance, above his head, he heard the sound of rushing water. If Two-Rabbit hurried, she would catch up with Tlacuache before night fell. "Go on! Quick, before anyone sees you!"

Two-Rabbit hesitated. "You'll be all right without me?"

"Of course. We're drunken rabbit gods! We're always all right!"

He touched noses with his sister, then Two-Rabbit hopped away to where the golden late-afternoon light was spilling into the warren. She didn't look back.

Eighty-Six was still holding the bottle of pulque he had confiscated from Two-Rabbit. He inspected it. Talking Two-Rabbit around had been hard, thirsty work. If ever a rabbit deserved a drink, he deserved one now.

"Come on, Eightsy!" Three-Twenty-Three scampered past him. "The first match is about to start!"

He put the bottle down, and lolloped after his brother. Maybe he'd feel like a drink tomorrow, and maybe he wouldn't. Maybe he'd party all night and maybe he'd stay in. There was room in his life for both. And for sunsets. Always for sunsets.

Who is the real super-hero? Rob Cantor or John Pierce?

Or both of them?

The Torch

by Chris "Sparf" Williams

Rob's hackles rose as he stared down the escalator at the wide hallway outside of the main ballroom that served as the autograph area. The multitude of people in a relatively small space produced a wide array of scents that was difficult for his canine nose to process. That said nothing of the occasional attendee who lacked some fundamental hygiene. No matter how many times he made these appearances he always had to fight down his instinctive desire to flee. The Dalmatian desperately wanted a drink. He adjusted his tan sport coat to distract him from those thoughts.

The fidgeting of the short, pudgy, young corgi standing next to him on the escalator as they descended snapped him out of thoughts of an early morning drink. He tried really hard not to drink while "on the job," and besides, the stuff was so strong that one drink was about all he could stand.

Rob leaned a little more heavily on the escalator railing for support than he used to. His lower back hurt him nearly constantly, and he'd lost some of the upper range of his hearing. The corgi was probably a third of Rob's age, if that, and nearly two feet shorter. Rob chuckled to himself; the handlers at these things kept getting younger. The corgi stared determinedly forward, risking little sidelong glances when he thought the older dog wasn't looking.

"So, you're my handler for the whole convention?" Rob asked. "What's your name?"

"I'm Jake. And yes, I'm with you for the whole convention. They wanted to assign staff on a rotating basis, but I told them that it was a good idea to keep a single staff member with a guest through the entire con, that way they get to know the person they're working with."

Rob reached behind him and rubbed futilely at the dull ache in his lower back.

"Sounds like a plan, Jake," he said, reaching out to shake the young corgi's paw. The corgi took his timidly but excitedly, giving it a firm shake.

"I hope you don't mind ending up a little bored. My table isn't so much a big draw these days."

"Are you kidding, Mr. Cantor? You're Captain Electron! Your show was awesome! I still pull out my old VHS tapes and watch the reruns I taped as a pup! I used to tell my little cousin about your adventures as bedtime stories! He liked them better than any old fairy tale."

The corgi was practically vibrating.

Rob chuckled and shook his head. "I was Captain Electron. Now I'm just this guy, you know? By the way, you can call me Rob if you want."

Rob pulled up his chair at the table and began placing neat stacks of publicity photos in even rows while he waited for Jake to stop panting madly. Rob glanced in both directions, taking in the lay of the land in the signing hall. His table was located in the corner of the end farthest from the escalators. Not the most ideal location, but the fans would make their way back to him.

* * *

"Mommy, Captain Electron's here, let's go! Let's go!"

The little Dalmatian's shouting caused Rob's ears to perk up. He sat up straighter in his chair and looked over the table at the pup, readying his biggest kid-friendly smile. The boy was just tall enough to see the copies of Rob's reproduction photos over the top of the table.

"Well, hello there!"

The pup paused, cocking his head.

"Who're you?"

"I'm Captain Electron! See?" Rob held up a photo of himself in the old costume, grinning and looking every bit the consummate superhero.

"You're not Captain Electron! You're too old!" the little boy barked. To their credit his parents, dressed the way parents who don't go to conventions dress when they go to conventions, reacted quickly. The mother shushed the child and led him away to the line to see the "real" Captain Electron. The father shuffled awkwardly, offering Rob a shrug and a forced smile.

"I'm sorry—"

Rob raised a hand. "No worries, son. It happens sometimes."

"I am going to get him started on your series soon, but I really wanted to see the new movie and I didn't have a pup sitter and—"

"Like I said, it's fine. Stop by later."

The father gave another quick nod and a smile, rushing to catch up with his wife. They wouldn't be back, Rob knew that. They were here to rush through, get John Pierce's autograph, and get out.

The former Captain Electron glanced down at the convention guidebook that had been left for him. Front and center on the cover was John Pierce as Captain Electron, with an old pulp-style cover design surrounding him and praising his virtue. Along the bottom, in what Rob always thought of as the "But wait! There's More!" area, a small, humble typeface announced that "Also featuring the legendary Rob Cantor, the original Captain Electron!"

Legendary? That was a nice flourish but probably untrue. His show might be legendarily campy, perhaps, but he himself? He'd really just done regional theatre since the show aired. His agent hadn't been able to get him seen for other parts. Sometimes, it was because of Captain Electron, sometimes just the bad luck that comes with a life spent as an actor. Being told 'no' became second nature to the Dalmatian long ago.

He cast his eyes down the exhibition hall, noticing a handful of other minor actors setting up at their tables. Most of them were younger than he was at this point. Maybe he'd been at this too long. The spotlight wasn't his anymore.

The line for Pierce's autograph was huge, and despite winding through a long series of velvet ropes and out through some glass doors to a below-ground concrete courtyard and then back inside, it still managed to block several tables.

In the line were dozens of parents of various species with their children, including the young Dalmatian. Rob felt a pang in his heart. Pierce had better take damn good care of those young fans.

He stretched out and leaned back in his chair to loosen the tension he hadn't realized was building.

Kids used to love him. They'd turn up with their store-bought or homemade costumes, their autograph books, and their Captain Electron comics, and smile so brightly when their hero—sent out in character by the studio—spoke to them. That had faded with the ending of the show, though, until he only got a few kids at the appearances any more.

The kids dropped off to a trickle, and then to nothing at his last few costumed appearances, but Rob did his duty, just as Captain Electron would have, and kept showing up. Occasionally he was rewarded by a particularly enthusiastic fan. Once he'd even given away Captain

Electron's prop badge. Rob had not been particularly fond of the choice to deputize the hero as a de facto police officer, but the studio had said they wanted no confusion for children about vigilante justice.

"Mr. Cantor, it's an absolute pleasure to meet you finally. Can I shake your paw?"

Rob snapped out of his thoughts and looked up to see a tiger, roughly half of the Dalmatian's age, grinning at him from across the table, paw extended. He wore the robes of some kind of space wizard that Rob didn't recognize. Probably something pretty new.

He shook the tiger's paw, and listened politely for a few minutes as the fellow, who spoke at a rate usually reserved for the legalese at the end of car advertisements, gushed over him.

"Well, you know what I mean, Mr. Cantor, I mean it's like, yeah, Pierce is all flashy, and he's got a super cool version of the car and all but I just love how simple and fun your show was."

"Well, thanks. I'm glad—"

"You're the real Captain Electron as far as I'm concerned. I just want you to know that."

Rob smiled and gestured towards the stacks of photos. "Could I interest you in any of these?"

"I can't, right now, but I'm thinking about coming to the photo session later so you can count on me!"

As the tiger scurried off to other pursuits, Rob turned his attention to his itinerary.

"So, what are my official signing times?"

"Well, uh," Jake paused, gnawing on his lip for the briefest instant. "We don't have any set times for you."

Rob's head jerked towards the corgi. "What do you mean? I always have at least one official time slot."

"Well the, uh, the con staff decided—this is totally off the record, by the way, sir—that they only had the budget to arrange the free signing deal with one guest. On the bright side, you can keep your own hours at your table." The corgi's ears were pinned flat against his skull.

Rob's spotted tail swished violently. "Which guest has scheduled times?"

"I...uh..."

"Just answer the question, kid."

"It's Mr. Pierce, sir."

Rob blinked. He'd been at giant conventions, tiny conventions, and everything in between. There had never been a one that hadn't arranged a time for him to sign. There was room for both Captain Electrons. He'd have agreed to concessions if he'd had to. This put him on the same level as some of the character actors and bit part players at the other tables in the signing hall. Not that they weren't talented, but they'd played Professor Moriarty once on a show that wasn't about Sherlock Holmes, or they'd been aliens or side characters or henchmen. They hadn't been the main character!

What did a big-shot like Pierce need with a tiny convention like this one? Rob had seen some glory hounds in his day. The guy who played Doom Bringer had been, as the British would say, an arrogant prat. He'd traded on a pawful of major theatrical roles for decades, until finally no one remembered them. He persisted even after that, and drove everyone on the Captain Electron set nuts.

Rob sighed, pushing away the uncomfortable thoughts. "Okay, so no official signing times. What events am I slated for?"

Jake wiped sweat from the tan and white fur of his forehead. "Well, there's the photo-op session this afternoon. You'll join Mr. Pierce for the joint photos at 2:30." Rob clenched his fists at that. Jake took no notice and continued. "Then from 3 until 3:30 are the solo pics with just you and the fans."

Rob sighed and offered Jake a wan smile. "Okay, terrific."

It really wasn't terrific. He'd turned down a decent one-night engagement in his local theatre's concert version of Coyote of La Mancha to be here. The fame from his years as Captain Electron had opened a few career doors for him (even if it had shut others). He owed the character and his fans this much.

"And then there's the Q&A session, of course."

"Of course." Even the character actors with the smallest, tangential careers usually got a Q&A for fans of their particular series.

"Oh, and there's a second Q&A tomorrow afternoon, but that's optional. Mr. Pierce's people wanted to offer you an invitation to share the stage with him for a big Captain Electron Q&A. That's if you're interested, of course."

Rob blinked. That was new. Probably they anticipated a lot of questions about the 'reboot' of Captain Electron, and figured there would be a lot of older fans who wanted to ask him what he thought. At least it would be a different set of questions than "Did you really kiss Ethel in the episode 'The Bank Robber's Daughter?'" or "What was it like on the set?" or the personal bane of the Dalmatian's existence: "How did you remember all those lines?"

Still, though, did he really want to put himself out there for a literal side-by-side comparison with Pierce?

"Anything else?"

The corgi's ear flicked uncomfortably.

"No, I think that's it. I brought this," he said, pulling out a thick vinyl banker's bag. "I'm also your cashier, that way you don't have to do anything but sign."

Rob sat and waited for autograph seekers and fans to make their way to his table. Over the span of about three hours, he was visited by exactly ten people. All of them were old enough to have watched him as Captain Electron in the show's first run. He smiled and talked with them, answering a few brief questions, and advised some people to bring their questions to his Q&A session. And, of course, he signed autographs.

That second Q&A weighed on the Dalmatian's mind. Should he do it? He really stood to gain nothing from it except helping promote the studio's new golden boy, but on the other hand, he had originated the role on screen. Though they were fewer and fewer with each passing event, he still had fans who looked up to him as some kind of mythic figure. He'd had cartoons making fun of his campy old series, and himself, for years, to the point that he and his version of Captain Electron might be more myth than mortal. If he went and did the Q&A, he could—what? What could he really do? He could legitimize the reboot, certainly. Maybe he could get some brownie points with the studio, maybe snag a cameo or a few lines in the sequel film which everybody and their brother knew was coming the way Hollywood handled franchises these days. It might, too, give him some final dignity in handing the role off formally.

No. The studio had made the decision to cut him out of involvement, and it wasn't like he was difficult to find for Pierce to get in touch. He was out there on all those social media things, and unlike John Pierce or Paul Vanzant, he didn't have an intern or manager handling his postings. The Q&A wasn't until tomorrow. He'd decide later. Maybe.

Thirty minutes after the last fan had dropped by Rob's table, John Pierce's line was still snaked outside and all through the hall. Jake fidgeted in his chair, holding onto the light cash bag. Rob couldn't see the new Captain Electron for the crowd. He found himself wishing that he'd looked up more information on the new movie, and maybe gotten some background on Pierce.

"I warned you it might be boring, Jake. I'm sorry it seems to be a ghost town."

"Oh, no! It's fine! I'm not bored! I'm sure more people will come by after the photo shoot and your talk."

"Sure. I'm…sure they will. Hey, I'm going to take off for a while, grab a drink and maybe a sandwich. Would you mind watching the table while I'm gone?"

"Sure, no problem. That's what I'm here for. If you want I could just go grab you something."

"No, thanks. I just need to think for a bit. I'll be back."

Rob shoved his chair back, slipped past some convention goers dressed up as rolling mechanized plumbers, and hopped on the escalator. There was a bar attached to the hotel's overpriced, and exceedingly pretentious, restaurant. He'd earned a drink, at least. Hopefully the bar had some decently aged single malt scotch. That might take the edge off of the growing sense that he really didn't belong at this convention.

From near the top of the escalator, he could see that a circle had formed around an open floor space at Pierce's table, and Rob, with his irritatingly less-than-decent vision, barely made out the rough outline of a Dalmatian kneeling down in the familiar red and blue.

Actors rarely came out in character any more, even the ones from the famous sci-fi shows and movies, so the fact that Pierce did struck Rob as a throwback to his own days in the costume. Curious indeed.

The lobby floor was packed with a few dealers that the convention hadn't been able to squeeze into the clearly overcrowded dealer's room, selling or displaying models of spaceships and custom painted holiday ornaments. Rob sidestepped them, trying to squeeze his way through the mass of various species in their outlandish costumes or their pop-culture mashup tee shirts to get to the bar. He got a few polite nods from some of the fans who had dropped by his table, though mercifully they all seemed to be polite enough not to interrupt a Dalmatian on a quest for scotch.

The bar teemed with convention attendees, as well as the occasional normal who'd wandered into town for a business conference, or some stop along a longer road trip, and who were all confused or amused or just plain bewildered by what they saw. The Dalmatian stifled a grin. No matter how long he came to these, the reactions from the normals always made him think of leaves being caught up in a hurricane.

A seat opened up at the bar, which Rob claimed. The bartender was swift and ruthlessly efficient in taking his order of a seventeen year old scotch, neat. As the Dalmatian sipped on the liquified peat bog, his mood darkened. He'd hoped it would be improved by getting some distance from his replacement's infinite autograph line, but instead it grew from grey skies to a rumbling storm cloud.

He hadn't asked much of the studio. He'd offered, in good faith, to consult on the new film and they'd ignored him. Well, to be more precise, they'd glad-handed him.

We'd be happy to talk about you consulting on the new movie! Of course! Don't call us though, we'll call you when we need you.

Two-faced studio executives had always been a way of life in Hollywood. That wasn't about to change. But it was different and somehow worse, when they took the only thing you were ever really known for and didn't even offer you a cameo appearance. Even the guy who stole Spider-Folf from his partner got a cameo in the movie.

He sipped his scotch again. No use crying over spilled milk. If truth be told, the studio had never had much support for either Captain Electron or Rob Cantor. After the show was canceled, they made such a halfhearted and half-assed attempt to get it picked up that Rob wondered whose daughter he'd accidentally jilted, or whose bratty nephew he'd snubbed.

The signing appearances had gotten smaller and smaller, going from big convention center venues and television interviews down to grand openings of furniture stores and costumed appearances in front of the cereal aisle at the chain supermarket. Those were usually the worst. People rushing past with a cart full of groceries, wondering why they were having to veer around this extra impediment.

Rob sipped at the scotch again, then downed the remainder of the glass.

He'd tried to stay positive in those days, hoping that if he just kept making the character look good that popular support would convince the networks to change their minds, and at least one of them would bid on returning the show to the airwaves. And those fans who turned up were always kind and genuinely seemed pleased to meet the great Captain Electron, especially the kids. He'd carried on for so long for their sake.

* * *

His scotch gone, the Dalmatian laid a twenty on the bar and slunk off in the direction of the escalators. Like it or not, bitter or not, he had a job to do and he didn't want to disappoint anyone who actually did turn up looking for a signature. The corgi, Jake, looked positively relieved as Rob reappeared and lowered himself back into the chair.

The ache in his lower back returned with a vengeance the moment he sat down, and he was forced to lean over on his knees, staring down at the ancient yellow and brown carpet. The pain lessened enough to sit up, and he passed a few minutes glancing around at the crowds and at the outdated, gaudy wood paneling of the hotel hallway, and his undisturbed stacks of photos, and his empty autograph line. Suddenly he felt his insides knotting up a little, and wondered if maybe he'd eaten something that disagreed with him. He stared mournfully down the concourse at where the throngs of people were dispersing from "Captain Electron's" table.

Rob closed his eyes briefly, to rest them. This was no good. He could sit and mope all he wanted and formulate all the reasons why the world was unfair and how dare that young whippersnapper steal his glory, but it wouldn't help. It wasn't John Pierce's fault that he was popular and that Rob was a mere afterthought. Hollywood didn't have a decent original idea in its collective brain; reboots and remakes were the norm. As he rubbed his eyes, a voice spoke from across the table. Blue eyes snapped open, and he sat up, like a clockwork toy freshly wound.

"Um, excuse me, sir. I'd like this picture, and if you could sign it 'to Jake'?"

He'd all but forgotten the pudgy little corgi who had now stepped around the table. He was holding out a twenty-dollar bill. Ten for the photo (he'd chosen one of Rob's favorites; his fight with Doom Bringer in the prime time special they'd done at the height of the series), and ten for the autograph. He stuffed the bill into the banker's bag and grinned sheepishly. Rob smiled and signed the photo, before giving it back.

"Thanks! Sorry for not waiting, but I figured you might get busy after your Q&A."

"No problem, Jake. Hey, I'll be right back, ok?"

"Sure thing, sir. Just remember that you've got fifteen minutes before you have to be on stage!"

Only fifteen minutes? Time had flown by already. He'd have to be quick. Rob strode through the crowds leaving John Pierce's table. Hopefully he could catch the actor before he was rushed elsewhere. At least to say hello and introduce himself properly.

Unfortunately, by the time he reached the table, Pierce was gone. A pair of security staffers and a convention handler tidied up the table. Rob slumped. He'd waited too long. He'd really wanted to bite the bullet and get the first meeting over with on his own terms.

The handler packed up Pierce's photos, placing them into one stack and leaving only the top one visible. On that one, Captain Electron was lit from above amid eerie, dark shadows, the outline of the costume's colors and the Dalmatian's own fur creating an ominous effect. Captain Electron is coming, it seemed to shout, and he isn't happy.

It fit with everything he'd heard in recent years: that the comic producer had taken the character, Rob's character really, in a dark, approaching anti-hero direction, which was pretty spectacular in Rob's mind for a character still named Captain Electron.

Having failed to catch Pierce, he trudged back to his table, feeling somehow abandoned by the universe. His rational mind fought that feeling back. He knew better. But his head knowing and his heart feeling were often irreconcilable. It didn't matter. He had to be on stage. That would perk him up. Hopefully.

* * *

"So, yes, I did actually kiss her in that episode, but neither of us enjoyed it very much, and afterward we each spent a week recovering from whatever plague we'd contracted."

The crowd, filling approximately the first third of the theater space, rumbled with laughter. The stage lights kept Rob from focusing on any one member of the audience aside from whichever person was lit at the house microphone, but they all seemed to be his older fans, most of whom had already dropped by the table, he figured.

"Are there more questions? I've got time for a few more, I think!"

The Dalmatian was all smiles and energy. Being on stage or on camera always brought it out in him. He'd probably pay for it with a mood crash later, but right now, it was important to keep the performance going. A heavy set badger waddled up to the mic and asked the question he'd been dreading.

"Hi, Mr. Cantor. Huge fan ever since I was a kid. I was wondering, um, well…did the studio consult you on the new Captain Electron film?"

Rob forced a big, energetic smile, though he could tell from the way it felt on his muzzle that it would've looked terrible on video.

"No. There were some discussions that I'm not at liberty to discuss, but in the end they decided that it would be best to go their own route."

The badger sunk, looking as if he'd lost a bet. "Um, well, a follow-up if I may?"

Rob glanced behind him. There was nobody waiting in line.

"Sure, go ahead."

"What do you think of the direction they're going? Your Captain Electron was a good guy through and through. I believe you were even legally allowed to hunt down criminals. What do you think of what they're doing, making him dark and brooding and, well, meaner?"

Rob took a sip of water from the provided glass.

Tread lightly

"This is a different Captain Electron, for a different time and a different fan base. By drawing on the more recent comics, I think the studio is doing what they think the fans want."

It was a good answer, and he felt some of the butterflies in his stomach dissipate with it. Diplomatic, unlikely to get him sued or have him show up on TMZ.

"Not all of us," the badger mumbled, then wandered back to his seat in the darkened theater.

Me either, friend. Me either.

Mercifully a few more creatures lined up at the mic to keep Rob from having to dwell on either the implications of the question or of his own response.

Rob answered a handful more questions, including the dreaded, "How do you remember all those lines," before time was up and Jake appeared in the wings to take him back to his table. The flashy M.C. Fox enjoined the audience to give the legendary—there was that word again—Rob Cantor a big round of applause, and while the roar of it didn't shake the huge theater the way a packed audience would, the sound of it made the Dalmatian grin just the same.

He gave a wave and strode confidently off stage, pausing in the wings to lean against a chair and catch his breath.

"So, we've got the photo shoot next, Mr. Cantor," Jake said, leaning down to look Rob in the face, probably to make sure the old dog wasn't about to keel over.

"Right, right… let's go. I'm feeling good and limber after that little bit of exercise. Maybe I can even hold up a prop or two this time!"

He patted the corgi on the shoulder, and the two made their way out the stage door.

* * *

Rob's grey-tinged ears perked up to better hear what was going on inside as he and Jake approached the photo room. The line was out the door. Creatures of every species and walk of life were there waiting to get their photo taken with the star. The mix was incredible, with everyone from Dalmatians to swift foxes to a couple of weasels and a sloth waiting their turn to step into the hotel suite which housed the photographer's equipment. Rob noted that the carpet here was plush and a rich crimson which contrasted with the beige, ribbed wallpaper. This area had either been added on after that god-awful convention space or it had been remodeled.

Of course, he didn't have to wait in the line. He was a few minutes early, but Jake ushered him through the crowd to the farther door, into the sleeping quarters attached to the suite. There were some murmurs of recognition among the crowd, and Rob felt some of his tension melting away. They remembered. At least some of them did anyway.

"Okay, they're on the last few single-shoot ticket holders for Capt— er, for Mr. Pierce. Then you'll go in and the people who bought the picture with both of you together will get taken. And then it's your individual photos."

"Right," Rob said distractedly. He was staring at the immaculately made, undisturbed bed, and at the electric blue bundle of fabric resting on it.

"We didn't figure you'd want to try to dress up in the full costume, so we got—"

"You got the mask and cape, huh?" The Dalmatian reached down and felt the material. It was a perfect replica of his old one, even down to the soft satin texture and its slight metallic reflectivity.

"You don't have to wear it if you don't want, sir, I—we just thought—"

"It's okay, Jake. I'll wear it. It's nice. You know, you guys do a pretty good job here. Lots of small conventions would have just had somebody cut a mask out of cheap blue felt and made a cape out of a towel." Rob forced a smile. The corgi was going out of his way to make him feel at least somewhat wanted, and that was golden.

An older vixen with a touch of grey in the dark fur of her ears, much like Rob's, stuck her head into the room. "We're ready for you now, Mr. Cantor."

Rob nodded and pulled the mask up against his face, tying it in the back automatically with a muscle memory that had not dulled over the years. Then he pulled the cape over the shoulders of his sport coat. He caught a glimpse of himself in the mirror and stifled a chuckle in spite of himself. He looked like some sort of modern day Coyote of La Mancha, a businessman gone mad and determined to live in a fantasy world.

The vixen—whose name was Dawn, Rob gleaned from her name tag—held the door for him from outside with one arm. He stepped into the room, squinting to adjust his eyes to the brightness of the space, enhanced to retina-scorching levels by the photographer's studio lights. The photographer had set up one of those grey backgrounds with the light area in the center and lit it with two big umbrella things and a couple of smaller lights from underneath. There was a huge set of French doors with gauze curtains letting the light stream in from the outside as well, and a few members of staff were manning some tables nearby where incoming subjects could place their bags and costume props and such to be picked up when the photo was done.

By the photographer's backdrop, standing slightly taller than Rob— even before age had taken its few inches—and in full red and blue Captain Electron costume, was John Pierce, flanked by his manager, a chubby pine marten who seemed to be glued to his smartphone, a very chipper young cacomistle with a very large and expensive looking camera dangling off his neck, and a female retriever making notes in an old fashioned leather date book.

Rob had to admit that the costume flattered the other Dalmatian. He was lean, muscular, and the costume showed off a superhero's physique. Rob had never been in that good of a shape. The popularity of the show at the time meant that he'd had a steady paycheck for the first time—and one of the only times, in his life as an actor—and he'd indulged himself a bit too liberally. After the first season aired, he remembered, they'd had to squeeze him into a girdle for a couple of public appearances, and from then on his contract contained an exercise clause.

The costume was a fairly faithful re-interpretation. The red was darker, a deeper and somehow more serious crimson, and the blue looked brighter by contrast. The texture of the fabric suggested something more like woven Kevlar. Even the gun had been given a less retro-futuristic look.

"Rob Cantor!" the other Dalmatian called excitedly, waving in his direction. Rob didn't move, caught off guard. "It is absolutely amazing to see you. Come on, come over here!"

Rob made his way over to the photographer's backdrop and shook Pierce's waiting outstretched paw. He'd expected a typical autographs-and-sunglasses movie star, not a warm and enthusiastic young male. As he approached the backdrop, Rob caught a whiff of something that smelled like paint. That probably answered the question of how long ago this room had been remodeled.

"Listen, before they let in the next group, could we, you know, get a picture of just the two of us, in the Justice Spots pose?"

Rob furrowed his brow but couldn't keep from smiling a little with nostalgia. The pose was stupid comic book mubfubbery, but it always looked great on camera somehow.

"Yeah, sure, why not."

"Great, over here! This tape mark! We good, Mr. Photographer?"

The cacomistle gave a thumbs up, and Pierce's manager meandered absently out of the frame, eyes still glued to his phone.

"Okay, ready?"

Rob nodded. He hadn't done this in a very long time. Right paw in a fist, against his left shoulder, bent at the waist, left arm straight at a 45 degree angle, paws slightly more than shoulder width apart, head up. Pierce took the same pose with his arms reversed, though with considerably less popping of joints and lower back pain.

"On the count of three, look defiant and say 'Justice'. Ready? One, two, three!" The two 'heroes' complied, and the lights flashed brightly. "And one more, one, two, three."

Again they repeated 'Justice' and again the lights flashed.

"Hey, Mr. Cantor, thanks so much. I'll get this signed before the con is over."

If your endless fans don't slow you down.

As Rob looked his young counterpart over he caught something wrong in the Dalmatian's left eye. It took Rob a moment to realize that it was an ice-blue contact lens slipping down and revealing a brown iris underneath. Masking heterochromia probably. Not a bad job.

The crowd for the double photo was older, though still younger than Rob had expected them to be. And there were quite a few of them. Males in their thirties who had grown up on reruns of his show. Most of them were canids but occasionally an otter or feline would pass through. Rob settled into his old habits, offering a warm smile and a paw on the shoulder for each photo.

"And that's it for the doubles," Dawn the vixen said from the doorway. "They're lined up now for your solo shoots, Mr. Cantor."

"Can't imagine this will take long," he muttered to himself.

"All right, I've got to go change. Are you going to be at the Q&A. I think it's tomorrow afternoon. Eh, Jean? Tomorrow afternoon, right?"

The retriever flipped the page of her organizer, "Yes, Mr. Pierce."

"Great! Think you'll make it?"

"I don't know if I'll be able to. These things take a lot out of me." He could tell just by the feel in his joints that he was going to be sore later, but really, he just wasn't sure he wanted to see a huge crowd cheering on this young new hero.

Pierce's ears pinned momentarily, and a faint whine reached Rob's ears. "It would mean the world to me if you'd come, but I understand if you can't.

And then he was gone, and Rob was left in the suite with Dawn the vixen, the cacomistle photographer whose name he didn't catch, and the four or five older folks who came in to get their photos with him.

* * *

After a quiet lunch the next day in the hotel's little overpriced cafeteria, Rob debated just going back to his room and taking a nap. It was nearly 4:00 in the afternoon, and if he was going to constantly feel old, he might as well act the part.

He thought about the Q&A offer with John Pierce, turning over the younger male's eagerness in his mind. He'd seemed genuine in his enthusiasm, but still. Would it be a good idea? Probably not.

He tossed the last few bites of his soggy, prepackaged turkey club into the trash on the way back out into the main autograph hall.

Jake trotted up in a tizzy, panting heavily and trying desperately to catch his breath.

"Oh, Mr. Cantor. Rob. Sir. Uh… yes… Um…"

Rob tilted his head, perking one floppy Dalmatian ear—his best one. "What's going on, Jake?"

"There's a Labrador at your table waiting for an autograph. He seems to be in a big hurry. I told him you'd be back soon but—"

"Ok, well, let's get over there."

The corgi turned on his heel and wove his way through the crowd of convention patrons, creating a tiny bubble of empty space in his wake which Rob fell into.

His table was at the other end and was obscured by the crowd admiring a spaceship model crewed by puppets on display outside the video viewing room. Rob never got that British stuff anyway.

When the pair had made their way close enough to Rob's table, there was no one standing near it, just a sign informing fans that Rob Cantor would return to his table soon.

"Oh gosh, sir, I'm so sorry! I told him to stay here and I'd be back quickly, but I guess he couldn't wait."

Rob gave a halfhearted nod and flopped back down behind his table, removing the "back soon" sign. He hoped the fan would come back. He'd hate to have caused the poor guy to miss his chance to say hello and get an autograph. Still, biological needs were biological needs. Lunch had to happen at some point. Now that it had, the Dalmatian felt a bit sleepy and so pulled out a well-worn paperback copy of The Adventures of the Scarlet Pimpernel to keep himself awake and focused.

He'd just read another delightful humiliation of M. Chauvelin by the crafty fox when he glanced up at the increased foot traffic and noted that the line for John Pierce was queuing up through the stanchions once more. Rob checked his watch, holding it closer to his nose so he could better read the hands through the scuffed crystal. He'd been reading for nearly two hours now!

Rob stood up once more, stretching and feeling the glorious popping of his joints.

"Back in a second."

Jake said something in reply, but Rob didn't catch what the corgi had said. He focused on the big time signing table beyond the sea of creatures lined up. He should probably let Pierce know that he wasn't going to join him on stage, just so he was warned ahead of time.

Trying to make his way around the crowd took some doing. Security let him through because of his badge's "guest" designation at least, but there were just so many people!

Finally, more out of desperation than cunning, he made his way out of the crowd and over to the outside wall, past which the fans who had received their autographs were walking on their way out. Rob sidled along it until he was finally able to see Pierce at the table being handed photos each in turn and personalizing each signature for each fan—probably with a pre-set group of phrases to pick from as Rob had learned to do.

He was dressed in the costume, that modern, stylish costume, just as he had been for the photo session. Rob noted that his energy level was just as high with the fans in line as it had been upon meeting him for the photo. He was all smiles and chatter, looking his fans in the face and chatting with them about where they'd come from, or what they did for a living. The convention staff and his personal aides managed, but only just, to keep the looks of annoyance off their faces.

Rob smiled and started to sidle back along the wall, but stopped short when the next fan reached the table in front of Pierce. It was a little pup, couldn't have been more than five or six years old, staring down at his paws and holding out his picture for Captain Electron to sign without even looking up.

"What do you have for me, there, little scout?"

Little scout? Rob blinked. He'd always called his young fans that, both because it fit and because it was what the fan club members were called. There hadn't been a fan club in decades though, at least not for children.

Rob watched as the little fox shuffled uncomfortably, looking everywhere but directly at Captain Electron. The fans in line fidgeted and checked their phones, while the attendant staff behind Pierce's table began to look at each other as the seconds stretched on. Pierce finally rose from behind the table and crossed around it to kneel down in front of the kit.

"Would you like me to sign your picture?"

The child sighed and nodded, holding it out and looking up for just a moment into the smiling face of the dashing Dalmatian.

"And what's your name, little scout?"

It took a gentle nudging from the boy's mother before he'd speak again. "Kevin."

"Well, Kevin," Pierce said, placing the photo on the corner of his table and uncapping his marker, "I'll sign this for you and—"

"Mommy says you're not real."

Pierce paused and looked to the mother, a nicely dressed vixen in her late twenties or so. She clamped both paws over her muzzle, her ears pinned and tail down, embarrassment evident.

A great writer once said, "These are the times that try creatures' souls," and this was one of those situations. Rob had been there. He kept his ears pricked and pointed sharply to pick up every bit of the ensuing conversation.

"Well, remember, little scout, Captain Electron has many enemies. Sometimes it's safest to pretend I'm not real, but you know what?"

The child perked up, daring to look, finally, at the superhero. "What?"

"I'm real as you are. You can even shake my paw if you want. So what do you say?" He extended his paw

"I knew it! I knew Mommy was wrong!" the kit yelped, bouncing up and down excitedly and looking at his mother with bright, shining eyes. The mother, for her part, looked relieved and mouthed a quiet "thank you" when the boy's back was turned and he was vigorously shaking his hero's paw.

Old memories tugged at Rob's heartstrings. The exchange felt so familiar. He knew every beat of the drama before it played out, and Pierce had played it perfectly. The line was moving again, he'd delighted a young child and soothed the embarrassed mother. He knew all the tricks already, and maybe, just maybe, better than Rob ever had.

With the crowd moving again, Rob took his cue to slip away, past the serpentine queue and the tables of occasionally engaged, occasionally bored, character actors, until he reached his own, with Jake sitting dutifully behind it.

"Jake? What time was that Q&A?"

* * *

Backstage once more, Rob felt the butterflies swarming in his stomach, not so much butterflies as angry bees now. This wasn't part of the plan. He should be having a glass of scotch in the bar right now, running through his travel checklist and preparing to get out the next day and return home, then deciding what to do about any future conventions.

Before seeing Pierce with the fox kit, that decision had been so clear. He'd gracefully retire from the convention circuit and focus his theatrical efforts on teaching or stage performance.

Now things were muddy. Hearing those words, seeing that interaction, tugged at the Dalmatian's heartstrings. He'd been that hero once, and Pierce was that hero now, in every sense of the word. Clearly there were still people who remembered Rob's Captain Electron and yet were still excited about the new.

The green room was abuzz with con staff, Pierce's personal staff, and security monitoring the door. Once again, his convention badge did its job, and he was ushered in past the overweight but muscular wolf security guard. Pierce was seated in front of a broad mirror surrounded by lights. Rob squinted to get a look, but the lights hurt his eyes, and he had to look away.

"Forty-five minutes, Mr. Pierce," said a badger, clothed in the black of a stage manager and wearing a microphone and earpiece.

"Thank you, forty-five!"

At his acknowledgement, the badger scurried off to her other duties.

Rob stood to one side of the door to stay out of the way of the bustling activity. He tried again to look over at Pierce, but the makeup lights were really something and left glowing green and red spots in the Dalmatian's vision.

"Mr. Cantor's here, Mr. Pierce."

The bright lights were shut off, and Pierce stood and faced Rob, who tried without success to blink away the spots in his vision.

"You made it! That's fantastic!"

"I saw you with the kid, earlier," Rob said, rubbing at his eyes. "You were really something."

Pierce stepped closer, a softer smile now sitting on his muzzle, one of warmth and not the glee of a fan. The lights must have really done a number on Rob's eyes because the other dog appeared to have all black fur on his muzzle and around his eyes. Rob's nose twitched. There was that paint smell again…

He stared long and hard at the grinning superhero, blinking as the glowing afterimage began to fade. The dog that stood before him bore the black fur and brown eyes of another breed entirely. The paint Rob had smelled, and smelled now, made more sense.

"You're not a Dalmatian?" Rob blinked.

"Nope! Labrador!" Pierce wagged his spotted tail. "But I can sure pass for one, huh?"

Rob gritted his teeth, fighting the sudden urge to tell this upstart mongrel off once and for all. Seriously? Changing your breed for the sake of a role? Sure, it wasn't like a fox trying to play a wolf. They were both still dogs, but just because it wasn't species prejudice, that didn't make it right.

The look on Rob's face must have been more apparent than he'd thought. Pierce took a step back, ears pinned. The room fell silent, all of the attendant staff staring at the scene unfolding.

"I know, it's pretty unusual, but the studio and everybody was cool about it—"

"Oh, I'll bet they were!" Rob snarled. "The Studio was cool with everything because The Studio only sees one thing: dollar signs. They don't see years of a person's life and hard work. They don't have any respect for the craft itself unless it makes them money. So what if you're not really a Dalmatian? As far as they're concerned, there aren't any Dalmatian actors out there waiting for a shot, so let's just get some other breed to fill in!"

Pierce looked wounded but stood his ground, backing up no farther. The security guard at the door had stepped inside, eyeing the situation tensely. The Labrador waved her off, though she stayed planted a few feet away, just to be certain.

"Who ever gave you the notion that this was a good idea?" Rob glared, the afterimage having faded completely from his vision now. The half-painted Labrador looked for all the world as if he were fighting back tears.

"You did," he answered softly.

Rob opened his muzzle to shoot off something else but was halted when Pierce lifted something off the side of his belt and held it out to Rob in offering.

Rob, now feeling a vibe of chill confusion swirling amid his white-hot rage, took the object without thinking, and stared at it. When he did, all of his rage melted away.

In his paw sat a five-pointed star made of shiny silver metal. The emblem at the center was Captain Electron's logo.

"Where did you get this?"

"You gave it to me, Mr. Cantor. You gave it to me when I was just a little pup, during an appearance at a big supermarket."

Rob looked up into the other dog's brown eyes. It had been thirty years. He'd seen lots of fans, but that time...that time he remembered very well.

"It was you?"

* * *

"Well, hello there, little scout," Rob had said, in his deep, booming "superhero" voice. "What can I do for you today?"

The little boy immediately looked down and fidgeted. His black ears could not decide whether they should be pinned back or perked up excitedly.

"What's your name," Captain Electron said, trying once again. It wasn't that he was in a hurry. Not at all. There was no pressure here. Most of the people passing by took no notice of him or his signing table. His manager was outside smoking and probably having a nip of brandy from the flask that he didn't want Rob to know he carried. He just knew, from experience, that he couldn't depend on the child to say something on his own. That either overeager parents would interfere or he would simply run off from sheer shyness.

"Um..." The boy turned his head to look behind him.

Rob looked up, following the boy's gaze until he saw a well dressed Labrador couple, quietly urging the boy on from a distance. Rob admired that. They wanted the boy to take the step on his own. The pup looked back in Rob's direction, still not making eye contact.

"I'm not s'posed to tell. It's my secret indemnity."

The masked Dalmatian's muzzle broke into a grin. Of course! Secret identity, or 'indemnity' as the case may be, was critical to any superhero, and the boy was completely dressed up, mask and all. He was playing an excellent game of pretend. Rob couldn't not play along. This was his favorite part, when the young ones really got into the swing of things.

"You're certainly to be commended," Captain Electron said. He dropped his volume conspiratorially as he leaned in closer and cocked a floppy black ear. "But if you can't trust Captain Electron, then who can you trust?"

The little boy looked up then, his eyes meeting Rob's, ears coming forward, tail wagging furiously. He was smiling now, and his brown eyes were full of wonder. "Okay," he said, excitedly. Then forcing himself back to proper superhero composure, leaned in and whispered, "It's Jonny. You gotta promise not to tell."

"My word as a member of the Justice Spots," Captain Electron whispered in return, winking.

"I have…um… a very important question to ask you, Mr. Captain Electron, sir."

Rob leaned across the table on folded arms. "Well, better ask, lad. I'm all ears."

"When are you gonna come back…um…on TV? They put on some stupid thing with a really creepy puppet at the time you used to be on."

Rob felt his heart sink beneath the costume's embroidered chest logo. This question was the worst.

"Well, you see… I've had to start doing more low-profile crime solving."

"Oh! Like a secret mission?"

"Yes, something like that." He hated that the boy was completely unfazed by the lie and took it as gospel truth. But he couldn't ruin the kids' fantasy by telling them the reality of the situation. CBS had decided to cancel the series.

"Will you ever come back on? It's boring without you."

Rob looked up, hoping to see the boy's parents coming to take him away, but they hadn't moved. The father's arm was wrapped around the mother's shoulder, whose paw was placed gently on his, admiring the imagination of their little pup.

"I can't say for sure, maybe one day."

"When I grow up, do you think I could join the Justice Spots…?"

This was safer territory for Rob.

"Well, normally, members of the Justice Spots are only Dalmatians. It takes someone of special character to be admitted otherwise. Do you think you have what it takes?"

The boy's tail lashed excitedly back and forth.

"I do, I do, I really, really do!"

Solemnly, Captain Electron came around the table and knelt before the child. He slipped his paw to his belt and lifted the heavy costume badge from its place. The shiny prop had been made by the same company that made a number of actual police badges. He didn't like wearing it, but the studio was insistent that a vigilante superhero like Captain Electron actually be shown as a duly deputized law enforcement officer, just so that kids weren't given mixed signals about lawbreaking.

The badge was splendidly detailed with Captain Electron's atom logo as the cloisonné design at its center and five rounded points extending outward like a marshal's badge from one of the spaghetti westerns. It sparkled in the fluorescent light of the supermarket.

"Then by the authority vested in me by the Justice Spots, I hereby induct you as an honorary junior member," he pronounced as he knelt, placing the badge into the pup's outstretched paws. "And maybe, when you're old enough, you can be a superhero too, just like me."

The kid practically vibrated with excitement, his eyes as wide as saucers staring at the badge in his paws. Impulsively, he wrapped both arms around his hero and hugged him tightly.

"I hope you come back on TV soon so I can watch you with my dad. He's a big fan too."

The little Labrador pup named Jonny turned and scampered off back to his parents. Rob couldn't hear what he was saying, but he was jumping up and down and showing the badge to both parents who grinned and laughed. They soon left, waving at Captain Electron for making their child's day.

* * *

Rob shook his head in disbelief. "It was you. I can't believe you held onto this." All the burning anger and humiliation he'd felt moments ago drained away, replaced now by a sense of shame at his outburst and a desire to reach out and hug the young actor.

"Are you kidding? I was obsessed with Captain Electron. He was always my favorite! You're the reason I got into acting in the first place. I mean, once I found out that your show wasn't actually real, that is."

Rob had been told that, occasionally, by some young creature at a signing table. He'd hear how he'd inspired them to chase their dreams, and even when they found out they couldn't be a real superhero, they wanted to be other people. It was a nice sentiment, but hearing it like this made Rob's old heart do some joyous backflips.

The staff and others in the room finally breathed a sigh of relief and returned to their bustling. The security guard stepped outside, holding the door as someone else came inside amid the flurry of activity.

"When I found out they were finally going to be rebooting Captain Electron, well, I hired a stylist and a makeup artist," he said, indicating the pair of foxes who had been dutifully grooming him before Rob had walked in. "And we worked out how to turn me into a Dalmatian. I'm just sorry that you didn't have time to be in the movie! I had a great scene for you all picked out!"

Rob's ears perked forward. "What are you talking about?"

"I asked the studio if we could have you in to play my father, but they told me you weren't interested."

Rob's face burned, his smile faltering. "That's really interesting. Nobody ever told me."

Pierce yelped. "What? I can't believe that!" He yanked out his cellphone and began dialing.

"Honestly, it's fine," Rob said.

"No, it's not fine. If they want me back for the next film, I don't care what contract I'm under, they'll put in the dad scenes! They're so important! Without them... You know what? They'll get an angry phone call on Monday."

"I still can't believe you stuck with being a fan all these years," Rob said, willing his voice not to break.

"Hey, listen. Meeting you meant everything to me when I was eight. You gave me permission to chase my dreams."

He reached out, lifted up the badge from Rob's paw, and held it up, grinning sheepishly. "They, uh, wouldn't let me wear it in the movie, y'know? I tried."

"So, now you're me. That's pretty impressive, kid," Rob said.

"Nah, I'm not you. I'm me. You're you. And we're both Captain Electron. But you're the legend, here."

That funny, loaded word again.

"So, are you still going to do the Q&A with me? I mean, I totally get it if you don't want to now," Pierce said, looking down at the carpet.

The indecision fluttered in Rob's stomach.

"I'll do it. You kept that dream of yours alive because of something I did. I think it's only fair that I keep doing this, for the fans, because of you." He nodded, tail wagging. The butterflies disappeared from inside, replaced by a warm glow.

"That means the world to me, Mr. Cantor."

"Call me Rob. I think you've earned it."

"Okay, then. Rob. So, uh, have you watched the movie?"

Rob shook his head and laughed, "Avoided everything about it. It all pissed me off so much at the time that I couldn't see straight."

"Tell you what, I'll have my manager drop off a Blu-Ray in my suite, and we can watch it together. You can give me pointers. They green-lit two sequels already, and there are talks for a new TV series." The Labrador's tail wagged.

"You've got a deal. But you supply the popcorn and the brandy, and I get to make fun of you as much as I want."

"Deal. Now, I gotta finish getting ready. I plan on talking about nothing but how much your show inspired me and colored my performance, and then I'm going to demand that everybody come and get your autograph."

The Dalmatian grinned. "Okay, but remember, I'm old. You're going to aggravate my arthritis by making me sign so much."

"Bah, occupational hazard when you're Captain Electron."

"When we're Captain Electron," Rob corrected. As Pierce returned to his makeup chair, the Dalmatian heard a strange, high-pitched noise from behind him.

He turned around to look for the source and nearly bumped straight into Jake, who was standing immobile, paws clasped firmly over his muzzle. He practically vibrated with excitement and made little whining noises to accompany his furious wiggling.

"Hey, Jake, calm down. You'd think you just saw a superhero or something."

Farad expects to wander alone in the desert until he dies. Instead he is invited to join a wandering Caravan of Fools, convinced that they have a map to Behesht—to Heaven.

Do they?

Behesht

by Dwale

When father died, I cleansed his remains and wrapped them in a sheet, then secured them in a sling I'd fashioned ahead of time. His thirty-five-kilogram corpse strapped to my back, I made the long climb up the dusty steel ladder of the surface access tube. The rungs were cold on the pads of my hands and feet. My efforts, my breath and heartbeat, the chimes and dings as I climbed, all resounded in the narrow confines.

Up above, I checked my compass to make sure his head would be facing the holy city, then said prayers and buried him in the sand. There were no animals or people to disturb his remains, which would quickly mummify once the sun rose, but it was our tradition to bury the dead in this way.

I thought of smashing the only solar array with the shovel while I was topside. Father's last words were, "Farad, my son, you must leave this place. Get married and, God willing, have children. You should not have stayed so long." I had told him to go to sleep and kissed the top of his head.

But in spite of my father's wish, I was tempted to spin out the rest of my days sustained by the hydroponics and insect farms that my great-grandfather had scrabbled together. I thought smashing the solar panels might hasten me along, until I imagined some desperate caravan would come hobbling into town only to find the pump inoperable and the water beyond their reach. So, I left the panels as they were and made my descent, back to the home where I had grown up, where my supplies were already packed.

The backpack was heavier than my father had been, but less bulky and therefore easier to handle, so my footsteps should have been light and quick, as a Jerboa's ought to be. But the further I walked, the more some vague unease stirred at the edge of my consciousness. The boulevard had been a quiet place even in my youth, when we had boasted a populace twenty persons strong; now it bordered on silence. As I passed the empty houses and storefronts where once we had played as children, the hairs on my back and ears stood on end, as though thousands of eyes were peering out from the dark and dusty windows on each side. I told myself it was only my imagination, a nervous response to being the only person within a hundred kilometers or more, but I quickened my pace nonetheless.

There was only one sound on the streets which did not originate with my person: the hiss of falling sand. It worked its way in through the old ventilation system, covering everything I had ever known. Now the dunes finally encroached on the last of the unburied structures. The sand would swallow everything in the end. Perhaps that was for the best.

A short time later and the maw of the underground highway loomed before me, the beam of my flashlight vanishing into its depths. As I steeled myself and stepped over the threshold, tears began to flow. I was the last inhabitant of New Fatimabad, below the ruins of Ardabil, and I was leaving forever...

Or so I thought.

I ran into the caravan mere hours after my journey started, a handful of individuals whose appearance reflected an assortment of cultures and phenotypes. Their leader, a short man of vole genetic stock, offered that I should join them before he even asked my name.

"Peace, my brother," he said. "Come with us, and leave these wretched places behind. Where we are going is far better."

When I inquired as to where that might be, he smiled and said a single word: "Behesht." Their destination was nothing less than Heaven itself, the hidden garden which is the reward of believers.

We ended up going back into New Fatimabad for water and the food I had been forced to leave behind. What we could not carry, my new half-starved comrades jammed into their mouths until their bellies were distended. While that was going on, I gathered up paper and ink from my father's articles. I had lived my youth in his books and reckoned it was time to try writing one myself. So, after traveling with the caravan and interviewing its members, I have set out to chronicle those stories which best reflect the world in which we find ourselves. It seemed the proper thing to do since we might be among the last people who will ever walk this earth.

The Clergyman

Their leader was a man named Shapur, a vole with a greying coat. He dressed in the simple fashion of desert nomads in times past, a knee-length shirt with a robe over it, and a turban, one wrapped in such a fashion as to expose his rounded ears. He approached me during our meal at the end of my first cycle with the group, there among the ancient vestiges of transports that would never again run on this road, what had once been a major thoroughfare but now aboded dust and silence.

"Peace," he said, smiling and taking a seat on the ground before me. His movements were stiff and abrupt, as though taken with a perpetual nervousness. His nose and whiskers wriggled in spastic contractions spaced some four or five seconds apart. "I wanted to welcome you formally to our group."

"And upon you, peace. May God reward you," I answered. "I wasn't sure if I would ever meet another person."

At that he laughed, and the laughter rang warm and earnest in my ears, such a strange sound as I had not heard in years, since before my mother died.

"You'll come to know all of us in time, and more people besides, once we get there." He must have read something in my face then, because before I could say anything, he added, "You have doubts. Do you lack faith?"

"I have faith in God. I have less faith in men. Do you truly believe we will make it to paradise?"

He smiled and said, "Paradise is always just around the corner for the righteous."

But of course, I could not be satisfied with that for an answer, so he continued.

"Tradition holds that the tomb in the holy city is considered a part of Heaven. You have heard this, no doubt?"

I nodded, remaining mute but seeing where this was headed.

"Then you must also know that a prayer made there is always answered."

"My great-grandfather's father was the last of our line to attempt the pilgrimage," I said. "He spent four years trying to find a tunnel westward that hadn't collapsed, and came home with nothing. So, what do you mean to do, sir? Will you build us a ship? Will you march us overland without environmental suits?"

My color must have risen, because his tone took on a conciliatory inflection when next he spoke.

"He would have checked the major roads, but could he know of every subway, access tunnel or pipe? Just because he could not find a way doesn't mean the way is lost. We have maps. It will not be easy, but we will get there."

The thought sparked a glimmer of hope in my heart, only to be snuffed out by the one that followed it.

"But what if the city is gone, what if the sand- "

"Brother!" he said, not shouting, but more than a little firm. He shut his eyes for a moment, and when he opened them again his smile had reconstituted. "If God, praise to Him, should so will, surely He could cover even the tops of the mountains. But should we believe His holy places are no more before we have seen it with our own eyes? Think about it for a while."

With that, he yawned and excused himself, the irony in his final question gleaming like chrome, but eluding him all the same.

The Newlyweds

Babak and Nadia were rabbits draped head to toe in bright clothes printed with intricate, spiraling vine motifs, such fine stuff as I had only seen before in books, but which must have been common in their oasis for them to put together entire outfits from it. Babak's shemagh had slits cut in it to admit the passage of his lanky ears, which was not uncommon; Nadia kept hers folded back and hidden beneath a scarf. But it was not their ears which most drew attention, but rather Nadia's protruding belly.

She noticed my staring and smiled.

"God has willed it," was what I said, referring to the kittens she carried. But I couldn't make myself smile. How could she think of bringing a litter into this dead world, to struggle and suffer in privation?

"Praise to Him," Babak addended. "Peace. I'm Babak and this is Nadia. Come, sit down." He took my hand and all but pulled me onto the large carpet he'd been spreading out.

"We found a little powdered tea," he said. "You must drink with us."

I refused five times, and still ended up with tea.

We talked for a while on small matters of personal history, our hometowns, our families. It may have been that they sensed my alarm and wanted to put me at ease. Babak and Nadia were from the same oasis, only three-hundred kilometers or so from my own, to the south, which was closer than I had expected. They were cousins.

"You're too gracious," I said after he forced a peach candy into my hand. My eyes kept wandering over to Nadia's bulging abdomen, however much I might try to stop them. I had never seen a pregnancy before.

"You are wondering," Babak said, changing the subject with a delicate air, "why my wife and I are… baking."

"Baking?"

"Yes. You know, the sort of baking for which rabbits are so well-known."

"Ah! Yes, of course," I stammered. He didn't seem offended at my curiosity, though other men might have been.

"When a doe is under stress, the bread…" he paused here to search out a word, "*returns*. The oven gives you nothing. My Nadia is the first in many years to come so far along. That's why we joined this caravan."

"You believe Shapur." I thought of the greying vole, the holy man leading this expedition, with his wary eyes and constant twitching, and did not see how anyone could be convinced by him. But then, I hadn't needed convincing to join; it could have been the same for them.

"I don't *not* believe him," he said, and laughed. "But about that, I have a theory. What if the world isn't ending at all? What if far away from us, who are isolated here in this tunnel system, the world continued on as it had before?"

The notion had occurred to me in idle moments over the years. The surface world, all sand and lethal heat in our region, might yet sustain survivors closer to the poles.

"Much was lost when the bombs fell," he said, his voice dropped down almost to a whisper. "It may be the case that this entire sector, or parts of it, were written off as a loss. We were cut off. Why would outsiders suffer the cost to excavate a wasteland? They forgot about us, and vice versa."

"Then you think we can reach it?"

"God willing," he said. "If we can, we will, for the sake of our children."

They were a charming couple and I often spoke with them when we encamped. Like her husband, Nadia was most cordial, but she rarely said more than a few words. Babak confided in me during our march one cycle that bandits had attacked her family's caravan and killed her parents when she was only a child. Her eyes, though, were clear and watchful. I sometimes wondered what went on behind them, and what she beheld when she lapsed back into her customary silence, staring off into the dark.

The Beekeeper

Ruzba was an oddity: a chimera with a reptilian phenotype. We shall assume his gender as male for the purposes of this story, but I couldn't be certain. He wore a white thawb, the ankle-length shirt which was not unusual for territories near the western mountains, and a plain white shemagh on his head. I would guess his weight at close to 60 kilos, which was a lot more than I had. He was only a bit taller than me, but stocky and powerful for his size. It was hard not to stare at his eyes, which were huge in proportion to his skull.

I think it was the jerboa DNA in me, but I was never entirely comfortable around Ruzba, which was unfair since I know he never willed me any harm. It must have been his teeth, which were not sizable , but were pointy, like his jaws were lined with stout ivory needles. Or it could have been his eyes. Unlike most geckos, the "leopard" variety possesses functional eyelids. More the pity, then, that Ruzba did not often think to employ them. The vertical pupils made his gaze even more unsettling. None of this was helped by the fact that his fingers ended with brutal hooks: claws like the blade of a jambiya.

There were two carts in our caravan, the labor of pulling them was distributed in shifts. But poor Ruzba, Shapur had explained, was, for all the human DNA in him, still too much a reptile for sustained physical activity in the cool temperatures underground. He could not even digest food without the aid of a heater. Whenever we went near a tube accessing the surface, he would always make the effort to go topside and bask, even during the day, which was flirting with death. We all understood, though no one ever mentioned it, that he wouldn't live long if he were to be cut off from surface access, and the batteries on his portable heater were exhausted.

But for all his woes, Ruzba would still take a short turn pulling one of the carts, then clamber on top of it to become part of the load. At first I could not understand why we would take the effort to haul him around when he was good for so little. But he was simple in manner, and quiet, bothering no one, and it was the charitable thing to do. And at dinnertime, he doled out a spoonful or two of honey to each of us, which inclined no few of us to favor him.

I had been with the caravan two days when we spoke. He had just finished his ephemeral turn hauling supplies, when I stepped in to take his place. He greeted me.

"Peace," he said. His mouth opened when he spoke, but his lower jaw didn't bob up and down. It was as if the sounds he made were produced all in his throat, and the mouth was only a channel for them. The words were distinct, but off, as though they were being played from a recording device rather than originating from his person.

"And upon you, peace. It's good to meet you, brother," I said, forcing myself to be civil. "I hear you were a beekeeper."

"Aye," he said, and licked his eye clean. I had begun to pull. The cart was not so bad once you got it going. I didn't begrudge his rest.

"You can keep bees underground?"

"We bring sunlight down for the plants with fiber-optic cable, same as any farm. Used to be a cable factory nearby, we had so much of the stuff we used it as rope. And our bees were specially engineered for that kind of life."

"I see." Even then, I had the thought that I would write this story someday, so I had a look around to see if anyone was in earshot, then put the question to him.

"Brother," I said, "Do you believe we will get to paradise?"

He didn't answer for some time and I began to think he had fallen asleep.

"What is paradise?" He asked dreamily, startling me back to attention. "For me, it's a warm, shady place with plenty of water and lots of food to eat. That's all I've ever wanted from life, and it would be so easy for God. It's not too much to ask, is it?"

The Djinn

We came across an abandoned oasis, the sign at the edge proclaimed it "New Doroud." The main transit tunnel we'd been following up to this point had suffered a cave-in some years before, so we were forced into the auxiliaries. When we emerged from one of these into a park or public square, our immediate response was to locate the residential area and fan out to scavenge for supplies. Most such localities were picked clean before any of us were even born, but there was always a chance some things might have been hidden or overlooked.

It must have been a thriving community at one time. It was by far the biggest city I had ever seen and must have sheltered two-hundred families or more. Judging by the four-centimeters-deep layer of dust on the floor, it was safe to say no one had been through for a long time.

As I searched a house, I became aware that my companions had spread out so far that I was quite alone. I held my breath and turned my ears this way and that, but heard only the slow passage of a draft, and the faint hiss of shifting sand. Then I caught movement from the corner of my eye.

I was not at first alarmed, but thought it was one of my fellow travelers come looking for me. I called out a greeting, to no reply.

"Who's there?" I asked.

Nothing.

I wanted to convince myself that it was only my imagination, but I was certain of what I saw. I slipped out the back entrance and found myself in an alleyway. A disused ventilation shaft had dumped sand onto the path to my left, blocking the way. Could they have gone back, taking care to duck under the windows so that I didn't see? But even if that were the case, why should anyone wish to move about in secret like that?

A chill ran up my back and every hair on my body stood on end. My hand wandered down to the jambiya on my belt; the blade sang a muted tone as the tip scraped free of its leather sheath. It was the first time I'd ever exposed the knife in a public place, as this was only permitted in our culture by the needs of self-defense. If ever there was a time, I thought, that time had come.

"Sir?"

I just about jumped out of my skin, but my composure returned at speed. It was a child's voice I had heard; I was certain. Taking care to replace my jambiya, I turned around. There was a chimera child standing in the middle of the road. I say "chimera child" because I could not, still cannot, identify her phenotype. She most resembled a jackal, sleek and fine-boned, but her coat was mottled shades of yellow and brown like the lifeless desert up above, which had once been scrubland, and her ears more resembled those of a ground squirrel, with tufts on the ends. Her tail was long and broad, like that of a skunk. At the time I took her for a hybrid, though of what, I couldn't discern. She was naked and smelled of ash and smoke.

"Hi, I'm Atash," she said.

"Girl, what are you doing? Put some clothes on!"

She ignored that and ran around me, out of the alleyway, into the road.

"Let's play! Come get me!"

Three seconds in and I already had enough of her. I prayed for patience and walked after her.

"Where are your parents?"

She went so still that if she had been lying down, I might have thought she died.

"They're gone," she said. "Long ago. The others, too. All gone."

"Well," I said, almost caught up with her, "I'm with a group. Poor thing, have you no clothes? Come with me and we will give you something."

"Where?" she asked. I pointed and we started to walk back together with me looking straight ahead, as much from embarrassment as from a concern to protect her modesty. She asked a few questions about the group, how many people, what sort, our method of transport. I answered her, but she continued uninterestedly, so that I was not sure if she was listening.

"You should all stay here," she said. Something in her speech had changed. It wasn't an issue of timbre, but of feeling. It was the same voice, but as though it issued from one who had already been on this world a hundred and more years, all of them weary. "You will never reach your destination."

"Ah," I said, unsettled by her change in tack, but still taking her for a child and willing to indulge her little game, "but you don't know our destination."

"Of course I do. You mean to go to the holy city and pray for paradise."

I stopped and whirled around in surprise. She had vanished.

"I'll show you..." she said, her words issuing from everywhere at once, and the world around me began to spin. How can I describe that feeling? It was like I had rollers on my feet, and the earth spun beneath me while I remained fixed in place. I was of a sudden on the surface, the multitude of stars shining down on the endless expanse of desert.

"Here is your refuge," she said, her words acidic, taunting, "Blasted ruins buried thirty meters deep."

Then the world rolled back over and I was standing in the ghost town, as I had been a moment before.

"We are the last of our peoples," she said. "Stay here. You will find only death out there."

Folks may berate me for this, but I ran away as fast as I could, and I didn't stop until I found someone. I didn't speak of the incident at first; I was afraid they would think I was crazy. There was talk of setting up camp there, but I wouldn't hear of it. I babbled on until Shapur relented and agreed to set up in the tunnel past the edge of town.

A week passed before I shared this story. It made its way around the caravan. Some said I must have dreamt it, others smiled and nodded but I knew they thought I was making it up. I guess I wouldn't have believed me either. I was surprised that Shapur did.

I found him sucking on a tube of fifty-year-old nutrient paste near the front of the caravan and poured out the whole story. He listened with a passive face until I was done.

"That was a djinn," the vole said, "in a child's form. Even as we were made from clay, so were djinn made from fire. The smoke and ash smell must mean it is near the end of its life. It would seem they are dying out along with us. Pay no mind to the vision it showed you. It was only an illusion meant to bring you to despair."

"Might it have been an angel?"

He scoffed and we left it at that. At times, I was not sure myself whether it was a dream, but I took care not to stray too far from my companions. I often thought of that girl, djinn or not, dying all alone in the dark, in that immense, inexorable stillness, and I pitied her.

The Highwaymen

We found the first body outside a formidable-looking structure that must have been a bank or government office in times past, which had been hollowed out of the living rock. Such architecture had been easier to produce with the assistance of machinery than it had been back in the days where it was all done by hand, but was still a colossal, labor-intensive sort of project spanning years. As such, there were not many of them.

The dryness and cool air had mummified him, this mole, who was shriveled but otherwise intact. He had a pistol in his hand and a wound in the side of his head. Near to his remains we found a shallow pit filled with bones, which were scattered in such a way that we could only discern how many people were involved by counting the skulls, of which there were three. Their teeth suggested they were all moles like their mummified friend. To judge by the holes, they'd been killed each with a shot to the back of the head. Everyone must have noticed, though we did not mention it, that the bones were covered with bite marks, and had been cracked open to extract the marrow.

There were bullet-holes in the door of the stone building, which wouldn't open. Circling for an alternate means of entry, we discovered that the windows had been blocked with piles of heavy furniture. We had just about resolved to give up and move on when I decided to throw my shoulder against the door to see if it would give. I am neither large nor strong, so this gesture was symbolic, yet, there was a crack and the door swung open, catching me so unawares that I almost bowled face-first onto the floor with all the excess momentum.

The door had been barred with a slab of some composite material which must have been rigid enough for the task when it was new, but had degraded with the years and become brittle. There was another mummy in this first room, this one laying prone with a pistol in its hand. The holes in the back of the shirt left little doubt as to the cause of this fellow's demise.

The last of them we found not far from that front area, sitting with his back to the wall, legs stretched out in front of him. He'd been shot three times in the upper torso. Stains on the floor indicated it had happened in the other room, after which he had dragged himself in here to die. He was clutching a pair of bags about the size of pillow-cases, full of canned food. We were excited about that until noting the way the cans had swollen up from bacterial activity inside.

Shapur insisted that we give the remains proper burial rites even though he conceded that these men had almost certainly been a family of highway robbers squabbling over the last of their stores.

"Murderers? Cannibals? Why should we?" I wasn't angry at the suggestion, but perplexed.

"God can forgive any sin if we turn to Him in sincere repentance," he said. "Only He knows what is in the hearts of men, and only He is fit to judge them now. Desperation can drive the best of people to an evil path. No man has the right to say who is or is not worthy of Behesht."

The Nomad

We lucked upon a caravanserai that had a pump in good condition. We believed we might top off our supply of water if only the power might be restored, so we made to locate a surface access to see if anything could be done for the solar panels. While engaged in this, however, the overhead lights sparked to life. There was only one conclusion: that we were not alone in this place.

It may have been a group like our own, but then it might also have been persons of less than noble intentions. A moment's talk and we took up a defensive position in the room with the pump, watching the doorway and waiting. Those of us with pistols had them ready. We did not have to wait long before the stranger made her appearance.

She entered the room with her head down. Chimera, being based on the human genome, fell within the limits of the human range of sizes, with those of smaller phenotypes tending towards the low end, and those of larger phenotypes tending towards the high end. But these tunnels and buildings had been made by and for chimera derived from slight, burrowing creatures, and this woman was a camel. We weren't in doubt about that, the famous hump, though reduced compared to that of their four-legged counterparts, was in evidence. She was well over two meters tall, the ceiling was just shy of it.

When she saw us, she startled and bumped her head, then clasped her hand over her heart.

"Peace," the she-camel said. "By God, you scared me!" To say her voice was like a man's would have been wrong. It was far deeper than that, a rumble that was felt as much as heard. She wore a long, white, hooded robe with trousers underneath, all made from some shimmering material I could not identify beyond saying it was no natural fiber that I had ever seen. There was a pistol at her waist but she made no move for it.

"Peace, sister," Shapur said. He gave us a look and we holstered our arms.

I was not privy to the conversation which followed, as she and Shapur went to speak in another room while I was summoned to assist in getting the pump to run. It was not until later that cycle, when we were encamped and taking our meal, that she came to me and exchanged greetings. Shapur must have sent her for me to interview, but whatever the case, I invited her to share my carpet.

"I was surprised to see a camel," I said. "I thought your kind was lost."

"My kind shall walk the earth until the final day." There was pride in it, but she could not conceal a twinge of sadness. She knew, as we all did, that day could well be imminent.

"Will you be joining us, then?"

She shook her head. "With these," she indicated her attire with a hand wave, "and our genetics, we can survive on the surface for days. It is dangerous, but because we can circumvent obstructions in the tunnels, we are able to range far when we scavenge."

"Ah." I thought about the civilization that had once graced the overworld, the great cities with buildings that seemed to touch the sky. "You must have seen so much."

She shook her head again and smiled. "Only sand, from horizon to horizon. We have been farther than you can imagine, and found nothing."

"You keep saying 'we,' do you have a herd?"

"Oh, yes," she said, confident. "We were attacked and became separated, but I'm sure I'll catch up with them soon."

"And when was that?"

She looked up at the ceiling, her lips moving as she performed the calculations.

"About ten years ago."

"I see." I didn't say what I was thinking, that her fellows were long dead. The both of us were chasing ghosts, and differed only in direction. "And is that why you won't come with us, because you're looking for them?"

"No," she said, and laughed. "I already told you, there's nothing out there. You fools are going to get yourselves killed."

The Executioner

Amir the hare stood out from the rest in many ways. He was just over one-hundred and eighty centimeters tall (not counting the ears), by far the tallest in our group. In dressing he was utilitarian, favoring slacks and baggy pullover shirts, eschewing traditional styles. He was the only male in our party who didn't wear any sort of head covering, and the only male to wear his hair long, which was not forbidden, per se, but so far removed from contemporary mores as to be peculiar. But the thing that stood out most of all was that he carried a shamshir. Swords had not been used in war for centuries, so I was curious as to its purpose.

But Amir was a hard person to approach: he took his meals alone and always sought the fringes whenever we encamped. It wasn't that he was rude when spoken to, people said, but rather that he preferred his own company. It wasn't until I had been with the caravan two weeks that I got a chance to speak with him in private.

It was our sleeping period and I was losing a battle with insomnia, so I decided to see if anyone else was conscious. Living almost all one's life underground bestows a certain awareness; we become accustomed to feeling our way along, seeing with our ears. I found the wall and followed it, not wanting to wake anyone with my lamp. I had the sense that a sleeping bag which had been occupied earlier was now empty, and a moment later I heard the clink of glass on glass and moved towards it.

A little while and I could see a glow emanating from a house we'd searched earlier that cycle. I'd always been told that it wasn't right to spy on people, so rather than creep up on whoever this was, I cleared my throat. The light inside the building changed, like someone wearing a lamp had turned their head. Then the light moved towards the doorway and there I met Amir.

"Ah," he said, and went back inside. I followed him.

Further in, he had pried up a piece of the floor, revealing a crawlspace. That was presumably where he had found all the bottles of liquor he had set up, and from which he was so nonchalantly sipping. My first reaction was to peek behind me to be sure I hadn't been followed, then to ask him a question.

"Are you crazy? Shapur will have you whipped if he finds out."

He smiled and shook his head, indicating his sword. "Let them try. The one who puts a hand on me surrenders it forever."

"They have guns."

He shrugged. "I never said they wouldn't shoot me. But you are right, if it pleases them to whip a dead man, they're welcome." That settled, he tipped the bottle in my direction, offering.

"No, thanks."

"Suit yourself."

As he did not appear to mind my presence, and would be more talkative on account of his inebriation, I decided to stick around. I had nothing better to do.

"So…" I began, but he never let me get started.

"You want to know about my shamshir." It wasn't a question.

"Yes. Yes, sir."

"I cut people's heads off for a living. Or at least I did. No courts anymore, that means no sentencing. Used to be, folks would catch a robber now and then. Bandits are parasitic, you know, but now there's no one for them to feed on. No host, no parasites."

"Oh. How did you get into that…"? I trailed off in thought, trying to find a tactful word, and came up with, "occupation?" He had already said more than I had ever heard him say. The liquor seemed to be doing its work already.

"You're born into it," he said. "One of my ancestors was a criminal, probably, who got stuck with it. From then on, his genealogical line became an 'executioner family.' That means we can only marry among other executioner families. How many of those do you think there are? God only knows how we made it this far. It stops here, though. No one for me to marry, executioner family or otherwise."

He took another drink and we were content to let the thread of conversation sleep a while. When he continued, he did so with a smile.

"The work is not so bad," he said. "The day before, I go to the aggrieved family and beg them to grant clemency. I beg mercy for murderers! If they don't forgive him, then at the beginning of the next cycle I sharpen my sword. It's just like swinging a pick, easiest job in the world."

I tried to imagine myself decapitating someone and decided I couldn't do it. By then, I was ready to change the subject. I asked him if he thought we would reach paradise, as I had done with the others, but he seemed not to understand that the talk had moved on.

"Well, why shouldn't I?" he asked, ears flat, his tone agitated. "God saw fit to have me born into this position. How, then, am I tainted? I'm just like this sword, an instrument for someone else's use. If the sentence is wrong, then that wrong falls on the authorities. And if a sentence is just, then what sin transpired?"

"Brother, I apologize, I didn't mean that. I'm asking if you think we'll ever escape these tunnels, if we'll ever reach the holy city."

Now that he understood the question, he settled back into thought, and his bearing softened. Then he laughed and gave me the answer for which I had been looking.

"I don't have any idea about that," he said, "but what would you have us do, sit on our hands?"

* * *

As I write this, the supplies are running low. Shapur pores over his maps and makes promises, but I felt it prudent to commence this project. Two cycles ago, Ruzba went on to his reward. His scales had gone from yellow and black to a greyish brown. We think it was the lack of sun. If you should stumble across this record, I hope you will pray for him, and for us.

So now I commit these pages to posterity. With this cool, dry air, they should last for many years. If you read this far, you have my thanks. Please return them to the box you found them in.

I had thought to write a warning here urging you to go back, but the fact is, you're going to die either way. You may not reach Behesht, but you definitely won't if you never make the attempt.

It's strange, but the more we search, the more certain I become that we will arrive in paradise. We are very close, I think we will find it any time now.

Little Fox falls to earth on Jamie's farm.

Where does Little Fox belong? He and Jamie find out.

The Moon Fox

by Amy Fontaine

Jamie lay in her bed. Warm summer air drifted in through the window along with cricket song. The moon was nowhere to be seen, but in the starlight she could just make out the shadowy shapes of the barn and the pasture fence.

A big shooting star streaked across the sky. She heard a crash on the other side of the house, then a thud …

Silence. Darkness. The chirp of crickets returning.

With a whispered prayer, Jamie tiptoed barefoot down the dark hall of the old farmhouse to the living room. Dimly, she saw something moving in the fireplace.

Jamie gasped. It was a little fox, with white-gray fur the color of memories and eyes as black as untold secrets. Two strange mounds were folded tight against his back like pillow down.

"Fire!" the fox cried, stumbling around dizzily in the fireplace soot. "Comets! They burned me! They burned my… my…" He keeled over and fell still.

Jamie stared, wide-eyed, at the limp, soot-covered animal. He was still breathing. She cleaned him as best she could, carried the furry form to her room, and laid him on her bed. She watched over him, hardly believing he was there, until she fell asleep.

* * *

At dawn, Jamie awoke to the smell of pancakes wafting in from the kitchen. The fox slept curled up at the foot of her bed.

"So I didn't dream you," said Jamie, patting his head.

The fox blinked awake and raised his head. "Where am I?"

Jamie's eyes widened. "And I didn't dream you could talk! You're in my home."

"What am I?"

"Don't you know?"

"I don't remember."

"Well, you're a fox, I think. A little fox. Can I call you that? Little Fox?"

"Sure!" Little Fox yipped, wagging his tail.

Just then, Jamie's father appeared at the doorway. He was in his overalls and boots, ready for work. "Come eat your breakfast, Jamie. We've got chores to do."

Little Fox yipped softly.

Jamie's father narrowed his eyes at the fox. "What in tarnation!"

Jamie gulped. "It's... it's a dog, Daddy! Found it scratching at the back door last night!"

"Lost, I guess. He's awful dirty. Why'd you bring him inside?"

"I... I thought maybe we could train him for herding? I could get him familiar with the sheep."

"Hmm. Looks too small and timid to me. But you can try." With a nod, Jamie's father clomped down the hall.

Jamie breathed a sigh of relief. "Let's go eat."

* * *

After she had scarfed down her pancakes and eggs, and passed some under the table to Little Fox, Jamie hurried to the pastures, her 'dog' trotting at her heels. Early morning painted the fields with a rosy glow.

"Is he mean?" asked Little Fox.

"You mean Daddy?" Jamie laughed. "No! Just a little rough around the edges, is all."

"Why'd you tell him I'm a dog?"

"Foxes aren't good for farms."

"Oh." Little Fox's ears drooped.

Jamie shook her head and smiled. "It's okay. I can tell you're a special fox."

Little Fox lifted his head high. There was a spring in his step as he followed Jamie across the farmyard and through a creaky wooden gate into a field. He saw huge white puffs drifting through the grass.

"Clouds! Beautiful clouds!"

"No, Little Fox. *Sheep.* Daddy wants to shear them today. Usually, I chase them through the gate one by one, yelling and banging a bell. It takes forever. But it'll go quick if you can be a herding dog."

"What does a herding dog do?"

"Just nip a little at the sheep's heels, and get them all moving together through the gate."

Little Fox gazed up at the sheep. Up close, they towered over him. He swallowed, standing as tall as he could. "I'll do my best!"

And with that, he charged, yipping sharply.

He soon forgot about herding, though. He pranced, almost danced, around the sheep and through the field. He was as graceful as a bird soaring through clouds. As he ran, he shook off the rest of the soot. The tips of his fur glowed.

But the sheep bleated fearfully and scattered. And then Jamie's father came running from the barnyard.

"Bad dog!" he shouted.

Little Fox hunched down and tried to look like a herding dog.

But when Jamie's father reached them, he could see that Little Fox was not a dog at all.

Back at the farmhouse, Jamie's father scolded her. Little Fox curled up into a ball in the other room and shut his eyes. When Jamie returned to him, her eyes glistened with tears. She held him close and stroked his fur.

"I told Daddy you were different, but he's sending you away," Jamie whispered. "I'm sorry."

Little Fox whimpered. "No! I want to stay with you! I'll be a good dog! I—"

Jamie's father came in carrying a small wooden crate. "Don't worry, Jamie. Joe's stopping by. He's driving past the preserve on his way to a delivery in town. Your friend will get to live in the woods, where he can't hurt any chickens."

"He doesn't belong in the woods."

"Where else would he belong?"

Jamie looked down at Little Fox, trembling in her lap. "Where he's safe and happy."

Jamie's father took Little Fox. "Sorry, Jamie, but I've gotta do this. C'mon, little guy." He put Little Fox in the crate and closed the lid.

* * *

The crate bumped along in the back of Joe's roaring truck. Little Fox could see flashes of light through gaps in the boards. In the cramped space, he felt squashed, his paws got scraped, and the mounds on his back ached as if they were on fire. He yowled, remembering the tears in Jamie's eyes. Eventually, he fell asleep.

When Little Fox awoke, his crate was open, and he could see light. But it wasn't sunlight, and the air felt stuffy. Gingerly, he placed his paws on the edge of the crate and peeked out into a strange, busy, noisy new world.

He was in the back of a stage. Red curtains rose up into darkness. Stagehands ran about with various items, including the old farm equipment that had been in the truck. Actors and actresses in wild costumes—kingly robes, scuba suits, fairy wings, animal suits—shuffled about, whistling, clapping, muttering lines. There were a lot of nooks and crannies where a little fox could hide. But Little Fox didn't want to hide. Leaping out of the crate, he shook himself and padded through a gap in the velvet curtains to the center of the stage.

A woman in bejeweled blue robes and a porcelain mask was fanning herself, speaking to a ballerina. In the bright spotlights, Little Fox could see couches, chairs, fake windows, fake portraits on a fake wall. The area out past the stage was very dark, with little lights sprinkled about, like the vast reaches of starry space. His heart fluttered, and the mounds on his back stirred with something other than pain. His fur began to glow softly and he ran in happy circles.

"Cut!" roared an angry voice from the dark.

Little Fox froze.

The director leaped onto the stage, his mustache bristling.

Little Fox yelped as he was scooped up by the scruff of the neck and lifted to the director's glaring eyes. "YOU are ruining my rehearsal!"

The woman in the blue robes and the ballerina stared at Little Fox. Stagehands, actors, and actresses gathered, circling.

Little Fox blinked. "I was supposed to go to a nature preserve, but maybe this is the wrong place."

"For you this is absolutely the wrong place! I've got a play to put on and there are no parts for talking animals."

"I'll just sit quietly right here."

"Not on the stage. The stage is for actors."

"I'll be an actor!"

The director snorted. "All our roles have been cast, except for the earthworm. Can you be an earthworm?"

"I could try!"

266

The director rolled his eyes. "Fine. Let's see. You're an earthworm. Go."

Little Fox wiggled across the stage. He pretended to burrow into the ground.

The director nodded approvingly, and Little Fox glowed with pride.

The director's face fell. "No glowing!"

Little Fox scrunched up his face. "Sorry!"

The director sighed. "It's all right. It's your first rehearsal. But don't glow, don't be a fox, don't run."

But later, Little Fox did run, around the stage with the children of some of the actors. He leaped over stools and raced around corners, laughing like frost shimmering on a tree. And he glowed brighter than a swarm of fireflies.

"Fox!" bellowed the director.

Startled, Little Fox crashed into a table. He wriggled out from under it, only to be grabbed by the scruff of his neck. The director hauled him back to the crate and dropped him in.

"Sorry," said the director, "but you can't be yourself here. Maybe the circus can use you." He slammed the lid shut.

Little Fox whimpered.

Little Fox was loaded into another truck. He shut his eyes and ignored the darkness but couldn't stop hearing all the angry things that had been said to him.

The crate jostled about in the truck. He bruised his tail, his paws, his nose, his ears, and the two crumpled mounds on his back. At least the pain in them had been lessening. He fell into a fitful sleep.

* * *

When Little Fox woke, someone had slid the lid off the crate. He poked his head out and looked around. Red and gold tents stood around him in a large field. He smelled popcorn, fried food, engine oil, perfume, sweat, lemonade, plastic, barnyard straw. He heard yelling, screaming, laughing, crying, buzzes, blares, whirs, and bleeps. The air tasted thick and smoky. People strolled about between the tents.

It was a cloudy night, but the lights of the Ferris wheel glowed like streaking comets as it spun. There were rides shaped like dragons that dipped and dove, tall slides, a carousel with fabulous wooden creatures. Little Fox felt drawn to a big ride shaped like a crescent moon. He watched it swing back and forth, mesmerized.

"Like what you see?"

Little Fox turned. A man was smiling down at him. He wore a red and gold suit that matched the circus tents, gloves and boots that gleamed in the lights flashing from the rides.

"I am Alfonso, the ringmaster. I hear you are a talking, glowing fox!"

Little Fox's ears perked up, and the growths on his back fluttered.

"Yes! Yes, I am!"

Alfonso laughed and patted Little Fox's head. "That's nice. But we already have one of those."

Little Fox jumped out of the crate. "Really? Where?"

Alfonso led Little Fox to a sideshow in a tent, to a fox puppet covered in gold paint, its puppeteer hidden behind a small wooden stage. A string waved the fox's paw.

"Hi, I'm Lloyd the Magic Fox!" the puppeteer said in a deep, goofy voice.

The children sitting before the stage laughed and clapped.

Little Fox's tail fell. "But I'm real! I should be your fox!"

Alfonso put a finger to his lips and led Little Fox outside. "Listen, fox, I don't want you stealing Lloyd's thunder, okay? What we really need is a goat. Our goat, Bertha, ran away two days ago. We could have just replaced her, but I said no, you people have no *vision!*" The ringmaster wagged a gloved finger. "Lots of circuses have goats, but none of them have a goat who's really a fox!" The ringmaster slapped his knee and chuckled. "Get it?"

Little Fox didn't get it but he smiled politely.

He followed the ringmaster into one of the tents. There were clowns with sad faces, lion tamers, and tightrope walkers in bright, sequined costumes. A woman balanced on the back of a galloping horse, and a man was swallowing fire. Little Fox's act was not hard. He just trotted and bleated in a very goatish way, while knowing he could do so much more.

But the audience liked his act. They clapped, cheered, and threw flowers to him. He blushed, the white fur on his face turning rosy. And then, as they continued to applaud, he glowed brighter, brighter than the lights of the tent until the crowd shielded their eyes and the ringmaster bellowed.

But a strange joy was humming in his mind, and Little Fox leaped through the air in graceful arcs that shimmered like rainbows. Laughing, he shot from one end of the tent to the other, jumping right over the woman on horseback. The horse neighed in alarm, thundered across the tent, and knocked against a tent pole. The pole began tilting, the tent began sagging, and people began screaming and running out. Little Fox froze, and his glow faded.

The ringmaster glared at Little Fox. "You're not supposed to act like yourself! You're fired!" He ran after the departing crowd.

Little Fox wandered sadly through the lanes between the tents. Lights dimmed, the Ferris wheel came to the end of its last spin of the night, and the game booths closed one by one. The circus was settling into stillness.

Little Fox walked to the edge of the circus, gazing out across miles of grass and starry sky. When he looked up, he felt like he was swimming in a sea of stars. Behind a drifting patch of clouds, he glimpsed something big and round and bright, and a shiver of delight went through him.

Suddenly, Little Fox heard rough voices and a girl's scream.

Jamie's scream.

Little Fox bolted back and careened around a corner into a lane behind some tents, where Jamie was struggling in the grip of two women.

"Let go of me! I don't want to join your circus!"

The women laughed. One of them put her face close to Jamie's and grinned a big, crooked, yellow-toothed grin. "But of course you do, dearie! We always use runaways in our magic act!"

Little Fox growled. Jamie saw him and a grin spread across her face, but the women dragged her kicking and screaming toward one of the trailers.

Little Fox lunged at the women, biting at their boots much better than he'd nipped at the sheep.

"Vermin!" one of the women shouted, kicking Little Fox. He yelped and crumpled. Gasping at the pain in his ribs, he watched as the women pulled Jamie to their trailer.

But now the full moon emerged from the clouds, pouring cool silver light over him. He looked up and smiled. A shiver ran through him, a good shiver, like nostalgia, like the taste of cold water on a hot summer day. The feeling spread through him from ear tips to tail tip, healing his bruises and the burned, bent feathers of his wings.

Wings!

Memories flooded back, and he knew. He was Moon Fox, the radiant Moon Fox. And he had wings! He didn't have to herd or trot or wriggle or bleat.

With a warbling bark, Moon Fox glowed, filling the circus grounds with light. Releasing Jamie, the two women stumbled back.

Blazing, Moon Fox flew at the women. They cried out and sprinted for their trailer, locking themselves in.

Moon Fox sailed through the air, relishing the midnight breeze, the freedom of his wings. Then he swooped towards Jamie. He hovered in the air before her, winged, shining. "I'm *Moon Fox!*"

Jamie thrilled to the sight of him. "Yes, you are!"

Moon Fox nudged Jamie. "How did you find me?"

Jamie took a deep breath. "We heard about the mix-up with Joe. Daddy and I went to the theater, but the director had already sold you to the circus. We were looking for you here when a lot of people ran out of one of the tents and I got lost in the crowd. I'm glad you're okay. More than okay," she added with a smile.

Moon Fox smiled back, nuzzling Jamie's hand. "Thank you for caring for me. I'm healed now, and I can go home. Let's find your dad so you can head home, too."

Jamie nodded. Once they spotted her dad, Jamie embraced Moon Fox. His body felt like a sparkling ray of light.

"I knew you were special," Jamie whispered, wiping tears on her sleeve. Reluctantly, she let him go, but a little glow stayed with her.

When Jamie had gone, Moon Fox looked up at the moon. With a yip of joy, he flew home.

He lives there to this day. He does not have to squirm or trot, bark or bleat; he flies, and he glows to his heart's content as he dances with the children of the moon.

Moon Fox feels he is always on center stage. He reflects the sun with radiant grace. He smiles, and the world smiles back at him.

Imperial Prime Agent Vix Pon Hallord (a weasel) arrives at an isolated space station, inhabited only by top-secret research scientist Doctor Liantro Pon Liskar (another weasel) and an Artificial Intelligence. Hallord finds the Doctor dead, apparently a suicide, and her space station only hours from irreversible self-destruction.

Can he learn why she killed herself, and stop the space station's destruction in time?

The Ouroboros Plate

by Slip Wolf

Imperial Prime Agent Hallord stepped from his ship through the space station's inner airlock. The scent that tickled his nose set his barren stomach growling. Six weeks of cryo during interstellar transit still had his brown ears cold and he was indeed on a mission, but the most urgent of directives couldn't be followed when he was all but starving since his awakening during final approach.

Hallord, being a weasel, could eat half his own mass of meat in a single sitting, but training and special metabolic drugs had prepped him for long stays in space with limited sustenance. After so long unconscious, he was ravenous. The sizzle of roasted meat combined with the bright bite of herbs and spices hooked him left, down a short hallway in the standard-layout remote military station to the dining nook, where a sumptuous feast of meat strips, ibex he guessed, awaited him.

Doctor Liskar, the station's solitary occupant, was nowhere in sight. Surely she'd be up to meet him soon, even if the nook's table was set for one. Likely she'd eaten earlier.

Hallord ate. The meat was the best he'd tasted in years, fully deboned, crisped and sauced. It was buttery on his tongue as it went down, lean meat with very little fat or gristle. "Computer," Hallord called out between bites.

"Yes." The voice that responded was deep, masculine and prim, devoid of emotion.

"Was Doctor Liskar notified of my ship's approach?"

"No. She is on the lab level. Her last request was to be undisturbed."

"Who prepared this meal for me then?"

"Kitchen processor."

"Processor? Amazing." The next bite was as sumptuous as the last. He chuckled. "If there's anything at all amiss, I'm not going to find it here."

"I take it that you have been sent by the Emperor to ensure the project is running smoothly."

Hallord nodded as he chewed, already feeling renewed. "In my typical role, I'd be out in the colonies helping put down livestock rebellions, but the Emperor has seen fit to provide me with a more agreeable assignment this time around." Hallord finished his repast with a flourish, all but licking the plate. He used a napkin to dab at his jaws and hoped there were more meals of its caliber ahead.

He stood, grooming down the chest fur between the straps of his rank harness. This, a tool belt and gray pantaloons piped in Imperial maroon were all the clothing he wore, all he needed for work in the climate controlled chambers of the Empire's transit ships and stations.

He hoped he cut a dashing figure in his vestments of office, showing off the dark chestnut fur that draped him from ear-tips to tail. Doctor Liskar was rumored to be quite a beautiful specimen of Imperial mustelid stock with a pelt like shimmering pearl. She'd been alone for as long as he had, developing her top secret project for the Imperial war effort in complete secrecy. Only scheduled progress report visits such as Hallord's broke the isolation that she had specially requested with her considerable influence and which she claimed to thrive on.

As for himself, Hallord thrived on company. No doubt Liskar was aware of the extremely formidable stature of the Emperor's personal field agents and the incredible responsibilities they took on. On his last mission out in the colonies, Hallord had wrapped up a livestock uprising by dining together with the general's daughter on the grilled flank of the rebellion's bison leader. Serving the Emperor's whims was difficult work that had its privileges, and Hallord's position as an elite in the Imperial forces netted him danger and reward in equal measures. His temporary presence would surely be no imposition. Hopefully quite the opposite.

"Where is Doctor Liskar now?" Hallord preened his ruff with sharp claws.

"She went to the laboratory antechamber, one level below."

"Have the maintenance bot clean up." Hallord tossed the napkin on the plate as he stalked back to the ladder by the lock. There was a lift a little further on, but he didn't want to use it, putting a bounce in his step to keep himself from getting post-meal lethargy.

Remote isolation Imperial space stations were primarily two level splits. Living quarters, kitchen, offices and docking port above with mission critical labs, storage and maintenance bays below. A tiny bay to access the fusion reactor lay below that. Hallord could navigate this facility with his eyes closed. Only modular chambers in the labs below had customizable layouts. With the project shrouded in whispers and his own secrecy sworn in the Emperor's presence, Hallord didn't know what lay below.

"The maintenance bot is offline. Failed main circuit. Cause unknown at this time."

Hallord frowned as he grabbed the ladder-well and hooked his paws on the rungs. "Has Doctor Liskar tried to repair it?"

The AI voice followed him through speakers in the ladder-well, sounding regretful. "It just happened an hour ago."

"Was she aware of it?"

"No."

Hallord's paws met the lab deck plates. He huffed as he turned to the laboratory entrance. The sealed door to the laboratory antechamber slid open silently, and there was Doctor Liskar, slumped low in an office chair.

The smell hit Hallord as fast as he saw her. Her sightless dead eyes had sunk back into her head, the sockets looking at nothing. Her slender jaws were open just slightly, exposing a tongue that had turned black. Two empty paws dangled towards the floor. Under the right, a syringe lay empty.

Hallord drew his sidearm. "What happened here?"

A security camera from outside the office whirred as it adjusted focus. "Doctor Liskar appears to be dead."

"How did this happen!"

"Unknown. The Doctor entered this room several hours ago and requested I prepare for your arrival. I have no other data." The AI sounded mildly annoyed by this.

"There were no other entrants to this facility then?"

"The last supply drop was two months ago. No station accesses logged between that linkage and the shuttle that brought the doctor here." Hallord realized it couldn't be otherwise. No transmissions could leave this station by design save an emergency call beacon. Its location orbiting a dead planet in a dwarf star's company was unknown to anyone but a minority of military planners. Hallord himself had surrendered his cryogenically suspended body to pre-programmed coordinates to even get wherever this system was.

Hallord holstered his weapon. "Why did you not tell me Liskar was dead when I first arrived?"

"I was unaware of this development until you opened the office door. The Doctor seemed tired when I last took instructions from her a few hours ago. I don't know why, but I have no additional information. Recorders in the office are disabled. I am observing you from the foyer."

Hallord gingerly set about examining Liskar's corpse. Her death had been very recent as the AI suggested. Lividity hadn't set into her dangling limbs.

A chill traveled through his limbs as he gazed down at the syringe on the deck at her feet. Whatever concoction had killed her hadn't been lying around. Death had not been a spur of the moment decision, but a plan. The Empire's very security had rested on her shoulders, and she had apparently divested herself of all that, even if a reason why escaped him.

Hallord caught a hiss in his throat. Regardless of what drove the scientist to die, so prominent a personage deserved decorum. He would not let himself embarrass her memory with tears or curses. He had to understand what had happened.

"Did you see anything at all?"

"Again, she had the recorders deactivated. I am unaware of the circumstances of her passing."

"Are there records of what she was working on?"

"There was a mass deletion of what she claimed was corrupted data several hours ago. I was strictly instructed not to attempt to back any of it up. All that remains is the project itself."

There was another sealed door beyond the office. A window next to it was also shuttered. Hallord passed Liskar's corpse and pressed a button, opening the shutter.

What he saw inside stole his breath for a moment. Inside the lab, surrounded by a wide array of terminals and power junctions, a featureless gray disc stood on its rim, reflecting none of the light from the banks of machinery around it. All was still in that room, like he was gazing in on a painting. The small hairs on his neck stood on end as Hallord gazed at the artifact for a few moments. When he forced himself to turn away, a sensation followed, a pang plaguing his full stomach. He felt something sightlessly cold at his back, like a specter at his shoulder, when he left the ante-chamber and the deceased Doctor behind. He couldn't explain why, but he did not want to be in there.

His metabolism high with a sense of urgency, he painstakingly began searching the facility top to bottom. Everything was nondescript; stock plain, as though the station had only come to life a minute before he'd arrived. Environmental control confirmed what the AI already told him, until the moment he'd docked, the station had been sealed for weeks, as per its painstaking design. Every useful clue that was on this station was still here.

Liskar's living quarters were sparsely appointed, her bunk neatly made. The desk contained a few electronic tablet journals on quantum physics, wormhole mechanics and one volume taken from the long-dead Humanian civilization whose ancestors had long been conquered and consumed by the burgeoning Predet Empire. A dry treatise on ancient myths was bookmarked on the legend of Ouroboros, a great snake who represented the cyclic nature of some human legend that held no interest for him.

A still image above the desk was prominent; Liskar being honored by the newly minted seventy-fourth Emperor Nore the August, his ample frame leaning forward at one of his weekly triumphal feasts. Hallord stopped to briefly study its details. He himself had only been in the young Emperor's presence once before receiving this assignment, at a recess in the public trial of a senatorial dissident. The August leader had been too engrossed in the proceedings to pay attention to Hallord's security report at the time. Nore seemed quite unlike his more reserved father Keasar, who had personally promoted Hallord and secured his oath. There was a fire in the new Emperor's eyes that Hallord never wanted to gaze straight into, and thus he'd kept his eyes lowered, much as Liskar did in the still.

The scientist standing diminutively before the Emperor here was slim in her formal wear, demurely accepting a medal of honor from his high dais which was surrounded with waiting dishes of bison meat, confectionaries, wine flagons and other delights. The sight of those dishes made Hallord's mouth water. In the image, the Doctor didn't seem to be hungry, rather her posture suggested a profound discomfort with the whole proceedings as a naked slave ceremoniously polished her foot claws.

She was rumored to hate crowds, hate the noise, the bustle of the capital. Out here, with nothing but her own voice and a computer to keep her company, she had done... something.

The lab was beneath his feet. That would come last.

His continued search through the station turned up the dead maintenance bot slumped around the corner from the kitchen near the exercise track, clawed limbs hanging limp as Liskar's, a slight score of carbon under its main plate confirming a critical motor failure. The scent of burnt silicone still lingered and a cursory examination confirmed that it would take a long while to repair.

In the kitchen there was no evidence of anything other than the meal that had been prepared. The place had been thoroughly scrubbed down, and a few sniffs confirmed that the bones removed from this meal by the processor had been ground down in the disposal along with the gristle. A single drop of blood had thawed on the preparation counter, just ten feet from where the freezer door was closed. Inside, Hallord found three dozen bison flanks dangling on hooks, with only a few hooks empty. There were too few empty hooks for the amount of time Liskar had been on the station. Even if she took metabolic drugs she would have to starve herself eating so few meals. This was especially evident in light of how large a meal had been prepared for Hallord's arrival. The refrigeration unit contained leftovers from the beast prepared for him, a meal they should have shared in celebration. The weight of Liskar's suicide hit Hallord once again, more forcefully now that shock wasn't a factor, and he realized she needed to be attended to.

He brought a medical gurney down in the lift. Without the maintenance bot it was tough work, but he got the doctor off her chair, onto the flat board, all the while keeping his eyes away from the object beyond the window, which inexplicably made his skin crawl even more than the corpse he handled. Working carefully, he brought her up the lift and into the kitchen's freezer. She would not remain here among the corpses of prey species long. Hallord would convey her back to the Empire along with the dire news of her passing. She would be buried in the halls of the ancestors and mourning feasts would be held to honor her life's accomplishments.

Including whatever it was that stood in the sealed lab.

Trying to stay focused, but with his mind drifting ever towards the lab, a familiar feeling of dread crept over him as though he'd seen it before in a dream. He kept on, checking terminal after terminal, including the AI's central memory core. Every data repository was empty, erased and formatted. Around him, the station was all but silent, the air conditioning muttering in ghostly breaths. Whatever had driven Liskar to insanity, was in here with him, haunting his every step. The feeling of inexplicable familiarity with this moment, with this place, plagued his awareness. Loath as he was to admit it, he wanted nothing more than to return to his cold ship, seal the hatch and leave here forever.

But he would not. He was a battle-hardened spy and soldier, and he would not return to his Emperor without answers.

Lights dimmed as he took the ladder down to the lab level again. "Is there a problem with the power?"

"The station has entered a power-save position to preserve essential resources."

"What's causing it?"

"Not sure. There is an issue with the reactor that I am not able to identify." Again, the dulcet AI sounded mildly put out by what it didn't know.

Hallord grimaced, tail lashing from wall to wall as he stepped back out of the well and turned. Reactor control was on this level. He quickly passed the laboratory ante-chamber and entered the environmental booth, bringing up the power-plant controls. He noticed something immediately.

"Coolant levels are off and there is a countdown marker. Why has a countdown commenced?"

More mild disappointment. "I don't know about any countdown. This is information I can typically access."

Hallord drew up controls for the fusion reactor and noticed the core temperature controls. They were rising. Hallord swore.

He tried to raise the coolant level in the reactor and found it wasn't responding. "This is a countdown to reactor failure, isn't it?"

"Again, I have been removed from environmental and power plant access. I do not know why."

Hallord growled. "I was being rhetorical." The scuttle command had been tripped and the alarms disabled. This command shut-off the coolant that kept the reactor powering the station from melting down. The countdown marked the expected time of containment failure, after which the station would become molten scrap. The control program to restore cooling had been outright removed. Imperators dammit! What had Liskar done?

The AI had learned at some point to simulate a sigh when it gave bad news. "Based on these temperature readings the reactor chamber is already too dangerous to operate within. Manual restoration of cooling is impossible without immediate fatality."

"So without the protocols to activate it I've got..." He looked at the board. "This timer has three hours and six minutes. Start a relative timer and keep me apprised every ten minutes."

His own anxiety at this new development made his stomach growl. He wanted to go back up and munch on something from the kitchen while he mulled over this impending disaster, but desperation was obviously clouding his judgment. He had time to get his ship a minimum safe distance away, but not much.

Something of vital importance was in the lab. He had to get answers first. Steeling himself against his rising dread, he re-entered the lab ante-chamber. A thorough search of it was brief, but turned up something surprising. There was a pistol in one of the nearly empty drawers, Imperial special issue, same model as his own. Hallord's nose wrinkled. If Liskar had a side-arm why would she not have used it on herself rather than poison?

He placed the weapon back where he found it and closed the drawer. It was time to start getting answers.

Environmental controls on the hatch labeled the lab safe. He was taking nothing for granted anymore. Hallord paused at the lock switch and gazed through the window at the standing gray disk among the range of readouts and relays. Once again, a chill, a shade, a presence just over his shoulder scraped at his senses. He turned back to the now empty chair that hours ago had held the doctor's livid corpse and shivered. He hated this place, sealed in from the universe, only work and exercise and food and solitude. This isolation had been Liskar's choice, he remembered, for months on end. Look what it was doing to him in just a few hours.

All over this. Taking firm hold of himself and stealing a breath, Agent Hallord opened the laboratory hatch, letting the buzz of slowly thinking machines and humming power relays float out over him. There was no smell in there, none at all. Not even the antiseptic cleave of chemical sterilization brushed his questing nostrils as he stepped over the threshold. Cool air tickled his whiskers and a crackle from the room's center stood his fur up.

Even close up, the disc in the center of the room was completely devoid of any sheen or visible texture, as though it only existed as a negation of space. He took a step towards it, noting the four brackets that positioned the disc vertically but didn't actually touch it. The artifact was suspended in space, weightless and unmoving.

Puzzled, Hallord walked around the disk, watching mathematical formulas recycle on the banks of computer screens around it. Unlike all the other computers in the facility, these didn't seem to be wiped. As he carefully moved around it, he saw the other side of the disk was also a formless void. Hallord accessed what appeared to be the primary interface board and saw a list of readings that made no sense. A single adjustable control referred to "dilation."

He checked the computer for any details. There was a single file in the computer's memory, a marked contrast from the vacant storage on every other terminal in the station. It was a video recording.

"Incidentally, two hours and fifty-six minutes remaining," the AI's voice drifted in from outside the lab, startling him.

Hallord swallowed. "Noted. There is a recording. She either missed this or left it here."

The AI said nothing as Hallord brought up the file.

The screen came to life. The snow-white weasel who stood in the recorder's field of view in the lab ante-chamber looked sickly and tired, her eyes dark with anguish. She looked as though she hadn't eaten in days, a sure sign of pervading sickness. Or perhaps a symptom of madness.

"I am Doctor Liantro Pon Liskar, chief physicist of the Predet Empire. Whoever should view this, and I can only assume you to be the field agent sent to check on my progress, will take note that this is the only entry to view as all others have been erased. This is by my hand, as have been all the other crimes perpetrated against nature here, past and future. I was commissioned to commit these against my eventual, better judgment."

The video Liskar took a deep breath. "My mission was to find a way to win the mass livestock rebellion against the Predat Empire using my extensive knowledge of temporal physics. Regardless of what is commonly reported, military setbacks have pushed many colonies to the brink of starvation. I have been tasked to correct this threat through the completion of my life's work: temporal-travel technology."

Hallord's ears perked and his tail began to twitch. Behind him, the disc hummed ominously. He took a step away from it.

Liskar continued. "It took years of research at three separate remote facilities to develop a way to send agents to points in history prior to the uprisings and prevent them. This has been the Emperor's top priority. Only his most trusted advisors are aware of how badly the Empire is faring, as the bison, ibex, and even rodent hordes continue to rebel against their place in the food chain. This knowledge released to the plebeians could undermine the Emperor's powerbase. To spread the truth has become a form of heresy, and therefore I have toiled in secret."

Hallord didn't believe her. He couldn't. He'd helped put down more rebellions than he could remember during his tenure and returned time and time again to feasts in the Emperor's palace so lavish it had taken three days of gorging to finish them. How could those celebrations be possible if outer rebellions were constant and colony worlds were starving? Why hadn't the news bursts talked of this?

"As a loyal servant you would not have cause to question, but here is something you must accept. We are a powerful race in decline and this technology could prevent these uprisings from spreading." Liskar broke off and gazed off into space with a heavy breath that stole her voice for a moment. She took a moment to collect her thoughts. "Which is why, I'm sorry to say, it cannot and must not happen."

Hallord's claws dug into his palms as he stared at the readout. Liskar kept on.

"Each of us can eat half our own weight in meat a day. Multiply this by billions of citizens in the finite number of habitable worlds we have been able to reach. I am a mathematician first, and the exact nature of objective reality is my domain. I have run simulations and had we won every single engagement that started the prey rebellion fifteen years ago, we would have expanded well past unsustainability. Our species is far too ravenous to allow only prey meat to sustain us, but the rations fed to livestock and slaves would never substitute for our needs, nor would Imperial pride ever accept a cessation of the meat frenzy. Mockery would greet any citizen who even suggested it. There simply isn't enough, rebellion or no, for the Empire to persist as it is. This is hard to accept. It was for me.

"What's worse, the presence of time travel, combined with the vast number of enemies the Emperor has accrued, would lead to catastrophic wars using the worst of weapons. Erasures of history or temporal paradoxes could become rampant as Imperial rivals are killed before their time, whole competitor dynasties gobbled off the plate of history in internecine wars. I began this work under the dynasty of the August Keasar, an uncompromising and hard ruler to be sure, but one tempered by wisdom and restraint where it was warranted. I have met his successor, Nore, twice. Though it is no doubt heretical to say, he is neither wise nor restrained. A member of his own family was killed for suspected sedition at the grand feast that honored my work, and orders were handed off to kill the rest of his line. He is cruel, paranoid and gluttonous. I am terrified of this power being wielded in his hands, but took too long to get past my own pride and enthusiasm to face it. What starvation fails to curtail, innate hunger for dominance will. We will bring ourselves to extinction with a vicious fool leading us every step. Once I realized the horror that this experiment would unleash, the folly of my work became clear, as did my responsibility to fix it."

She swallowed. "I desperately wanted to end the experiment, to undo the horrors that I've brought. But I can't. The time disc, once expanded and initiated, cannot be shut down. It connects two points in time much like a wormhole, but which cannot be ended without creating a singularity. I find it a hideous irony that of all the changes this technology can be used to make, the one unnegotiable paradox is that I can't prevent this monstrosity from being made. Its existence is required for me to go back and warn myself of my overzealous stupidity." Liskar seemed to blink away tears at this point. But she maintained her composure, her voice unwavering.

"So what to do? I know that simply ending my life in the destruction of the station is not an option as other Imperial scientists would follow in my footsteps, unaware of what transpired, unaware of what I've discovered. That which keeps this station safe is that which keeps me a prisoner here. Nothing gets out. This station is completely self-contained, and not a single molecule can be removed from it without a ship to ferry it. That, my friend, is where you come in. You are the key. The fate of everything rests on you. You must bring this record back and open the Emperor's eyes to what my folly could cost everyone. For whosoever sees this and hears my words, the only choice is clear.

"Leave."

"The reactor will explode and can't be stopped. You have ample time to place survival provisions on your craft for the return trip and get to a safe distance before the explosion, which will result in a radioactive molten sphere surrounding the time-travel portal for all time. There will be nothing of value to extract from it then. There are no files to recover and the time travel apparatus cannot be dismantled for movement. I know as you hear this you will object, that this defies the Emperor's will, that you may even think me a traitor. If you are one of his trusted, loyal field agents, and he would send no one else, then you also would be compelled to take me back to the Emperor to be interrogated, then tortured, for what I will refuse to divulge. Duty would demand no less. You most likely have the skill-sets to extract the information on the portal from me yourself." She gritted her teeth and glared defiantly into the lens.

Hallord swallowed, his throat suddenly dry. What she assumed was absolutely true. Hallord was duty bound to wring every word from her. He forced the surprising ache of that avoided choice aside and kept his focus on her.

"Well," Liskar said with a swallow. "I'm still considering my options. I certainly don't want to die, but if you are the creature I worry you are, I will have to save us both from that anguish by any means necessary. My failures die with me. I won't recreate this monstrosity from a cell in chains."

She took a deep breath, gathering her composure. "If you are smart, if you are reasonable, you will realize that this is the only sensible path. Anything else will... well, let's not dwell on it.

"I'm sorry it has to be this way. I hope it will never be again. It was an honor to serve my Emperor for as long as I was blind to this truth. Now I serve the Empire posthumously. If you fail to see how we will destroy ourselves, you will discover it for yourself. That I promise you."

Liskar sighed deeply, seeming to ponder if she should say more. Abruptly her white paw reached toward the pic-up and the recording ended.

Hallord sat stunned, unmoving as her words reverberated through his head. She had built a time machine. A time machine! The ultimate weapon against the Emperor's enemies, one that could win all the wars Hallord had been sent to fight in every dank corner of the Empire's hundreds of stars. It could end all conflicts past and future. Yet she had, of her own volition set its destruction in motion.

All to protect the Empire from extinction. Hallord sniffed the empty air, feeling the potent forces of destiny crackle in space behind him. The sense returned that he was not alone, that something waited just out of reach, beyond his perception, like a ghost, watching him from another place.

Another possibility.

The doctor couldn't be right, could she? She had sacrificed her very life on the certainty that she was. It was something an insane person would do, but could an insane person build something like this?

No, they couldn't.

Despite all she believed or came to believe, out here with only her own voice echoing back at her, Liskar could still easily be wrong. Another forceful voice, deeper seated within Hallord insisted that all this didn't matter. He was a servant of the Emperor, his hand beyond the throne, an extension of divine will, as was Liskar by oath; an oath she had betrayed. Even if the doctor truly believed that the end was in store for them all, she had no right to defy the patriarch of the whole galaxy. This was not her decision to make.

Nor was it Hallord's. There was nothing to consider here, no horrible truth to mull over beyond the immediate threat to what was simply the most important war asset the Empire had ever gained. The video contained nothing more than the last ramblings of a starving traitor.

"Two hours and forty-six minutes."

"We have to restore the reactor manually," Hallord muttered, pacing frantically around the lab and its irreplaceable contents. "I'm prepared to die to accomplish this."

"You would not survive long enough to complete the task," the AI commiserated. "Radiation leakage will start burning through the compartment shields soon."

Hallord's mind worked frantically. He couldn't restore the reactor himself, and the maintenance bot that was capable would take far too long to repair. Liskar had likely trashed it to prevent him from using it for that purpose. It would be impossible to move the disc and its attendant machinery to his ship one level higher. Was it possible that she had lied about it being unstoppable and unmovable? No, of course not. She would never have killed herself if she could have simply shut it down, dismantled it and declared it a failure. But the full extent of its secrets were lost with her death.

Hallord accepted the obvious conclusion with a heavy but resolute heart. "I have to use this machine. I have to go back."

The AI was silent. If it had a contrary opinion to voice, it demurred from saying so. He stared into the featureless gray disc and restrained the urge to shiver. "There must be instructions to this machine's use."

"The Doctor kept her work in that lab and myself out. All the usual observation devices were disabled."

Hallord studied one panel to the disc's left that contained some form of interface. "These readouts are all but gibberish to me, but this here seems to be a control unit. The only adjustable feature seems to refer to dilation. Right now it has a setting of six."

He picked up something loose on the desk, a reader pad that was wiped like everything else here. Good a test subject as any. He approached the disk slowly, seeing nothing of note in its murky gray. As he took a step, he heard something clatter to the ground in the lab. Turning, he saw nothing. "Emperor protect us all," Hallord whispered with a wince and hurled the pad. It disappeared into the gray soundlessly without marring the disc's face.

He waited for a moment. Nothing happened. Slowly, he walked around the object, passing the disk's edge and came to see what lay on the other side. The pad lay on the deck and he realized what the clattering sound had been. The pad had come out and hit the deck before he had even thrown it.

Six. Six seconds. The setting on the panel was for seconds.

Hallord worked the control panel, drawing the dilation wider. A standard interstellar day was defined as the twenty-four hours of the Imperial throne-world, sixty seconds per minute. He dialed the number higher and higher, until it abruptly stopped at over 3500, unable to go further. By his hasty math, that was nearly one day. "I have to go through," Hallord said reluctantly, tail curling in worry. That gray, featureless surface terrified him, but he had conquered fear before. This was the solution. Go back, fix the reactor before it was too deadly to fix, stop the station from exploding. With any luck, he could do it before his ship arrived. As for running into himself, he fingered the flange gun on his hip. Hopefully he could explain things in spite of his own hair-trigger reflexes.

The AI was silent for a few moments, then in taciturn tones that would have come with a shrug it said, "Please be cautious."

Hallord would have laughed if he wasn't terrified. He could only hope Liskar was as brilliant as she was traitorous. He took a deep breath. Would he even feel anything happen?

"Two hours thirty-six minutes," The AI said.

In four quick bounds, Hallord leapt against the gray.

Glacial void in all directions. A formless expanse of—

His cheek and chest slammed the deck, knocking the wind out of him. Pain hammered through every cell in his body, as though a million teeth had chewed through him. He lay groaning on the deck for a full minute before slowly rising to his knees. The lab was sealed, the machinery humming in a drone. He was alone.

Had he actually gone back? When was this? Hallord blinked away tears as he patted himself down, feeling a cold not unlike the cryo unit on his ship. His limbs felt stiff as steel rods, his torso like it was on fire. He took several precious minutes to pick himself up and crawl to the laboratory's exit. He thumbed the door switch and felt his blood chill as he rose and stumbled through.

The ante-chamber office was empty, its lone chair sitting unoccupied. A full day. He'd gone back a full day. If Liskar wasn't here…

"Who are you?" The AI demanded, its voice emanating from the desk speaker.

No sense in deception. It would simply sound the alarm. "Imperial Prime Agent Vix Pon Hallord, Special Commission. Quickly, tell me, where is Doctor Liskar?"

"How did you come to be here?"

Hallord's chest heaved as he checked the office chronometer. His shuttle hadn't even approached yet. He had to lean on the desk for support. Random nerves in his body screamed at him, while the rest filled with pins and needles. He could only hope this didn't last long.

"The doctor will know. Where is she?" For one bright, painful moment, he felt a flush of triumph through his queasiness. He had dared to break the laws of time, to go back and protect the greatest asset ever created, and now he would succeed. He wondered deep in his resolute heart if the brilliant female whom he would soon put in chains would have a moment of wistful satisfaction that her greatest invention—

There was a bloodcurdling hiss from the doorway. Hallord spun around queasily, his paw fumbling for his gun as a white-furred form rushed him, knocking the wind out of his already taxed lungs and bringing him to the deck. The scent of her breath was potent in his flaring nostrils. "Damn you, damn you!" Liskar screamed. "Why! Why didn't you listen?"

Hallord forgot his pistol, a mistake in his weakened state. He weakly reached out with spasming limbs, trying to grab her arms with his paws, trying to get his feet under her mass to kick her off. There was a familiar object in her right paw that prickled the skin of his raw throat. He went still as he realized what it was. "Don't!"

Liskar's tears felt salty in his mouth as she straddled him, her teeth bared in a feral hiss and her lab tunic askew. "Didn't you see the recording? I gave you a chance to fix this. I gave you the opportunity to prevent a catastrophe. Now you've ruined everything! Why can't you see what has to be done?"

Hallord bared his chattering teeth and concentrated on getting his limbs under control. "You had no right to take this from us. You had no right. Stopping you was my duty. How could you not know that?" He screamed as the needle pushed home and the syringe depressed. His already spasming limbs shook even more in panic as Liskar glared down at him.

"I had faith in you, in the kind of man you could be. I hoped, I knew, that if you didn't come back through, that I would know you took the offer I have waiting for you, to save us." She released the syringe and it clattered to the floor. "To end this."

Hallord swore at her and spat, spittle landing on her neck. She wiped it away. "You still can. You can still save us from this. I locked the machine so that it couldn't go any further back than now, so I'd know when to expect you if the worst happened. But it doesn't. Every turn of the circle is a new chance. You will return there again, but you don't have to return here. Do you understand? You don't have to—"

Hallord's freed hand shot out, grabbed the syringe and jabbed it in her side. Liskar cried out and rolled away, the syringe dangling between her ribs. Hallord struggled to rise as she plucked it out and gazed hollowly at the instrument before putting it in a pocket. "Well," she sobbed and then laughed. "I don't have to consider those options." She coughed. "This time around, anyway."

She stood up, kicking Hallord's paw away when it tried to draw the pistol. It clattered to the deck and came to a rest. "The pain of traveling back will pass just in time for the poison to start working. Ironically, that will be far gentler. For both of us."

She collected the pistol and placed it in the ante-room drawer. Hallord realized as pain gave way to queasiness that there was no way for her to dispose of that pistol, no means of throwing it overboard.

Nor him.

"The locks are sealed!" He rasped as Liskar grabbed his ankles and dragged him through the office hatch towards the deck lift. The fully functioning maintenance droid accepted her order to pick him up off the deck and follow her. "You can't hide me anywhere my body won't be found. I'll find my own corpse in this timeline you've created and I'll figure it out. I always figure the truth out." Hallord shivered and forced breath through his lungs as the lift rose them to the main deck. "You've lost! Nothing will prevent me from completing my mission, nothing! You were stupid to even try."

Liskar sighed as they came up to the main deck, holding the hallway handrail and weaving while they made their way to a place Hallord's fading vision could not see. He was completely blind by the time the machine slid him onto a flat metal surface. Her raspy breath, as the poison worked slowly but certainly within her too, came as a gentle whisper.

"I have faith that things will not always be this way, that you will find wisdom to help me prevent us from eating our own tails until we cease to exist. Until then, ensuring you leave no evidence for yourself to find is a matter of... irony. Till we meet again."

She placed a paw on his forehead then, a coolness that stole away Hallord's already dying fury before she slipped away. The peculiar final words imprinted momentarily on his fading mind as desperation fled his limbs and he went completely limp in purposeful mechanical hands. His vision would never return, but his remaining senses delivered him one final cold moment of horrifying clarity.

As his clothes were unceremoniously cut away and he heard the sharpening of robotic knives, he caught a familiar tinge on the stale station air. "Please, no. You can't..."

The rising scent of ground spices wafted tantalizingly from the sizzle of a kitchen's grill as the first steel found his flesh.

Hours passed as knives and ovens worked. Files were wiped and a scientist quietly died. A drone signaled in the docking bay as a ship completed its final approach maneuvers and mated with a staccato of clangs.

Imperial Prime Agent Hallord stepped from his ship through the space station's inner airlock. The scent that tickled his nose set his barren stomach growling. He was indeed on a mission, but the most urgent of directives couldn't be followed when he was all but starving.

Hallord, being a weasel, could eat half his own mass of meat in a single sitting, but training and special metabolic drugs had prepped him for long stays in space with limited sustenance. After so long unconscious, he was ravenous. The sizzle of roasted meat combined with the bright bite of herbs and spices hooked him left, down a short hallway to the dining nook, where a sumptuous feast of meat strips, ibex he guessed, awaited him.

Doctor Liskar was nowhere in sight, the nook's table set for one. Likely she'd eaten earlier.

Hallord ate. The meat was the best he'd tasted in years, fully deboned, crisped and sauced. It was buttery on his tongue as it went down, lean meat with very little fat or gristle. "Computer," Hallord called out between bites.

"Yes." The voice that responded was deep, masculine and prim, devoid of emotion.

"Was Doctor Liskar notified of my ship's approach?"

"No. She is on the lab level. Her last request was to be undisturbed."

"Who prepared this meal for me then?"

"Kitchen processor."

"Processor? Amazing." The next bite was sumptuous as the last. He chuckled. "If there's anything at all amiss, I'm not going to find it here."

The Cóyotl Awards

A History

The Cóyotl Awards are nominated and voted upon a ballot with up to five nominees by the membership of the FWG, in the categories of Best Novel, Best Novella, Best Short Story, and Best Anthology. In their first year, 2012 (for 2011 works), there were two divisions within each category; General and Mature. These were merged the following year. The Best Anthology category was added in 2013. The Cóyotl Awards are announced at a presentation ceremony at a furry fandom convention the next year; currently Furlandia in Portland, Oregon.

The Cóyotl Award trophy is a certificate illustrated with the Cóyotl logo, and a small coyote pup plush doll wearing a red bandana with the Cóyotl logo and category sewn upon it. The plush dolls with bandanas are store-bought, with the Cóyotl logos and category name sewn on the bandana. The coyote dolls for the four categories are unofficially named Neve for Best Novel, Ella for Best Novella, Shorty for Best Short Story, and Anthony for Best Anthology.

The winners in the Best Novel category have been:

2011—General: *Inchoate Carillon, Inconstant Cucold* by Charles Mathias (The Metamor Keep website, added October 23, 2011; electronic edition only).

Mature: *Sixes Wild: Manifest Destiny* by Tempe O'Kun (Sofawolf Press, June 2011).

2012—*By Sword and Star* by Renee Carter Hall (Anthropomorphic Dreams Publishing, February 2012).

2013—*God of Clay* by Ryan Campbell (Sofawolf Press, September 2013).

2014—*Off the Beaten Path* by Rukis (FurPlanet Productions, July 2014).

2015—*Barsk: The Elephant's Graveyard* by Lawrence M. Schoen (Tor Books, December 2015).

2016—*The Digital Coyote* by Kris Schnee (CreateSpace, July 2016).

2017—*Kismet* by Watts Martin (Argyll/FurPlanet Productions, January 2017).

The winners in the Best Novella category have been:

2011—General, *Real Dragons Don't Wear Sweaters* by Renee Carter Hall (Kindle, October 2011).

Mature, *Science Friction* by Kyell Gold (FurPlanet Productions, September 2011).

2012—*Reach For the Sky (The Battle of Britain—A Novel of Lt. Corn, Book 1)* by Vixyy Fox (Kindle, April 2012).

2013—*Indigo Rain* by Watts Martin (FurPlanet Productions, January 2013).

2014—*Huntress* by Renee Carter Hall (in *Five Fortunes*, edited by Fred Patten; FurPlanet Productions, January 2014).

2015—*Koa of the Drowned Kingdom* by Ryan Campbell (FurPlanet Productions, September 2015).

2016—*The Goat: Building the Perfect Victim* by Bill Kieffer (Red Ferret Press, September 2016).

2017—*Dragon Fried Cheese* by Madison Keller (Hundeliebe Press, May 2017).

The winners in the Best Short Story category have been:

2011—General, *The Canoe Race* by Daniel and Mary Lowd.
Mature, *Best of Breed* by Renee Carter Hall.
2012—*Chasing the Spotlight* by Tim Susman.
2013—*Fox in the Hen House* by Mary E. Lowd.
2014—*Jackalope Wives* by Ursula Vernon.
2015—*The Analogue Cat* by Alice "Huskyteer" Dryden.
2016—*400 Rabbits* by Alice "Huskyteer" Dryden.
2017—*Behesht* by Dwale.

The winners in the Best Anthology category have been:

2013—*Hot Dish 1* edited by Alopex (Sofawolf Press, March 2013).

2014—*Abandoned Places* edited by Tarl Hoch (FurPlanet Productions, December 2014).

2015—*Inhuman Acts: An Anthology of Noir* edited by Ocean Tigrox (FurPlanet Productions, September 2015).

2016—*Gods With Fur* edited by Fred Patten (FurPlanet Productions, June 2016).

2017—*Arcana: A Tarot Anthology* edited by Madison Scott-Clary (Thurston Howl Publications, November 2017).

About the Authors

Malcolm Cross

Malcolm F. Cross lives in London and enjoys the personal space and privacy that the city is known for. When not misdirecting tourists to nonexistent landmarks and standing on the wrong side of escalators, Malcolm enjoys writing science fiction and fantasy.

A member of SFWA, his work has appeared in *Strange Horizons*, he's contributed to the *Afterblight* and *Extinction Biome* shared universes by Abaddon Books, and is the author of the 2016 novel *Dog Country*.

He can be found online at http://www.sinisbeautiful.com.

Alice "Huskyteer" Dryden

Alice "Huskyteer" Dryden has been writing furry fiction since 2010. Her short stories have appeared in anthologies including *Heat, ROAR, Hot Dish* and *The Furry Future*, and have won two Cóyotl Awards, two Ursa Major Awards, and one Leo Literary Award. You can find a complete list of her published works at huskyteer.co.uk

She lives in south London, owns a motorbike and too many books, and is a black belt in karate. She can bark well enough to confuse most dogs, but has no idea what she's saying to them. She enjoys travelling to other countries to sample their alcohol, cheese, and aviation museums.

Come and say hello on Twitter, where she's @Huskyteer. She doesn't bite.

Dwale

Dwale is a semi-sapient congeries of dross and shadow-play who walks the path illumed wherever the moon touches the sea. Producing works at once abstruse and aggressively pretentious, its stories have received critical acclaim and multiple award nominations. Dwale has stories in thirteen furry anthologies: *Allasso, volume 1: Shame; Civilized Beasts 1* and *2; CLAW volume 1; Claw the Way to Victory; Dogs of War II: Aftermath; Fragments of Life's Heart; The Furry Future; Hot Dish 1;*

ROAR volume 8; Seven Deadly Sins: Furry Confessions; and *Typewriter Emergencies, September 2015* and *December 2017.* Masochists may also follow on Twitter: @ThornAppleCider

Amy Fontaine

Amy Fontaine is a wildlife biologist who has studied wolves, hyenas, and other creatures in the field. As an author of fantasy, science fiction, and poetry, she loves to write about magic, animals, and adventure.

Amy's writings have been featured in the *ROAR* anthology series and other furry anthologies, as well as in mainstream speculative fiction markets. Her first novel, *Mist*, a young adult fantasy about shapeshifters, elemental magic, and being the change you wish to see in the world, was published by Thurston Howl Publications in 2017. Currently, Amy is writing an interactive novel about mythical fox spirits (known in Japanese as *kitsune*) for Choice of Games.

Amy is a member of the Codex Writers' Group and the Furry Writers' Guild. She also works as an assistant editor for Ottercorrect Literature Services and an editorial assistant for *Cosmic Roots and Eldritch Shores.*

Along with writing and chasing wild animals, Amy enjoys stargazing, drawing, and playing guitar. She likes to see the world, not only as it is, but as it could be. You can connect with Amy and find her published work at https://amyclarefontaine.com.

Vixyy Fox

I have been writing as Vixyy Fox from somewhere around the year 2000. Oddly enough, or not so oddly, it was the finding of Dark Natasha's artwork that solidified who I am as the funny little Fennec who is everyone's grandmother. Vixyy is my totem, and when we found her image, she told me, 'That's me… that's who I am.' It's times like this where one might question their sanity, but personal things like this touch the soul. I asked Dark if I could use the image and she agreed. [Note from FP: *Tales of the Fur Side*, with text by Vixyy and art by Dark Natasha, was published by United Publications in June 2006.]

Since that time I have never stopped writing. After several books and countless short stories, I can now look back and say with certainty, 'You don't have to be crazy to be a writer, but it certainly does help.'

Renee Carter Hall

Renee Carter Hall's short fiction has appeared in a variety of magazines and anthologies, including *Strange Horizons, Daily Science Fiction, Podcastle*, and the furry anthologies *ROAR, An Anthropomorphic*

Century, and *SPECIES: Wolves*, among others. She is also the author of the furry fantasy novels *By Sword and Star* (Anthropomorphic Dreams Publishing, February 2012) and *Huntress* (FurPlanet Productions, September 2015), both of which won Cóyotl Awards, and she served as the president of the Furry Writers' Guild from 2014 to 2016.

Renee lives in West Virginia with her husband, their cat, and more books than she will ever have time to read. Online, she can be found at www.reneecarterhall.com and on Twitter as @RCarterHall.

Daniel Lowd

Daniel Lowd likes dogs, unicycles, and researching artificial intelligence. By day, he is a computer science professor. By night, he is also a computer science professor, because he tends to work odd hours. At various other times (dusk? gloaming? teatime?) he writes a few words of fiction or the occasional song

Mary E. Lowd

Mary E. Lowd writes stories and collects creatures. She's had more than one hundred short stories published, and her novels include the *Otters In Space* trilogy, *In a Dog's World*, and *The Snake's Song: A Labyrinth of Souls Novel*. Her fiction has won an Ursa Major Award and two Cóyotl Awards. Meanwhile, she's collected a husband, daughter, son, bevy of cats and dogs, and the occasional fish. The stories, creatures, and Mary live together in a crashed spaceship disguised as a house, hidden inside a fairy's garden in Oregon. Learn more at marylowd.com.

Bill "Hafoc" Rogers

I was born in Michigan shortly after the end of the last ice age. I was educated in the public schools where my parents worked. In college I studied geophysics and oil exploration techniques, but ended up with a career in air pollution control enforcement. Spent the job interview telling them how they couldn't use me, and let them convince themselves that they could and would, I guess. Go figure.

I backed into anthropomorphic literature late, sliding across from my lifetime love of science fiction. I always thought the nonhuman characters were the most interesting, especially if they didn't think like humans. I'd guess a fair number of those who read this would agree with me on that one.

Sean Silva

Sean Silva is a non-writer, video game collector and sports fan living in San Antonio, Texas with his partner and a couple puppies. His stories have been featured numerous times on the Anthro Dreams Podcast, as well as the anthologies *ROAR volume 4* and *Different Worlds, Different Skins*. He is also the founder of the Furry Writers' Guild.

Slip Wolf

Slip Wolf has spent the last six years combing the literary universe for story ideas to conquer for the greater Furry Empire. Of course, come writing time, the rebellious bastards mount resistances, disobeying narratives and blowing up words counts with abandon. It's enough to drive a wolf to eat his own tail.

You can read peace treaties to the voices in his head through Sofawolf Press, FurPlanet Productions, Rabbit Valley Books, and Weasel Press. Catch snippets of his campaigns at http://www.furaffinity.net/user/slip-wolf/ and keep tabs on his rantings on Twitter @Slip_Wolf

Tim Susman

Tim Susman started a novel in college and didn't finish one until almost twenty years later. In that time, he earned a degree in Zoology, worked with Jane Goodall, co-founded Sofawolf Press in 1999, and moved to California, where he lives with his two partners. Since publishing *Common and Precious* (Sofawolf Press, January 2007), he has attended Clarion in 2011 (arooo Narwolves!), published short stories in *Apex Magazine, Lightspeed*, and *ROAR*, among others, and recently released the second in his Revolutionary War-era fantasy series, *The Demon and the Fox* (Argyll Productions, July 2018). Under the name Kyell Gold, he has published multiple novels and won several awards for his furry fiction.

You can find out more about his stories at timsusman.wordpress.com and www.kyellgold.com, and follow him on Twitter at @WriterFox.

Ursula Vernon

Ursula Vernon is the real name of T. Kingfisher. Both of them write books, mostly involving talking animals, magic, and a great many random plants.

Chris "Sparf" Williams

Sparf is a writer of anthropomorphic fiction currently residing in the Washington, D.C. area. His work has previously been featured in several anthologies from FurPlanet, as well as in *Trick or Treat vol. 2: Historical Halloween* from Rabbit Valley. In addition to his writing, he is also a stage, film, and voice actor who received his MFA in Acting from The Catholic University of America. His thesis production, "What the Fur?!" can be found on his YouTube channel (Sparf1) and on Vimeo.

He can be found on SoFurry, Furry Network, and Weasyl as Sparf. This story is dedicated to the attendees and instructors of the first RAWR (Regional Anthropomorphic Writers' Retreat), without whose critique and support the story would not have taken the shape that it did.

Ianus J. Wolf

Ianus J. Wolf is an author who writes in multiple genres, usually focused in horror and other macabre areas or adult material. Aside from writing, he also acts, does voice work, and has been known to lead fun historic tours in the heart of his home city.

His work has previously appeared in *Abandoned Places*, *Will of the Alpha*, *Bleak Horizons*, *Altered States*, and other anthologies from FurPlanet. He is also the editor of *Trick or Treat* and *Pulp!* from Rabbit Valley. He lives in the Seattle area with his two mates and their two dogs where he enjoys horror movies, books, theatre, and studies into the sapient condition.

About the Artist

Kacey Miyagami

Kacey Miyagami is an illustrator with a background in fine arts and animation. She specializes in traditional media, favoring fluid acrylics and Copic markers, but she dabbles in a wide variety of media, including digital. She is known for her cute and colorful anthropomorphic and animal characters, as well as her detailed semi-realistic environments. Her inspirations often come from some of her other interests, including music, traveling, anime/animation, video games, and audio books.

She is originally from Southern California, having grown up in Los Angeles, and attended art school at the University of Southern California. She currently lives in Aloha, Oregon with her wife, Noriko.

Electric Keet

The Cóyotl Awards logo was designed by Jessie "Electric Keet" Tracer.

About the Editor

Fred Patten

Fred Patten (1940-2018) joined the Los Angeles Science Fantasy Society in 1960 while in college, and was an active s-f & fantasy fan throughout his life. He began writing for and publishing fanzines in 1961 (see http://www.zinewiki.com/Salamander), and wrote over a thousand reviews of anthropomorphic literature since 1962, irregularly for s-f fanzines in the 1960s, 1970s, and 1980s; for Yarf! from 1990 to 2003, for Claw & Quill in 2004-2005, for ANTHRO from 2005 to 2008, for Renard's Menagerie in 2008, for Flayrah from 2011 to 2014, and for Dogpatch Press since 2014. He wrote four non-fiction books and edited sixteen anthologies of furry fiction. He founded the Ursa Major Awards and served on its administrative Anthropomorphic Literature and Arts Association since 2001. He was a member of the Furry Writers' Guild and the Furry Hall of Fame. He was awarded the Comic-Con's Inkpot Award in 1980 for helping to introduce anime to America. He wrote a weekly column on animation, Funny Animals and More, for Jerry Beck's Cartoon Research from 2013 to 2017. A stroke in 2005 left him hospitalized, from which he continued his fanac until his death in 2018.

www.ingramcontent.com/pod-product-compliance
Lightning Source LLC
Chambersburg PA
CBHW071859020726
47502CB00003B/813